DAWN OF THE JEDI

INTO THE VOID

BY TIM LEBBON

NOVELS

Mesmer

Hush (with Gavin Williams)

Face

The Nature of Balance

Until She Sleeps

Desolation

Berserk

Dusk

Hellboy: Unnatural Selection

The Everlasting

Dawn

30 Days of Night

Mind the Gap
(with Christopher Golden)

Fallen

The Map of Moments
(with Christopher Golden)

The Island

Hellboy: The Fire Wolves

Bar None

The Chamber of Ten
(with Christopher Golden)

30 Days of Night: Fear of the Dark

Echo City

The Shadow Men
(with Christopher Golden)

The Secret Journeys of Jack London: The
Wild (with Christopher Golden)

The Secret Journeys of Jack London: The
Sea Wolves (with Christopher Golden)

The Cabin in the Woods

The Heretic Land

Toxic City (book one): London Eye

Coldbrook

Toxic City (book two): Reaper's Legacy

Star Wars: Dawn of the Jedi:
Into the Void

NOVELLAS

White

Naming of Parts

Exorcising Angels

Changing of Faces

Dead Man's Hand

Pieces of Hate

A Whisper of Southern Lights

The Reach of Children

Children of the New Disorder
(with Lindy Moore)

The Thief of Broken Toys

COLLECTIONS

Faith in the Flesh

As the Sun Goes Down

White and Other Tales of Ruin

Fears Unnamed

After the War

Last Exit for the Lost

Nothing as It Seems

STAR WARS®

DAWN OF THE JEDI
INTO THE VOID

Tim Lebbon

BALLANTINE BOOKS • NEW YORK

For Ellie and Dan, my young Padawan

Published in the United States by Del Rey,
an imprint of The Random House Publishing Group,
a division of Random House, Inc., New York.

DEL REY is a registered trademark and the Del Rey colophon
is a trademark of Random House, Inc.

ISBN 978-0-345-54193-2

Printed in the United States of America

ACKNOWLEDGMENTS

Thanks to everyone at Del Rey, LucasBooks, and Dark Horse for their help and encouragement. And as ever, a big thanks to my agent, Howard Morhaim.

The STAR WARS Novels Timeline

BEFORE THE REPUBLIC
37,000-25,000 YEARS BEFORE
STAR WARS: A New Hope

c. 25,793 YEARS BEFORE STAR WARS: A New Hope

Dawn of the Jedi: Into the Void

OLD REPUBLIC
5000-67 YEARS BEFORE
STAR WARS: A New Hope

Lost Tribe of the Sith†
Precipice
Skyborn
Paragon
Savior
Purgatory
Sentinel

3954 YEARS BEFORE STAR WARS: A New Hope

The Old Republic: Revan

3650 YEARS BEFORE STAR WARS: A New Hope

The Old Republic: Deceived

Lost Tribe of the Sith†
Pantheon
Secrets

Red Harvest

The Old Republic: Fatal Alliance

The Old Republic: Annihilation

2975 YEARS BEFORE STAR WARS: A New Hope

Lost Tribe of the Sith†
Pandemonium

1032 YEARS BEFORE STAR WARS: A New Hope

Knight Errant

Darth Bane: Path of Destruction
Darth Bane: Rule of Two
Darth Bane: Dynasty of Evil

RISE OF THE EMPIRE
67-0 YEARS BEFORE
STAR WARS: A New Hope

67 YEARS BEFORE STAR WARS: A New Hope

Darth Plagueis

33 YEARS BEFORE STAR WARS: A New Hope

Darth Maul: Saboteur*
Cloak of Deception
Darth Maul: Shadow Hunter

32 YEARS BEFORE STAR WARS: A New Hope

STAR WARS: EPISODE I
THE PHANTOM MENACE

Rogue Planet
Outbound Flight
The Approaching Storm

22 YEARS BEFORE STAR WARS: A New Hope

STAR WARS: EPISODE II
ATTACK OF THE CLONES

22-19 YEARS BEFORE STAR WARS: A New Hope

The Clone Wars
The Clone Wars: Wild Space
The Clone Wars: No Prisoners

Clone Wars Gambit
Stealth
Siege

Republic Commando
Hard Contact
Triple Zero
True Colors
Order 66

Shatterpoint
The Cestus Deception
The Hive*
MedStar I: Battle Surgeons
MedStar II: Jedi Healer
Jedi Trial
Yoda: Dark Rendezvous
Labyrinth of Evil

19 YEARS BEFORE STAR WARS: A New Hope

STAR WARS: EPISODE III
REVENGE OF THE SITH

Dark Lord: The Rise of Darth Vader

Imperial Commando
501st

Coruscant Nights
Jedi Twilight
Street of Shadows
Patterns of Force

The Last Jedi

*An eBook novella
**Forthcoming
† Lost Tribe of the Sith: The
  Collected Stories

THE STAR WARS NOVELS TIMELINE

NEW JEDI ORDER
25–40 YEARS AFTER
STAR WARS: A New Hope

Boba Fett: A Practical Man*

The New Jedi Order
Vector Prime
Dark Tide I: Onslaught
Dark Tide II: Ruin
Agents of Chaos I: Hero's Trial
Agents of Chaos II: Jedi Eclipse
Balance Point
Recovery*
Edge of Victory I: Conquest
Edge of Victory II: Rebirth
Star by Star
Dark Journey
Enemy Lines I: Rebel Dream
Enemy Lines II: Rebel Stand
Traitor
Destiny's Way
Ylesia*
Force Heretic I: Remnant
Force Heretic II: Refugee
Force Heretic III: Reunion
The Final Prophecy
The Unifying Force

35 YEARS AFTER STAR WARS: A New Hope

The Dark Nest Trilogy
The Joiner King
The Unseen Queen
The Swarm War

LEGACY
40+ YEARS AFTER
STAR WARS: A New Hope

Legacy of the Force
Betrayal
Bloodlines
Tempest
Exile
Sacrifice
Inferno
Fury
Revelation
Invincible

Crosscurrent
Riptide

Millennium Falcon

43 YEARS AFTER STAR WARS: A New Hope

Fate of the Jedi
Outcast
Omen
Abyss
Backlash
Allies
Vortex
Conviction
Ascension
Apocalypse

X-Wing: Mercy Kill

45 YEARS AFTER STAR WARS: A New Hope

Crucible**

*An eBook novella
**Forthcoming

DRAMATIS PERSONAE

Lanoree Brock; Je'daii Ranger (Human female)
Dalien Brock; dreamer (Human male)
Tre Sana; rogue (Twi'lek male)
Dam-Powl; Je'daii Master (Cathar female)
Lha-Mi; Je'daii Temple Master (Dai Bendu male)
Kara; troublemaker (Human female)
Lorus; Kalimahr Police Captain (Sith male)
Maxhagan; gangster (Human male)

A long time ago in a galaxy far, far away. . . .

At the heart of any poor soul not at one with the Force, there is only void.

—Unknown Je'daii, 2,545 TYA (Tho Yor Arrival)

CHAPTER ONE

DARK MATTERS

Even at the beginning of our journey I feel like a rock in the river of the Force. Lanoree is a fish carried by that river, feeding from it, living within it, relying on the waters for her well-being. But I am unmoving. An inconvenience to the water as long as I remain. And slowly, slowly, I am being eroded to nothing.

—Dalien Brock, diaries, 10,661 TYA

She is a little girl, the sky seems wide and endless, and Lanoree Brock breathes in the wonders of Tython as she runs to find her brother.

Dalien is down by the estuary again. He likes being alone, away from all the other children at Bodhi, the Je'daii Temple of the Arts. Her parents have sent her to find him, and though they still have some teaching to do that afternoon, they've promised that they will walk up to the boundary of the Edge Forest that evening. Lanoree loves it up there. And it scares her a little, as well. Close to the temple, near the sea, she can feel the Force ebbing and flowing through everything— the air she breathes, the sights she sees, and all that makes up the beautiful scenery. Up at the Edge Forest, there's a primal wildness to the Force that sets her blood pumping.

Her mother will smile and say that she will learn about it all, given time. Her father will look silently into the forest, as if he silently yearns to explore that way. And her little brother, only nine years old, will start to cry.

Always at the Edge Forest, he cries.

"Dal!" She swishes through the long grasses close to the riverbank, hands held out by her sides so that the grass caresses her palms. She won't tell him about the walk planned for that evening. If she does he'll get moody, and he might not agree to come home with her. He can be like that sometimes, and their father says it's the sign of someone finding his own way.

Dal doesn't seem to have heard her, and as she closes on him she slows from a run to a walk and thinks, *If that was me I'd have sensed me approaching ages ago.*

Dal's head remains dipped. By his side he has created a perfect circle using the stones of chewed mepples, his favorite fruit. He does that when he's thinking.

The river flows by, fast and full from the recent rains. There's a power to it that is intimidating, and, closing her eyes, Lanoree feels the Force and senses the myriad life-forms that call the river home. Some are as small as her finger, others that swim upriver from the ocean almost half the size of a Cloud Chaser ship. She knows from her studies that many of them have teeth.

She bites her lip, hesitant. Then she probes out with her mind and—

"I told you to never do that to me!"

"Dal . . ."

He stands and turns around, and he looks furious. Just for a moment there's a fire in his eyes that she doesn't like. She has seen those flames before, and carries the knotted scar tissue in her lower lip to prove it. Then his anger slips and he smiles.

"Sorry. You startled me, that's all."

"You're drawing?" she asks, seeing the sketchbook.

Dal closes the book. "It's rubbish."

"I don't believe that," Lanoree says. "You're really good. Temple Master Fenn himself says so."

"Temple Master Fenn is a friend of Father's."

Lanoree ignores the insinuation and walks closer to her brother. She can already see that he has chosen a fine place from which to draw the surroundings. The river curves here, and a smaller tributary joins from the hills of the Edge Forest, causing a confusion of currents. The undergrowth on the far bank is colorful and vibrant, and there's a huge old ak tree whose hollowed trunk is home to a flight of weave birds. Their spun golden threads glisten in the afternoon sun. The birdsong complements the river's roar.

"Let me see," Lanoree says.

Dal does not look at her, but he opens the pad.

"It's beautiful," she says. "The Force has guided your fingers, Dal." But she's not sure.

Dal picks a heavy pencil from his pocket and strikes five thick lines through his drawing, left to right, tearing the paper and ruining it forever. His expression does not change, and neither does his breathing. It's almost as if there is no anger at all.

"There," he says. "That's better."

For a moment the lines look like claw marks, and as Lanoree takes a breath and blinks—

A soft, insistent alarm pulled her up from sleep. Lanoree sighed and sat up, rubbing her eyes, massaging the dream away. Dear Dal. She dreamed of him often, but they were usually dreams of those later times when everything was turning bad. Not when they were still children for whom Tython was so full of potential.

Perhaps it was because she was on her way home.

She had not been back to Tython for more than four years. She was a Je'daii Ranger, and so ranging is what she did. Some Rangers found reasons to return to Tython regularly. Family connections, continuous training, face-to-face debriefs, it all amounted to the same thing—they hated being away from home. She also believed that there were those Je'daii who felt the need to immerse themselves in Tython's Force-rich surroundings from time to time, as if uncertain that their affinity with the Force was strong enough.

Lanoree had no such doubts. She was comfortable with her strength and balance in the Force. The short periods she had spent with others on retreats on Ashla and Bogan—a voluntary part of a Padawan's training, should they desire to go—had made her even more confident in this.

She stood from her cot and stretched. She reached for the ceiling and grabbed the bars she'd welded there herself, pulling up, breathing softly, then lifting her legs and stretching them out until she was horizontal to the floor. Her muscles quivered, and she breathed deeply as she felt the Force flowing through her, a vibrant, living thing. Mental exercise and meditation were fine, but sometimes she took the greatest pleasure in exerting herself physically. She believed that to be strong with the Force, one had to be strong in body.

The alarm was still ringing.

"I'm awake," she said, easing herself slowly back to the floor, "in case you hadn't noticed."

The alarm snapped off, and her Peacemaker ship's grubby yellow maintenance droid ambled into the small living quarters on padded metal feet. It was one of many adaptations she'd made to the ship in her years out in the Tythan system. Most Peacemakers carried a very simple droid, but she'd updated hers to a Holgorian IM-220, capable of limited communication with a human master and other duties not necessarily exclusive to ship maintenance. She'd further customized it with some heavy armor, doubling its weight but making it much more useful to her in risky scenarios. She spoke to it, its replies were obtuse, and she supposed it was the equivalent of trying to communicate with a grass kapir back home. She had even named it.

"Hey, Ironholgs. You better not have woken me early."

The droid beeped and scraped, and she wasn't sure whether it was getting cranky in its old age.

She looked around the small but comfortable living quarters. She had chosen a Peacemaker over a Hunter because of its size; even before she'd flown her first mission as a Je'daii Ranger, she knew that she would be eager to spend much of her time in space. A Hunter was fast and agile but too small to live in. The Peacemaker was a compromise on maneuverability, but she had spent long periods living alone on the ship. She preferred it that way.

And like most Rangers, she had made many modifications and adaptations to her ship that stamped her own identity upon it. She'd stripped out the table and chairs and replaced them with a weights and tensions rack for working out. Now, she ate her food sitting on her narrow cot. She'd replaced the holonet entertainment system with an older flatscreen, which doubled as communications center and reduced the ship's net weight. Beside the extensive engine compartment there had been a small room that housed a second cot for guests or companions, but because she had neither she had filled the space with extra laser charge pods, a water-recycling unit, and food stores. The ship's four laser cannon turrets had also been upgraded, and it now also carried plasma missiles, and drone missiles for long-distance combat. At the hands of the Cathar master armorer Gan Corla, the cannons now packed three times more punch and were effective over twice the range as those standard to Peacemakers.

She had also altered and adapted the function and position of many cockpit controls, making it so that only she could effectively fly the ship. It was hers, it was home, and that was how she liked it.

"How long to Tython?" she asked.

The droid let out a series of whines and clicks.

"Right," Lanoree said. "Suppose I'd better freshen up." She brushed a touch pad and the darkened screens in the forward cockpit faded to clear, revealing the star-speckled view that never failed to make her heart ache. There was something so profoundly moving to the distance and scale of what she saw out there, and the Force never let her forget that she was a part of something incomprehensibly large. She supposed it was as close as she ever came to a religious epiphany.

She touched the pad again and a red glow appeared, surrounding a speck in the distance. Tython. Three hours and she'd be there.

The Je'daii Council ordering her back to Tython meant only one thing. They had a mission for her, and it was one that they needed to discuss face-to-face.

* * *

Washed, dressed, and fed, Lanoree sat in the ship's cockpit and watched Tython drawing closer. Her ship had communicated with sentry drones orbiting at thirty thousand kilometers, and now the Peacemaker was performing a graceful parabola that would take it down into the atmosphere just above the equator.

She was nervous about visiting Tython again, but part of her was excited as well. It would be good to see her mother and father, however briefly. She contacted them far too infrequently. With Dal dead, she was now their only child.

A soft chime announced an incoming transmission. She swiveled her seat and faced the flatscreen, just as it snowed into an image.

"Master Dam-Powl," Lanoree said, surprised. "An honor." And it was. She had expected the welcoming transmission to be from a Je'daii Ranger or perhaps even a Journeyer she did not know. Not the Cathar Je'daii Master.

Dam-Powl bowed her head. "Lanoree, it's good to see you again. We've been eagerly awaiting your arrival. Pressing matters beg discussion. *Dark* matters."

"I assumed that was the case," Lanoree said. She shifted in her seat, unaccountably nervous.

"I sense your discomfort," Master Dam-Powl said.

"Forgive me. It's been some time since I spoke with a Je'daii Master."

"You feel unsettled even with me?" Dam-Powl asked, smiling. But the smile quickly slipped. "No matter. Prepare yourself, because today you speak with six Masters, including Stav Kesh's Temple Master Lha-Mi. I've sent your ship the landing coordinates for our meeting place thirty kilometers south of Akar Kesh. We'll expect you soon."

"Master, we're not meeting at a temple?"

But Dam-Powl had already broken the transmission, and Lanoree was left staring at a blank screen. She could see her image reflected there, and she quickly gathered herself, breathing away the shock. *Six Je'daii Masters? And Lha-Mi as well?*

"Then it *is* something big."

She checked the transmitted coordinates and switched the flight computer to manual, eager to make the final approach herself. She had always loved flying and the freedom it gave her. Untethered. Almost a free agent.

Lanoree closed her eyes briefly and breathed with the Force. It was strong this close to Tython, elemental, and it sparked her senses alive.

By the time the Peacemaker sliced into Tython's outer atmosphere, Lanoree's excitement was growing. The landing zone was nestled in a small valley with giant standing stones on the surrounding hills. She could see several other ships, including Hunters and another Peacemaker. It was a strange place for such a meeting, but the Je'daii Council would have its reasons. She guided her ship in an elegant arc and landed almost without a jolt.

"Solid ground," she whispered. "Ironholgs, I don't know how long we'll be here, but take the opportunity to run a full systems check. Anything we need we can pick up from Akar Kesh before we leave."

The droid emitted a mechanical sigh.

Lanoree probed gently outward, and when she sensed that the air pressures had equalized, she opened the lower hull hatch. The smells that flooded in—rash grass, running water, that curious charged smell that seemed to permeate the atmosphere around most temples— brought a rush of nostalgia for the planet she had left behind. But there was no time for personal musings.

Three Journeyers were waiting for her, wide-eyed and excited.

"Welcome, Ranger Brock!" the tallest of the three said.

"I'm sure," she said. "Where are they waiting for me?"

"On Master Lha-Mi's Peacemaker," another Journeyer said. "We're here to escort you. Please, follow us."

"I'm here representing the Council of Masters," the Talid Temple Master Lha-Mi said. "Forgive us for not welcoming you back to Tython in more . . . salubrious surroundings. But by necessity this meeting must be covert." His long white hair glowed in the room's artificial light. He was old and wise, and Lanoree was pleased to see him again.

"It's so nice to be back," Lanoree said. She bowed.

"Please, please." Lha-Mi pointed to a seat, and Lanoree sat facing him and the other five Je'daii Masters. This Peacemaker's living quarters had been pared down to provide a circular table with eight seats around it, and little more. She nodded a silent greeting to Lha-Mi, Dam-Powl and the Cathar Master Tem Madog, but the other three she did not know. It seemed that things had moved swiftly while she had been away, especially when it came to promotions.

"Ranger Brock," Master Dam-Powl said, smiling. "It's wonderful to see you again in the flesh." She was a Master at Anil Kesh, the Je'daii Temple of Science, and during Lanoree's training there, she and Dam-Powl had formed a close bond. It was she more than any other who had expressed the conviction that Lanoree would be a great Je'daii one day. It was also Dam-Powl who had revealed and encouraged the areas of Force use at which Lanoree was most skilled—metallurgy, elemental manipulation, alchemy.

"Likewise, Master Dam-Powl," Lanoree said.

"How are your studies?"

"Progressing," Lanoree said. There was a hidden place in her Peacemaker ship, and a container holding a very personal experiment, and sometimes she spent long hours at work there. Her alchemical skills still seemed fledgling sometimes, but the sense of accomplishment and power she felt while using them were almost addictive.

"You're a talented Je'daii," Master Tem Madog said. "I can sense your experience and strength growing with the years." It was a durasteel sword forged by this master weapons smith that hung by Lanoree's side. The blade had saved her life on many occasions, and on other occasions it had taken lives. It was her third arm, a part of her. In the four years since leaving Tython she had never been more than an arm's reach from the weapon, and she felt it now, cool and solid, keen in the presence of its maker.

"I honor the Force as well as I can," Lanoree said. " 'I am the mystery of darkness, in balance with chaos and harmony.' " She smiled as she quoted from the Je'daii oath, and some of the Masters smiled back. Some of them. The three she did not know remained expressionless, and she probed gently, knowing that she risked punishment yet unable to break her old habit. She always liked knowing who she was talking to. And as they had not introduced themselves, she thought it only fair.

They closed themselves to her, and one, a Wookiee, growled deep in his throat.

"You have served the Je'daii and Tython well during your years as Ranger," Lha-Mi said. "And sitting before us now, you must surely believe that we mean you no ill. I understand that this meeting might seem strange and that being faced with us might seem . . . daunting. Intimidating, perhaps? But there is no need to invade another's privacy, Lanoree, especially a Master's. No need at all."

"Apologies, Master Lha-Mi," Lanoree said, wincing inwardly. *You might have been out in the wilds,* she berated herself, *but be mindful of the Je'daii formality.*

The Wookiee laughed.

"I am Xiang," one of the strangers, a female of the Sith species, said. "Your father taught me, and now I teach under him at Bodhi Temple. A wise man. And good at magic tricks."

For an instant Lanoree felt a flood of emotion that surprised her. She remembered her father's tricks from when she and Dal were children—how he would pull objects out of thin air, turn one thing into another. Back then, she'd believed he was using mastery of the Force, but he had told her that there were some things not even the Force could do. *Tricks,* he'd said. *I'm merely fooling your senses, not touching them with my own.*

"And how is he?" Lanoree asked.

"He's fine," Xiang said, her red skin creasing with a smile. "He and your mother send their best wishes. They'd hoped you could visit them, but given the circumstances, they understand why that would be difficult."

"Circumstances?"

Xiang glanced sidelong at Lha-Mi and then back at Lanoree. When she spoke again, it was not to answer her query. "We have a mission for you. It's . . . delicate. And extremely important."

Lanoree sensed a shift in the room's atmosphere. For a few moments they sat in almost complete silence—Temple Master Lha-Mi, five other Je'daii Masters, and her. Air-conditioning hummed, and through the chair she could feel the deeper, more insistent vibration of the Peacemaker's power sources. Her own breath was loud. Her heart beat the moments by. The Force flowed through and around her, and she felt history pivoting on this moment—her own history and story, and that of the Je'daii civilization as well.

Something staggering was going to happen.

"Why do you choose me?" she asked softly. "There are many other Rangers, all across the system. Some much closer than me. It's taken me nineteen days to reach here from Obri."

"Two reasons," Xiang said. "First, you're particularly suited to the investigations required. Your time on Kalimahr brokering the Hang Layden deal displayed your sensitivity in dealing with inhabitants on the settled worlds. Your actions on Nox saved many lives. And your defusing of the Wookiee land wars on Ska Gora probably prevented a civil war."

"It was hardly a defusing," Lanoree said.

"The deaths were unfortunate," Lha-Mi said, "but they prevented countless more."

Lanoree thought of the giant apex trees aflame, countless burning leaves drifting in the vicious winds that sometimes stirred the jungles there, the sound of millennia-old tree trunks splitting and rupturing in the intense firestorm, and the screams of dying Wookiees. And she thought of her finger on the triggers of her laser cannons, raised and yet more than ready to fire again. *It was me or them*, she thought whenever the dream haunted her, and she knew that to be true. She had tried everything else—*everything*—but in the end, diplomacy gave way to blood. Yet each time she dreamed, the Force was in turmoil within her, dark and light vying for supremacy. Light tortured her with those memories. Dark would let her settle easy.

"You saved tens of thousands," Xiang said. "Maybe more. The Wookiee warlord Gharcanna had to be stopped."

"I only wish he had not fought to the end." Lanoree glanced at the Wookiee Master and he nodded slowly, never taking his eyes from hers. He had great pride, and carried his sadness well.

"You said two reasons," Lanoree said.

"Yes." Xiang seemed suddenly uncomfortable, shifting in her seat.

"Perhaps I should relay the rest of the information," Lha-Mi said.

"The mission first. The threat that has risen against the Je'daii, and perhaps even Tython itself. And when you know that, you will understand why we have chosen you."

"Of course," Lanoree said. "I'm honored to be here, and keen to hear. Any threat against Tython is a threat against everything I love."

"Everything we *all* love," Lha-Mi said. "For ten thousand years we have studied the Force and developed our society around and within it. Wars and conflicts have come and gone. We strive to keep the dark and the light, Bogan and Ashla, forever in balance. But now . . . now there is something that might destroy us all.

"One man. And his dreams. Dreams to leave the Tythan system and travel out into the galaxy. Many people desire to do so, and it's something I understand. However settled we are in this system, any educated being knows that our history lies out there, beyond everything we now know and understand. But this man seeks another route."

"What other route?" Lanoree asked. Her skin prickled with fear.

"A hypergate," Lha-Mi said.

"But there is no hypergate on Tython," Lanoree said, "only tales of one deep in the Old City, but they're just that. Tales."

"Tales," Lha-Mi said, his eyes heavy, beard drooping as he lowered his head. "But some people will chase a tale as far and hard as they can, and seek to make it real. We have intelligence that this man is doing such a thing. He believes that there's a hypergate deep beneath the ruins of the Old City on the continent of Talss. He seeks to activate it."

"How?" she asked.

"A device," Lha-Mi said. "We don't know its nature or its design. But our source tells us it will be fueled by dark matter, harnessed through arcane means. Forbidden. Dreaded. The most dangerous element known to us, and which no Je'daii would ever dare attempt to capture or create."

"But if there's no hypergate—"

"Tales," Lha-Mi said again. "He chases a legend. But whether it exists or not is irrelevant. The threat is the dark matter he intends using to try to initiate the supposed gateway. It could . . ." He trailed off and looked to his side.

"It could destroy Tython," Dam-Powl said. "Exposing dark matter to normal matter would be cataclysmic. It would create a black hole, swallowing Tython in a heartbeat. The rest of the system, too."

"And if there *is* a hypergate, and it *does* work?"

Silence for a while. And then one of the three Masters she did not know spoke, her first and last words of the meeting. "Then the danger to the Je'daii would be very different but equally severe."

"So you see the dire threat we face," Lha-Mi said.

"Just one man? So arrest him."

"We don't know where he is. We don't even know which planet he's on."

"The little intelligence you have is sound?" Lanoree asked, but she already knew the answer to that. Such a gathering of Je'daii Masters for this purpose would not have taken place otherwise.

"We have no reason to doubt it," Lha-Mi said, "and every reason to fear. If it does transpire that the threat is not as severe as it appears, then that's a good thing. All we waste is time."

"But the hypergate," Lanoree said. "Protect it. Guard it."

Lha-Mi leaned forward across the table. With a blink he closed off the cabin—air-conditioning ceased; the door slammed shut and locked. "The hypergate is a tale," he said. "That is all."

Lanoree nodded. But she also knew that talking about a simple story would surely not require such care and such an arrangement as this. *For later*, she thought, guarding her thoughts.

"And now to why it's you we've chosen for the mission," Xiang said. "The man is Dalien Brock, your brother."

Lanoree reeled. She never suffered from space sickness—the Force settled her, as it did all Je'daii—but she seemed to sway in her seat, though she did not move; dizziness swept through her, though the Peacemaker was as stable as the ground it rested upon.

"No," she said, frowning. "Dalien died nine years ago."

"You found no body," Xiang said.

"I found his clothing. Shredded. Bloodied."

"We have no reason to doubt our sources," Lha-Mi said.

"And I have no reason to believe them!" Lanoree said.

Silence in the room. A loaded hush.

"Your reason is that we order this," Lha-Mi said. "Your reason is any small element of doubt that exists over your brother's death. Your reason is that, if this is true, he might be a threat to Tython. Your brother might destroy everything you love."

He fled, I found his clothes, down, down deep in the—the Old City.

"You see?" Lha-Mi asked as if reading her thoughts. For all Lanoree knew he had, and she did not question that. He was a Temple Master, after all, and she only a Ranger. Confused as she was, she could not help her thoughts betraying her.

"He always looked to the stars," Lanoree said softly.

"We hear whispers of an organization, a loose collection of people, calling themselves Stargazers."

"Yes," Lanoree said, remembering her little brother always looking outward to the depths of space as she looked inward.

"Find your brother," Lha-Mi said. "Bring him back to Tython. Stop his foolish schemes."

"He won't come back," Lanoree said. "If it really is him, he'll never return after so long. So young when he died, but even then he was growing to . . ."

"To hate the Je'daii," Xiang said. "All the more reason to bring him back to us."

"And if he refuses?"

"You are a Je'daii Ranger," Lha-Mi said. And in a way, Lanoree knew that was answer enough.

"I need everything you know."

"It's already being downloaded to your ship's computer."

Lanoree nodded, unsurprised at their forwardness. They'd known that she could not say no.

"This is a covert operation," Xiang said. "Rumors of the hypergate persist, but the knowledge that someone is trying to initiate it might cause panic. We could send a much larger force against Dalien, but that would be much more visible."

"And there's a deeper truth," Lha-Mi said.

"You don't want people supporting his cause," Lanoree said. "If news of what he plans spreads, many more might attempt to initiate the gate. More devices. More dark matter."

Lha-Mi smiled and nodded. "You are perceptive and wise, Lanoree. The threat is severe. We are relying on you."

"Flattery, Master?" Lanoree said, her voice lighter. A ripple of laughter passed around the assembled Je'daii Masters.

"Honesty," Lha-Mi said. He grew serious once again, and that was a shame. A smile suited him.

"As ever, I'll give everything I have," Lanoree said.

"May the Force go with you," Lha-Mi said.

Lanoree stood, bowed, and as she approached the closed door Lha-Mi opened it with a wave of his hand. She paused once before leaving, turned back.

"Master Xiang. Please relay my love to my mother and father. Tell them . . . I'll see them soon."

Xiang nodded, smiled.

As Lanoree left the room, she almost felt her little brother's hand in her own.

On her way back to her Peacemaker, a riot of emotions played across Lanoree's mind. Beneath them all was a realization that was little surprise to her—she was glad that Dal was still alive. And this, she knew, was why she had been chosen for this mission. There were her past achievements, true, and though only in her midtwenties, she had already served the Je'daii well. Her affinity with the Force, and the Je'daii's purpose and outlook, was pure. But her personal involvement might be her greatest asset.

Because she had failed to save her brother's life once, she would not let him go again. She would do everything she could to save Dal—from danger and from damnation—and that determination would serve her mission well.

But she knew that it might also compromise her assignment.

She breathed deeply and calmed herself, knowing that she would have to keep her emotions in check.

Two young Je'daii apprentices passed her by. A boy and a girl, they might well have been brother and sister, and for a fleeting moment they reminded her of Dal and herself. They bowed respectfully and she nodded back, seeing the esteem in their eyes, and perhaps a touch of awe. Lanoree wore loose trousers and wrapped shirt, shimmersilk jacket, leather boots and equipment belt. Her flowing red scarves were from one of the finest clothing stores on Kalimahr. The silver bangles on her left wrist bore precious stones from the deep mines of Ska Gora, a gift from the Wookiee family she'd grown close to during her time there. Her sword was carried in a leather sheath fashioned from the bright green skin of a screech lizard from one of Obri's three moons. Add these exotic adornments to her six-foot frame, startling gray eyes, and long, flowing auburn hair clasped in a dozen metal clips, and she knew she cut an imposing figure.

"Ranger," the young girl said. Lanoree paused and turned, and saw that the two children had also stopped. They were staring at her, but with a little more than fascination. They had purpose.

"Children," Lanoree said, raising an eyebrow.

The girl came forward, one hand in the pocket of her woven trousers. Lanoree sensed the Force flowing strongly in them both, and there was an assuredness to their movements that made her sad. With her and Dal it had been so different. He had never understood the Force, and as they'd grown older together that confusion had turned into rejection, a growing hatred . . . and then something far worse.

"Master Dam-Powl asked that I give you this," the girl said. She held out a small message pod the size of her thumb. "She said it's for your eyes only."

A private message from Master Dam-Powl, beyond the ears and eyes of the rest of the Je'daii. This was intriguing.

Lanoree took the pod and pocketed it. "Thank you," she said. "What's your name?"

But the girl and boy hurried away toward Lha-Mi's Peacemaker, a gentle breeze ruffling their hair. The ship's engines were already starting to cycle up.

Ironholgs stood at the base of her ship's ramp. It clicked and rattled as she approached.

"All good?" she asked absently. The droid confirmed that, yes, all was good.

Lanoree paused on the ramp and looked around. The Masters' Peacemaker and several smaller escort ships were already lifting away, and further afield there were only the hillsides and the ancient standing stones, placed countless millennia ago to honor long-forgotten gods.

The feeling of being watched came from elsewhere. The Je'daii Masters. They were waiting for her departure.

"Okay, then," Lanoree said, and she walked up the ramp into the comforting, familiar confines of her own ship.

But she was distracted. This short time on Tython, and hearing of Dal's mysterious survival, was waking those troubled memories once again.

CHAPTER TWO
THE GREAT JOURNEY

In your early years, the flow of the Force might seem frightening, shocking. Find balance between its light and dark facets, and the flow will become a powerful stillness. Struggle against the Force, and your body rebels; fight with the Force and you have the universe on your side.
—Temple Master Vor'Dana, Stav Kesh, 10,441 TYA

Two years, Lanoree thinks. *It'll be at least that long before I see Mother and Father again.* But such is the training of a young Journeyer. Their time at Padawan Kesh over, teenagers now, she and her brother Dal are embarking on their Great Journey. And they have returned home to say good-bye.

Close to the sea on the southern coast of Masara lies Bodhi Temple and its surrounding settlement, her home since birth. Her parents are Je'daii and they teach at the temple, instructing young Force sensitives in the arts. Her mother specializes in music, prose, and poetry. Her father is a talented sculptor and artist. They made their own Journeys years before Dal and Lanoree were born—indeed, they enjoy telling the story of how they met as Journeyers—and they were both drawn to Bodhi, the Force exposing and celebrating their particular talents and strengths.

Now it is time for Dal and Lanoree to journey across Tython to the other Je'daii temples, there to learn the ways of the Force. Science and combat, meditation and healing, the raw talents Lanoree has now will be honed and practiced throughout the coming two years. She is excited and nervous. And when her mother calls her close and asks that they walk across the grassland until they are alone, she almost knows what to expect.

It is a fine, sunny day, and the sky is clear. Tythos blazes above, giving them heat and light. The Force binds her and her surroundings together, and she wears her Je'daii training sword on her hip. Though nervous, she is at peace. Until her mother begins to speak.

"Look after your brother, Lanoree."

"I'm only two years older than him, Mother."

"True. But the Force is *strong* in you. You welcome it, and it nurtures you. Your father and I both sense your strength, and we also sense Dal's weakness. He and the Force . . . there's little love lost."

"He'll learn, Mother. He has you and Father to look up to. You're powerful Je'daii, and he'll be the same."

"You are destined to follow us, I believe," her mother says. She smiles at Lanoree, but there is little joy here. "But my worries for Dal are genuine and heartfelt. His interest in the distant past, our ancestors and history outside the system, places on Tython like the Old City . . . I'm afraid his fate leads away from the Force. Away from Tython." Her voice hitches, and Lanoree is startled to see tears in her mother's eyes, glistening on her soft brown cheeks.

"I'll make sure that *doesn't* happen! I'll guide and help him, I promise. That's what we're traveling for, after all."

"You're traveling to learn to control and expand your powers. If the Force isn't there to begin with—"

"It *is* there," Lanoree says, interrupting her mother. "I see it in his eyes. I think Dal just has trouble letting go."

"He wants to be his own master."

"And he will," Lanoree said. "You know the teachings, Mother. 'The Force is neither light nor dark, master nor slave, but a balance between extremes.' Dal will find balance."

"I hope so," her mother says.

Lanoree frowns, pouting slightly. It's a little unfair, she knows, using the look that her mother can so rarely resist. But it might be the last time. She is leaving as a child, and when she returns she will be a woman.

"Fine, Lanoree," her mother says, smiling. "I'm *sure* he'll find the balance he needs."

Lanoree smiles and nods, and a little while later she and Dal take the first symbolic steps away from their parents. They look back along the river several times and their mother and father remain there, watching them go and waving them on their way.

Dal says nothing. Neither does Lanoree. Lost in their private thoughts, hers are troubled. *I'm sure he'll find the balance he needs*, her mother said of Dal.

Buried deep beneath her childish enthusiasm, in truth Lanoree is far from certain. And yet unsettled by whatever future her brother might face, she also leaves her parents and home behind with excitement burning in her heart. This is the start of a real adventure, and one that every Je'daii on Tython has to undergo at some point during their training.

Balance in the Force is essential to become a great Je'daii, and to achieve that one must also gain balance in one's abilities and talents. Being adept at Force skills is nothing if you do not know how to use them. Having a great talent in channeling the Force through writing and art is fine, but if you cannot also protect yourself in combat, then you will never reach the heights of Je'daii Master. Ashla and Bogan cast their light and dark shadows upon the surface of Tython, and true balance exists within as well as without.

Lanoree can feel the Force thrumming through her sometimes, matching the beating of her heart or, perhaps, vice versa. And she is looking forward to every day that follows. She and Dal often wander together, and they're very familiar with Bodhi, the nearby ocean, and the lands around it. But other than their time at Padawan Kesh, they have never gone beyond.

The start of their journey will take them northwest across the large island continent of Masara to the other coast. A flight by Cloud Chaser eight hundred kilometers over the Thyrian Ocean will follow; and after their arrival on Thyr, they will journey across rocky plains and through extensive forests until they reach Qigong Kesh, the Temple of Force Skills. It lies beyond the forests and three days' walk into the Silent Desert, that mysterious place where sound is soaked up by some unknown quality in the constantly drifting sands. The winds are relentless there, and it's said that some of the sand sculptures that persist sometimes for mere seconds are sentient, part of a species that has existed on Tython for millions of years. No contact has ever been made with these sculptures—indeed, there are those who believe they are simply another unusual quality of the Silent Desert. But Lanoree is always ready to believe.

Beneath the desert, in deep caverns, they will undertake the first lessons in their journey of learning.

They crest a gentle hilltop around midday and turn to look back down upon Bodhi Temple in the distance. The sea shimmers beyond it, constantly moving yet at peace. The Tho Yor at the temple's center reflects the bright sunlight, and the river snaking inland is a dancing rainbow of light.

"When we return we'll be real Je'daii," Lanoree says. "Aren't you excited, Dal? Isn't it just thrilling?"

"Yeah," he says. He grasps her hand and squeezes, but never quite meets her gaze.

"Mother and Father will be so proud."

Dal shrugs. "I suppose."

Lanoree knows of their parents' hopes—that their journey will imbue Dal with more of the Force, that he will come to know and love it, and that perhaps he is simply a late starter. *It happens*, they said. *Sometimes it just takes time and experience.*

But Lanoree also knows that a Journeyer has to *want* it to happen.

"Come on," she says. "Race you to that fallen tree!"

They run down the slope, and soon Bodhi is out of sight behind them. Neither of them comments on the fact. And for a while, as they race each other through long flute grasses and listen to the gentle hum and hoot of the breeze around them, they are young children again.

Lanoree let the Peacemaker's computer fly them out of Tython's atmosphere, and this gave her time to look down upon the planet that had once been her home. To reach escape velocity they passed over Tython's largest continent, Talss, and even from this distance she could see the vast wound in the land that was the Rift. Six hundred kilometers east of the Rift was Anil Kesh Temple, and it was here, on her Great Journey, that she had truly found her peace with the Force for the first time. It was also here that her brother's doom had been sealed.

But she wished she could look down upon Masara, home to Bodhi, the Temple of the Arts. There, her parents still lived and taught. They mourned the son they had believed dead, but who now seemed to have become an enemy of the Je'daii and a danger to everyone. Her parents now knew that he yet lived, of that she was certain—Master Xiang's comments about their understanding the circumstances made that obvious. But she would have liked to speak to them and tell them to continue mourning their son. Whatever the outcome of her mission, the Dalien Brock they had known and loved was no more.

He had shunned his family, and let them continue for nine years believing he was dead. *Not everyone is lucky enough to finish their Great Journey*, her mother had said to her at Dalien's memorial ritual. It seemed now that luck had little to do with it.

"Little shak," Lanoree said. She laughed bitterly. She'd used the term before to describe Dal, but only to herself, when he got his own way with their parents or infuriated her so much.

The ship shuddered with its efforts to tear itself from Tython's pull, and she wondered why leaving did not trouble her equally. She'd spent four years believing it was because she was a wanderer, a seeker of knowledge and enlightenment, and the farther she went, the more she knew. A large part of that was true; her passion in the Force made it so.

But she also suspected that in ranging beyond Tython, she had left behind the lingering guilt that Dal's death had been her fault.

Where could such feelings reside now?

She withdrew the message pod from her pocket and slipped it into the ship's computer. The flatscreen snowed and then a picture faded in from the darkness. Master Dam-Powl's face, though this time she seemed more tense than before.

"Lanoree, I'll be brief. By the time you view this message you'll have stood before me and other Je'daii Masters and been given a mission. What I offer you now—privately, the reason for which I'm sure you will understand—is help. Your ship's computer now contains all we know of your errant brother and his intentions, though, as you will see, that's precious little. A rumor, a warning, a few words of worry from our Rangers and spies out in the system. On Kalimahr you should proceed to the city-state of Rhol Yan, where you will meet a Twi'lek called Tre Sana in Susco's Tavern. He lives close by, just ask the tavern's owner. Tre will tell you more. He's not a Je'daii. Indeed, many of his interests are on Shikaakwa, and on any other occasion you might seek to arrest him rather than take his advice. But he's served me well several times before. Greed drives him, and I pay."

She sighed, and looked for a moment incredibly sad. "I hate to go behind the backs of the other Je'daii Masters in this, because no one on the Council wanted a non-Je'daii involved. But I justify doing so in the knowledge that it will help. You'll know more than most that some on the settled worlds don't trust the Je'daii, even though perhaps they hold us in awe. Some actively dislike us. A few harbor hate, still nurtured and fresh following the Despot War twelve years ago, and I suspect it is these levels of society where your investigation will take you. Tre might help you past this mistrust. He *knows* those levels. But . . . be wary of him. Stay alert. He has his own interests at heart, and only that. He's as dangerous as . . . Well"—Dam-Powl smiled—"almost as dangerous as you."

She touched the corner of her mouth with one finger, a habit Lanoree knew well—the Master from Anil Kesh was thinking. "I hope your studies go well," she said softly. "I hope you're still learning. I've never seen such potential in anyone. Go well, Lanoree Brock. And may the Force go with you."

The message ended and the screen faded to black. The computer ejected the message pod, but Lanoree sat for a while in the cockpit, seat turned away from the windows and the amazing views beyond.

"Kalimahr it is, then," she said. Over four years spent mostly alone, the habit of talking to herself—or Ironholgs, which was almost the same—had grown. "But I don't like the idea of a *partner*." She liked her own company. Sometimes she spoke to the second, empty cockpit seat beside her, though it had never been occupied.

She swiveled the pilot's seat and looked to the stars. There was already much to absorb and muse upon, and she had the time it would take to reach Kalimahr to do so. All these secrets being entrusted to her should have made her feel honored. But instead she was unsettled. There was so much she still didn't know.

After running through standard checks to ensure that her Peacemaker was not being tracked or followed at a distance—being alone was more than habit—she turned to the flatscreen once again.

"So let's see what *all* the Masters wanted me to know." She lifted a keyboard onto her lap, tapped in some commands, and started to view the information that had been loaded into the ship's computer.

Lanoree and Dal's parents told them that the ritual of visiting each temple would be best done under their own steam as much as possible. Not for them the ease of a speeder or the comfort of a shire, one of the most common beasts of burden on Tython.

Walking, their parents said, will bring them closer to Tython, which itself is incredibly rich in the Force. It will make them understand, experience, taste, and smell their surroundings instead of viewing them through a speeder's windshield or from the high back of a shire. And sometimes it means there will be dangers to confront. Dreadful dangers.

Forty days and twenty-four hundred kilometers from home, on the strange continent of Thyr, they reach the expansive Stark Forests that lead eventually to the Silent Desert. The trees of these forests store water in pendulous, leathery sacs, useful to travelers and constantly refilled as the skeletal branches suck what moisture they can from the air. It is here that their lives are threatened for the first time.

Tythos shines down on them, the weather neither too hot nor too cold. The going through the forest is gentle, and they are following a shallow stream that meanders lazily toward the desert some kilometers ahead.

"I'll harvest ground apples for dinner," Dal says.

"I'll catch a rumbat to cook," Lanoree says.

And then a flight of hook hawks swoops out of the high trees and attempts to hypnotize Dal and Lanoree with their sweet song. Carnivores, these birds hunt in packs, singing their prey to a somnolent standstill and then tearing into eyeballs and throats with their wickedly hooked beaks and sharp talons. They hover in a rough circle around the brother and sister, wings beating a gentle rhythm, voice glands whistling and humming in practiced harmony. Their eyes are dark and intelligent. Their claws shine.

Lanoree has heard about these creatures but has never seen them before. She is terrified. Never has she faced such danger, and the knowledge that their lives are at risk strikes a heavy blow. And yet a thrill rushes through her as she thinks, *This is what the Great Journey is all about!* "Quick," she says, "down to the stream!"

"What good will that do?" Dal asks. She realizes that he is also afraid, and she feels a rush of protectiveness.

"The splashing of water can sometimes smother their song."

"Really?"

"Don't you listen in *any* of our lessons?" She grabs Dal's hand and tugs, but already his eyes have taken on a hazy sheen, the corners of his mouth lifting in a lazy smile. "Dal!"

"I'm fine. . . ."

A single hook hawk drifts down, slow and casual, still singing as it aims its claws for Dal's eyes.

Lanoree punches wildly, and in her panic she feels the Force flailing within her. It is against everything she has learned, but she does not have time to berate herself—her fist ruffles feathers, and she feels the cool kiss of the hawk's claws across her knuckles.

It screeches in anger as it flaps back, and in that moment she manages to calm, focus, and flow with the Force.

When the bird swoops down once more and turns its beak toward her eyes, Lanoree reaches out and Force-slaps it aside. This time her hand hardly touches the creature, barely a kiss of feathers across her fingertips. But the impact is much greater. Bones crackle, and with a single weak cry its body disappears into some undergrowth, leaving only a few feathers dancing on the air.

"Come on!" she says, dragging Dal with her.

The hook hawks are still singing, and their voices silence the rest of the forest. A cool cascade, a pleasing symphony, and though Lanoree tries to close herself to their influence she can feel a distance growing around her. She is dragging Dal along, and when he trips and falls, his hand is jerked from hers.

She turns back, and her brother is lying on his back, smiling up at the Stark Forests' canopy. They will never reach the stream in time. The hook hawks are coming close. This is all on her.

Lanoree feels like screaming in fury and fear, but instead she finds serenity and balance. She draws her consciousness inward and crouches, breathing deeply. Perhaps the hook hawks see this as her succumbing to their charms. But they could not be more wrong. As the first of the birds swoop, Lanoree stands and sends an air-splitting Force punch their way. Two creatures are knocked from the sky with broken wings and ruptured innards, and a third is smashed into a tree trunk in an explosion of feathers. The surviving birds change their song to one of panic, and fly up through the canopy and away.

Lanoree smiles at Dal, who is still shaking with fear. His eyes are distant.

"But they were so . . ." he says.

"Beautiful? A trick. They'd find beauty in your flowing blood and open flesh." Pleased that she has protected them, yet wary of pride, Lanoree helps Dal stand.

"Your hand," he says. It is bleeding. He tends his sister's wound silently, dripping in medicines from his rucksack that will clean the talon cuts. Then he wraps her hand in a bandage. All the while, Lanoree listens for a return of the hook hawks, and a small part of her *wants* them to come back. Her heart is beating fast, and she delights in her success. But the birds have finished hunting for the day.

Dal leads the way through the diminishing forest, and as dusk starts to fall they see the sparse desert landscape visible on the horizon. The edge of the forest leads down a gentle hillside, and the boundary between forest and desert is a gradual lessening of undergrowth, a greater spread of creeping sand. They pause for a while, filling their water canteens.

And as they move out into the desert they are cocooned within a deep, encompassing silence.

Lanoree speaks her own name, and feels it only as a vibration in her chest and jaw. It is as if the desert does not wish to hear. She looks at

Dal and he is wide-eyed and afraid, and Lanoree thinks, *I have already saved him once.* Pride swells once again. She tries to push it down, because pride is distracting.

That first night they camp on the cooling sands. They have eaten and are seated close to the campfire, blankets huddled around their shoulders, packs resting beside them, sleeping rolls already laid out. Yet neither of them wishes to sleep. This place is so strange that they relish each other's company as never before. Lanoree fears the dreams such utter silence might bring.

Reflecting on the fight with the hook hawks, she stares across the fire and sees movement in the shadows beyond. Tensing, nudging Dal, she realizes that he is also alert to the movement. Lanoree stands. Dal crouches. Firelight flickers from something, and a nightmare slashes into their camp.

Silik lizard! she thinks. Rare but deadly, these silicon-based creatures absorb energy from the sand itself, but have been known to supplement their diets with mammalian spinal fluid. The size of a human adult, they are viciously spiked beasts, six limbed and capable of charging on their hind legs. Encounters with them are often fatal. For some, siliks are much-prized hunting trophies.

For the second time in half a day, they must face a terrible danger.

Lanoree is so shocked by its appearance that she freezes. Sparks scrape from its extremities as it lopes toward her; its curved claws dig into the sand and splash up fleeting flames; and its mouth falls open to display crystalline teeth beyond counting. The complete silence of the attack is perhaps the most shocking aspect, and Lanoree opens her mouth in a soundless scream.

The lizard leaps through the fire, scattering burning brands around it and throwing up a confusion of sparks.

Force-punch, push it back, shove it back! Lanoree thinks, but her instincts are petrified by disbelief. That she will die so soon after beginning her journey, victim of such a beast—

A flash lights up the night, and the scattered campfire seems to erupt with new life. The terrifying creature twists and squirms away, slicing shadows with its limbs and slipping through them to safety.

One heartbeat it is there, the next gone, and Lanoree turns a quick circle to try to see where the next attack will come from.

Dal is holding his laser blaster. Its muzzle is still warm. *No*, she wants to say, because she is meant to protect *him*. Her limbs quiver in fright, and as she starts to draw in her senses and balance herself within the Force, the darkness beyond Dal sparkles with a hundred dancing stars.

Lanoree opens her eyes wide as she tries to form a Force punch. But her fear is still a barrier, seemingly muting the Force as this desert mutes sound.

Dal crouches and spins, alerted by Lanoree's reaction, and the night is lit by three blaster shots in quick succession.

The silik lizard spins a full circle as it powers from the darkness. It hits the ground close enough for Lanoree to kick. Dal's gunfire and the creature's fall are silent.

Her brother is still aiming the weapon at the lizard. He's shaking slightly, his eyes wide as if he can't quite believe what he's done. It is an old weapon, bequeathed him by his grandfather, and Lanoree has always dismissed it as clumsy and unreliable compared to the Force. Now, though, it has saved them both. The lizard's head hangs by a thread. Its blood is dust.

She embraces Dal and tries to speak into his ear, *Thank you.* Even as she does so, she is troubled and ashamed at her hesitation. Perhaps after the hook hawks she was too confident in her abilities. Misplaced pride has no place in the heart of a true Je'daii.

They drag the silik lizard away from their camp and bury it to prevent interest from carrion creatures. The burial is silent, even the shush of sand between their fingers unheard. Before sand covers its face, the beast stares past them at the glorious night sky with violet eyes.

Forty days out from home, not having even reached the first temple, and already their lives have twice been endangered. Lanoree thinks of the long journey still ahead; the perils they will face; the distances they will travel on water, in the air, and largely on foot. For the first time since leaving their parents, she wishes for home.

That night in her dreams Lanoree sees great shapes rising out of the desert, sculptures in sand that live in a manner beyond her comprehension, feeding on sound and taking sustenance from every whispered word, each expression of love or fear. In the morning the desert around them has changed in profile, there are three humped mounds of sand close by, and she wonders what watched them sleep.

They march hard for the next two days. In the afternoon of their third day in the desert they see curved rock spires rising from the landscape far ahead, and know that they mark the location of Qigong Kesh. Lanoree feels a rush of excitement, but she has also seen the holos about this place. As the desert steals sound, so its dry, scorching atmosphere also muddles distance; the temple could still be another four days away.

They walk on, traveling by day, camping by night, watchful for danger and barely sleeping.

When they arrive at last they are tired, hungry, disoriented. The silence has become a great weight crushing them down. Even communicating by sign language is an effort, and for the last two days Lanoree has felt so alone even with her brother constantly by her side.

But the sight of the giant rock spires, and the mysterious Tho Yor floating between them, brings a sense of anticipation.

We're here at last! Lanoree thinks. *Qigong Kesh!* The temple is belowground in a network of natural caverns and tunnels. Beneath the desert, they will be able to speak, to hear once more. As they pass within the shadow of one of the massive rock spires, several Je'daii guards emerge from a cavern in its vast base. They look Lanoree and Dal up and down; smile; and hold out two canteens of cool, fresh water.

Then they take the exhausted brother and sister down beneath the desert. Here, in a huge cavern, lies the majestic Temple of Qigong Kesh where the arcane, mysterious, and enlightening training in Force Skills will commence.

It is here that Dalien Brock's fall will begin.

CHAPTER THREE
THE GOOD AND THE GREAT

Not every Journeyer will complete their Great Journey. Some will fall victim to Tython's many dangerous landscapes or creatures. Some will lose themselves. Some may even lose their way in the Force and leave Tython far behind, scattering out to the system, lost in a much more fundamental way. But as Je'daii we must accept this, because this is not an existence of absolutes. Life is a challenge, and facing that challenge is what makes the good great.

—Master Deela jan Morolla, 3,533 TYA

Even though she had been away from home for four years, Lanoree still kept to Tython time. She was used to it, it suited her natural sleep patterns, and she saw little point in adapting her ship to Standard Time. In her less-guarded moments she might also admit that it reminded her of home.

The computer calculated the optimum flight path from Tython to Kalimahr for the time of year and current planet alignments. And before committing to the route Lanoree also calculated it manually. The computer was never wrong in such matters—the navigational elements were programmed and designed by the Je'daii's most experienced space travelers—but she was always pleased when her calculations came out the same. Rather than questioning the computer, she was testing herself.

Pushing her Peacemaker to its limits, it took a little over seven days to reach Kalimahr. She used this time to meditate, prepare herself for the coming mission, exercise, and review every aspect of the information downloaded to the Peacemaker's computers. There wasn't much. Whatever contacts had informed the Je'daii of Dal's scheme had not been very thorough. Rumors, speculation, and a few hazy images. But even in those grainy images of covert meetings and mysterious exchanges, she recognized the face of her brother.

He looked older, of course. But she was surprised at how *much* older, as if he'd lived three lifetimes since she had last seen him, not nine years. He was taller, thinner, his child's sadness translated into adult bitterness. His dusky skin had turned darker and more rugged. And there was something haunting about his blurred visage. Lanoree berated herself for letting her thoughts of his death cloud how she viewed him now. Yet the idea remained. Seeing those images of Dal felt like looking at a ghost.

"We'll meet again," she said to the screen, "and I'll ask why you let me think you were dead all these years."

For the first few days of the journey she left Dal's image on the cockpit flatscreen, also feeding it through to a screen in the living quarters directly behind the cockpit. A reminder of who she sought and who she had lost. But seeing him there only confused her more, so by day five she left the screen blank.

Lanoree had visited Kalimahr twice over the past four years. The first time was to act as mediator in a troublesome deal between three landmass developers, all of them bickering over an island called Hang Layden in the planet's vast Southern Ocean. Normally a Je'daii would not have been concerned with such matters, but the Je'daii Council had sent Lanoree because of the island's suspected archaeological importance. Though the island appeared bare, it was believed that an ancient structure—possibly of Gree origin—existed a kilometer beneath the surface. Her presence had been resented, but she had taken an active role in the negotiations, ensuring that each of the three interested parties had a portion of land to develop. More important, she had covertly protected the cave network that might lead deep down to that ruin from ancient history. The Force illusions she had left behind of rockfalls and impassable ravines would last for a hundred years.

Her second time on Kalimahr had been less peaceful. That time, her sword had been wetted with blood.

Even so, she did not pretend for a moment that she knew this place. A good Je'daii was always on guard and ready for surprises. Especially a Je'daii on a mission as important as hers.

As she entered the atmosphere and her computer contacted air traffic control, she saw two Kalimahr Defense ships shadowing her thirty kilometers away. They would be no threat. It was more likely that the pilots were excited at spotting a Peacemaker, and they'd go home that night to tell their families and friends that they'd seen a Je'daii arrive! They followed for the next hour, and just before peeling away they made contact. She replied with a gentle push of grace and humor, responding to them while revealing nothing. *If we met in a tavern, we might even be friends*, she thought, smiling. It was a subtle Je'daii talent, but one that often served her well. They disappeared from her screen when she was more than a hundred kilometers from her destination.

She approached Rhol Yan above a startling azure sea. The Peacemaker shuddered as she passed across the waves. She was so low that spray from the sea misted the windows, but she enjoyed flying like this. Out in space there was no context—she could fly for days with the starscape changing hardly at all. Depth was infinite, and distances were so vast that her mind could barely grasp them. But down here she was *close* to something. Sometimes closeness mattered.

Rhol Yan had been built on an archipelago stretching out into the Southern Ocean. There were five large islands and countless smaller ones, all of them developed, and hundreds of bridges both large and small spanned the spaces between landmasses. Gleaming white spires reached stark fingers to the sky, and several classes of Cloud Chaser airships drifted between them like lazy birds flocking around ak trees back on Tython. Lower down, buildings and streets clung to the islands and sometimes protruded out over the ocean on slender stilts, and beautifully wrought bridges stood in isolation over the waterways.

Ships dotted the ocean, and the inner waterways were busy with smaller watercraft. The white metal spires pulsed here and there with colored lights, illuminated even during daytime to identify an island, a building, or a street. It was an attractive city, and most of its money came from tourism. People traveled from all over Kalimahr to holiday on Rhol Yan. And with tourists came the vultures and parasites who preyed on them.

She was directed to a landing platform on a high tower on one of the outer islands. There were scores of gracefully wrought landing pads and bays around the tower, and exterior elevators whisked up and down its uneven sides. Even the city's air and spaceport were beautiful.

As the Peacemaker settled, Lanoree prepared herself for what was to come. Her mission started here.

"Keep an eye on the ship," she said to the droid. It grumbled and clicked. "Yes, I'll have my comlink." She felt the sliver of tech in her lapel just to make sure. Then she stood within the cabin and smoothed down her clothing, checking that her sword was strapped correctly to her thigh, ran fingers through her hair. She used her metal Je'daii star to fix her cape around her neck. For now, there was no need to hide.

She was surprised to realize that she was nervous.

Somewhere at the end of this mission, her brother waited.

Like any visitor who had landed on one of the spacecraft platforms, Lanoree was directed through to a large room with lines of interview pods. One entire side was a window offering staggering views across Rhol Yan and the glimmering sea beyond, and the opposite wall was splayed with extravagant artwork that labeled it the Welcome Hall. But its real purpose was obvious. Kalimahr's security services were efficient and discreet, and even a Je'daii was not simply waved through. She respected that. And by the time she was ushered from her interview pod, the three officers inside also respected her privacy. A subtle push, a gentle word. Perhaps in a few days' time they might start to question their decision to let her in so lightly, although by then she would be long gone.

But by the time she had traveled on three elevators down through the tower to ground level, Lanoree began to suspect that she was being followed.

She paused in the vast lobby of the port tower, bought a drink from a vendor droid, and melted into the shadows beneath a wide, low tree. There were tables and chairs there, and a massively fat Zabrak woman was harvesting large insects from the tree's lower canopy, flash-frying them, and selling them to eager customers. Lanoree decided she was not hungry.

As she drank, she watched the bank of elevators she had just left. Her sense of being followed was strong, but though she waited for a while, none of those exiting the elevators seemed to be looking for her. Strange. She was certain it was not one of the customs officers.

"Lady, you're a fine one," a voice said. A tall robed figure had approached, and she was annoyed with herself for not noticing.

"I'm drinking," she said.

"So drink with me."

"No, thanks."

"Come on, Ranger. You're young. I'm almost two hundred years old. Got experience. Got three bottles of chay wine in my rooms, almost as old as me, just waiting for a special occasion."

She rested her hand on her sword's haft. The Force was calm and settled, and the weapon was part of her. "Would losing your life constitute a special occasion?"

He stared at her from beneath his hood, amused, uncertain. Then he waved a hand and turned to leave. "Ach. Je'daii. So tightly wound."

She finished her drink, then moved out across the lobby area. There were hundreds of people there, a varied mix of the many species who had spread out from Tython to colonize the system. Humans and Wookiees mingled with Twi'leks, with their prominent head-tails, and red-skinned Sith. Near-human Zabrak, with their vestigial horns, walked alongside Iktotchi, whose heavy horns gave them a fearsome appearance. Kalimahr had been the first planet settled after Tython and its moons, and it remained the most racially mixed and diverse. It was proud of its diversity, and it was a pride well earned. Even on Tython it was rare that so many species were seen in one place at any one time, and Lanoree paused for a moment in the center of the lobby to feel the ebb and flow of so many people in transit.

She paused also to try to spot any pursuer. Still nothing. She'd seen no one obviously stop when she had. And although some people looked at her as they passed by, she sensed that it was only out of interest when they recognized the Je'daii star. And on occasion, perhaps even distaste. She knew well enough that some Kalimahr thought themselves above the Je'daii.

I'm alone too often and for too long, she thought. Perhaps a subtle paranoia was a natural part of being among so many people once more.

Leaving the spire's lobby, she passed a group of Dai Bendu monks chanting one of their strange, haunting ululations. A small group of travelers had settled around them, and some were swaying slowly in time with the song. Just outside the main doors, down a wide, long ramp that led to street level, a circle of feline Cathars was meditating upon an image of their god painted on the ground. The image was beautifully wrought, and their meditations had drawn several smoke snakes up from the ground to dance in a slow, hypnotic pattern. Lanoree had heard of the Cathars' smoke snakes but had never seen them.

Such diverse beliefs being celebrated in such close proximity. Her immersion in the Force meant that she believed neither, but it was still pleasing to see such inclusivity.

The streets outside were bustling with people, trade stalls, performance artists, religious groups, speakers, security officers, and children and adults alike pointing and chattering in delight at their surroundings. She felt almost unnoticed, and she welcomed that. But she also knew that it was an ideal environment in which to be followed, and that feeling persisted. Though she cast her Force sense around, there were so many people that her thoughts were confused. She would have to remain alert.

Cloud Chasers floated above, and occasionally drop ships came down to pick up passengers. But Lanoree had studied maps on her ship and knew that the tavern she sought was close by. She chose to walk.

"Bet you've never seen one like me, eh? Eh?" Tre Sana grinned at her over his glass of wine. His yellow eyes and blazing red skin gave him a fearsome appearance, but she perceived a gentle intelligence behind the startling exterior.

"Your coloring is quite rare," Lanoree said. "Rarer still for a Twi'lek, the extra lekku."

"Rarer? Oh, yeah, rarer indeed." He stroked the third head-tail that grew behind the usual two. "Least you use the right terminology. You wouldn't *believe* what some people call these things."

"I probably would."

"They call me freak." He growled suddenly and leaned forward, baring teeth that seemed to have been filed down to points. "A scary freak!"

"You don't scare me," she said.

"Hmm." Tre's lekku—those three long, curious tentacles growing from the back of his skull—twitched a little, one tip stroking over his left shoulder, the other two pointing like fingers tapping at the air.

" 'Yeah, well, *this* bitch is a Je'daii,' " Lanoree translated.

Tre's eyes opened wide. "You know Twi'leki!"

"Of course. That surprises you?"

"Huh. Huh! Nothing about the Je'daii can surprise me."

"Oh, don't be so sure." Lanoree took a drink and looked around Susco's Tavern. With more than fifteen settled planets and moons and spread over sixteen billion kilometers, there were places like this all across the Tythan system. Places where people gathered to drink, eat, and talk, no matter what their color, species, creed, or breed. Where music played in the background—either a local tune or perhaps something more exotic from another continent or another world. Where travelers found common ground, and those who chose not to travel could hear outlandish tales of faraway places. And it was in these taverns that tongues could be loosened, news spread, and secrets overheard. Lanoree loved places like this, because often after a drink or two she could have been anywhere.

The drink she was sipping now had been recommended by Tre—a local wine, made from deep-sea grapes and fortified with swing dust from some of the air mines at Kalimahr's north pole. It was incredibly strong, but she used a gentle Force flow to make sure the potent drink did not impede her senses. She might enjoy such taverns, but she had been attacked in places like these. And she had also killed in them.

"Master Dam-Powl vouches for you," Lanoree said.

Tre Sana's eyes glimmered with humor. "Oh, I doubt that."

"Well, she says to watch you. And that I should kill you the first moment you display any hint of betrayal." Lanoree looked around the tavern but probed for Tre's reaction. Strange. She felt nothing. She turned back to him and said, "But Dam-Powl assures me you don't have a traitorous bone in your body."

Tre raised his brows and his lekku, resting now over his shoulders, performed a gentle, almost sensuous touch along their tips.

"Good," Lanoree said, smiling. "Then let's take a meal and at the same time share some information."

"The sea beef is very good here," Tre said. He raised a hand and caught the attention of the barman. A wave and a click of his fingers, and the barman nodded back, grinning.

Lanoree probed outward and touched the barman's mind. She took a startled breath—she could never really prepare for experiencing another's thoughts, as the first rush was always overwhelming—but she quickly filtered out the random, the violent, the sick and disgusting, and narrowed to what she sought. *Tre so cool so calm so red sitting there with her that Je'daii and he'd be lucky, she'd eat him alive.* She broke away and stared at Tre until he averted his yellow eyes. But she said nothing. She knew she was attractive, and if he *was* thinking of her that way, there was no real harm.

"I'll be very open with you," Lanoree said, "very honest. That's a good way to begin, for both of us. There's something about you I can't read, but I don't need the Force to understand people. You're haughty and superior. Maybe that's just you, but right now I think it's because you think you have me at a disadvantage. Perhaps because Dam-Powl has told you most, if not all, of what I know and why I'm here."

Tre blinked softly, his lekku touching in gentle acknowledgment.

"And so, you know whom I seek. You'll know that he's my brother. I have rumors and stories told in taverns, secondhand information from sources I can't verify and don't trust. And the sum of all the information I have gives me virtually nothing to go on. I don't even know what planet he's on right now."

"You can't"—he waved his fingers, raised his arms up and down—"*Force* his location?"

Lanoree glared at Tre. His childish display did not warrant a response.

"Master Dam-Powl sent me to you and said you might be able to help. I hope so. Because I don't know how much more of this piss I can take." Lanoree emptied her glass in one swallow.

"And now I'll be very open with you, too," Tre said, suddenly serious. "Along with talk of your brother, I hear rumors of Gree technology."

Lanoree inclined her head, raised an eyebrow.

"I don't mean the hypergate. Anyone with half a mind knows of the theories about the Old City being of Gree origin." Tre leaned in closer, glancing around. "I mean what *drives* the hypergate."

"I don't understand," she said, but already she was thinking of what the Masters had told her back on Tython. *Dark matter* . . .

"I mean there are whispers of design plans. Tech details." Tre shrugged. "Blueprints. And all Gree."

Lanoree leaned back in shock. Gree? Really? So little was known about that ancient people. There were theories that the Gree had once inhabited the Old City on Tython, but theorists were split as to whether the Gree had built it themselves. Though the Gree were long gone from the galaxy, it was suggested by some that the Old City was even *more* ancient. Lanoree had met a man on Tython—not a Je'daii but someone allied to them in outlook—who had spent his life researching the Gree and their legacy, and even what he knew could be relayed in little more than an hour of talk. And now this mysterious Twi'lek who, if what Dam-Powl had told her was true, undertook criminal activities, was claiming that Dal had found something the Gree had left behind.

"Blueprints?" she asked.

"Only what I've heard. More wine?"

Lanoree bristled. He was toying with her. Playing a Je'daii Ranger as he would a weak-minded petty criminal looking to muscle in on some nefarious deal. She leaned back in her chair and feigned tiredness, but behind her drooping eyelids she felt the Force flow, stirring her senses, boosting them, and she probed outward once again to touch Tre's mind.

But he was closed to her.

Tre's eyes went wide, and for a moment he looked unaccountably sad, shoulders dropping and lekku slumping down exhausted. *He looks like a battered pet*, Lanoree thought. She wasn't sure where the image came from, but she had grown to trust her first impressions. The Force resided in her subconscious, too, and sometimes it spoke.

He would not meet her gaze, staring instead into his half-empty glass.

She sensed around the fringes of his mind but could not get in, and it was something she was not used to. Some species were very hard to read—the Cathars' minds worked in a very different way, thinking in symbols and abstracts rather than words and images—but usually she could at least touch another's mind, whether human or alien.

Tre's had a wall. It seemed to encircle his consciousness, and her efforts rebounded from it, almost hinting that there was no mind at all. Yet she knew that was not the case. Tre was very much his own person, intelligent and alert, harboring desires and aims, and she could see that he knew himself well. Very well.

"Tre, what's been done to you?" she asked, because she sensed that he wanted to talk. The feeling was nothing to do with the Force; it was merely the empathy of one sentient being for another.

"Just another slave spy used by the Je'daii."

"You're altered," she said, realizing the startling truth. "Genetic?"

"Deep and permanent."

"No Je'daii would do that," she said.

"Ha!" Tre spat. A few people nearby glanced around at his outburst, and he stared them down, red and ferocious when he wanted to be. They went back to their drinks.

"But it's . . ." Lanoree said, but she did not finish her sentence. *Forbidden*, she was going to say. But she had that ongoing alchemy experiment on her ship, and she knew that some Je'daii would frown on that. What was considered forbidden to some was exploration to others.

* * *

"I'm Dam-Powl's toy," Tre Sana said, quieter now. "There are promises made to me." He sat up straighter, proud. "And they'll be kept! Money. A new identity. An estate on a Ska Goran city ship." He nodded firmly but his lekku writhed, displaying uncertainty and vulnerability.

Lanoree wasn't sure what to make of him, and the fact that he was closed to her gentle probings unsettled her. But she could also not help admiring Dam-Powl's work. Whatever subtle genetic adaptations she had performed, whatever strange alchemies kept Tre's mind purely his own but made him very obviously hers, were perhaps immoral, yet startlingly brilliant.

"And you'll get all that," Lanoree said. "Master Dam-Powl is a Je'daii of her word."

Their food arrived. Tre started eating immediately, chewing and swallowing with barely a pause. He seemed ravenous.

"The Gree," Lanoree asked. "The blueprints. I need to know more."

"And now you're here, we *can* know more," Tre said, spitting half-chewed meat across the table. Some of it landed on Lanoree's plate.

"When?"

"I need to find someone," he said. "Someone who's not easy to find. But . . . on my own. A Ranger will attract attention. You know the saying, 'When a Ranger comes calling, trouble quickly follows.' Well, so, they hear of you with me and they'll melt away. Maybe for a long time. So leave it to me, meet me here at dusk. I'll know where they are by then."

"Who is this person?"

"A rich Kalimahr. A dealer in swing dust and other air spices. And a Stargazer."

"That word again," Lanoree said.

Tre wiped his mouth and took a drink. "Not one that many know. Don't use it too freely." He nodded down at Lanoree's plate. "You going to eat that?"

"No. Help yourself."

Tre pulled her plate across to him and started eating. It was as if every bite was his first.

"So, here, at dusk," Lanoree said.

"Hmmm." He nodded without looking up from the food. He exuded indifference, yet he had called himself a slave. A conflicted character, complex, troubled. Exactly who she would not want guiding her during her investigations.

"Fine," she said. As she stood to leave, she saw faces turning away from her, and she walked to the doorway in a bubble of silence broken only by awed whispers of *Ranger!* and *Je'daii!* and darker mutterings of *trouble*. She hoped the old saying Tre had reminded her of could be put to rest on Kalimahr.

But hope alters nothing.

And soon after leaving Susco's Tavern Lanoree knew that she was being followed again.

"The first day is always the worst," the human Master Ter'cay says as he leads Lanoree and Dal toward the surface. "The Silent Desert can be an unsettling place."

We know, Lanoree thought. *We know for sure.*

They climb up through the vast cavern.

It's more like a city than a temple, Lanoree thinks, and Ter'cay glances back at her.

Listen when I'm talking, or you'll learn nothing, he speaks in her mind. He's not angry. More amused, if anything. Her surprise at how easily he silently communicates is obviously evident in her expression. Force telepathy is well-known to her, but such control and command must have taken many years of meditation and study to master.

Ter'cay laughs aloud, and Lanoree smiles sidelong at Dal. He's frowning. He didn't hear a thing.

She is still stunned at the size and scope of Qigong. She's heard all about it, of course, from her parents and from those Journeyers venturing through Bodhi Temple after having visited Qigong previously on their travels. Their talk is always of the temple first—its incredible size, the complexity of its caverns and tunnels, the strength of the Force in this natural nexus—and then inevitably they will finish with stories of the Silent Desert.

A haunting place. Almost unnatural.

She and Dal have already spent days crossing the desert to Qigong and encountering some of its dangers. But she senses that their real experience of those strange sands has only just begun.

"It's cool down here," Ter'cay says. "Sometimes the sands are hot enough to melt your shoes and a slightest breeze will blister your skin. But that's usually later in the day. Down here we're protected from the sun, and the climate is controlled by six conditioners. There's one over there." They are crossing a wide cavern bounded on three sides with sheer walls, each of them speckled with ledges and stairwells, people bustling all about. Ter'cay points at the fourth side of the plaza, and there stands a huge machine, the height of thirty people, with curved protuberances that flex and bulge like something biological, not mechanical. It steams, groans; and moisture speckles its surface and pools around its base.

"That's a machine?" Dal asks.

Of sorts, Ter'cay sends. He glances at Lanoree, raises an eyebrow, then speaks the words aloud.

He expects Dal to be hearing all this, Lanoree thinks. Her brother seems unaware, enrapt as he is with the giant conditioner.

"Of sorts?" Lanoree asks.

"Many of its inner working are . . . grown at Anil Kesh."

"So it's alive?"

"Far from it." Ter'cay turns and strides across the cavern floor, and they have to hurry to catch up.

When we reach the surface, all will fall silent, Ter'cay says in Lanoree's mind. *But silence is subjective. You and I can communicate as we are now, and this is the first lesson. Force telepathy is a talent that some Journeyers already have when they arrive here; but those who don't, pick it up quite quickly.* He glances back over his shoulder at her, grim faced. *It's a fundamental talent. Not like farsight, or using the Force to cast illusion. If you flow with the Force, then so can your words and thoughts. But your brother . . .*

He shrugs as they continue walking.

"He's . . ." Lanoree begins, but Dal looks at her. She coughs, pretending to have swallowed some dust. Then she tries to speak without words.

Her mother had taught her the basics. Sometimes her father touched her mind when it was late and they were tired, giving her a bedtime tale. Now was Lanoree's chance to use those lessons.

He's slow with the Force, she sends, and she knows that Master Ter'cay hears. *But he wants to learn.*

No, Ter'cay says. *I sense no eagerness in him. Only resistance. No delight, only suspicion.*

He'll do his best.

They reach the edge of the cavern, where a large opening in one wall leads to small, busier tunnels. Six-armed droids amble back and forth offering drinks. Taller droids provide physical care to a group of people who are dressed in grubby clothing, their skin sun reddened, faces drawn, and eyes haunted. They don't stop talking, as if it's a novelty. Lanoree suspects these are Journeyer students having just finished another surface lesson.

If he will do his best, then so will I, Ter'cay says, but Lanoree already hears his doubt. It seems to echo her own.

Master Ter'cay speaks then, including them both. "The main climb to the surface. There are elevators and rising tubes, but I like my students to walk. Physical exercise." He thumps his chest and laughs. "Good for the lungs! The heart!" And he strokes his forehead. "The health of the body feeds the health of the mind."

They start climbing the naturally formed stairway. Lanoree counts more than a thousand steps.

Their first evening, as the sun blazes red across the western desert and the sands come alive with scorpions and serpents and other shadowy things, Lanoree Forces an illusion before Master Ter'cay. A shire with graceful veined wings and a single horn protruding from its head dances in the sand, beating its hooves against shadows that do not notice, snorting, and she hears every beat and breath. Ter'cay smiles at the solocorn that prances before him, and he nods once at Lanoree. *Good work*, he speaks silently. *But you'll find that making an illusion of reality that much harder. You know the solocorn is a creature of myth, rich in your mind, and so an illusion is easy to form. Try something more mundane. A rock, a fruit, a shoe. Not so easy.*

Lanoree lets the illusion flitter away in the dusk and does as Ter'cay suggests. She cannot do it.

Your lessons have only just begun, Ter'cay says. He turns away from her and sits close to Dal, holding the boy's hands in his own, touching his cheeks and his temples, and then the Master closes his eyes and Dal's own eyes grow wide.

He hears him! Lanoree thinks, delighted. *He feels the Force, and hears with it!* But her excitement is short-lived.

Dal stands and kicks at the sand, sending it spraying into Master Ter'cay's face. He reacts like he has been invaded or touched by something disgusting. Then he turns and walks away into the twilight. Lanoree wishes she could call her brother back.

Their first dawn camped in the Silent Desert with Master Ter'cay is one of the strangest times of Lanoree's life. Camping with Dal on their way here had been nothing like this; they were times of fear and worry, not wonder. Perhaps being so close to the temple—a natural nexus of the Force—drew life to that place.

As the rising sun sets the eastern horizon aflame, the desert comes to life, and the silence seems more staggering than ever before. Night creatures have already gone to ground an hour before dawn, as if aware that sunlight will soon expose them. Shadows retreat, the coolness of the night is burned away, and shimmering heat haze dances across the sands. Desert birds take flight from wherever they sleep. A small species of shire—thinner than those elsewhere on Tython, with water humps on back and neck—moves in herds across a distant hillside. Lizards frolic and dance around rocky areas; gliding pendles flap their mighty wings as they ride the dawn air currents; and she sees a giant mankle stalking in the distance, its vicious spines raised for the hunt. Yet this magnificent display of life and diversity exists in the desert's unnatural silence, the cries and calls, the flapping of wings, the growls and roars of the hunt, all unheard.

There, toward the hills. Look. Blink and you might miss it. She was not even aware that Ter'cay had risen; his tent looks undisturbed, untouched. Yet as he speaks in her mind she sees him hunkered down south of the camp, as motionless as the rock pile beside which he sits.

She looks where he said, and sees.

There seems to be no wind lifting the sand, no disturbance in the ground that might raise such a thing. The sculpture looks about the size of a human, though distance can be deceptive. It seems fluid, moving and dancing as the billions of sand particles within constantly shift and flow. The shape is ambiguous.

Dal should see this, Lanoree thinks. Yet she knows she cannot wake him with a thought, and to move him might break this moment.

Reach, Ter'cay says, and Lanoree reaches. The Force is alive within her and she probes outward with her senses, feeling that distant sand sculpture is slightly warmer than the surrounding sand, its smell is like something long buried exposed at last. And, most amazingly of all, within its confines the sand sings out loud. The sound is confused and seems to make no sense. There are no words there that Lanoree knows. Yet she can sense something of unbridled freedom and passion in the noise, and for a few beats of her heart she is filled with a blazing optimism that puts the sun to shame.

Then the shape disintegrates, and with one more heartbeat it is returned to the desert. The sound has vanished. The movement has ceased. Lanoree is left breathing hard with excitement, and as she glances across at Ter'cay she catches his smile.

What is that?

A mystery. You should wake your brother. Your training starts again now.

They spend the rest of that day, and the two following, training in the Silent Desert. Lanoree is delighted with the talents she possesses and those she is introduced to, and thrilled at how adept she already seems. Ter'cay pushes her. Tests. And she performs, pushing back with silent requests for harder tasks, more complex problems. Her relationship with the Force expands rapidly in that silent place, and she feels fully a part of it for the first time. Suggestion, telepathy, control, her skills grow and expand with each passing moment. She enjoys her time there with Master Ter'cay. And yet many times she realizes the strength of her pride when she forgets that Dal is not finding any of this easy.

He cannot flow with the Force, and the more Ter'cay works with

STAR WARS: DAWN OF THE JEDI: INTO THE VOID 49

him, the less Dal wants to try. Lanoree becomes frustrated and annoyed with his frequent displays of petulance. In the evenings, when they are eating and relaxing, she tries communicating with him. A sisterly touch on his mind, borne of love and concern. Yet she's met with a deluge of chaotic thoughts—frightening, furious, and yet scared.

As dusk falls on the third day and they make their way back to the temple, Lanoree is enlivened by her successes and saddened by Dal's failures.

She takes his hand, surprised when he holds on. And she smiles at him.

She has an idea.

A subtle push and—

They are walking along the river back at home, close to Bodhi Temple. This is the one place where Dal feels most at peace with himself. Weave birds have been here recently, and countless golden threads are carried on the breeze. The river flows fast and heavy, swollen by recent rains in the hills of the Edge Forest. The air smells of blossom and hangs heavy with the promise of a family meal that evening, when their father will cook rumbat stew and their mother will read some of her poetry. It is beautiful.

It is false.

Dal squeezes her hand so tightly that she feels bones grinding, and the hook hawk wounds start to bleed again. Then he crumples to his knees in the sand and vomits.

Lanoree kneels beside him, wondering if she has done wrong. He *hates* her touching his mind, using the Force to invade his thoughts. They have fought about it more than once. But after so long in this strange place, she'd thought that perhaps he would have welcomed those thoughts of safety and calm, those images of home.

When he looks up at her, she sees the venom of his gaze.

She cannot touch his mind again to say sorry.

CHAPTER FOUR
HIS OWN MAN

Never place all your reliance in the Force. It's always there, but that does not mean it can always be called upon. Each Je'daii is his own person with his own talents. Learn to use them. Nurture them. If the Force is the dream, you are the dreamer, and sometimes you have to wake up. Sometimes, you are all you have.
— Master Shall Mar, "A Life in Balance," 7,523 TYA

Tre Sana had already told her more than the Je'daii Masters who had sent her on this mission. They had mentioned a loose network of rich Kalimahr apparently involved in Dal's Stargazer sect, and Tre had backed that up with talk of tracking down a particular person to question. They had spoken of dark matter being used to attempt activation of a supposed hypergate. But they had not mentioned the Gree at all.

What was known about the Gree was so far back in history, so deep in time, that it had taken on the sheen of myth and legend. Lanoree wanted to get back to her ship's computer to find out what she could.

But first she had to discover who, or what, was following her.

She imagined that this district of Rhol Yan must be somewhere at the lower end of the tourist experience—the streets were grubby; some vendors very probably dealt in illegal goods, services, or substances; and the clientele of the various establishments displayed little evidence of being mere visitors. A rough area, but not one in which Lanoree felt out of place. Every city on every planet had them, and she had visited many.

Sometimes, she fit right in.

Cloud Chasers drifted above, speeders buzzed along a slightly raised roadway in the center of the street, and several types of indigenous beasts of burden carried people on their backs or limbs. But Lanoree chose to walk. It meant that she had complete control of her movements, and it would be easier to keep watch. She wanted to draw her follower out, not escape from him or her.

She used the polished shine of speeders, the glass of display windows, and the reflections in the eyes of those passing by to look behind her. And when she could not see, she blinked slowly, casting her senses back to try and discover who and where her pursuer was.

It was frustrating. She felt observed, and it could no longer be the usual curiosity for a Je'daii Ranger; she had removed her Ranger star to try to blend in.

The end of the street opened up into a large market, stalls built across a wide marble-paved square and suspended on three massive treelike structures around the square's perimeter. Small Cloud Chasers moored at some of these trees, ferrying people and freight to and from the larger vessels that buzzed and drifted above. Lanoree trotted down the curved stone steps that led to the square. Then she stopped, turned, and ran back up.

She paused on the top step and looked around. The street she had walked along was bustling. She looked at people walking toward and past her, human and otherwise. She watched many more walking away. Probing with her senses, touching the pulse of the Force, she felt for any image of herself in someone else's regard . . . and found it.

Just standing there, watching, don't forget she's a Ranger, dangerous, mysterious—

She touched the haft of her sword and pulled it partway out of its sheath, turning, seeing a Cathar family paused twenty paces from her while the mother and father fussed over their six children. Standing just behind them, pretending to be a part of their group and yet so obviously not, was a shape that did not belong.

The man was small but stocky, wearing an expansive gray robe and a large mask. Lanoree was sure he was Noghri—reptilian, skilled fighters, prized assassins. As she laid eyes on him, he looked up and met her gaze.

She raised one hand, ready to Force-push him to the ground for the moment she'd need to reach him.

He pulled a laser blaster and fired into the family group.

Screams. Panic. People running, fleeing, falling. The Noghri fired again, shooting at random.

Lanoree drew her sword and ran at the shooter. He was already fleeing, blaster in one hand and something else in the other. She could not make out what the device was. She reached for him, shoved, but he dodged sideways, and her Force punch tripped a beast of burden, spilling its three passengers.

As she passed the Cathar family, she glanced down and saw the woman on the ground, blood pulsing from a terrible, black-tinged wound in her furry scalp. The father was trying to pull the children away while crying out in mad grief. Lanoree wanted to stay and help, but there would be others to do that.

She would best serve the dead woman by catching her killer.

The Noghri had flowed down the steps and was sprinting toward one of the mooring stations. When they saw him coming, most people moved away, his violent intent obvious. But when two militia crouched before him and aimed long, spearlike weapons at him, he shot them both. The movement was almost too quick to be seen, and as they fell back dead the killer was already entering the shadow of the mooring tree.

He was well trained. It would take someone who knew what he was doing to bring down those two guards without pause.

She was gaining on him as he entered one of several doorways into the Cloud Chaser mooring structure. He was still doing something with the object in his other hand, and she paused and reached for him, concentrating, willing the Force his way, her clawed hand closing slowly as she struggled to grasp him. But there were too many other people around, and the panic was too great.

More laser blasts erupted from the interior lobby of the mooring platform, and more screams.

Lanoree used the Force to increase her speed, willing her muscles to stretch and contract faster, pumping her arms, pushing blood through her veins. There were a hundred travelers and merchants in the lobby, and two people were on the ground with blood spattered around them, others rushing to help. But she saw the Noghri immediately.

He was plugging the device into a comm column. He glanced back over his shoulder but did not raise his blaster.

More concerned with sending whatever he has to send, she thought. And as she ran at him she reached for the comm column, probing, frowning in concentration. She had to stop him sending, and if—

She heard the dry cough of a blaster and raised her sword, and it was only that instinctive reaction that saved her. The shot struck the sword and she stumbled backward, then fell, her weapon clanging against the marble floor. She still grasped its haft—she would never let it go—and she could feel the heat dispersing from the exquisite blade.

Lanoree shoved, and forty paces away the Noghri was lifted from his feet and smashed back against a wall. The blaster dropped from his hand and skittered away across the floor.

The crowd of people had scattered and hidden as well as they could, leaving only the two shot people behind. Lanoree sensed that they were both dead.

Anger throbbed through her but she reined it in. It would feed her action, but it could also cloud her senses. Using the Force while harboring rage could upset the balance within her, and that would lead to mistakes.

She jumped to her feet, and she was the only person standing.

"Stay down!" she shouted. She held out her hand and Force-pressed her observer to the ground. Heard him gasping for air. Pressed a little harder.

Walking forward, sword held protectively before her, Lanoree glanced at the comm column and the device he had attached there.

A flurry of movement and she knew what was coming, lifting the sword to deflect the blast a blink before it came. Another followed.

She shifted to the left and raised her blade to the right. The shot was swallowed by the hot metal.

He'd been carrying a second, concealed blaster.

Lanoree grunted in frustration, then reached out and lifted the Noghri above the ground, grasping him there, tight, tighter.

"Drop it," she said. Though quiet, her voice carried all across the open lobby.

He dropped the weapon. She raised him even higher . . . then let go.

The sound of breaking bone as he struck the ground was followed by the collective gasps of those watching.

Lanoree ran to him. He was writhing, his gray-skinned leg twisted, protruding bone visible beneath his loose robe. Keeping an eye on his big, clawed hands and feet, and conscious of the Noghri's reputation as fighters and killers, she kept her sword drawn in case he had other concealed weapons. And as she knelt by his side, she reached for his mask.

"Hold him!" someone called. Militia. Lanoree cursed inwardly, knowing that this would now get complicated. She wanted to get him somewhere quiet to interrogate him, and handing him over to Kalimahr militia would gain her nothing. She sighed and looked up at the two uniformed women running her way, wondering if she could persuade them otherwise.

"He shot them and just—"

"She chased him in here, and she *threw* him, she must be *Je'daii* and—"

"Dead, my brother's *dead,* and leaking his brains all across—"

There was a flood of voices as terrified people started speaking around the edges of the concourse. And in that cacophony, one shout from a child that saved Lanoree's life.

"Look out!"

As she looked back down at the injured Noghri, she saw the shell of his mask peel back and a wisp of smoke from within. *Voice activated!* she had time to think, and then she put every shred of strength and every measure of power she had in the Force into shielding herself from what came next.

She barely heard the explosion.

* * *

For a moment, as she saw the Wookiee's face and felt its strong, furry hands hauling her to her feet, she thought she was back on Ska Gora with her fingers hovering over laser cannon triggers. Then she remembered what had happened and smelled acrid smoke on the air.

"I'm fine," she said. Dizziness swept over her and she composed herself, breathing deeply. The female Wookiee grumbled a question, and Lanoree nodded. "Really. Fine."

The few people around her—the Wookiee; several humans; a tall, eyeless Miraluka with slatted mask—observed in stunned silence. When Lanoree looked beyond them, she understood their amazement at her survival.

The Noghri had packed quite a blast. There was nothing left of him, and the site of the explosion was the center of a wide swath of blackened and broken marble. Detritus littered the lobby. He had killed himself without a second thought, and it was incredible that no one else had been caught by the blast.

I was there, Lanoree thought, looking at the small, cracked crater in the marble floor. She had been blasted across the lobby, protected and shielded by the Force that she was so rich in, and for a few moments she tingled with something approaching ecstasy. She took a deep breath and felt a rush of well-being. Perhaps it was relief. Or maybe she was simply realizing that it was good to be alive.

"You!" a voice called. "Je'daii!" It was one of the militia who'd been approaching when the Noghri had killed himself. The other was bloodied and being helped to her feet. As the woman drew closer, Lanoree glanced quickly around at the comm columns. One side of it had taken some of the blast, but it remained standing, though bent and twisted. She could see the comm point in which the Noghri had plugged his device.

She ran.

"Stop!" the militia woman called again, angry. Lanoree would have to be careful. The woman was shaken, and in the confusion she might decide to take a shot.

Lanoree raised one hand, smiled, then slowed to a walk. "Just here," she said, pointing. "Just going here."

"Stop or I'll—"

"You'll wait for me," Lanoree said, pushing softly.

"I'll—I'll wait for you," the woman said, frowning even as she stopped running. She looked around as if confused, and then Lanoree reached the comm column.

She examined the device briefly, then plucked it from the socket. It was a small black box with several connectors and a screen on one side. A camera, among other things. Lanoree tapped the screen and scrolled down the list of stored images.

They were all of her.

"When a Ranger comes, death always follows," the man said.

"I thought the saying was 'danger always follows'?"

"Whatever."

They had taken her to the nearest militia post, and Lanoree had gone without argument. Her assignment had already become more complex than she had hoped, and making herself a fugitive would mean answers would be even more difficult to come by. People were dead. She owed it to the Kalimahr authorities to answer their questions.

Besides, she would be meeting Tre again at dusk. She had time to kill.

The captain was Lorus, a tall member of the proud Sith species, powerfully built and obviously used to being a leader and having his orders obeyed, and demands met, without question. He seemed unperturbed at holding a Je'daii in his restraining cell. He must have known that she could likely escape at any moment, but that would cause a diplomatic incident. So for now there was a gentle balance between them, an act from which both sides might benefit. The fact that they both knew this made things easier. At any other time it might have been amusing.

"Something funny, Je'daii?"

"No, not really. And I've told you my name."

"I prefer to call you Je'daii."

"Very well, Lorus."

"You should address me as Captain Lorus."

"I should?"

The captain sighed and leaned against a wall. The two human militia who had brought her in stood in the corners of the room at either side of the door. They both looked afraid, and stared at her in open wonder. Probably the first time they had seen a Je'daii in action.

The room was a little larger than the main control room on her Peacemaker, with one door, several chairs around the edges, and the single containment cell at its center. The cell was too small to lie down in, and consisted of an archaic heat field instead of bars. Lanoree could feel a touch of heat where she stood—the generator was old and leaking—and knew that she'd be singed to a crisp if she moved too close to the shimmering walls. She also knew that she could knock out the generator with a single thought, and with a little more effort she could shield herself and walk straight through the heat field.

But she had no wish to fight Captain Lorus and his constables.

"Five dead," Lorus said.

"Six, sir," one of the militia women said. Lorus stiffened but did not turn around, and the woman became suddenly nervous. "Er . . . including the bomber."

"I don't care about the bomber," Lorus said. "There are five people dead who I care about, including two of my militia."

"Sir," the woman said, quieter.

"I didn't kill any of them," Lanoree said.

"They're dead because the bomber was following you."

"Yes."

"Why?"

"I'm here on Je'daii Council orders," Lanoree said.

"Why?"

"I can't reveal the purpose of my assignment."

"Why?" Lorus smiled.

Lanoree did not respond. She looked down at her feet and probed softly, so gently that she hoped he would not feel. What she discovered did not surprise her. He enjoyed the power his position gave him. He was something of a bully toward his staff. And though he had been in the presence of Je'daii before, he had no love for them.

"I've done nothing to make you hate me," Lanoree said.

Lorus's face fell.

"I know your mind. And there's more I can do."

"Not if I press the purge button on your cell and fry you to a crisp."

Lanoree said nothing. Silence was more effective. It projected confidence.

Lorus snorted. "Je'daii. Rangers! I knew a Ranger once, several years ago. Vulk. Did you know him?"

"No," Lanoree said. But she remembered the name and the sadness of people she loved. "My parents knew him."

"Arrogant. Superior. He moved me out of the way once. I was a constable then, still in training, and he'd arrived close to here with two younger Je'daii. Those you call Journeyers. Too young and unable to control the powers you give them. Troublesome. There was a dispute at the time, two of the richer Kalimahr families bickering over mining rights for some distant asteroid or other. Vulk said he'd come to settle the dispute before it came to blows. Never did know why the Je'daii were involved, don't care. But when I confronted him in the street— told him I had questions and that he and his young troublemakers would have to follow me—he told me there wasn't time. Said he had a meeting to attend and a gift to make, otherwise blood would be spilled. And then he lifted his hand and . . . moved me aside. Picked me up, almost throttled me with that damned Force you people mess with. Dropped me out of his path. Walked on, without giving me another glance."

Lanoree smiled. She could not help it, even knowing it would only enrage this proud, simple man more. But she had heard her parents talking of Vulk, and this sounded exactly like the man he had been. He had never permitted anything to obstruct what he thought was right.

It was a lesson her parents had taught her well.

"You'd laugh at me, Je'daii?" Lorus said.

"Only at Vulk's memory."

"You *did* know him, then?"

"No. Like I said, my parents did. And it was more than several years ago. Vulk died eight years ago in a Cloud Chaser crash a thousand kilometers from here. But I guess you're so parochial you won't have heard about that. He'd already killed fourteen Xang terrorists by then, and he was mortally wounded. He steered his ship away from populated areas, saving hundreds, maybe thousands. He crashed into the sea." Lanoree said no more. But she watched Lorus's expression change, subtly but definitely, and she was glad. It seemed the man had some measure of honor after all.

"So tell me about the dead Noghri," Lanoree said.

Lorus grunted.

"I'll not move you out of the way." She smiled, pleased to see a twitch of response on Lorus's lips. He stared at her for a moment, then nodded at one of the militia. The woman pressed switches on a control panel on the wall. The heat field imprisoning Lanoree shimmered and then faded, whispering away to nothing. Lorus sat and gestured at a seat opposite him.

"He's known," Lorus said. "There wasn't much left of him." Grinning, he pointed back over his shoulder at the female militia. "Ducianne found one of his toe claws snagged in her uniform. We identified him from security footage taken from the docking tree. What we don't know is why a preacher would become a killer."

"A preacher?" Lanoree asked. "He was Noghri, wasn't he? Preaching isn't something they're known for."

"A cult," Lorus said. "There are many across Kalimahr, too many to keep track of. Unlike your Tython, we're inclusive here. We welcome any species, creed, or breed."

"As do we. But Tython is a challenging place for a non-Je'daii."

"Yeah. Well. The Noghri was a Stargazer."

"What do you know about them?" Lanoree sat down, at ease, comfortable. She was loading her questions with the subtlest of Force pushes, barely a suggestion. And perhaps now she was getting somewhere.

"Not much," Lorus said, shrugging. His red Sith skin looked strange in the artificial light, the color deeper, bloodier. "They're one of the lesser sects, hardly any members, no real influence. One of many who seek to look beyond the Tythan system, way back into history. I've had no dealings with them before. They've never caused trouble." He frowned. "Until now."

"They want to go home," Lanoree said, remembering Dal once saying, *One day I'll find my way home.*

"There are many who maintain an interest in where our ancestors came from. Who resent that we were ever brought to Tython at all."

"Are you one of them?"

"Not at all," Lorus said. "I've got it good here."

Lanoree asked more questions about the Stargazers, information held on them, and any prominent members. She barely touched Lorus's mind, and he seemed not to notice. Without hesitation he consulted an old computer in the wall and gave her a name and address.

"Ah, yes. Kara. She's not openly affiliated with the Stargazers. But she's incredibly rich—made her fortune in swing dust mining—and it's whispered that she funds them, lets them stay in properties she owns around Rhol Yan and beyond. But these are just whispers. I've found no proof."

"Really?" Lanoree raised an eyebrow.

"I've had no need to look. The Stargazers haven't done anything wrong."

"Five counts of murder?"

"And that's for me to investigate. Please, Je'daii, don't explode this one. She's one of Rhol Yan's elite, and it would leave much more of a mess."

"I'll do my best," Lanoree said. "I'm grateful for your time." And with a nod to the two militia she exited the holding room. She glanced back once to see Lorus staring into the inactive cell, frowning, and probably already wondering who had interrogated whom.

Leaving the militia post, Lanoree quickly lost herself in the bustle of late afternoon.

"Someone tried to kill me," Tre said.

"Seems quite common around here."

"You, too?"

Lanoree shrugged. "Who was it?"

"I didn't see. A shot, then they were gone."

"You don't seem overly troubled."

"It's not the first time it's happened." Tre Sana tried to exude calm, but there were signs of his being flustered—his clothing a little awry, eyes flickering left and right, lekku unsettled.

They had met outside Susco's Tavern and then walked through the streets. It was evening now, and everywhere was a different kind of busy. Earlier, the walkways had been thronged with residents and visitors all going somewhere, a purpose in their strides. Now the ebb and flow was less urgent, destinations less certain. They drank and ate, and music emanated from many establishments, vying for the greatest volume and subtlest lure. It was a more relaxed scene than earlier but more chaotic.

Dirigibles floated above the city, the larger intercontinental ships higher up illuminated with extravagant displays that danced and pulsed light across the sky. Smaller craft drifted down and rose again, ferrying people from docking trees up to the larger vessels. Several were moving away to the east, and Lanoree wondered what lay in that direction.

She had already contacted her Peacemaker to ensure that everything there was as it should be. Ironholgs had spat and buzzed as if annoyed at being disturbed, but all was well. She yearned to be back in the ship, alone.

"Easy for someone to follow us out here," Tre said.

"I'll know," she replied. And perhaps she would. She was much more alert now, and she kept her mind open to threatening thoughts, sudden movements, being the focus of attention. The Noghri had been more than willing to kill innocent bystanders to get away from her—until he'd made his broadcast, at least—and she could not let crowds be protection. But she could not know everything. And there were people like Tre who had been altered specifically so that they could not be read.

Master Dam-Powl, you should have told me more, Lanoree thought.

"My brother knows I'm coming," Lanoree said.

"And he's trying to kill you?"

She did not answer. The Noghri's camera had been plugged into the comm column to send the images of her, and it seemed likely that they were sent to Dal. From what the Je'daii Masters had told her, he appeared to be the head of the Stargazers, or this faction at least. But why would the Noghri be so willing to kill himself rather than be captured? Lorus had called them a cult, but they worshipped nothing. They craved a single purpose, but that made them more like a criminal gang than a group of twisted fundamentalists. They were an enigma she had to solve.

"So when are we seeing Kara?" she asked.

Tre's surprise was obvious. His extra lekku twitched in annoyance because she'd found out something he'd believed was a secret. Perhaps concealing something from a Je'daii had given him a sense of power. Either way, his brief display of petulance did nothing to endear him to Lanoree.

"Don't worry—I didn't pluck her name from your mind."

"I know," Tre said, trying to smile again. "So where *did* you hear about her?"

"I have my sources." It would do no harm to let Tre think he was not her only contact on Kalimahr.

"I spoke to her people earlier, as I said I would," Tre said. "Before the bastard took a shot at me. She'll see us at midnight."

"Where?"

"You don't know everything about her, then," Tre said, confidence restored a little.

"Only her name and where she lives."

"And never leaves. Rumor has it she hasn't left her apartments in thirteen years."

"Why?"

"She can't. Come on. Time to introduce you to some Kalimahr culture. It's close to where she lives—we can kill a couple of hours."

Lanoree didn't like his turn of phrase, but she followed as he led the way, always on guard, keeping her mind open, listening and sniffing for trouble. She sensed plenty. But for now, none of it was for them.

The Pits was aptly named. A subterranean tavern deep beneath one of Rhol Yan's more salubrious quarters, it displayed more than anything Lanoree had yet seen of the mix of cultures, people, and philosophies that existed on Kalimahr. She had heard of gladiatorial combat on Nox; and once on one of Mawr's moons, visiting the Je'daii recluse Ni'lander, she had witnessed the results of a contact knife fight. Ni'lander had told her that the fights were often arranged for money or standing, and that the losers did not always survive. On such an outpost as Mawr and its moons this had not surprised her. On Nox, such brutality was commonplace. But she'd believed Kalimahr was better than that. More settled. More civilized.

On the surface only, it seemed.

Even as they descended the freestanding spiraling staircase that led down through a large, poorly lit cavern, the scent of violence, excitement, and desperation reached her. Human sweat, Krevaaki must, the sweetness of a Sith's blood—the smells filled the cavern, rising on wafts of noxious heat from the tumult below.

The tavern was built across the cavern floor thirty meters beneath the streets. Its focal point was a deep trough in the floor, a natural pit in which two combatants fought. One was a big human with an extra set of arms grafted on his hips. The other was a Wookiee, pelt patchy, hide lacerated; and around his neck was a heavy control collar, lights flickering as electrical pulses urged him into greater fury. His screams were as much of pain as anger. He carried a metal-studded club, and it was already glistening with scraps of the human's flesh.

"This is culture?" Lanoree asked as they descended the last curve of staircase.

"The ass end of it," Tre said. "You grow used to it. They use mostly criminals and murderers. That's what they say, anyway. I try not to question it." He glanced back at her, and his three lekku touched and turned, telling her, *A good place to remain anonymous.*

And much as she hated to admit it, that was probably more true than even Tre knew. Because not only was the Pits filled with all manner and race of people, it was also somewhere that leveled everyone. Every patron was here for the drink and the fight. A person not riled up, drunk, and filled with bloodlust would stand out.

It would be easy for Lanoree to see anyone following them.

They reached the floor and Tre shouldered his way to the nearest bar. There were several placed around the pit, and most were doing brisk business. Lanoree followed, senses alert, hand on her hip close to her sword.

A thud, a gargled scream, and a shout. Hands waved, and the crowd roared. Betting chips were illuminated; and across the other side of the pit, several gambling pods were rushed as people went to claim their winnings.

Lanoree had no desire to see, but still she stood on tiptoes to look down into the pit. The Wookiee was leaning against one wall with blood caking his ragged beard. For a moment she thought he was the loser, but then a mechanical arm swung down and speared the human's corpse, hauling it out, swinging it over the heads of the crowd, and flinging it into shadows at the cavern's extremes.

She heard a splash, and then a frenzy of movement as unseen creatures made short work of the vanquished.

She closed her eyes and breathed deeply. Every decent shred of her Je'daii self wanted to close this place down. And her very basic human side wanted only to leave. But this was an easy place to cast her senses around, and every mind she touched was transparent to her. Base emotions flooded the Pits. Unpleasant emotions, true, such as she had learned to control many years ago during her Je'daii training. But simple to read for any threat or sense of being observed.

Tre nudged her arm and handed her a drink. "Not the best wine on Kalimahr."

"You surprise me." She took the glass and looked around. "You come here often?"

"No," Tre said. Perhaps that was disgust in his voice.

"These places are allowed?"

"Tolerated. They channel aggression, and the Council of Rhol Yan welcomes that. So they turn a blind eye."

"How civilized," Lanoree said. "You really are an inclusive society."

"It's not *my* society. I just come here from time to time." He took a sip. "Anyway, don't judge Kalimahr from this, Je'daii."

"Difficult not to." She initiated comm to the Peacemaker, asked if there were any communications from Tython or elsewhere. There were none.

"Next bout's beginning," Tre said, and this time his distaste was obvious. Perhaps he downed his rough wine to dull his senses. He was becoming more of an enigma than ever.

In the pit, a wretched-looking Cathar, naked but for the spiked manacles around his wrists, stood shivering. And as three barred gates were opened and human-sized, gray-skinned creatures slithered shrieking through curtains of fire, Lanoree was reminded of the second time she had saved her brother's life.

*   *   *

Heading south across the Strafe Plains toward Stav Kesh, Lanoree hopes that she and Dal will find common ground. Away from Thyr and the Silent Desert even she breathes a sigh of relief, though in their time at Qigong Kesh she made great advances in her understanding of Force Skills. She tingles with the Force. Her mind is awash with it. Yet she has to remember her promise to her parents.

This journey is as much for Dal as for her.

"Getting colder," she says.

"Good. I like the cold." Dal is quiet, but when they do talk, she senses no animosity from him. Perhaps he is just thinking things through. Trying to settle himself, find balance. *I wish Mother and Father were here*, Lanoree thinks, because they might be able to make sense of their son.

Since leaving Qigong Kesh he has seemed much more at peace, and she hopes this is a good sign. Their journey to the southern coast of Thyr was an interesting one, meeting people on the way, sharing stories with Journeyers undertaking their Great Journey in the opposite direction, and having the opportunity to see some of Tython's great sights. And once at the coast, the great Cloud Chaser airport was a wonder to behold. High on the cliffs above the roaring ocean, they sat together to watch several big airships launch, drifting down and out across the ocean in silent majesty.

Their turn had come, and the flight south to the tumultuous continent of Kato Zakar had been their last chance to rest.

Kato Zakar was often referred to as the Firelands because of its extremes of volcanic activity. But much of this volcanism was located in the continent's heartlands almost thirty-two hundred kilometers south of the coast where they landed. Their destination was much closer. In the high mountains almost five hundred kilometers inland lay Stav Kesh, the Temple of Martial Arts.

The Strafe Plains are a tough, cold environment—windswept scrubland prone to frequent localized Force Storms and scattered with leaning columns of ice-sharp silica and dangerous magma-filled swallow holes that can appear without warning. Molded largely by the elemental Force itself, the Strafe Plains are a manifestation of what draws every living thing together. The Force as a tactile thing. Powerful. Sharp.

As the landscape rises steadily into the high mountains, Lanoree remains alert, watching the wildlife of the Strafe Plains. It's said that the common spinner birds can sense a swallow hole's imminent emergence, and that they will fly spirals around any area about to erupt.

But it is not a hole that almost kills them both.

In places, piles of detritus thrown up from the holes form homes to creatures drawn by the ease of tunneling through loose material. It is from one of these large, uneven mounds that the attack comes.

Lanoree has never seen a flame tygah, but she's heard of them. When she was a child she believed them a myth made up by her parents to scare her. As she grew older, she heard stories and saw those few rare holos made of the elusive creatures. And days before their journey began, their parents warned them both.

It bursts from a hidden hollow in the top of the mound, broken trees and shattered stone erupting as it lopes down the slope toward them.

"Dal!" Lanoree shouts, but he is already stepping forward to meet the beast. "No, Dal, I can—"

"Shut up!" he shouts. He has drawn the old blaster from his belt.

The flame tygah is a big one, its length easily twice Lanoree's height, its head as high as her shoulder, each of its six heavy paws the size of her head. Fire drips from the tips of its claws and shimmers in the prints it leaves behind. Its scaled, oily hide flexes and reflects the sun in multicolored swaths; its tail swishes white fire through the air; its eyes blaze; and its tooth-filled mouth glimmers with heat haze. It is as beautiful as it is deadly.

Dal fires when the beast is thirty paces away. It does not even pause. He crouches and shoots again, and Lanoree can see the recoil of the old weapon. The tygah grumbles, a splash of blood scorches the air above its shoulder, and it speeds up its attack.

Lanoree could stop it, she is certain. She has a Force punch ready to stun it, and once immobile she can move forward and cramp the muscles in its legs, breathe the Force, and drive so much pain into the creature that it will turn tail and flee.

If needs must, she can kill it.

But she hesitates. Back in Qigong Kesh she shamed Dal, placing that image of home in his mind when he had not even invited her in. He needs to recover from that. If she defeats the flame tygah for him, it will be just another display of how inadequate he is and how strong she is becoming.

So she pauses but stands ready.

Dal dodges sideways, and fires almost point-blank into the creature's flank. It roars and shakes itself, and he leaps over its back, shooting once more even before he lands. It is athleticism and strength that drives him, not power of the Force, but the effect is still the same. The creature is confused and pained. As it swings around to lash out with one huge paw, Dal is already crouched and ready to deliver the final shot into its eye.

It rears up, fire shimmering from its claws in searing whips.

Dal smiles. Pulls the trigger.

Nothing happens.

As Lanoree sees the surprise on Dal's face, the tygah lurches forward and slashes at him with one big paw.

Dal is driven sideways, scraping and bumping across the rough ground. Snakes of fire curl around his arms and shoulders.

Lanoree drives a heavy Force punch at the tygah and knocks it onto its side. One eye on Dal—he is writhing on the ground now, rolling to extinguish the flames—she drives another punch into the beast's chest, pushing hard, feeling the Force power through her and into the enraged animal.

It screams in pain, a surprisingly human sound. Fire erupts from its mouth and hazes the air. Ash falls.

One chance, Lanoree thinks, and she pauses and pulls back. She keeps her hands raised, readying to throw a heavier, harder shove than she ever has before. For a moment she meets the creature's gaze, and it understands the pain she can deliver.

"Go," Lanoree says, pushing against the thing's mind even as she speaks.

The flame tygah glances once at Dal and then leaps away, bounding around the mound it emerged from and then disappearing into the distance.

Lanoree lets out a relieved breath and then goes to Dal.

"I could have killed it," he says.

"Your blaster misfired. It was almost on you." Lanoree is surprised at the anger in his voice, hurt.

"*I* was fighting it, not you."

"I saved you, Dal," she says.

"No." He stands unsteadily, clothing still smoking where he has beaten out the flames. He looks furious and sad at the same time. "No, the Force saved me." He's shivering now from the burns he has suffered.

I can heal those, Lanoree thinks. "You might have died." She's crying silent tears.

But Dal only looks bitter. "At least I'd have died free. My own man." He turns his back on her, and his coolness does more than make her sad.

For the first time, her brother scares her.

CHAPTER FIVE
SHARP EDGES

It will be the Great Journey. Journeyers may walk, or ride on beasts or in mechanical vehicles, but it will be their first self-sustained adventure across Tython's surface, visiting each temple to learn and refine their talents in the Force. Tython is a tumultuous place, and our new home still has countless hidden corners and depths unplumbed. Every Journeyer will encounter different dangers. Many will find their travels treacherous and troubling. And there are inevitably some who will not survive. But to exist in smooth balance within the Force, one must first confront its sharp edges.
—Nordia Gral, first Temple Master of Padawan Kesh, 434 TYA

"I like the sense of floating. For someone like me it's . . . freeing. Almost like there's nothing to me at all. I sometimes think I'm one of the cloud creatures that live deep within the Obri atmosphere. Huge, immaterial. That's what I sometimes think."

"They're speculation," Lanoree said. "A mystery. No one's ever really seen one."

"I know," Kara said. "I like the idea of that, too."

Lanoree was not sure whether Kara was a poet or a madwoman.

Either way, perhaps she would tell Lanoree what she had come to discover.

After leaving the Pits, Lanoree and Tre had traveled to the base of this tower. Tre had announced their presence to the sentry system. An air elevator had whisked them up to the two-hundredth floor. The view as they rose was staggering, and they had both stared silently from the clear elevator pod. As Lanoree had felt the silvery light of Kalimahr's three moons purging the stink of the Pits from her skin, she had meditated on the Force. Cleansing her mind. She would not forget the smells and sounds, and the deaths she had witnessed, but she no longer carried them with her.

"Well, it scares the shak out of me," Tre said. He was standing close to one of the inner walls, back pressed to it, hands splayed flat. His lekku were wrapped protectively around his throat.

"Thank you for seeing us," Lanoree said. "I understand you value your privacy."

"I do," Kara said. "But how could I turn down a request from a Je'daii Ranger?"

"Many do," Lanoree said.

"The system is filled with fools." Kara glided across the clear crystal floor of her apartment's huge main room and approached a low table that was adorned with all manner of food and drink. "Refreshments?"

"Water, please."

A droid poured, but Kara brought Lanoree her drink. This close, the Ranger saw just how huge the woman was. She was human, but her immense size made her appear like a different, unique species. She rode on a suspension unit that was hidden by her flowing robe. She was bald, as if her head had outgrown her hair, and where her robe parted Lanoree saw rolls of heavy flab and pale skin. There was a perfume to her that was not unpleasant, but beneath that was her own natural stench. Her arms had been artificially lengthened so that they could reach around her girth. Her face was so bloated that her eyes seemed to stare at each other. But however freakish she appeared, Lanoree knew that she could not underestimate Kara for one moment.

Handing the drink to Lanoree, Kara held on for just a moment too long, staring into the Ranger's eyes.

"What?" Lanoree asked.

"A Je'daii, so pure," Kara breathed. "Forgive me. It's been years." Those enigmatic words hanging in the air behind her, she floated back to the table and started eating.

Lanoree took a sip to steady her nerves, looking down at her feet as she swallowed. This large main room of the apartment was cantilevered over the top of the high tower, and its floor was composed of a thin, incredibly clear crystal. It gave the impression of standing on air, and at midnight the view below was staggering. Lights shifted and moved on the ground below, passing along the network of streets and squares surrounding the immense structure. And closer to the floor's underside, the flashing nav beacons of small Cloud Cruisers and other craft darted back and forth around the tower.

Lanoree glanced at Tre. He was still at the edge of the room, trying his best not to look down. But he was also close to the door. She thought perhaps it was not only fear that kept him there but caution, and for the first time she was grateful for his presence.

"You'll know why I'm here," Lanoree said.

"I will?"

"My reasons already seem more widely known than I'd like."

"Ah, yes. I heard about the attempt on your life."

"Is that what it was?" Lanoree asked.

"A Noghri assassin explodes himself close to you. What else could it be?"

Unwillingness to be caught, Lanoree thought, but she did not reply.

"Yet you have me at a disadvantage," Kara said. "I never leave here. I exist for myself and by myself."

"I'm sure you have a long reach," Lanoree said. She saw Tre breaking a smile behind Kara, but kept her own expression neutral.

"I make provisions to know what I need to know," Kara said. She laughed softly. "I'm very, very rich. My businesses run themselves, but I still feed off information. It's my obsession. And the only true universal currency."

"Stargazers," Lanoree said. She watched for any reaction, but other than a slight pause before replying, Kara gave nothing away.

"I know of them. Little to do with me."

"You fund them."

"I donate. They're a charitable cause."

"A sect of madmen," Tre said.

"Only to those who don't understand."

"You'd seek to leave the system?" Lanoree asked.

"You wouldn't?"

"No." Lanoree shook her head, confused. A strange question. "This is home."

Kara stared at her, and for an instant Lanoree felt something strange, as if an outside consciousness were scratching at the wall of her mind. Then the feeling was gone. But she tried to grab hold of it, analyze. It was like nothing she had ever felt before.

"Have you ever been to Furies Gate?"

"No," Lanoree said.

"I have," Kara said. "Many years ago, before I became like this, I was quite a traveler. It's a minimum of three hundred days to reach that small planet, and not many make the journey. There's really no reason to go there. But I felt . . . the need. The urge to push my boundaries. I've always felt that way, and I've done so physically as well as mentally. Even my appearance is a product of that urge. I spent twenty days there, at Fury Station, and most of the time I simply . . . looked. Out, into the Deep Core. Out, beyond anything anyone in the Tythan system knows. I wanted to see the glimmer of a Sleeper ship returning, one of those craft sent out over the millennia to return to the wider galaxy. I wanted to travel onward myself but knew that death would likely be the result. But even since turning my back on Fury Station and returning here, I have continued to look outward."

"Gazing at the stars," Lanoree said, and she remembered so much about her young brother—his anger that their ancestors had been brought to Tython, his wishes, his interests. They had never been her own. And yet there had always been that place inside her, the troubling presence of dark and light dancing their own fight.

"I'm not ashamed of it," Kara said. "Many in the system look outward. Most only in their dreams, because day-to-day life doesn't allow otherwise. But me . . . I'm rich. I can *invest*."

"So you give the Stargazers money to seek a way to leave."

Kara shrugged, and her immense body shivered and shook with waves of flab.

"You know my brother."

"Brother?" Her confusion seemed genuine.

"Dalien Brock."

That shuddering shrug again. "Honestly, I've never even met them. I fund several of their small temples around Kalimahr, give them somewhere to meet and talk. I pay for their contemplations." She turned away from Lanoree, perhaps to lie. "They are only one of my interests."

Lanoree tried to touch Kara's mind but could not. The woman was a riot of feelings, thoughts, sensations; and if there was sense in that white noise Lanoree could not find it.

"They're more than just a project to you," Lanoree said.

"I'm a dreamer with money," Kara said.

"So you fund them out of pure philanthropy."

"Yes." Kara continued grazing at the table, eating such dainty amounts for a woman so huge.

"I hear of Gree technology," Lanoree said. Again, she watched for a reaction. Again, that strange scratching at her mind. Perturbed, she reached out, trying to sense who or what might be trying to read her. But there was nothing. Perhaps the feeling really did come from the inside. Maybe such questions were touching hidden desires planted there all those years ago by her younger brother's interests. However much she tried, she could not deny her fascination with what had come before Tython.

Kara glanced at her and then started eating some more.

"The Gree," Lanoree pressed.

The woman turned her back on Lanoree once more and settled closer to the table, her hover system gently touching the crystal floor. She sighed heavily, seeming to change shape within her clothes. Her shoulders relaxed.

"I'm tired," she said. "Your audience is over. Speak to the Stargazers, if you must. Their nearest temple is in the eastern quarter of the Khar Peninsula. An old abandoned Dai Bendu temple that I own. Now leave."

"I haven't finished," Lanoree said. "Tython, the whole system, might be in terrible danger from what your Stargazers are doing."

"Leave!" Kara continued eating. And just for a moment, Lanoree recognized something about her. A manner, a presence, a bearing.

"You're Je'daii?" Lanoree gasped. It seemed amazing, and yet it would explain that strange, insistent scratching at her mind. The shadow of Bogan passed across Lanoree's mind, and she was even more confused.

"Once," Kara said, laughing bitterly. "But no more. The Force is stale within me. Now leave, Ranger. I have my security, and they're the best money can buy."

And now suddenly she threatens me, Lanoree thought.

A cough, a thud, and Kara slid over onto her side, rolling from the hover platform and seeming to spill across the floor. Breath rattled in her throat.

"What have you—?"

"She's out, that's all." Tre was holding a small weapon in one hand, barely the size of a finger. Stun tube. It carried one charge, but was effective for several hours. Or maybe less for someone of this size. He raised an eyebrow. "So now that you've spoken with her, do you want to find everything she *wasn't* telling us?"

"You'll bring her guards down on us!" Lanoree looked around the large room. She could not help partly agreeing with Tre's actions. And whether she liked it or not, the time for talk was over. "Now that it's done, we won't have long."

They started searching. Tre was haphazard, pulling open cupboards and throwing aside cushions from the several huge, low seats that lay around the place. But Lanoree tried to concentrate her efforts.

She let the Force flow and sought where a Je'daii might hide her secrets.

Was she once really Je'daii? she wondered. *Or did she merely say that to confuse me?* Kara was a player of games, that was for sure, answering some questions and dodging others. She seemed very open about her desires and ambitions. Yet there was still a mystery to her, and something far deeper and more complex than this fat woman confined to her own apartment. Rich she might be, and powerful, and she undoubtedly had a long reach. But Lanoree's recognition of something about her—something Je'daii—was even more confusing.

There were some who trained with the Je'daii but then left Tython. It was usually at the Padawan phase, when children once strong with the Force seemed to lose that strength as they reached adulthood. There was no shame to it. And the Je'daii themselves admitted that on occasion they might make mistakes and take into training those who would never be comfortable and at balance with the Force.

My brother, for one, Lanoree thought. She stared at the slumped figure of Kara, rich benefactor of the Stargazers, and wished she could ask her more.

"Hurry!" Tre said. "The sentries might be coming even now."

"Why would they?"

"Like she said, the best security that money can buy. They'll have sensors for weapon discharges."

"Oh, great," Lanoree said. More conflict was the last thing she wanted here. Her brief time on Kalimahr had already been more eventful than she had hoped.

She looked down past her feet at the ground far below. A chaos of lights swarmed around the base of the tower, but there were three white lights rising quickly up the tower's outer wall. Air elevators. She touched her collar and activated her comm.

"Ironholgs, I need you to bring the ship. We're on the two-hundredth floor of Gazz Spire, eight kilometers southeast of the landing tower."

Nothing.

"Did you hear me?"

Ironholgs answered, a splutter of static and groans. As usual, he sounded like an old man being woken from a comfortable sleep, but she already heard the background whine of the Peacemaker's engines being prepped.

"What?" Tre asked.

"Company. We'll be leaving soon."

His wide-eyed fear could not have been feigned. "Leaving how?"

"Let's worry about that when the time comes. Now search." Lanoree turned and faced the wide panoramic windows looking out over Rhol Yan archipelago, trying to relax, remembering her Force-skills training and relishing the balance she could feel inside. Darkness and light, seeing and seeking. She surveyed the vast room, looking for where something might be hidden. A woman like Kara had plenty to hide, and not all of it the currency of secrets. She was a rich woman with a grand apartment and material wealth. She would have *things* to hide, too.

At the far corner of the room was a wall display of martial objects—blades, spears, maces, other striking weapons, all of them powered by the bearer alone. It did not surprise Lanoree that Kara might be a collector of such antiquities, and they did not interest her. What might be behind the display did.

There was no obvious door, but she sensed a hollow beyond the wall.

And she did not have time to find the hidden opening mechanism.

Lanoree drew her sword and struck. Sparks flew, and an intense surge of energy webbed across the display of old weapons, lighting them briefly with the Force. She struck again and a wall panel gave way. Several crossbows clattered to the floor.

Lanoree shouldered her way through the opening into the narrow space behind the wall.

"Those elevators are pretty close!" Tre called.

"Lock the doors. Barricade them. Give us as much time as you can." Her voice sounded muffled in the small, unlit room, as if swallowed by something soft. Lanoree took a small glow rod from her belt and flicked it on.

The light flooded the room, and seeing what was in there gave context to the curious musty smell.

Books. Perhaps a dozen of them, each sitting on a plinth in a separate display case. It had been a long time since she'd even seen a book. Her parents had one—an old instruction tome written by the great Je'daii Master Shall Mar more than three millennia ago—and they showed it to her whenever she asked. She loved the printing, the care and attention that went into the production processes. But these . . .

She opened the first case, caught a whiff of must and age, and as she opened the book she realized that it was unique.

Not printed. Not mass-produced. This was handwritten.

Tre's voice called, muffled by the wall between them. "They're outside!"

Lanoree knew they did not have very long. "Ironholgs, how far away are you?" Her droid replied that the Peacemaker was moments away. "Good. Drop low, wait until you see me, then come in close." A quizzical buzz from the comm. "Don't worry. You won't be able to miss us." Opening the rest of the display cases, she winced at the damage she might be doing to these books. But time was not on her side. Flipping pages, her heart settling yet her mind moving faster than ever, at last she found what she was looking for.

She slipped the thin book into her jacket and left the room.

"Quickly!" Tre whispered. He was in the center of the large room, standing on one of the low seating areas so that he did not have to look down. Lanoree thought he was actually shaking with fear, his lekku touching nervously beneath his chin.

Kara groaned, her bulk shifting in a sickly, fluid movement. A comlink on the table beside her was glowing softly, call unanswered. Her security would already know that something was very wrong.

Lanoree dashed across to the wide, tall windows and beckoned Tre Sana after her.

"There?" he asked.

"You think we can leave any other way?"

Something crashed against the wide doors, three heavy impacts. A low table that Tre had upended against the doorway tilted and fell, smacking against the crystal floor.

Lanoree squinted through the window at the sea of lights below and around them, and then she saw the shape she wanted. She breathed a sigh of relief.

"Battle droids," Tre said, arriving by her side. "All the rich hire them, private security, get them chipped and reprogrammed, more heavily armed. Some of them fought in the Despot War. I've even heard that some retain memories of their battles with the Je'daii, don't like them, *hate* them, and some even dream of—"

"You're babbling," Lanoree said. "And droids don't dream."

"I told you, I don't like heights."

More impacts from beyond the room. And then a louder, deeper thud vibrated through the floor and the doors burst open in a blast of smoke, flame, and torn metal.

Lanoree drew her sword again and faced the door. Three droids entered, short, thin units designed for speed and offering narrow targets for any aggressor to hit. Their fist-sized heads twirled as they scanned the room.

Lanoree pressed her hand to Tre's chest to still him, and she felt his heart hammering against her palm.

And then without warning the droids opened fire.

Lanoree swept her sword left and right, catching and deflecting blasts from their weapons. Tre shrank down behind her. She concentrated, her stance perfectly balanced, and with her free hand she Force-punched a droid back against the wall. It struck, fell, and then quickly rose again. It was scarred with several old blast injuries. Battle hardened.

"Get ready!" Lanoree shouted.

"For what?"

"You'll know when it happens." She angled the sword and deflected several blasts back against the window. Crystal shattered, and a large slab of the window burst outward with a heavy *crump!* Wind whistled into the room, sweeping food-laden plates from the table, and Lanoree saw Kara's eyes flicker open.

Sword still shifting before her, Lanoree clawed her left hand, lifting one droid and flinging it at another. A blast caught it and it blew apart, a brief shriek of tortured metal followed by a hail of white-hot components ricocheting around the room.

Lanoree knew she didn't have much time. She could Force-jump across the room and take on the two remaining battle droids, but right then destroying them was not the priority.

The priority was escape.

She turned, grabbed Tre around the waist, and leaped from the shattered window.

The wind stole her breath. It grabbed them and spun them around as they spiraled down from Kara's overhanging apartment, drawing them in close to the tower so that windows flitted by in a blur. It roared in her ears. Lanoree squinted, ignoring Tre's scream of terror as they plummeted, struggling to hold him.

Laser blasts flashed by them and there was nothing she could do, no way she could gather her thoughts to protect them from the sustained fire coming from the shattered window above. She only hoped—

The Peacemaker drifted from the shadow of the tower and dipped below them, dropping, engines roaring, matching their speed so that the impact as they struck its upper surface was as gentle as possible. Lanoree grunted and clasped Tre as they hit, flailing with her other hand that still held the sword. Given a choice of which to drop, she knew the weapon would win out. But she hoped she did not have to make that choice.

Laser blasts ricocheted from the ship's curved hull, but Ironholgs remote piloted the ship perfectly. They flew a gentle circle around the tower so that the droids could no longer hit them with fire from above, then the craft hovered to give them the chance to get inside.

The Peacemaker's top hatch whispered open.

"After you," Lanoree said.

Tre scrambled across the ship's smooth back and tipped inside headfirst.

Lanoree dropped in beside Tre, landing softly on her feet, and the hatch closed above her. At home once more, she hardly even swayed as the ship powered away from Rhol Yan and out across the dark sea.

"Are you mad?" Tre shouted. "Insane? What if your ship hadn't been there, what if—"

She raised one hand, silencing him, and took a deep, calming breath. "A simple thank you would be fine."

With the Peacemaker's computers patched in to Kalimahr's nav sats and the ship flying across the ocean toward the Khar Peninsula, Lanoree wanted to use the time to take stock. At first Tre Sana tried to talk, but she held up a finger in warning and nodded at her cot.

"Sit. Still. Quiet. You're on my ship now. It was easy getting you on board. It'd be even easier for me to fling you off."

"You call that *easy*?" he spat.

"The cot! And silence."

Tre sat, his lekku so pale they were almost pink. He was all front, but Lanoree could see his relief at having a chance to rest.

She turned the cockpit seat toward the front and sat back for a moment, staring at the sea flashing by below. Moonlight caught the waves. Ships' lanterns speckled the surface, and here and there the navigation lights of airborne craft moved across the night. It was clear, and a swath of stars smeared the sky. Her ancestors had come from somewhere out there, and now her brother was preparing to risk everything to travel there once again.

Her brother, and others.

Lanoree was aware of the dreadful danger Dal's efforts might be putting Tython and the wider system in, and it chilled her to even imagine him getting close to his aims. But at moments like this, looking up at the stars, she could not hold back her interest. Her fascination. In many ways she was as curious as anyone about their origins, but she went about feeding that curiosity in different ways.

Kara had appeared quite open about her affiliation with the Stargazers. Her Je'daii past was a mystery, especially as she now exuded dislike for their society and beliefs. If the information she'd imparted was correct, she had willingly sent them to a Stargazer temple, and perhaps one step closer to Dal. Yet she had also been hiding secrets.

Lanoree had brought one of them with her.

Quietly, she took the book from her jacket and placed it on the control panel before her. She sensed no movement from Tre. If he so much as stood from the cot in the living area behind her, she would be aware, and she did not need any Je'daii senses to know this. The Peacemaker ship was as much her home as the one with her parents had ever been, and she knew every waft of air, every creak of loose paneling, and every shadow cast by the ceiling lights or control panel indicators. She was safer here than anywhere.

The book was leather bound, its cover worn around the edges and blank. It was thin; perhaps fifty pages. Age emanated from it, a combination of its hand-worn appearance; the faint smell of dust; and the mere fact that it was a book of paper, card, and ink. There were those who still produced books, but only as novelty or special items.

This was the real thing.

How many have touched this? she wondered. *How many have stared at it as I am now, readying themselves to see inside?* Haunted by history— the scent of lost times, the feel of ages—it represented something that no flatscreen or holo display ever could.

She opened the cover and looked at the first page. The little that was printed there was in a strange symbology she only faintly recognized. She ran her fingertips across the page and felt grittiness beneath them, the dust of ages.

Stroking a pad on the arm of her seat, she listened for Tre as a small globe rose from the Peacemaker's control panel. He was silent and still.

Lanoree picked up the globe and twisted it to aim at the book. It floated beside her right cheek, and when she touched the pad again it flickered on and started to hum softly. A faint blue light splashed on the book, and beneath it the symbols started to shiver.

It took longer than she had expected. The print seemed to flow and shift, though only within the globe's blue light, and at last the shimmering settled into words she could read.

The Gree, and Everything I Have Found of Them in the Old City. The name below was Osamael Or. And that name rang in Lanoree's memory.

Frowning, she leaned back in her seat and closed her eyes to concentrate. Who was it? *Where* did she know that name from? She looked again, out at the stars so far away from everything she knew and loved, and the concept of exploration came to her. What was she, if not an explorer? A Ranger of the Je'daii, a traveler of this system that still contained countless unknowns even though it had been inhabited for ten thousand years. There was so much more to know—mysteries, confusions, ambiguities. There were . . .

"There are depths," she whispered. These, too, were the words of Osamael Or, and she remembered where she had heard them before. A bedtime story from her father, told so long ago and never remembered again until now. Even after everything that had happened with her and Dal, the Je'daii temples, the search, and what she had found of him. Even then she had not thought of that time almost twenty years before when her father sat in the chair beside her bed, long hair loosened to flow across his shoulders, hands folded on his chest as he relayed the cautionary tale of Osamael Or and his final, greatest adventure—in the depths of the Old City, where he insisted there were secrets still to be found. So he embarked on his next expedition alone, because by then no one wanted to go with him anymore. They said he was mad. They said there were more important things to do across Tython, and that the surroundings were too dangerous. This was nine thousand years ago, you have to remember, back at a time when dreadful Force Storms still ravaged the planet and the Je'daii were sometimes swept along with them, instead of taking power and balance from them. There were many like Osamael Or back then. Frontiersmen, they called themselves, but for Osamael Or the greatest frontiers did not necessarily exist at the greatest distances. So he went down into the Old City on Talss alone. And he was never seen again. They searched for him. His family felt a sense of responsibility, though they thought him mad as everyone else. So they looked, but nothing was ever found, and no one was willing to go deep. "There are depths," Osamael had told his sister the night before he went, and she repeated his final words whenever anyone asked her about her brother. Because she was the one member of the family who insisted he was still alive. "He's still exploring down there, in those depths," she'd say. "He's going deeper, and finding more, and one day he'll emerge with news that will astound us all." But he never did come back. And that's why the Old City is such a dangerous place, my sweet Lanoree. Because there are depths.

"Osamael Or's diary," Lanoree whispered, awed. For her to be holding this, now, nine thousand years later . . . he must have come back.

A chill went through her, as if someone from a great distance touched the deepest part of her, and knew her.

She turned the page and started reading.

CHAPTER SIX
OLD MYTHS

No one can fight without balance.
                    —Master Rupe, Stav Kesh, 8,466 TYA

Stav Kesh. The name itself inspires a shiver of anticipation, a frisson of excitement. For Lanoree, Qigong Kesh was a place of contemplation and immersion in Force Skills, nursing and nurturing them, and considering what the Force meant to her. At the Martial Arts Temple of Stav Kesh, she will learn to fight.

It is dawn as Lanoree and Dal approach the temple. They'd camped several kilometers to the north, and breaking camp when the sun rose above the eastern horizon is an incredible moment. The air here is thin, the mountains high, and they are both dizzy with breathlessness. But the thin air seems to purify the amazing colors of dawn.

Dal seems excited. He was always good in a fight, as several arguments with the children of other Je'daii at Bodhi Temple had proved. Lanoree hopes that he will find the Force here and truly welcome it at last. When he sees what it can do . . . when he feels how it might help . . .

"This is my time," he says as they stand on a rocky cliff path, a shallow ravine to their right. Snow had fallen in the night, and a light covering softens their harsh surroundings. "Don't try to be my teacher here, Lanoree. And don't try to be Mother and Father. You're my sister, that's all. Whatever happens to me here is my responsibility."

"Our parents made you *my* responsibility."

"We're not children anymore. And I'm my own man." It's a surprising thing for Dal to say. But as he walks ahead of her toward the temple, and she sees the strength in his stance and the determined set of his shoulders, it does not seem ridiculous at all.

The breeze is picking up. Snow dances through the air. The landscape is harsh, weather likewise. Lanoree knows that Stav Kesh is never an easy place to be.

"My name is Tave, and I'm one of the Masters of the temple. We've been expecting you. How was your journey south from the sea?"

"No problems," Dal says. He does not mention the fire tygah, and when Master Tave glances at the healing burns across his forearms, Dal says nothing.

After a brief pause, the Noghri Master smiles. "Good. Wait here and I'll send a droid to show you to your quarters. You have the morning to perform breathing exercises, acclimatize to the altitude. After lunch your training begins. This afternoon, Force breathing."

"Breathing?" Dal says. "I thought this was the Martial Arts temple."

Master Tave stares at Dal, glances at Lanoree, then turns his back on them both.

"Dal!" Lanoree whispers. "Don't be rude!"

"Rude?" he asks, but at least he's keeping his voice low. "But—"

"Don't you think Master Tave knows what he's doing?"

"Yes. Well. But breathing?"

"I'm sure it'll all make sense." She walks past Dal and between the wide temple doors, suddenly afraid that they will swing closed and shut her outside. *Perhaps this is how Dal sometimes feels*, she thinks. Her brother follows her inside, and together they take in their surroundings.

She has seen plenty of holos of Stav Kesh, and heard many stories from those Journeyers who visited there before Bodhi Temple in their own Great Journeys of learning. But nothing could have prepared her for the real thing.

The strength of the Force, for a start.

Lanoree can feel the Force here as an almost physical presence, Ashla and Bogan exerting a gravity upon her that seems to stretch, pull in all directions, and give her body an incredible lightness. It is easy to let herself fall into the flow, and the talents she honed at Qigong Kesh feel even more refined here. The Force is close, and it takes so little effort to become one with it.

She glances at Dal. He is looking about him in wonder, and she hopes that some of it is recognition of the Force. But after what he said outside, she will not ask him.

Stav Kesh does not so much cling to the mountainside as form it. Rocky outcroppings are visible here and there, but most of what Lanoree can see above her are buildings. They start at her level and rise up the slope of the mountain, projecting out over heavy buttresses and elsewhere forming sheer cliffs of smooth gray stone. Windows pock wide facades, and balconies held up by slender, incredibly strong supports stretch out over long drops. Canvas window shades are already flapping in the dawn breeze, lending splashes of a dozen colors to the sandstone city. A waterfall tumbles from high above, leaving glittering icicles on the buildings and rocks it passes by. A series of wheels are driven by the fast-moving water. Spray hazes the air, and the newborn sun casts several rainbows across illuminated parts of the city. As Lanoree watches the sun line move around the mountain's girth, the rainbows seem to be driving shadows before them. The scene is beautiful, and she remembers at last to draw a breath.

On the mountainside below them sits the Tho Yor. They passed it on their ascent, mysterious, enigmatic, and the recent snowfall coated it with a glittering layer.

"Bet our room's right at the top," Dal says. Lanoree laughs more than the comment warrants, because she is so pleased at hearing even a hint of humor from her brother.

A floating droid arrives and utters their names in an electronic buzz. They follow. By the time they reach their quarters, Dal is laughing hard, and panting, and perhaps crying just a little.

"One thousand three hundred," he says, gasping. "I lost count of the steps after that."

"Good training," Lanoree gasps. They glance into their room—beds, benches, little else. Their training robes are laid on the beds, and she can already tell how rough they are, and how cold they will be wearing them. *Toughening us up*, she thinks. She asks the droid where their afternoon session will take place.

"Master Tave always takes his classes in the lower training levels," the droid burrs.

"Of course he does," Lanoree says. "Of course."

"Attack me," Master Tave says, "with anything you can."

The students are hesitant. Even Lanoree pauses, though she knows that the Master will not suggest anything he does not mean.

Then she walks to the weapons rack, picks up a slingshot, and fires a stone at the Master's head.

He steps aside and it misses.

She pushes a Force punch his way and he defects it with a flick of his fingers.

Lanoree dashes to the left, and her sudden movement seems to bring the room to life. There are six Journeyers in the training courtyard, including her and Dal, and they take her enthusiasm as permission to attack.

The Cathar twins go at Master Tave with heavy spiked chains that he easily avoids, leaving them tangled and useless. Dal darts in low and fast, swinging a mace at his legs . . . which are no longer there. Tave shoves Dal onto his back and kicks the mace aside. A Wookiee roars and swings two short, heavy clubs that Master Tave ducks and swerves around before planting a boot in the Wookiee's rump and sending her spilling to the floor. The last student to attack is a Twi'lek, who fires a Force punch so powerful that it even takes Lanoree's breath away.

Master Tave deflects the punch back against its originator, and the Twi'lek staggers back with a bloodied nose.

The large courtyard rings with their heavy breathing, their bodies still unused to the thin air. The fight drives their hearts, pumps blood, sharpens senses. But it is far from over.

"Again," Master Tave says. He is not even breathing hard.

This time Lanoree, Dal, and the Wookiee attack simultaneously from three different directions, gasping, grunting—Lanoree trying to sweep Tave's legs from beneath him with a sly Force punch, Dal aiming a flying kick at his head, the Wookiee clumsy yet strong with her deadly clubs—and within moments they are all on the floor, clasping bruises and wallowing in wounded pride.

Lanoree and Dal lock eyes, and her brother grins.

They go again. The courtyard is a confusion of spilled bodies and bloodied noses and swirling snow, and as Lanoree is casually cast aside for the third time, she sees the Twi'lek go at Master Tave with a surprisingly adept combination of Alchaka moves, the vigorous Force martial art. Tave seems to never be where a punch lands or a foot kicks, and moments later the Twi'lek spins through the air toward a far wall.

The Master raises a hand and softens the flying boy's impact.

Lanoree is sweating even in her thin robe, her heart racing, breathing hard. Dal looks the same, but he also appears more alive than he has in a while. It's good to see him like that, but worrying, too. Each of his attacks was traditional—not once did he try to channel the Force.

"You all try too hard," Master Tave says. He walks among them with his hands behind his back, and there's no sign at all that he has expended any strength in holding off their attacks. "You give in to effort and let it rule your moves." He points at the Cathar twins. "You both held your breath as you attacked, and your hearts will not like that." At the Wookiee. "A roar will not distract an enemy strong with the Force, but it will steal your breath, empty your lungs, tire you quicker." And at Lanoree. "And you. You stumble, rather than flow. With every move you expend three times the energy you should." He stands in the middle of the scattered, panting, bleeding students and sighs. "So. Breathing."

For the rest of that afternoon Master Tave teaches them how to breathe. To begin with, it feels unnatural and goes against everything Lanoree thought she knew, because breathing is something she never thinks about. She has done it forever. It simply happens, like her heart beating, her blood flowing, her mind working both when she is awake and asleep. But by the time they stop at midafternoon for drinks and a handful of local fruit and nuts, she realizes the truth. Tave is showing them how to breathe with the Force as well as with air. Perhaps later she will have to revisit her heart, her blood, her thinking.

The students enjoy the session, but Lanoree does not allow herself to draw too close to the others. Usually gregarious and willing to make friends, she feels the pressure of her responsibility for Dal. And now that he has emphasized his independence from her and their parents, that pressure feels even greater.

Dal also remains somewhat aloof. He's enjoying the training, she can see that, but he is also selective about what he is taking from it. The more Master Tave tells them that the Force is their friend, their protector, the balance that they must find, the more she perceives Dal's attention wandering.

Perhaps he's simply way out of balance, she thinks.

And once she grasps this idea, Lanoree lets it grow. It's uncomfortable, but something she understands. Something that can be resolved. In her mind it's far better than the alternative.

That Dal truly hates the Force, and is doing everything he can to tear himself away from it.

"Your first training session in Stav Kesh is almost at an end," Master Tave says later that afternoon. "This evening you will prepare food, scrub the kitchens, and then return here to clear the training yard of snow and mud. You might also visit the Tho Yor and meditate for a while. Meditation is a part of fighting. Centering yourself, finding and ensuring your balance. And so attack me once more, with everything you can."

This time there is little hesitation. Lanoree and Dal are the first to react. Lanoree uses the Force to send a piercing whistle at Master Tave's ears, upsetting his physical balance, but her follow-up attack with an Alchaka kick combination is parried and countered, and her face meets the stone pavement. She feels her nose gush blood—the second time that day—and rolls onto her side in time to see Dal spinning through the air, victim of a Force punch from Tave.

The others attack, too, using combinations of the Force and the physical. This time there is no panting and roaring, groaning and grunting, and the only sounds echoing across the courtyard are the rustling of loose robes, the whisper of bare feet on snow-covered stone, the impacts of flesh against flesh. Master Tave stands tall and fights off every attack. His expression remains impassive, and his movements are fluid and confident.

It is Dal who scores the first and only hit of the day. With Tave warding off a sword attack from the Cathar twins, Dal feints a clumsy Alchaka assault, but then slides within Tave's reach and delivers an elbow to his face. Master Tave takes a step back and his head turns to the side, spots of blood splashing his shoulder.

The courtyard grows suddenly still. Dal lowers his elbow, rubbing it slightly from where it contacted Tave's heavy brow. There is a stunned silence.

Master Tave smiles. "Good," he says. "Very good, Dalien." He slings one arm over Dal's shoulder and presses one clawed finger against his chest. "You're learning to breathe well, deep and gentle from the stomach instead of the chest. You're learning to control your body instead of letting your body control you. Now imagine what you could do if you were willing to let in the Force."

The silence in the courtyard goes from stunned to awkward. Dal says nothing.

But Lanoree can read his expression, and his thoughts, as he looks at Master Tave's bruised temple.

Who needs the Force?

"He let you get the hit."

"No!"

"Of course he did. That's Master Tave! You think he'd be fooled by a move more suited to a tavern scrap?"

"He was tired, he let his guard slip. I got him. I hit him!" Dal is angry, she can see that. But Lanoree cannot let him believe something like this. It will only add impetus to his fleeing the Force.

"I've heard stories about him. He can hide in the Force! Slip away. Come back again." She smiles softly. "He wanted to let you gain confidence. You were the clumsiest of all of us there, and he didn't want you—"

"Are you serious?" Dal asks. "Don't treat me like a child, Lanoree. I might be younger than you, but I see more. I know more truths. And the truth is, strength doesn't only come from your stupid Force."

"*My* Force?"

Dal snorts. They are high up on the wild, windswept top of the temple. It's night, and the views over the plains are amazing. But Dal looks at the sky.

"None of this is for me," he says, and he sounds almost wistful. "None of this down here."

Even as Lanoree walks away, Dal is still gazing at the stars.

For a long while Lanoree stared up at the night sky. Alone out in the Tython system she sometimes sat staring at the stars, letting the Peacemaker fly itself, and wondering what was out there. It was part of the reason why being a Ranger suited her. One day she would advance to Master, and then perhaps she would spend more of her time on Tython, contemplating the Force, instructing and guiding others, and eventually becoming an elder Je'daii. But youthful curiosity still drove her, and being alone in space she had the time to dream.

Besides, she liked the adventure. In that regard, perhaps she and her brother were alike.

She glanced back into the living area and saw that Tre Sana was asleep. A pang of annoyance hit her that he slept so easily on her cot. But it was the best place for him right now. As they powered across the Kalimahr sea toward the Khar Peninsula, Lanoree needed to report in. There was much to tell.

She lowered the volume on the flatscreen and then keyed in Master Dam-Powl's code. The soft chiming went on for some time, and then the screen flickered and Dam-Powl's face appeared.

"Ranger Brock," Dam-Powl said. She looked as though she had been asleep. "I wasn't expecting to hear from you so soon."

"Master Dam-Powl," Lanoree said, bowing her head briefly. "I have a quiet moment. And there is progress. Troubling progress."

After the brief time delay, the Je'daii Master heard her words and appeared suddenly more alert.

"My brother Dalien is aware that I'm pursuing him," Lanoree said. "He has his spies, and they followed me from the moment I landed. I'm on the way to one of the Stargazer temples right now. I believe he might be here, right on Kalimahr."

"Did you make contact with Tre Sana?"

"I did."

"He's proved useful?"

Lanoree considered this for a moment, then nodded. She chose not to mention Dam-Powl's genetic manipulation of Tre. It seemed irrelevant, and perhaps even intrusive. She was a Je'daii Master, after all.

"Have you questioned any of those close to your brother and the Stargazers?"

"Yes, a woman called Kara. Rich, revered in Kalimahr society. Something of a hermit, though she seems very aware of any events that have interest for her. She funds the Stargazers. Didn't seem concerned about letting us know that."

"Hmmm," Dam-Powl said. "It's from someone like her that we received some of what little information we have. It seems not all those who fund the Stargazers agree with what they're now attempting."

"I think Kara does."

"She said as much?"

"Not in so many words. But we searched her apartment. And I found something."

Dam-Powl shifted as she became more interested.

"Master, are you familiar with the tales of Osamael Or?"

"Should I be?"

Lanoree smiled. "Perhaps not. A story my parents used to tell me when I was a little girl. He's something of a myth, from at least nine thousand years ago. An explorer from the very early days of our ancestors' time on Tython. It's said he developed an interest in the Old City and disappeared down there, never to be seen again."

"And the relevance?"

"He was real. And when I searched Kara's apartments, I found a secret room that contained several very old books. There was trouble—

her security droids came, and I had to make a creative exit. But I took one of the books with me."

"And?"

"And it's Osamael Or's diary from his time exploring the Old City. One of them, at least."

"One of them?"

"It's incomplete. But it contains something that . . ." She pursed her lips.

"Ranger?"

"It seems he found something of the Gree down there," Lanoree said. "And if my translation of the diary's obtuse wording is accurate, the technology your spies heard about—the dark matter device— might well be of Gree origin."

Dam-Powl was silent for a while, and she did not hide her shock.

"It contains instructions?" she whispered.

"No," Lanoree said. "Much of what it says is obscure and does lead me to believe the stories of Osamael's madness. But there are three mentions of something that translates as 'step to the stars.' And toward the end of the diary—it's very short, and I suspect much more once existed—he says he's searching for designs."

"Did he find them?"

"Right now there's no way of knowing."

"Designs for a device to initiate a hypergate," Dam-Powl said.

"So does it exist?"

Dam-Powl did not answer. It was as if she had not even heard the question. "Very little is known of the Gree," she said instead. "If these Stargazers *do* have technical plans for something of Gree origin, they're toying with technology way beyond us."

"You really believe that?"

"Even though the Gree have been gone for millennia," Dam-Powl said, "technology that old might as well be ten thousand years ahead of us instead of ten thousand behind. It's obscure. Arcane. Not to be touched."

"I'm doing my best to track him down."

"This might be worse than we thought," Dam-Powl said. "I must speak with Temple Master Lha-Mi, and he will want to contact the Council."

"There's one more thing," Lanoree said. "The Kalimahr, Kara. I think she was once a Je'daii."

"Once?"

"It's confused. I couldn't read her at all. But not in the same way that I can't read Tre Sana."

One corner of Dam-Powl's mouth lifted in a half smile. Unspoken acknowledgment of whatever was between her and Tre.

"She claimed that the Force was stale within her."

"Her name, again?"

"Kara. That's all I have. Human, perhaps seventy years old. And big."

"Big?"

"Huge."

"Did she fall hard?"

"Master, I didn't kill her."

"Then how did you search her apartments?"

"We have your friend Tre to thank for that."

Dam-Powl nodded, but she seemed more distant now, mind working. "Lanoree, take care," she said. "I have heard of such people, but they're very, very rare. Most end up on Bogan for a time and then come back to us. One remains."

"Daegen Lok."

"Yes, him. But a few . . . we in the Council call them Shunned. People in whom the Force can never settle, nor find balance in light or dark, and who develop a disgust for the Force itself. Most of them flee way out into the system, broken mentally and physically, die."

"I've never heard of the Shunned."

"Few have. They're not a group . . . just a name." Dam-Powl stared from the screen for a moment, smiling uncertainly. "Your own studies?"

"On hold," Lanoree said. "But . . . Tre Sana is impressive."

"He has his uses. Dangerous, damaged, there's a lot of good in him. Drowned by selfishness, unfortunately."

"Well, he's suitably annoying," Lanoree said.

"Tell him he'll get what he's promised."

"And will he?"

Dam-Powl seemed surprised. "Of course, Ranger. You think I'd not keep a promise?"

It was Lanoree's turn to smile instead of reply.

"Find your brother," Dam-Powl said, leaning closer to the screen. "Stop him. Any way you can, and however you must."

"You'll be guarding the Old City, just in case?"

"Just in case," Dam-Powl said. "May the Force go with you, Ranger Brock."

"Master Dam-Powl," Lanoree said, bowing her head.

The screen flickered to darkness. The Peacemaker's nav computer chimed softly. Tre Sana woke up.

"Where are we?" he asked.

"Closer to the Stargazers," Lanoree said. She heard the static-filled mumble of contact from Khar Peninsula's landing towers, but she turned them off and took manual control of the ship. There was no time for political niceties now. "According to the computer there's only one old Dai Bendu temple in this quarter no longer used by them. If anything Kara said was true, that'll be where the Stargazers are."

"So we land and get transport there," Tre said.

"No. I'm landing us on the temple."

"*On* it?"

"Strap yourself in. This might get bumpy."

CHAPTER SEVEN
SAFE AND SOUND

Tython is beautiful and powerful, enigmatic and dangerous, filled with mysteries and open to those comfortable with the Force. It was here long, long before us, and these mysteries persisted with no eyes to see them, no minds to contemplate them. And that is why I fear Tython. It means everything to us, and yet we are nothing to it. We are merely passing through.

—Je'daii recluse Ni'lander, 10,648 TYA

Dawn was breaking as they glided over a stormy ocean toward the Khar Peninsula. And if Rhol Yan was impressive, Khar was stunning.

The peninsula itself was around nineteen kilometers long and a kilometer and a half wide, protruding from a much larger island out of sight over the horizon. Seven towers reached up from its spine, incredibly tall, graceful, beautiful. Their upper levels caught the sunlight, and as the Peacemaker approached, Lanoree and Tre could see the sun's influence slipping down the towers' exteriors. Beneath them were countless other tall structures, dwarfed by the more-than-one-kilometer-high towers yet impressive in their own right. Almost every building was ivory-colored, the only exceptions being many flat-topped buildings that seemed to serve as gardens and parks. These gave splashes of exotic greens across the Khar's otherwise uniform hue.

The peninsula looked like a jewel cast into the sea. But Lanoree did not have time to be impressed.

"What's that?" Tre asked. He was standing behind her cockpit seat, leaning on its back and annoying her every time he moved. She was concentrating too much to berate him. He hadn't yet had the audacity to sit in the spare flight seat beside her, and for that she was pleased.

"Khar law enforcement," she said. She'd already seen the four small, sleek ships, rising ahead of them and was readying to give them the slip.

"They won't argue with a Peacemaker."

"Probably not. But I've not responded to flight control. Far as they're concerned, I'm coming in blind. Hold on." Lanoree braced herself and punched a button.

The acceleration pressed her back into the seat, stealing her breath, trapping her limbs, compressing her stomach and chest, and yet she still managed a low chuckle when she heard Tre's startled cry and the sound of him tumbling back into the living area. He grunted and Ironholgs rattled, and Lanoree knew the droid had caught Tre. Probably to prevent him from damaging anything in the ship. She laughed again.

The four Khar ships flashed past and disappeared from view. Lanoree checked their positions on the scanner screen and made sure they weren't swinging about to fire on the Peacemaker. Then she swung low and sharp into the built-up conurbation of the Khar Peninsula.

She twitched the ship left and right, passing around buildings, dodging airships and smaller craft flitting here and there, and all the while glancing at a map display on a small screen to her right. It showed the layout of this quarter, and at the edge of the screen a green light pulsed. If her ship's computer was right, that was the location of Kara's unused Dai Bendu temple, home to the Stargazers.

"You could have warned me," Tre said.

"I did."

"But you didn't give me time to—"

"Hold on." Lanoree swung the ship to the right, curving tightly around the wide base of one of the seven massive towers. It filled her field of vision, and a series of openings just above ground level provided parking bays for ground speeders. They swarmed in and out like insects to and from a hive.

Tre picked himself up again and then jumped into the spare flight seat beside her. She glared at him. He stared back.

"You did that on purpose," he said.

"We don't have time to mess around with landing permissions."

"You're Je'daii. Do you ever?"

"When it's needed. I don't like you sitting there."

"So you do what you want, and shak on the natives?"

"Natives?" Lanoree slewed them around a big Cloud Chaser that had drifted down low, careful not to get too close. "That's demeaning. Is that how you think we think of everyone else?"

"Isn't it?"

"No," she said. But she frowned. She'd experienced antagonism from the settlers on worlds other than Tython, and she usually attributed it to leftover opinions and allegiances from the Despot Wars. But perhaps she had been fooling herself and picking on a simple and clear reason for some people's dislike of the Je'daii. Maybe it really was deeper and more complex than that. "We only ever do our best for everyone."

"You intrude. You serve yourselves and your Force. You fling me around your ship rather than telling me what you're doing." He pointed from the window at the beauty and complexity of Khar. "You'll land and leave again, without permission and without telling anyone why, and there will be another reason for everyone's distrust."

That troubled Lanoree. But only a little. She was on a mission to prevent a possible system-wide catastrophe, and whether everyone in the system knew that or not did not detract from its importance.

"You deal with us," she said. "With Master Dam-Powl."

"Do you think I have any choice?" Tre asked.

"Yes," Lanoree said. "Plenty."

"I'm a businessman," he said. "I suppose . . . I'm as mercenary as the Je'daii in achieving my aims."

"You're a criminal," Lanoree said. "And I didn't warn you about that turn because I needed a laugh."

"The complexity of a Je'daii," Tre said, and she could not help smiling at his light tone. He annoyed her. But there was something eminently likable about Tre.

"I still don't want you in that seat," she said.

He glanced across at her but did not reply.

A chime from the control panel—proximity alert. "Please hold on, Tre," she said pointedly. Then she put the ship into a dive. They drifted beneath one of the wide, garden-topped buildings, dodging between the stocky feet that held the amazing structure upright, and then she turned a sharp right and quickly climbed again.

"The temple is a kilometer ahead." She checked the map, where the Dai Bendu temple was marked a hazy green.

"You're really going to land on the roof?"

"No. Changed my mind. Too exposed."

"Good!"

"I'm going to take us in the front door."

Tre did not even reply, but his shocked silence was enough. He grasped the seat restraints and secured them across his chest and hips.

Lanoree knew that this was a tricky, risky maneuver, but they needed time. They'd be far too visible on the roof of the temple; and right or wrong she had already made the decision that there was no time to handle this through diplomatic channels. Dal and the Stargazers knew she was here, and whatever their plans, they would be accelerating them. She had to be creative.

The building was low, large, rectangular, with spires on four corners and a steeply pitched roof. As Lanoree lowered the Peacemaker into the wide courtyard in front of the temple she probed inside for Dal. She had no idea whether or not she'd be able to sense him, but she had to try. She was nervous. Afraid of what a confrontation might bring.

Another warning chime from the ship brought her around, and she realized that her concentration had been drifting. She'd almost flown them into the ground.

People scattered away from the ship, dropping belongings, rushing for cover as its powerful engines kicked up violent storms of dust. Benches were blown across the courtyard. Trees were bent over and stripped of leaves. Lanoree floated the Peacemaker along the front of the temple until she saw its main wooden doors. Wide enough. They were closed. But the ship was tough.

She nudged them forward and smashed the doors aside with the Peacemaker's nose, taking a significant chunk of masonry with them. Then she settled the ship down, nose inside the temple, the body of the ship in the courtyard. Hardly inconspicuous, but she didn't plan on being here for long.

"Ironholgs, keep the engines powered up. We might be leaving in a hurry. Tre? Coming?"

He looked across at her, lekku forming a series of words that might have made his mother blush. Lanoree grinned.

Dal was not there. No one was. But until very recently, they had been.

Inside the temple was one large central room with many smaller rooms around its edges. The main room itself was full height, the walls and ceilings extravagantly decorated with frescoes relaying Dai Bendu religious tales and history, tall windows allowing in multicolored dawn light through stained-glass symbols. The nose of the Peacemaker ship cooled and ticked, hull dappled with colors, the temple's ancient wooden doors smashed on the floor around it.

It was in some of the smaller rooms that they found evidence of recent habitation.

Sleeping rolls were scattered across the floor. Meals lay half-eaten on several long tables, cold but not congealed. Candles still burned in some of the windowless inner rooms. Here and there lay the remains of hastily smashed equipment.

And in one small room, Lanoree found something of Dal.

"Check the other rooms," she said.

"They've gone," Tre said. "Kara must have warned them."

"Why tell us where they are and then warn them? Check the other rooms. I need to know where they're going." Tre must have sensed something in Lanoree's voice because he did not argue, did not reply with another quip. He melted away, and she heard his footfalls echoing through the temple room.

It was the smallest of things. Dal had always loved fruit, and mepples were his favorite, the tangy, sweet flesh complemented by the spicy zing of many small seeds. He always chewed right down to the long core stone, and then when he finished the small fruits, he placed the stones end to end until they formed a circle. Sometimes there were only five or six making the shape, on occasion fifteen or more.

There were nine now on the floor, and the circle was incomplete. If he'd left this as a sign for Lanoree he would surely have finished the circle. But the last core had been flung aside, as if he'd departed the temple in a hurry.

Lanoree stared at the almost circle and wished the ends would meet. At least then Dal might be welcoming her pursuit and drawing her on, some sibling rivalry remaining.

"Not like this," she whispered. "Not desperate." She touched one fruit stone gently, then moved around the small room. It was a mess. Clothing lay scattered across the floor, plates were speckled with dried remnants of old food. On the stone wall a network of metal pins showed where something had been on display. Plans? Maps? There was no way of knowing.

She picked up a jacket, pressed it to her face, inhaled. But there was nothing there that she recognized.

She had to know where he was going, how much information—if any—he had about those old plans, how far along the device might be. Perhaps even *with* the blueprints it would be impossible to replicate Gree technology to the detail required. But there was little here to indicate anything one way or another, and Lanoree felt a flush of desperation. She had come so close, and yet now Dal might be heading anywhere.

Looking around the small room one more time, she tried to remember the last good times she and her brother had spent together. Her thoughts drifted this way often, usually when Dal intruded unexpectedly in her mind. She knew it was long before their journey across Tython. Maybe as far back as when they were children, younger and more innocent to the truths of things.

But even then he had been different.

"I should have listened to you," Lanoree whispered. She had always harbored guilt about his death, because she believed it was her reveling in the Force—and her determination to push him toward it—

that had ultimately driven him away. Now that same guilt sang in once more, but it was over something worse than death.

She might have made him whatever he had become.

"Anything?" she shouted. She left that room quickly, kicking the mepple stones apart. "Tre? Anything?" Emerging into the main room, she glanced at the Peacemaker's nose blocking the shattered doorway at the other end. The vessel's engines pulsed with potential.

Tre darkened a doorway across the temple and ran toward her. He was carrying something. He looked pale. "We've got to go."

"Why?"

"They left quickly, but not before setting a timer."

Lanoree's senses sharpened, her veins flooded with energy. "How long?"

"Moments."

They ran to the ship, up the ramp, and even as Lanoree jumped into the flight seat, the window lit up with an incredibly bright light.

"Ramp!" she shouted, but Ironholgs was already closing it. A wave of fire roared across the temple and engulfed the ship. The explosion blasted in, incredibly loud inside the ship, hull shaking and everything outside blurring as walls shook and part of the roof was lifted from the huge building.

Tre shouted, voice barely heard.

Momentarily blinded by the fire flash Lanoree coaxed them aloft. Impacts sounded across the hull as the building started to collapse. The flight stick shuddered in her hand and she eased back, trying to remember the layout of the courtyard. If she backed them into another building they'd be in just as much trouble.

Another explosion pounded against them and Lanoree pressed her lips together, grabbing the stick with both hands. The time for caution was over. She pulled and turned, eyes scanning the instrument panel. Proximity alerts sounded and a wall of blazing masonry smashed down across the window, ancient stones bursting apart. Then they were away, vision clearing, and the ship almost seemed to lighten in relief as she lifted them away from the courtyard.

Tilting them slightly to dislodge any detritus left on the hull, she looked down in time to see the temple implode—roof collapsing, spires tumbling inward and adding to the billowing clouds of dust and flame that roared up and out.

"That was close!" Tre said from the other seat. He was gripping the armrests, his lekku pale and agitated.

"The old girl can withstand more than that."

"I mean us!"

Checking the scanner for law enforcement, knowing they'd be here soon, Lanoree glanced one more time at the burning ruin of the old Dai Bendu temple. "I think Kara might be upset."

"I think maybe she knew exactly what was going to happen."

Lanoree did not reply, but she couldn't help agreeing with Tre's assessment. So far she'd been steered here and there, guided by words from people she didn't know or trust. Kara deserved another visit.

But not yet.

"What did you find?" she asked.

"What was left of a comm unit," Tre said. "They smashed things up pretty bad, but I think one of the memory cells is whole in this one."

"Give it to the droid." She offered Tre a half smile. "Don't worry, that was nowhere near close."

"Compared to things you've done, perhaps. But I value my skin. I don't do 'close.' I don't even do 'near.' I do 'safe and sound.'"

"Then why did you agree to help a Ranger?"

"I didn't have much choice."

"There's always a choice," Lanoree said. And she thought of Dal again, the choices he had made, and how perhaps she had forced some of them upon him.

She flew them high, arcing up from the Khar Peninsula and back out over the ocean, where there was not so much traffic. Tre left her alone, and Lanoree spent some time assessing the ship's condition and checking for damage. There was nothing significant. Drifting up until they were skimming the edge of space, she left the ship to fly itself and went back to see what Ironholgs had found.

Tre was seated on the cot, and the droid was still working. The comm unit was more smashed up than Tre had believed, and Ironholgs whistled that it might take some time to extract any information remaining in the memory cells.

Lanoree realized for the first time how cramped the Peacemaker felt. It was designed to carry two pilots and four passengers with ease, but it had been her home for so long, and hers alone. She was not used to sharing this space with anyone or anything other than Ironholgs. And she could switch him off.

"So, this is cozy," Tre said, as if reading her thoughts.

"Fresher's through there," she said, pointing at one of three hatches leading from the back of the main compartment. "Middle door's to the engine room and laser cannon charge unit. You stay out of there. The third door's to spare living quarters, but it's my storeroom. Food, water, spare laser charge pods. I suppose you *might* be able to clear enough space to sleep."

"I'm fine here," Tre said. His lekku twirled slightly, random movement that betrayed little.

"For now," Lanoree said. "You've got to know, I don't like passengers."

"Hey, I didn't ask to come along."

She could not argue with that. Lanoree opened a compartment and took out two drink sachets. She flung one at Tre and it bounced from his shoulder. He caught it, examined it briefly, then ripped the corner and drank. He raised it in a silent toast and nodded his thanks.

"So what's your story?" Lanoree asked. "Dam-Powl told me you were dangerous."

"You don't believe her?" he asked.

"Maybe you've been bad. Perhaps you're dangerous to some. But not to me."

Tre Sana looked down at his hands as if considering what they had done in the past. His smile was contemplative. "I've done things I can never tell you about," he said, "to people you'd never want to know."

"Not much can shock me," Lanoree said.

"No. Of course not. You're a Ranger." Something of his defense dropped then—she thought perhaps he let it—and she saw behind the slightly awkward, scared-of-heights Twi'lek to the man beneath. And his eyes were ice, his heart a solid lump, and she suddenly believed every word Dam-Powl had told her.

"Fresher," he said softly. "If you'll excuse me."

"Don't get lost," Lanoree said. She turned her back on him and faced the living area, and as she heard the fresher hatch open and close behind her, she breathed a silent breath. *Dam-Powl, just who have you burdened me with?*

"Droid. Get busy."

Ironholgs snickered some choice abuse at her, melted more wires, made more connections. The compartment smelled of electrics, and Lanoree turned the climate conditioning to full to clear the air.

She sat in the flight seat and watched the scanners for trouble.

"Oh, great," Tre said. "That's just great."

Lanoree jerked from a gentle doze, angry with herself for drifting off. *That's not professional,* she thought. *That's not good.* She climbed from the cockpit and went back to where Tre was looking down at Ironholgs.

The droid had wired a small mobile screen to the shattered comm unit, and now several lines of broken information glowed softly.

"Safe and sound?" Lanoree grinned at him.

The screen showed seventeen recent communications between the Stargazers and an unnamed recipient on Nox.

Nox. Third planet of the system, it was also the most polluted, rich in mineral deposits, and now home to dozens of cities devoted entirely to manufacturing. Five centuries before, the atmosphere had become so polluted that the cities were enclosed with giant domes, and ironically the richest conurbation was now Keev Crater, which manufactured dome components and charged a heavy premium to oversee their upkeep and maintenance. The air outside the domes was acidic and poisonous, and heavily corrosive to any craft exposed to it for too long. Skirmishes were not unknown between competing domed cities. During the Despot War, some had sided with the Despot Queen Hadiya and some with the Je'daii and a few with whomever paid the most. Many of those divisions still ran deep.

Lanoree had been to some dangerous places, but Nox might well be the most dangerous planet in the system.

"Well, drop me off before you go," Tre said.

"Sure. I'll open the door."

Tre glared at her. "I mean it."

"So do I. They have a head start on us already, and there's no telling what sort of ship they have. If Kara funds them, there's a good bet there's money from elsewhere, too. It won't be some old space freighter they're riding to Nox. If I land to—"

"I'm getting off this ship."

"I'm getting off this planet." Lanoree turned her back on Tre and slipped into the flight seat. "Come up here and strap in," she said. "No time to worry about niceties."

The Peacemaker shuddered and roared as it escaped Kalimahr's gravity, and the cool embrace of cold, dead space had never been more welcome.

Their time at Stav Kesh is the most intense period of learning Lanoree has ever experienced, both psychologically and physically. She and Dal train hard all day—meditation, combat, Force movement—and in the evenings they prepare food, clean the training classrooms and halls, wash clothes, and learn how to care for weapons. They also descend to the caves beneath the temple, places warmed by deep magma lakes, and here they tend the fruit and vegetable crops grown in vast hydroponic gardens. Food, cleaning, maintenance, water, clothing . . . no one is simply given things at Stav Kesh, and they have to work together to ensure the temple's smooth running.

Dal seems to find some form of acceptance in their training. Lanoree can still feel the turmoil of the Force around him as he fights its influence, but for the most part his childlike smile has returned.

For a while, she starts to believe that he is almost at peace.

Until the Darrow sphere.

"The Darrow sphere is your next great test," Master Kin'ade tells them one morning. The Zabrak Master has taken over from Master Tave several times now, and Lanoree likes her very much. Short, slight, her tattooed skin as dark as Bodhi caf, she might be the most deadly person Lanoree has ever met. Yet with that talent for combat comes an easy manner and a gentle balance, evident in her smooth movements and tranquil expression. Her relationship with the Force is as natural as breathing.

Master Kin'ade has taken them high up toward the top of Stav Kesh, close to the mountain's top. It is even colder up here than elsewhere, exposed to higher winds and with a thinner atmosphere. There is very little actual climbing to do, but the walk is long and energetic, and by the time they reach the small plateau at the mountain's top they are all sweating. More accustomed now to the thin air at these altitudes, Lanoree still feels light-headed and adrift. The wind starts to freeze their sweat. Their thin training robes are ineffectual. None of them wants to be there.

Except Master Kin'ade. She lowers the rucksack she has been carrying to the ground and turns to face them all. "No time for sightseeing," she says. "Here. Watch." She upends the rucksack, and something falls from it.

But it does not hit the ground.

The sphere glows, hums, shines. It darts up past Kin'ade's horned head and hovers high up, drifting left and right as if looking at the views. It is the size of a human's head . . . and then larger . . . and then smaller again, fistlike, hard. It flits from place to place and glides. It is smooth, and glimmers like a fluid, hard and spiked with countless protuberances. There are so many contradictions to the sphere, it is so ambiguous, that when it attacks, it takes Lanoree a few moments to figure out what is happening. By then her leg is bleeding and her arm aches, and the other students are in disarray.

The Darrow sphere attacks and then retreats, rises and falls, fires darts of light, and impacts against flesh. One moment it seems intent on killing them all, the next it drifts away, glowing an almost serene shade of blue as it seems to contemplate the views.

It sweeps toward Master Kin'ade, who performs an Alchaka move and kicks the sphere aside.

"Concentrate," Kin'ade says. "Don't panic. Don't get flustered. Let the Force flow with you, sense the sphere's movement. Know its intent."

Lanoree tries. She calms her mind and breathes long and deep, remembering all that Master Tave has taught them. The Force within her is perfectly balanced. She feels at one with it, neither master nor servant but—

The Darrow sphere sweeps behind her and delivers a paralyzing charge to her leg. She groans and tips to the ground, massaging the spasming muscle and angry at herself. She remains there for a while as the pain dissipates, watching the other students fall to the sphere. The Wookiee manages to get a hit in with one heavy fist. But perhaps the sphere let her, because she cries out as the hairs on her arm stand on end and her fist sparks and sizzles.

"Enough," Master Kin'ade says. She performs a graceful gesture with her hand and the sphere sinks to the ground, fading until it is almost transparent. Lanoree has the impression that it is still of its own mind, and that Kin'ade is barely controlling it at all.

"What *is* that thing?" Dal asks. He is crouched across the small plateau from the rest of them, nose bleeding, knuckles raw from where he has been trying to fight the sphere.

"This is the Darrow sphere," Master Kin'ade says. "I created it myself to help student training here at Stav Kesh, and this is the only one. A student of mine several years ago called it Je'daii's bane, and I almost changed its name. I like that." She looked up at the sky, smiling. "And like anything with two names, the sphere has its ambiguities." She nods at where the sphere came to rest, and Lanoree is not surprised to see it gone.

"Where is it?" Dal asks.

"There," Kin'ade says. "Or perhaps not. Are you too trusting of your senses, Dalien Brock?"

"They're all I have."

A loaded hush falls over the breezy plateau, even the wind seeming to die down at Dal's words.

"No," Kin'ade whispers. "They're the very least of what you have. And so you can go last."

"Go last for what?"

Master Kin'ade ignores Dal and gestures Lanoree forward instead. Lanoree walks to her, and as she approaches, the Master starts talking quietly. "Remember, the Force does not lie, although if you're out of balance you can make lies from it. Feel the flow. Relish the balance." She delves into her rucksack and brings out a blindfold, a nose clip, earplugs, and a mask.

"If I wear all those—" Lanoree protests, but Master Kin'ade cuts in.

"Then you have to trust in the Force."

Taking a deep breath, Lanoree nods. She puts them on, and it is like cutting herself off from the world. The blindfold gives perfect darkness. The earplugs mold to her ears and cut out all sound, leaving only her beating heart. The nose clip steals all smell. She can taste snow on the air, but the sphere—

An impact on her leg and she cries out, staggering to the left. She can hear no instruction from Master Kin'ade and realizes this is intentional. Lanoree tries to center herself, breathing long and deep, sensing the Force within her and being a part of it, balanced and level. She draws her sword and waits.

A sting on her shoulder. She shrugs it off.

Something moves past her face, close and quick.

She reaches out and senses everyone else around her, and then—

Spins on her left leg, crouching and lashing out with her sword. She feels the connection and the impact travels up her arm. She rolls forward, then back onto her feet, holding her left hand up with fingers splayed, throwing a Force punch, sensing it strike the Darrow sphere. Her heart is thumping, breathing increasing, and she feels the flow of blood and Force through her veins. It is ecstasy.

The sphere impacts against her back and knocks her sprawling. The blindfold is torn from her eyes, the clip and plugs taken from her nose and ears. Input floods her senses, and the pain kicks in.

"Not bad," Master Kin'ade says. "Although you did let pride get the better of you. Never assume the danger is gone unless you know for sure."

Lanoree nods and sits up. The other students are all looking at the Je'daii Master and the sphere floating at her shoulder, pulsing, shifting. All but Dal. He is looking at Lanoree, and she cannot quite read the expression on his face. Resignation? Determination?

"Very well," Master Kin'ade says, hand stroking accumulated snow from her vestigial horns. "Next."

They all try, and then there is Dal.

Lanoree watches him having the blindfold fitted and the earplugs and the nose clip. He stands still and patient while Master Kin'ade does so, and she cannot sense any tension or displeasure in him. Though he has seen each Journeyer suffer to some extent at the mercy of the Darrow sphere, he seems calm. She does not probe—that would be wrong, to try to touch his mind before such a test—but he exudes confidence.

Kin'ade steps back and glances at Lanoree, and then says, "Begin."

Dal ducks left and right, scampers across the ground, tilts his head as if listening. But it is all a show. The sphere drifts in slowly and then powers into his left ankle. He does not see or sense it coming. Its movement is almost smug, and Lanoree wonders how it knew that Dal was faking everything.

He hits the ground. Rolls. And she sees him pulling the blaster from his jacket.

"Dal!" she breathes.

He starts shooting. His shots are wild and aimless, and Lanoree and the others hit the ground, Force-shielding themselves as stone splinters and erupts, falling snow sizzles to steam, someone screams. She feels heat and pain across her hand and arm.

Dal shouts and drops the blaster. Lanoree can see its glow from where it has been superheated, and then Master Kin'ade twists her clawed hand in Dal's direction. He rises and is immediately thrown back, spinning, fading from view in wafts of snowflakes. For a moment she thinks the Master has thrown Dal too far and that he will plummet over the parapet, falling three hundred meters to find his end on one of the rooftops below.

Then he strikes the ground with a heavy thud. As she reaches for Dal with her mind his fall into unconsciousness becomes, for a moment, her own.

CHAPTER EIGHT
THE MEMORY OF PAIN

A Je'daii needs nothing but confidence and comfort in the Force. Clothes for warmth, a ship to travel in, food for energy, water to slake thirst, a sword to stab, a blaster to shoot . . . all these are luxuries. The Force is everything, and without it, we are nothing.
—Master Shall Mar, "A Life in Balance," 7,538 TYA

Lanoree relaxed in her reclined flight seat. She had plotted the fastest course she could from Kalimahr to Nox, and now she was eager to see if Ironholgs could download more information from the damaged memory cell. Nox was a big planet, and of its almost ninety domed manufacturing cities, almost half might conceivably be capable of taking on a commission for the Gree device. Lanoree had no doubt that the specific expertise required would reduce that number to a mere two or three, but as yet she had no real idea what that ancient technology might entail. She was flying blind into a storm, but that was the only direction to take.

She'd contacted Master Dam-Powl and told her of the situation.

The Je'daii Master had promised that she could instruct those few Je'daii currently on Nox to monitor incoming off-planet traffic, but it was a notoriously renegade planet, and the majority of travel to and from Nox was unregistered. Finding Dal and the Stargazers' ship would be like finding a particular pebble on a beach, especially considering Lanoree still had no clue what type of ship they might be flying.

Dam-Powl had asked if Tre was still with her, and Lanoree had nodded. The resulting silence had been loaded. But the Twi'lek had not moved from Lanoree's cot to speak to the Je'daii Master, and Dam-Powl had nodded and then signed off.

Lanoree stared at the stars and stroked the scarred mass on the back of her left hand. She still remembered the day Dal had given her that. The beginning of the end.

"So you actually *live* in this thing?" Tre Sana asked.

"It's my ship, yes."

"It's a bit . . . bland. Not much of a home. Don't you get claustrophobic?"

"With this view?" Lanoree hadn't even raised the back of the flight seat.

But perhaps Tre was growing bored, and confrontation would pass the time.

"I never did like space travel. Always makes me feel sick. We weren't built to travel through space. However well shielded a ship is, I'm not convinced I don't get baked by radiation every time I leave the atmosphere. Your grav unit's configured wrong, too. I feel twice my usual weight, and that's making me feel even sicker."

Lanoree raised and turned her flight seat, smiling. "Is that all?"

"No. It stinks in here. I know you're probably used to it, but . . . electrics and grease and the smell of *you*. And let's face it, your ship is *small*. You sit where you sleep when you eat. And that fresher . . . I have to tell you, Je'daii, I've been in some of the seediest taverns in the worst of the Nine Houses on Shikaakwa, and even they have better amenities than you. How can you wash in recycled water? Where's the shower?" His face fell as if he had just recognized a terrible truth. "And what do you eat?"

"Ah," Lanoree said. "Food. Good idea." She stood and entered the living area, opening a small cupboard set in one wall. As she did so she nudged the droid where it worked at a drop-down bench. "Anything yet, Ironholgs?"

The droid did not even reply. It was tweaking and adjusting a delicate arrangement of wires and chips on the broken end of the memory cell, and it paused briefly as if disturbed, then continued.

"I'll take that as a no," Lanoree said. "Now then, Tre. Here. Take your choice." She threw a handful of packets across her cot, several of them landing on Tre's legs.

"What's this?"

"Dried food. What, you think I'm hiding a hydroponic pod somewhere at the back of the ship?"

Tre picked up a silvery packet and looked at it in disgust. His face wrinkled, lekku drawing back as if from something poisonous. "You eat this stuff?"

"Hot water, some salt. Some of it can be pretty good. Although you've got dangbat stir there. Got to admit, that's not the best."

"How long do you spend in this thing?" Tre asked, looking around, feigning disbelief.

Lanoree was starting to get annoyed. She hadn't really wanted him along—didn't trust him, especially since she'd seen the true, harder Tre behind the quips and false face he displayed. But she was stuck with him now, and he with her. Civility didn't cost much.

"Once, I was in deep space for over two hundred days, tracking a Special Forces cell from Krev Coeur gone mercenary."

"Two hundred . . ." Tre shook his head in despair.

"I don't need what you need," Lanoree said. She slipped a food packet into a metal pocket behind the cupboard hatch and charged it with hot water. Delicious smells filled the cabin, soon whisked away by the climate conditioner. "I know what Dam-Powl's promised you, and I'm sure you'll get it. But vast estates don't interest me. Fast ships, great wealth, prominence, standing in the community. Overflowing credit accounts on a dozen worlds." She took the packet and started eating. "Men. Adoration. Even respect. I don't need any of that."

Tre laughed. "Then you're—"

"Because I know there's more to life," she said, cutting him off.

She was tired of his inanities and angry that he could be so superficial. In the face of everything she knew, and all that he must know, such shallowness offended her. "There's the Force. It binds and holds us, and makes everything precious to me. It's our reason for being. There is no ignorance, there is knowledge. And that's much more precious than fine foods or somewhere comfortable to wash."

"You sound like one of the clans on Kalimahr praying to one of their Sprash Gods."

"Difference being, I know the Force exists."

Tre Sana smiled and nodded, never taking his eyes from hers. It was a strange moment. Dam-Powl had made him unreadable, and Lanoree wondered why the Je'daii Master had employed such a dangerous man. Or perhaps what she'd done to him that had made him this way.

"But there's not always balance, is there, Je'daii?" he asked, as if he knew everything.

"Eat," she said. "It's really not that bad." She turned her back on him again, sat in her cockpit seat, and thought of those experiments she had put on hold. There was darkness there, if she did not use caution. But she was comfortable. She was balanced. There was no reason at all to worry.

Lanoree stayed there for some time, and Tre must have read her need to remain undisturbed. She was glad of that. She didn't like having someone else in her ship, and despite all her best efforts, being constantly reminded of his presence was putting her on edge.

Ashla and Bogan were out of sight, along with Tython, a hundred sixty million kilometers away on the other side of Tythos. Yet she felt their pull and presence, as did every Je'daii wherever they might be in the system. Ashla was light and Bogan dark, and they tugged at her with a comforting gravity, as if she were suspended at the most perfect balancing point between the moons, influenced by both yet pulled in neither direction.

It had not always been like this. After she had lost Dal, halfway through her Great Journey, she had experienced a period of unbalance. Returned home. Learned from her parents to be trusting and trustworthy in the Force once again. It had been nowhere near serious enough to warrant exile, but it had troubled her greatly then, and still did now.

And Dam-Powl had warned that her experiments had the potential to upset the balance once more. The alchemy of flesh—genetic manipulation of cells that, though seeded from her own body, had a life of their own—held such dangers. But Lanoree could not help playing to her strengths. Ignoring them would be like trying to deny the Force itself, and she had already seen the results of that.

Death, she had believed. But now in Dal maybe something worse. A terrible kind of madness.

Perhaps at some point during this mission she might find cause to return to her studies.

"Greenwood Station," Lanoree said. "The Stargazers were communicating with someone there. That's not good."

"It's not?" Tre asked.

Lanoree looked at the partial communications Ironholgs had managed to extract from the damaged memory cell. All of them had been encoded, and even when deciphered by the droid they had used mundane language that was beyond any code breaker. But the origin and destination of each signal had been scrambled with military-level ciphers.

"Greenwood Station is one of the worst places on one of the most dangerous planets in the system," Lanoree said. "If there's a general dislike for the Je'daii on Nox, they *hate* us there. It's surrounded by three destroyed domes, bombed by the Je'daii during the Despot War. I was only young then, thirteen. But my parents went to war, and my father served some of his time on Nox. A terrible place, he told me. Acid rain, corrosive gas storms. We warned the domes the bombings were going to happen—they were supplying Hadiya with weapons, however much nonmilitary pressure we exerted—but thousands still died. Many thousands. No one has ever really known how many."

"I'm older than you," Tre said. "I seem to recall Greenwood Station being bombed as well."

"But not destroyed. The original dome was breached but quickly repaired. It's a damaged place, and everything around it is ruin."

"But it's still where they make the most advanced military tech outside Tython," Tre said. It seemed he'd known everything about Greenwood Station, but had feigned ignorance and let her say it anyway. Another one of his games.

"And how would you know that?"

"I've had cause to use them, from time to time."

"You've been there?" Lanoree asked. She had no interest in Tre's business or his reason for using high-end tech. Not then.

"Of course not! I told you, I hate space travel."

"But you'll be known there?"

Tre raised an eyebrow, shrugged. "Not by anyone who'd help us."

"Why not?"

"You're Je'daii."

"Great," Lanoree said. It was a perfect place for the Stargazers and Dal to flee when they knew she was on their trail. And yet . . .

This was not about escape. Some of the older communications her droid had plucked from the damaged memory cell proved that. They were going to Greenwood Station for one reason, and that could only be the construction of the Gree device. How complete their plans were, Lanoree could not tell. The old Osamael Or diary was far from comprehensive, and there was no way of knowing whether he had ever found those Gree plans. If he had, perhaps they existed in another diary. One that Kara had been too sensible to leave even in her hidden room. And even if the Stargazers *did* have the plans in some form, whether they could build the device effectively—and make it actually *work*—was something no one could know. Her mission remained one of unknowns and ambiguities.

One thing she *was* certain of: this had already gone further than she could have hoped. The dangers were too great, the chances of Dal's success too dreadful to comprehend. The chase had to end on Nox, and there she would face her brother.

"I'll plot a course," Lanoree said. "Then we'll find you somewhere to sleep."

Tre feigned surprise and held his hands out, indicating the narrow but comfortable cot.

"Don't even think about it," Lanoree said. She pointed at the door she'd shown him before.

"With the laser pods? And the food stores? There might be space rats in there."

"I keep a clean ship," Lanoree said. "And I'm sure you've slept in worse."

"Well . . ." His three lekku stretched in amusement. Lanoree tried not to smile; she sensed that he wanted to make this as painless as she did.

"Come on," she said. "Let's just get by. I'll fly us there as quickly as I can."

"I'm not sure I *want* to get there that quickly," Tre said, and his tired smile might have been the first genuine one she'd seen.

"We'll be fine. I'll look after you."

"And who's looking after you?"

The Force will be my guide, Lanoree thought. She turned her back on Tre and went up into the cockpit again to chart the fastest, safest course to Greenwood Station on Nox. All the while she was thinking of Dal, and that as a Journeyer she had never truly understood how dangerous he might be.

Not until close to the end.

Even though Master Kin'ade is adept at healing, Lanoree's arm and hand still hurt. *It will for some time*, Kin'ade told her. *I can fix the damage, but the scarring will remain, and the memory of pain is stronger than you think.*

The memory of pain means that she can barely sit still, even in Temple Master Lha-Mi's chambers.

Dal is also there. His own wounds are less serious than hers—bruises and lacerations from impacting the ground—but Master Kin'ade paid them just as much attention.

"You are not here to be punished," Temple Master Lha-Mi says to Dal. Even though the chambers are large and impressive, Master Lha-Mi sits in a simple wooden chair, his sword propped beside him. Lanoree has heard many tales of this man, and this sword. "You are here so that I can hear what happened at the top of Stav Kesh. I've learned through my long life that stories are . . . fluid. And that the truth is often found in the sum of the parts. So I'll have each of you tell me your own version of events."

"It's very simple," Dal says. He is sitting before Lha-Mi alongside Lanoree, and on his other side sits their instructor. "Master Kin'ade took away all my senses and expected me to shoot straight."

"I haven't yet asked you to speak," Lha-Mi says. His voice is not stern, but it carries the authority of age and experience. "Master Kin'ade. If you will begin?"

She stands and bows her head. "Master. I was training a group of students with the Darrow sphere." She goes on to relate events exactly as they happened, expressing no opinions, simply relaying the facts. Lanoree cannot perceive any elaboration to her story—it is exact and correct in every detail. Kin'ade finishes and bows again.

"And now you, Lanoree Brock," Lha-Mi says.

"It's as Master Kin'ade described. I did my best to feel the Force and fight the sphere, but I admit to becoming overconfident. The others did well, mostly. Some bruises, burns, bloody noses, and one or two hits on the sphere, too. And then it was Dal's turn. He moved well, and at first I thought he was seeking the Force, and I felt . . . proud. Pleased for him. But then the Sphere took him down easily, and he pulled his blaster. He got off several shots before Master Kin'ade stopped him."

"She flung me to the ground and almost broke my arm," Dal says. "I almost went over the parapet."

Lha-Mi does not even look at Dal. He is still staring at Lanoree, his old eyes almost closed as he listens and thinks. "And your thoughts when one of those blaster shots passed close to your arm?"

"I was frightened for Dal," Lanoree says.

"Because of what Master Kin'ade might do to him?"

"No. Because of his own loss of control."

"And now *your* version of events, Dalien Brock."

Dal sighs deeply, an almost petulant breath. But Lanoree can sense his fear.

"Go on, Dal," she says. He glances sharply at her, then his gaze shifts to her bandaged arm and hand, and he looks wretched.

"I tried," he says. "I tried to find the Force."

He's lying, Lanoree thinks. *I know him so well, I can hear it in his voice.*

"I tried my best—and when the sphere hit me, I went for my blaster, tried to . . . follow the Force, shoot where it told me." He shrugs. "It didn't work. I'm sorry, Lanoree."

"Every scar tells a story," she says, repeating something their father once told them.

Temple Master Lha-Mi nods. "It's fortunate that no one was killed. Master Kin'ade is adept at healing, and I consider myself lucky that she chose Stav Kesh instead of Mahara Kesh. She can mend flesh wounds and knit bones, given time. But no Je'daii can defeat death. Your actions were foolish, Dalien. Led by impetuousness, not guided by the Force. I put that down to youth's enthusiasm. Perhaps some more traditional weapons training might be in order for the next few days, Master Kin'ade."

"Just what I had in mind," Kin'ade says. She stands as if at a silent signal and motions Lanoree and Dal to stand, too.

"Stay with me, Lanoree," Lha-Mi says. The other two leave, and then Lanoree is alone with the Temple Master. He is old and strong, but not intimidating. There's a kindliness to him that makes her feel comfortable, and she can sense his concern.

"Your brother," he says, and then he says no more. A question?

"He's trying," Lanoree says. "He knows what our Great Journey is for, and he's doing his best."

"No," Lha-Mi says. "I fear he has already given up. For some, the Force is never comfortable or easy to find balance within."

"No!" she says, standing before the Temple Master. He remains seated and composed. "Our parents are Je'daii, and we will be also."

"You already *are*, Lanoree. I sense a great future for you. You're strong, sensible, mature, and you have—" he held out his hand, tilted it left and right "—balance, give or take. But your brother is different. He carries a darkness within him, and his shunning of the Force makes it too dark to penetrate, too deep for me to plumb. There *may* still be a way back for him. But you have to realize how dangerous he might be. You have to be careful."

"I made a promise to my parents. He's my brother, I love him, and I'll save him."

"Sometimes love is not enough." Lha-Mi rises and takes her hand. He speaks no more. But she feels a touch on her mind, brief but potent, that shows her a blink of what Dal had been thinking in the Temple Master's chambers.

Deep, dark thoughts.

CHAPTER NINE

SCARS

*The Je'daii say, "There is no ignorance; there is knowledge." But they are
ignorant of your lives, your struggles, and their superiority blinds them.
They say, "There is no fear; there is power." Yet in their power they are
smug. And I will make them fear me.*

—Despot Queen Hadiya, 10,658 TYA

Even from a distance, Nox looked like hell. Lanoree plotted a route
that brought them into the planet's atmosphere well on the opposite
hemisphere from Greenwood Station, swinging them in an arc around
the planet and approaching from the nightside. The seas were a heavy,
sullen gray, the landmasses mostly covered by sickly looking yellowish
clouds that glowed and pulsed with interior storms. The small patches
of land she could see between the clouds were of a uniform bronze
color. There was no green. She wondered what Greenwood Station
had been like when it had been named, or whether the name was bitterly ironic.

Tre sat in the copilot's seat again. He hadn't said much for quite a
while, and Lanoree was starting to fear that he was succumbing to

space sickness. If that happened, he'd be no use at all and she'd have to leave him in the Peacemaker. And she would *not* leave him here with her ship alone and awake.

She knew exactly where to hit him.

"Pretty," he said as they started skimming the atmosphere.

"Not very. It's going to get bumpy."

She'd taken them in a steeper descent than was normal, eager to enter the atmosphere as quickly as possible. The longer their approach, the more likely they'd be noticed. She could see at least seven other craft on the scanners, all describing different descents to various parts of the planet, and she'd heard no hailing on the comm. But that didn't mean they weren't all being tracked. And maybe those other seven were expected.

Heat built around the Peacemaker's nose, shimmering their view and then hazing it out completely. The window's shields closed automatically, and Lanoree kept her eyes on the scanners to maintain manual control.

"Really," she said. "It'll be bumpy."

"Trying to get rid of me?" Tre asked. "Don't worry. I think I'll stay here. Strapped in."

Even after six days, she *still* didn't like him sitting in the cockpit beside her, because she couldn't talk to herself anymore.

The Peacemaker started to vibrate as it carved its way down into the planet's toxic atmosphere. Lanoree swung the ship to the left and down, increasing the speed and angle of descent, and every now and then she glanced sidelong at Tre to see how he was taking this. Space-flight was simple compared to the traumas of entering an atmosphere. And despite all he'd said, he seemed calm and confident with what was happening.

"Almost there," she said.

"Good." He exhaled deeply, as if suddenly aware that she was watching. "Don't like this at all."

They dropped, and soon Lanoree leveled them out, flying above Nox and feeling the ship's responses at being back in an atmosphere again through her hands. The Peacemaker was rattled but unbroken. It cruised.

Lanoree skimmed them along the coast of one of the largest continents, flying low enough to avoid basic radar-based scanners but not too low to be dangerous, and a while later she edged them inland toward their destination.

There was no saying whether Dal and the Stargazers were here yet. Just as when they'd entered Nox's atmosphere, Lanoree knew that they were flying blind.

The destruction was worse than she could have imagined.

Lanoree remembered some of the Despot War. She'd been only thirteen at the time, but she would never forget watching her parents leaving home, false smiles hiding the fear that they might leave their children as orphans. She had watched the holos and heard the reports, but her real knowledge of the war came from what she'd read and seen of it down through the intervening years. At the time it was happening, war was always confused. The truth emerged afterward.

She'd learned about the Despot Queen Hadiya uniting Shikaakwa's crime barons under her charismatic rule and then attempting to exert her influence across the rest of the settled worlds. There had been a surprisingly enthusiastic rallying to her cause, as she promised safety and wealth and a freedom from Je'daii interference. Denying the Force, demonizing it to all who followed and listened, her aggression had been brutal but short-lived. The Je'daii swore to confront any moves made against them, and also to protect all those who did not wish to be subjugated beneath Hadiya's rule.

After a period of phony war, during which there were many small skirmishes in space and on some of Kalimahr's moons, Hadiya had taken the war to Tython. Working in secret she had built a formidable army, well equipped and heavily armed, and had taken the Je'daii somewhat by surprise. The invasion was massive, brutal, and the battles fierce. But the Je'daii had the Force on their side, and everything Hadiya hated had worked against her. The defining moment of the war had been catastrophic. Following Hadiya's death at Kaleth and the defeat of her armies, it had taken a long time to count the true cost of the conflict. A hundred thousand Tythans dead. Ten times that many of Hadiya's forces, and many more seriously injured. Wounds ran deep, and remained so even now, more than a decade later.

Before Lanoree now was one such wound.

She knew about the manufacturing domes on Nox that had been bombed by the Je'daii—attacked for providing arms and weapons for Hadiya's armies—and she had seen holos of the act itself. But holos were at a distance, imagination was limited by experience. Nothing could prepare her for seeing the truth with her own eyes. It was startling to see how effective a Je'daii military strike could be, and though Lanoree had seen plenty of combat, she had never been involved in a full-scale war.

She didn't even know the name of the first ruin they passed. Her Peacemaker flitted quickly by, but the scale of the devastation was still staggering. The city must have been eight kilometers in width, and now very little of its original protective dome remained. The ruins inside were a charred, melted mess, holding lakes of rancid water and pointing accusatory slivers of wrecked buildings at the sky.

It was a relief to pass the destruction and fly across undisturbed ground, even if that landscape was so obviously polluted and poisonous. Very little grew here. And if any creatures were able to live and breathe in the rank air, they did not make themselves known.

They passed another dome on their starboard side, several kilometers distant yet still plainly visible as a scar on the landscape. *Every scar tells a story*, Lanoree thought, and this tale must have been terrible. A portion of the dome remained, shattered and starred by multiple projectile impacts, and detritus from the city was scattered across the surrounding plains. The explosions that had finished this dome must have been immense.

She felt sickness welling inside, and a sense of hopelessness enveloped her. The Force offered so much, yet still there was the need for conflict, pain, and death. A thousand people might be peace loving and committed to living their lives well, but it took only one to plant a seed of poison that would spread through the population. How many of the Despot Army's million dead would still be alive today were it not for Hadiya? Perhaps most of them. Some might harbor dislike of the Je'daii or some vaguely unsettled sense of mistrust. Hatred, even. But without someone with Hadiya's charisma and determination, such feelings remained inside, unfocused. She had made them manifest, and on her hands was the blood of a million victims on both sides.

"Seeing it really brings it home," Tre said. He sounded so distressed, so genuine, so not like Tre Sana. Lanoree could almost like him.

She turned the Peacemaker and tracked Greenwood Station on her scanner. It was a riot of movement—ships lifting and landing, and large ground transports moving around the massive dome. But she was more concerned with traces of ships closer to her. If Greenwood Station had anything like an organized military, or a defense force funded by the great manufacturing conglomerates, they would detect the Peacemaker soon.

And her arrival had to remain covert. That was essential, because if Dal and his Stargazers knew where and when she had arrived, their reaction would be instant. This was a much wilder place than Kalimahr, and they had hardly been careful there.

Twenty-six kilometers out from Greenwood Station, two small sentry ships rose from the landscape a kilometer ahead and accelerated toward the dome.

Lanoree reacted instantly, flicking a switch to block their communications systems. She heard a few panicked words—

"Greenwood Four? Greenwood Four, you reading this? Je'daii incoming, Peacemaker class, must be the one we've been waiting for! We'll lead it in but I'm not engaging that, no way, we'll leave it to Greenwood's pulse cannons to—"

—before shutting off the comlink.

"They sound friendly," Tre said.

Lanoree ignored him. She stroked a pad on the joystick and the weapons system fired up, casting a gleaming blue grid across the cockpit window. The two sentry ships were outlined in red, and a series of readings down the left-hand side showed the Peacemaker's readiness. Three lines turned quickly from white to green—targeting, plasma missile, laser cannon, all online.

"Really?" Tre asked.

"I'm not here to start a war," Lanoree said. "And you heard them. They're expecting me. Dal must have warned them, maybe lied about why I'm here. If Greenwood Station gets to know I'm here, war's what it might be."

She relaxed into her seat and felt the Force flowing through her, nerve ends tingling, senses sharpened. She tweaked the joystick to the left and stroked the trigger, and one of the ships exploded in a haze of fire and smoke.

The second sentry took evasive action, swinging up and to the right in an attempt to drop back behind the Peacemaker. But fast though they were, these small atmospheric craft were not designed for such complex maneuverability. Lanoree followed, and as the ship reached the apex of its arc and slowed with the increased effort, she fired the laser cannons. The sentry's right wing exploded, and the craft started a long spin to the ground.

Lanoree drifted around and finished it off. No need to let the pilot suffer any longer than was necessary.

She breathed deeply and thought briefly of the people she had killed—their lovers and friends, their families and stories. Je'daii were taught to empathize with anyone they were forced to injure or kill, but Lanoree never attributed these thoughts to the Force. They were all about being human.

"Great shooting!" Tre said. He clapped his hands together once, lekku meeting above his head in a celebratory embrace.

"I just killed two people," Lanoree said.

"But you had to!"

"Doesn't make it any nicer. We'll be landing soon. Part of Greenwood Station's northern sector was bombed during the war, we'll get in through there."

"You mean we're landing *outside* the dome?"

"Do you think they'll welcome a Peacemaker into their landing bays?"

Tre fell silent as Lanoree flew them toward the distant dome.

The ship settled, ticking and creaking as its engines wound down and its hull began to cool. Lanoree usually liked this part of a long flight, imagining that the Peacemaker was sighing with satisfaction at a job well done and slumping, ready to recharge its muscles. But this was nowhere near the end of her journey.

She'd changed her clothes, donning a long flowing robe that hid her sword but made her feel like a Dai Bendu monk.

"Ready?" she asked.

"Honestly?" Tre Sana asked. "After everything I've said, I still think I'd rather stay on board than go out there."

"Come on, Tre. You said my ship stinks." She grinned and keyed the code for the ship's hatch.

A hiss, a groan, and the hatch swung down into a ramp, a breeze swirling around them as atmospheres equalized. Even behind the air mask she wore, Lanoree swore she could smell the rancid atmosphere of this place. And if she hadn't been able to smell how toxic it was, it was easy enough to see.

They exited the ship into a drifting yellowish haze. Tre followed her down the ramp, the spare mask she'd found for him clinging to his face in all the wrong places. It was made for a human, not a Twi'lek, but it would have to do. She didn't plan on their being outside for any longer than was necessary.

They'd landed in a dip in the ground, and Lanoree had skillfully drifted the ship in against an overhanging spur of rock. It rested in shadow, but anyone looking even casually would be able to find it easily. She wished she had time to camouflage it somehow—dust, or even some of the ragged creeping plants that she now saw grew here and there. But time was not on her side. She was very aware of the march of time and that each moment moved Dal closer to carrying out his insane plan.

She signaled the ship to seal up behind them, and paused to watch the ramp fold in and shut tightly. She caught a glimpse of Ironholgs just as the hatch closed. The droid would protect the ship with everything it had, but she was still worried. This might well have been the most hostile environment she had ever landed in.

Greenwood Station was a smooth curve in the distance, just visible through the haze. She'd confirmed with Tre that this was indeed dawn on Nox, Tythos a blur just above the horizon past the dome. The atmosphere was so heavy with toxic pollutants, pumped out over millennia of mining and manufacturing, that Nox was denying the star itself.

Lanoree probed outward, sensing for trouble. There were lifeforms close by, but not many, and they were not sentients. She felt nothing dangerous, although she would never lower her guard. Her senses and caution were heightened now, and would remain so every moment she was here.

"This is nice," Tre said, voice muffled by his mask.

"Keep quiet," Lanoree said. "These masks don't carry much air, and you'll waste it."

They walked across the desolate landscape toward the dome. By all accounts Nox had once been a verdant world, and although much warmer than Tython, it had supported vast forests of giant trees with huge leaves to bleed heat to the sky, beneath which complex ecosystems existed. It was rumored that one large island on Nox had been home to more species of birds and mammals than the whole of Tython. But settlers had quickly made use of its rich metal deposits and endless wood supplies to build giant smelting plants, extracting 90 percent of the metals used across the system. Over the space of a thousand years, most of the forests had vanished into ash, and with them the creatures they had supported. It had been a merciless despoliation of the planet, but at the time the system had been a new, mysterious frontier, and those brought there by the Tho Yor were desperate to make a home for themselves. The Je'daii were finding their own path on Tython, and Nox's settlers had let need, and greed, guide their hands. It was desperately sad, but Nox was now beyond saving.

Anything left was clinging to life. Mutation had increased, and there was little plant or animal life left on Nox that would have been recognizable by someone from seven thousand years before.

Trees were gone, and the only plant life remaining was a low-growing, creeping scrub, thin leaves gasping carbon dioxide from the tortured air, roots growing deep in their search for nutrients. Small lizards scurried here and there. Lanoree saw snake trails in the dusty soil, though she never spied a serpent. She guessed they kept themselves out of sight, perhaps living most of their lives belowground where the air could not kill them, the rains could not melt.

By the time they were halfway to Greenwood Station, her skin was already starting to itch and burn where it was exposed to the atmosphere.

As they drew closer and the settlement emerged from the haze, the damage to the dome's structure became apparent. It was as if a giant foot had stamped on the smooth dome, crushing the regular curve, reducing its surface area by a tenth, and cauterizing the damage with an uneven blackness. Closer still, and Lanoree could see that this blackness was a layer of twisted metal and melted panels, the damaged structure propped by giant buttresses of gray rock and thick, roughly formed stanchions. The repair work seemed slapdash and haphazard, but Greenwood Station's business was tech, not construction. And its specialization was war.

She held up a hand and paused by a lake of sickly yellow water. Greenwood Station took up half of their view, and this close Lanoree was wary of guards or security droids.

"I want to go home," Tre said, voice muffled.

"We'll be inside soon," Lanoree said. "It's . . . huge." She knew how large the domes were, of course. She'd seen the remains of those bombed by the Je'daii, and had viewed many holos during her time at Padawan Kesh. But being this close to Greenwood Station brought its true size home to her. The brief research she'd carried out on her way here meant nothing to seeing it herself.

Knowing that it was a space enclosed by one huge dome had perhaps given it limitations in her mind's eye, but the truth was, this was a city. More than eight kilometers across, the dome structure rose sharply from the ground and then curved gently toward the pinnacle, a place out of sight that was supported by a giant tower. This interior tower housed the city's ruling council, business owners, and other elite. Spread out from its base for more than three kilometers in every direction were the factories, transport roads and canals, habitation blocks, and leisure parks of this massive manufacturing city. Countless chimneys pierced the dome and rose higher, all of them spewing smoke and steam that billowed southward.

"The thought of being inside that is no comfort," Tre said. "So do we just knock at one of the gates?"

"No. We sneak in."

"Through the Scar," Tre said.

"How do you know they call it that?"

Tre shrugged. "I thought it was common knowledge."

More and more suspicious of Tre Sana, Lanoree led the way toward the smashed span of dome.

* * *

Though the bombing had been almost twelve years before, the rubble and remains were still scattered over a wide area. The dome's survivors had repaired the breach and sealed the damaged area, but no one had seen any need to clear the ruins. It seemed that anything outside the boundary of Greenwood Station was irrelevant.

There were defensive positions across the dome's curved surface. Lanoree could see pulse cannons and plasma mortars nestled in indentations in the structure, but she did not believe the positions were manned. She had heard of skirmishes between manufacturing domes—sometimes concerning resources or business, other times over causes unknown—but Greenwood Station was now so isolated by the ruins around it that it usually worked in peace.

"We'll climb up there," she said, indicating a path that rose through the debris. "Hopefully there'll be air locks through the structure."

"Good," Tre said. "Let's move. My skin's on fire and my lekku are itching."

They climbed an uneven mountain of debris—shattered rock, twisted remnants of structural material, and some opaque sections of the dome's shell that had been blasted and half-melted. The transparent material was almost as thick as Lanoree was tall, and the shattered fragments were sometimes thirty meters across.

Soon they were inside the perimeter of the ruined section of dome. The going got tougher as the ruin became more confused, with fallen buildings mixed with melted rock and jagged sculptures of distorted material. Pools had formed here and there, some of them covered with such thick layers of ash and dust that they resembled solid ground. Lanoree had to pull Tre out of one pool, and he started shivering, soaked to the waist in rancid water.

"There," Lanoree said at last, pointing to a cliff of fused dome and metal.

"What?"

"Air lock." She Force-probed, sensed no one. "I don't think it's guarded. Come on."

The air lock only became obvious when they were ten steps away. Lanoree lifted her hand and tried to gesture the door aside. She grimaced and concentrated harder, and the door finally obeyed with a tortured whine. It can't have been used very much.

She was aware of Tre watching her with a mixture of fascination and fear of her talents, but she did not acknowledge his attention.

Air whooshed past them and they entered, Lanoree closing the door behind them. Pressures equalized. Several small lights came on and the air cleared, and then a fine mist sprayed all over them. Decontamination complete, Lanoree waved open the inner door.

She readied herself for confrontation. If there *were* guards beyond the door, the questions would come thick and fast, and she would dip into the guards' minds, confusing them for long enough to put them out of action. She had no wish to kill anyone else unless she had to. But she would not hesitate if it meant getting one step closer to Dal.

And stopping him, of course. That was her mission. Sometimes she had to remind herself that this was not simply a search for her long-lost brother.

But there were no guards beyond the door, and no indication that this entrance was even monitored. A dilapidated corridor with flickering lights led away from the air lock, and they followed until they reached another door.

They removed their masks, and Lanoree hid them as well as she could above a loose ceiling panel.

"This must have all been built after the bombing," Tre said. "I heard that Greenwood Station's council sanctioned the murder of a Je'daii for every hundred city inhabitants killed in the attack."

Lanoree was aware of the series of assassinations that went on for two or three years after the Despot War. Rangers were lured into traps and killed, diplomatic missions attacked; and even on Tython there had been deaths.

"They lost about two thousand here," Tre continued.

"You're knowing more and more about this pit," Lanoree said. "Makes me wonder whether you have business interests here I should take notice of."

"No interests."

"But you've *done* business here."

"Only by necessity."

She rounded on him. "Then do me a favor, Twi'lek. Let me conduct *my* business with no more talk of the past."

Tre smiled in apology and inclined his head.

"Come on," she said. "We're wasting time."

They worked their way through a series of roughly built corridors and halls, all deserted and stinking of disuse. Lanoree remained alert, and was more aware than ever of the comforting weight of the sword beneath her robe.

The air became heavier. The taint of burning grew and a hint of hot metal, and the sweeter smell of something perfumed the air, as if added to distract from the other smells. As they crossed one large, featureless room, Lanoree began to hear the sounds of a city.

Beyond the room, a short walk to a doorway. And then they were out of the repaired zone and standing on the rise of a hill at the inner edge of the dome, looking out across the vast, filthy, yet wondrous vista of Greenwood Station.

"Whoa," Tre breathed beside her, and in that one word Lanoree was certain he had never actually been here. She almost said the same.

A couple of kilometers distant was the massive central tower upon which the graceful, curved structural ribs of the dome rested. Its dark facade glinted with countless lights that Lanoree assumed were windows, and larger openings might have been launch bays for the small airships that drifted back and forth through the confined space. Beyond that, just visible in the hazy distance, she could make out the far wall almost eight kilometers away.

Buildings crowded the ground all across the dome. Roads trailed here and there, and in a few places wide-open areas that might once have been parks seemed now to act as refuse dumps, with broken machinery or useless spare parts piled in reckless abandon. Fires burned on these dumps, and smoke from the conflagrations was being sucked up by mobile air cleansers, floating machines that vented to the outside via long flexible pipes.

Elsewhere, more solid chimneys rose and pierced the dome. There were hundreds of chimneys, and all were illuminated with bright neon strips. There seemed to be no relevance to the color of light used—

greens, blues, reds, yellows, harsh whites—the whole aerial part of the dome was lit garishly, and perhaps beautifully. The sight shocked Lanoree, and for a moment she felt a lifting of her heart.

But the true purpose of this place became obvious when she examined the buildings, roads, and storage structures more closely. She drew a small, powerful telescope from the discreet utility belt she wore beneath her robe and held it to her right eye.

At the foot of the slope they stood on was an open area used to park military vehicles. They looked newly made. Some were large and cumbersome, bearing heavy guns and massive, spiked wheels. Others were sleek and small, designed for infiltration rather than full-on attack. A few bore bulbous shells on their backs, inside which would be balloons ready for rapid inflation to lift the craft out of harm's way. Many ran on wheels, others on segmented tracks, and some were equipped with repulsor units that would enable them to glide and float just above the ground.

Farther away the factories began.

"Busy place," Tre said. His voice was high and loaded with shock. "Where's the demand? I mean, for all this? It's like they're readying for war."

"There's always demand," Lanoree said. "Some of Shikaakwa's crime barons can never have enough hardware. Kalimahr has its needs. And there are places on Ska Gora that even the Je'daii don't know much about. Someone's always readying for war."

Factories churned and roared, rumbled and throbbed. A gray haze hung in the air, even though countless chimneys vented the steam and poisonous gases caused by this endless, heavy manufacturing to the toxic outside atmosphere. Trains trundled on tracks along the center of wide thoroughfares, high wagons packed with raw materials or finished hardware. Three kilometers from where they stood, one train passed into a tunnel that must lead outside. It seemed that, though cut off by the result of the war, Greenwood Station was still very much involved in import and export.

Maintenance drones buzzed through the air, and Lanoree noticed that there was a huge amount of construction work going on. Some buildings were being extended or repaired, while others were being torn down, materials salvaged and set aside for new buildings. The noise from this work was a constant background rumble, and even from here she could see at least five locations where major construction was under way. But impressive though the sight was, her mind was already working on the problem at hand. Greenwood Station was almost forty square kilometers of industrial buildings, living quarters, storage warehouses, spaceports, and other built-up areas. Whether or not Dal and his Stargazers were already here, the task of finding them seemed immense.

"Ringwood petals," Tre said. He breathed in deeply.

"What?"

"Can't you smell it on the air? Beneath everything else, the scent of ringwood petals. They must pump it into the air to overcome the stench. It's a flowering shrub from Kalimahr. Beautiful."

"You like flowers," Lanoree said, voice flat.

"Doesn't everyone?"

Tre was becoming more of an enigma to her, not less. She had the sudden urge to ask about his history, his family and ties, get his true story out of him.

"You know people here," she said. "You've done business here, so you know people."

"Like I told you, I've never been myself."

"That's not a denial."

Tre looked uncomfortable. His lekku waved and touched, until he remembered that she could read them and he brought them under control. But his red face seemed to shine redder than ever, and she saw shame rather than anger.

"What?" she asked.

"The people I dealt with here . . . they're not nice."

"I wouldn't expect them to be."

Tre looked away and nodded absently, as if conversing with himself. He frowned. Then he looked back to Lanoree and seemed to have made a decision.

"Don't judge me," he said.

She raised an eyebrow in surprise. He didn't seem like someone who cared what people thought about him.

"I mean it," he said. "I'll take you to someone, if I can find him. But he's . . . unsavory."

"Compared to you?" Lanoree asked, immediately wishing she hadn't. Tre had done nothing in her eyes to deserve that.

"Compared to him, I'm a space angel. He's a scumhead. And whether he helps or not, please don't judge me by his company."

"I won't," Lanoree said. "But why do you think I need your help?"

"Why else did you bring me along?" Tre's confident smile returned, and Lanoree was surprised by how pleased she was to see it.

CHAPTER TEN
EMPTY SPACES

Pride is a dangerous indulgence.
—Temple Master Lha-Mi, Stav Kesh, 10,670 TYA

They spend fourteen more days in Stav Kesh, and sometimes Dal is taken away and taught on his own. This worries Lanoree. She wants to remain close to keep an eye on him, and when they are apart she can't seem to reach him. She tries, but he is blocking her out. Only the weak-minded are always open to a Je'daii's sensings, and Dal is far from weak-minded. He has had years to learn how to exclude his sister's gentle probings.

Master Kin'ade continues to teach Lanoree and the others, but on those occasions when Dal is taken, it is the Temple Master Tave who takes him. In the evenings when Dal chooses to return to their room, Lanoree asks him where he goes and what he does.

"Weapon training," Dal says. "They see my talents as a warrior and Tave is giving me one-on-one attention." But she sees that even Dal does not believe that. When the group is being instructed on Force use of weapons, they are keeping him apart. Maybe they're afraid that he will let loose with a blaster and hurt someone again.

Even worse, perhaps they believe he did that on purpose.

On their final day there, Masters Kin'ade and Tave welcome them into the Grand Hall. This is a structure built deep in the mountain, and it has become something of a legendary place among Journeyers over the centuries. It is said that Temple Master Vor'Dana fought and killed thirteen Sand Assassins in the hall more than two hundred years before, and sometimes when the wind is right lonely grains of sand still whistle and hush against the ancient stone.

Now, the hall is cool and still, illuminated by an array of burning brands and expectantly silent. The Journeyers stand along one wall as instructed, and Tave and Kin'ade are together, whispering and waiting for something.

What is this? Lanoree wonders. She glances sidelong at the Cathar twins, and they look back and smile. There is a special bond between the two of them that is deeper than the Force, and they trouble her. She looks in the other direction at Dal. He is relaxed and calm, glancing around the hall at the tapestries and the array of old weaponry hanging on hooks and resting in display cases around its perimeter. He catches her eye and grins.

"Master Kin'ade—" she says, but the Zabrak holds up one hand, fingers splayed.

Someone is coming. Lanoree can sense it, and she feels an approach in the flow of the Force. Moments later a shadow appears in a doorway across the hall. Temple Master Lha-Mi enters, walking confidently toward the students. The two Masters bow slightly, and then Lha-Mi pauses and examines the Journeyers. He spends some time looking them up and down, and when he reaches Lanoree, she can feel the strength of his regard. *Sometimes love is not enough,* Lha-Mi told her, but today there is no special message. He moves on to Dal, and then after a glance at Masters Tave and Kinade, says one word.

"Fight."

The two Masters maintain ultimate control. When a Force punch is thrown with a little too much vigor, Master Tave reaches out and absorbs some of the impact. When a series of overenthusiastic Force shoves thuds along the floor toward the Wookiee, Master Kin'ade snatches them from the air and dispels them with little more than a grunt.

Lanoree avoids fighting with her brother for as long as she can. But soon she finds herself standing side by side with Dal, and, as they swap glances, she sees how much he's enjoying this.

"No sides here," Dal says. He leaps toward Lanoree in a clumsy, yet strong Alchaka move, and what happens next plays on her mind for a long time afterward. She lets him strike her down.

She tumbles, sliding across the stone floor and bruising her back, hips, elbows. She uses the Force to prevent herself slamming into a wall. Then she stands, and Dal is already charging at her again.

She ducks beneath Dal's kick, slides past him as he spins and lashes out with his fist, trips him, stomps on his ankle, then drops astride him with one fist raised, ready to hammer down on his face.

"I need no Force to bring you down, brother," she says, smiling. She is trying to lighten the mood, appealing to their close bond. But his eyes are filled with anger.

He punches Lanoree in the temple and she falls to the side, shocked more than pained. A kick to her ribs, another punch to her stomach. She rolls away from him but he is always there, and then she thinks, *Why shouldn't I use the Force? Am I holding back simply because of his sensibilities?*

She punches out, hard, and a great thud! reverberates around the hall. Dal is powered back away from her, arms and legs splayed as he flies through the air. Someone catches him and drops him, hard, before he smashes against the wall. Lanoree does not see who but assumes it is Tave or Kin'ade.

She stands, holding her head and willing the heavy throbbing pain from her insides. But sometimes even the Force cannot dull such agonies, and in her studies she has come to trust pain. It is there for a reason, and to mask it can lead to more damage and worse pain later.

"You lower your defenses," Kin'ade says, and at first Lanoree thinks she's speaking to Dal. But she is actually addressing her. "You should be able to anticipate such clumsy attacks, and counter them. Your brother's Alchaka moves are rudimentary at best, and he does not use the Force to wield them."

"I know," she says softly, facing Master Kin'ade but glancing sidelong at Dal. He is standing across the hall from them, and he looks dejected, defeated.

"Cease," Lha-Mi says, and the fighting ends. The Cathar twins embrace, bloody and smiling. The Wookiee and Twi'lek draw close together and slap each other's shoulders.

Lanoree looks to Dal, but he has already turned his back on her.

Kin'ade walks ahead of Lanoree, saying nothing. Lanoree has been told to follow her, and she suspects that she is being taken to Lha-Mi one last time before they depart in the morning. Tomorrow, she and Dal commence their long, dangerous journey to Anil Kesh.

The Temple of Science lies more than a thousand kilometers to the east on Talss. They will have to cross the Moon Islands to reach Talss, and once there they'll be faced with a long hike across a wild land. Lava arcs burst from ancient volcanic tunnels; mountain slopes are smothered with ash trees; and strange, sometimes deadly creatures stalk the valleys and ravines. Wilder still is Anil Kesh itself, straddling the mysterious and deadly Chasm high in the mountains. No Je'daii has ever descended to its bottom and survived, and many of those who have tried were driven insane. Daegen Lok, the Prisoner of Bogan, is one such man—his fascination with the Chasm led to his downfall. All young Padawans are told his story.

Lanoree was looking forward to time on her own with Dal. Yet now, she is fearful as well. Of Dal, what he is becoming, and what he might do. She is desperate to not let her parents down. And though she still tries to believe that her brother can be saved and brought to the Force, deep down she knows the truth.

His days on Tython are numbered.

"Wait here," Master Kin'ade says. She rests a hand on Lanoree's shoulder. "This is the last time we'll see each other, for now at least. I hope your onward journey is safe, Journeyer. May the Force go with you."

"Thank you for all your training," Lanoree says.

Master Kin'ade looks as though she wants to say more, and Lanoree is surprised when she senses doubt exuding from the Master. But then the room beyond where they wait is no longer empty, and Kin'ade merely smiles.

"Enter," a voice says, and Lanoree recognizes Lha-Mi once more.

The small, hexagonal room is lined with images of people Lanoree does not know. There are a mix of people, all species and colors, and at points around the walls there are also empty spaces. Lha-Mi stands in a doorway on the far side of the room.

"Everyone I have let down," the Temple Master says. "All those people—Je'daii and not—whom I have failed throughout my long life. I keep the room open for anyone to view, because it's important to know we are not all perfect. Pride is a dangerous indulgence. I'm a Temple Master now, but even that doesn't exclude me from failure. In many regards, my failures are greater, because as a Temple Master there is so much more expectation put upon me, and responsibility brings more risk." Lanoree says nothing. She is being spoken to, and Lha-Mi invites no response.

"It's down to me, of course, whose images I place here," the old man continues. "Some would argue that there are those here who let themselves down, rather than being let down by me. And there are others who might name some images that are missing." He walks slowly around the room. "There are spaces. Gaps yet to fill. I hope to still see areas of bare wall here when I am older and closer to death, but . . ." He shrugs and touches cold, bare stone.

"You don't want to see Dal's image here," Lha-Mi says. "You're learning well, and your experience shines through. But it's *your* face I have no wish to see on the walls of this room, Lanoree. So heed this warning. Ignore it, suffer the consequences, and I will have let you down. Your brother grows more unstable and dangerous every day. Be wary of him."

"I will, Master Lha-Mi."

The old man sighs. "There was a time when people like Dalien . . ." He trails off.

"What?" Lanoree asks.

"Harsher times," Lha-Mi says. "No matter. Go safe, Lanoree Brock, and may the Force go with you."

Lanoree watches the Temple Master turn and leave the room of his shame, and when he has gone she spends some time looking around at the faces staring back at her. She wonders what became of them. Dead, banished, fled out into the system?

She hopes to never find out.

And she swears that neither her face nor her brother's will fill one of those empty spaces.

Down in Greenwood Station, Tre Sana became someone else.

Lanoree sensed it when they emerged onto the first bustling street of shops, taverns, and other places of pleasure. Not in any Force way, because whatever Dam-Powl had done to the Twi'lek had rendered him almost immune to Lanoree's probings. But in the way he carried himself. His manner, his bearing, his interaction with the world shifted subtly. The Tre Sana she had met on Kalimahr and with whom she had spent days cooped up in her Peacemaker turned into the man Dam-Powl had warned her about.

He became dangerous.

They walked along the street side by side, and Lanoree kept the hood of her robe raised. A few people glanced at them but only casually. Most were too involved in their own lives to be concerned with anyone else. Sellers displayed their wares on metal market wagons—food, drink, and an array of drug slips that promised a temporary escape from the reality of this wretched place. People stood outside drinking establishments, trying to lure passersby inside with promises of the best drink. And all the while, farther toward the center of the dome, the chimneys throbbed and pumped, the machines thumped away, the ground shook, and great trains trundled in or out with raw materials or finished products. The people were the oil that kept the dome working, and Lanoree sensed that safety and sanity here rested on a thin skein of smoke.

While they walked, she kept her senses open for any sign of Dal. But she wasn't even sure she would recognize him anymore.

"There," Tre said. He pointed along the street.

"What?"

"Listing point." He walked forward, shoved a tall man aside, and pressed several buttons on a box mounted on a short, stumpy pole.

"I was using that!" the man said. He might once have been human, but some terrible growth had eaten at his face, and gleaming artificial eyes were set in the remains of eye sockets.

"How about using this?" Tre said. He shifted his jacket aside and displayed the small blaster on his belt. *I didn't even know he had that!* Lanoree thought.

"You're carrying!" the man said. "No one's allowed to carry in Green—"

Tre shoved him hard. Arms pinwheeling, the man stumbled back into a group of women wearing dull red worksuits, and one of them tripped him. They laughed.

Tre turned his back on the fallen man and started working at the listing point. Its small screen showed a map of Greenwood Station, and as Tre tapped at the keys, the map zoomed in to a sector, then a small network of streets. A green glow pulsed. Tre swiped the screen clear and nodded at Lanoree.

"The scumhead is listed?" Lanoree asked.

"No, but someone who knows someone who knows him is."

"Right. Easy."

Tre started walking.

"You could have waited to use it," she said, walking alongside the Twi'lek.

"Just keeping up appearances."

"I thought you hadn't been here before?"

"I haven't. But I know how to get by here. Trust me."

Lanoree tried to smile and roll her eyes, but Tre was not even looking at her.

Someone had been run over by a train. Lanoree saw the commotion as they approached a wide road that led to a tunnel mouth beneath the dome's lower edge. A woman was screaming in grief, and a small crowd had gathered around a sickening red smudge on the road's rough surface. Most people quickly walked on. The trains must have been huge and heavy because there wasn't much left.

"No security? No help?" Lanoree asked.

"There's some, if you can afford it," Tre said. "But Greenwood Station is like any other city on Nox—run by the Corporations. They're the law, and the people work for them. What security does exist is con-

cerned with maintaining production, ensuring the safety of Corporation members—most of whom probably live in the central tower—and
protecting the city from attacks from other cities."

"That still goes on?"

"More often than you think. Come on. Nothing to see here." They
walked on, and Lanoree spared one final glance for the grieving
woman.

"Sounds more like Shikaakwa," she said.

"Oh, it's nowhere near as organized," Tre said.

They crossed the wide train track and entered a district closer to the
central manufacturing zones. The ground shook with a constant vibration, and the workers' accommodation buildings were much more
regimented. People moved through the streets, red-clad workers on
their way to or from work; and here and there were groups of armed
guards, watching for trouble but apparently expecting none. Their
weapons were obviously displayed, and they all looked mean.

Lanoree touched the weight of her sword and kept her face down.
It was doubtful that anyone would identify her as Je'daii simply by
looking at her, but she could not disconnect from who she was so easily. She feared her eyes, her expression, would betray her.

"Here," Tre said, nodding at a gray accommodation tower. "Not
the scumhead, but an associate. Equally unpleasant."

"Can't wait," Lanoree said.

Inside the tower, up fourteen flights of stairs because the elevator was
broken, and when Tre knocked at a door, there was no answer. Lanoree
kicked it in. The person who'd been pressed, listening, to the other
side fell back and tripped over a piece of furniture, spilling drug slips
and bottles of a rancid-smelling drink. Lanoree Force-shoved the door
closed and pressed it into its broken frame.

"Well," Tre said. "Lanoree, meet Domm, a business contact of
mine."

"Still keeping fine company I see, Tre Sana," Domm said from the
floor.

"She's virtually asleep right now," Tre said, going with the flow.
Lanoree was impressed. "You'd hate to see her awake and angry."

"I know a Je'daii when I meet one."

Lanoree was on the fallen man in an instant, sword drawn and pressed across his throat before he could draw another breath.

"You know one of these, too?" she asked.

"No," Domm said. He was Zabrak, but terrible wounds disfigured his face, leaving a tracery of scars behind. His breath stank of chemical staleness. "But my father did. One of your sort parted his head from his shoulders twelve years ago."

"Where?"

"Kaleth."

"Then he shouldn't have been there," Lanoree said. "We were protecting our own. That's what I'm doing now. And you know the Je'daii . . . protecting their own, we're more than happy to take heads." She pressed down on the sword, knowing exactly how much pressure to exert before drawing blood.

"I'm looking for Maxhagan," Tre said.

"So?"

"Come on, Domm."

"Find him yourself."

"You tell us, it'll save us time," Lanoree said. "Don't be like your father."

A flash of fear was replaced by defiance in Domm's eyes. He even managed to smile against the sword's pressure. "You won't just slaughter me," he said.

Yes, she will. Lanoree pushed the thought. *She's mean and desperate, and she'll take my head from my shoulders without even breathing heavily.*

Domm's smile dropped and he looked nervously back and forth between Tre and Lanoree. He smiled, defeated. His anger faded away, and Lanoree wondered if he really cared about his dead father at all. Maybe it was just a convenient reason to hate.

"Let me up," Domm said.

"No."

"I need to stand and—"

"No," Lanoree said again. "You'll get up, feign weakness, lean against that cupboard over there. Then you'll try to distract us and take the blaster that's stuck beneath its upper table. You might even get off one shot. But then I'll kill you, and that'll be an inconvenience to me. So, no, you're not getting up. And now my pressure on this sword will continue to increase until you tell us where Maxhagan can be found."

Domm's eyes had grown wide as he heard the thoughts plucked from his mind.

Lanoree smiled. "And if you could read my thoughts, you'd know I tell the truth." She leaned down on the sword and its keen edge pressed against the heavy scar tissue on his throat. Skin split. Blood flowed.

"District Six," Domm said. "Market. He runs a stall . . . selling . . . imported water."

Lanoree frowned, but could sense no lie in Domm's words.

"Hiding in plain sight," Tre said. "I think he's telling the truth."

"He is," Lanoree said. She started to ease back on the sword.

"You should kill him," Tre said. His words were light, unburdened by feeling.

"Kill him?"

"He knows you're a Je'daii. Knows we're here. And we're already at a disadvantage. One call from him to anyone in Greenwood Station and we're compromised."

Lanoree never looked away from the man beneath her sword. There had been many whose flesh had parted around this blade, but all of them had been fighting back at the time. Shooting down the pilots had been unavoidable, though their deaths pained her. She was not in the habit of killing for killing's sake.

"There's another way," she said. She sheathed her sword and sat up astride Domm's chest. He did not move; he seemed to sense that this was far from over.

"We don't have time!" Tre said.

"This won't take long."

Lanoree calmed herself and gathered the Force, and Master Dam-Powl's face and voice came to her. *There are some who are troubled by what you and I excel at, but they don't understand the potential. Maintain control, keep yourself balanced, and it will serve you well.*

Lanoree felt the power of the Force swirling and flowing within and around her, personified by Ashla and Bogan, their attraction and repulsion perfectly balanced, and Lanoree suspended weightless, fault-less, between them. She lifted skin dust from the floor and chose four particles, and they became her servants. Concentrating on them, ex-panding them in her vision and giving them a touch of the Force, she dropped them into Domm's upturned eyes.

He blinked and cried out, but could not move. His eyes watered, and then he squeezed them closed. But by then it was too late.

"I'll wait outside," Lanoree heard Tre say, and he sounded like a child afraid of the dark. But her eyes were closed, and she did not see him leave.

"Keep calm, keep quiet," she whispered with a slight Force push, and Domm grew motionless beneath her. She delved down, vision growing dark, the sense of touch intense and shocking as the dust particles forged through his eyes and back into his brain. She felt the warm wetness of his insides. She sought, the dust sought; and when she found the places she wanted, she paused, gathering strength and molding the Force to her will. This was the dangerous part. She felt Bogan looming and darkness closing, and balance drifted. Power grew around her, and she breathed deeply, trying to ward off the ecstatic sensations flooding through her. The pleasure of control. The ecstasy of darkness.

The dust transformed into elements of her will, and Domm started to choke as her will was done.

Keep calm, Lanoree thought, and this time she was speaking to herself. Bogan grew large and heavy, and she felt the irresistible lure of shadow—freedom from constraint, reveling in power.

And she fought her way back to balance, the denial of Bogan diffi-cult but ultimately triumphant. The sense of loss was staggering for a time, but it quickly faded.

This was her talent, Dam-Powl had told her. The alchemy of flesh, however minute that element of flesh might be. Transformation, tran-sition, and Lanoree tried to hold down the sense of pride at her achievement. She had not touched the experiment on her ship since the start of this mission, but she had not lost anything that she had learned.

She stood from Domm and went to the door that Tre had left open behind him.

"It's done," she said, and Tre's voice answered from the corridor beyond.

"You had the face of Dam-Powl. Her darkness."

"And her control," Lanoree said. Of course. Dam-Powl must have performed something similar on Tre. But Lanoree didn't mind frightening him. Tre afraid might serve her well.

"Is he . . . ?"

"I seared his memory. For a time he'll remember nothing, not even his name." Domm writhed on the floor and struggled to stand.

"For a time?" Tre asked.

"I'm not sure how long." And she was not. It could be mere days, or perhaps much longer until Domm returned to the damaged person he had been, a dark shadow in his mind where the memory of what had happened was a charred emptiness. "Better than murder."

"If you say so." Tre was standing in the corridor, back against the wall.

"Now tell me you know where District Six's market is," she said.

Tre nodded. There was no easy smile this time.

CHAPTER ELEVEN

SLAVES

There are depths.

—Osamael Or, circa 1,000 TYA

Part of a Journeyer's pilgrimage is to learn how to survive in the wild, and now they are hunting.

Lanoree stalks through the forest of giant fungi, breathing through her mouth so that the meaty scent of the huge mushrooms does not throw her senses. Her footfalls are completely silent; she can sense the areas of dried fungus skin that might crackle when she steps, or those places where a hollow in the ground is covered with moss. Her breathing is light and slow. And her mind is connected with their quarry: a small mammal. She can feel its rapid heartbeat and breathing, and if she really concentrates, she can see through its eyes. It perception is so much different from hers. Everything it sees is shaded by the Force.

It used to trouble her that so much wildlife on Tython was so in tune with the tides of the Force. But she has grown to learn that theirs is a passive relationship. It is only Je'daii who can harness the Force and use it to perform great deeds.

Her movements urge the mammal onward, down into the shallow ravine, past the growth of pink mushrooms that blankets one wall, and then she sees a flurry of movement ahead.

A whistle in the distance, and then Lanoree runs between the milky white stems. She revels in the silent movement, the breeze riffling her loosened hair, sweat lifted from her brow. When she arrives at the edge of the ravine and looks down, Dal is holding up the creature pierced on a spear he fashioned himself. She smiles. *We make a good team*, she thinks. But then that familiar pang of guilt stabs in once again.

They are six days out from Stav Kesh, and every moment that passes Lanoree knows she is lying to herself.

Dal will never accept the Force, nor adjust to its ebb and flow.

Silently he skins, guts, and butchers the creature, builds a fire, and starts cooking the meat. Everything he does is methodical and skilled. He's learning so much. Lanoree remembers overhearing their father talking to their mother once. *He's like a sponge*, their father said. *Every question of his I answer inspires two more. His thirst for knowledge is insatiable. He's going to be a great Je'daii one day.*

It saddens her how her parents could have been so wrong.

Dal's skills hide a deeper void within him. A dark void, where all around expect the Force to dwell. And at last, as he starts serving the meat with a soft, sweet root vegetable they gathered earlier, she asks the question that has been burning at her.

"Are you sad?"

He gives her a plate. The food smells wonderful. Dal's expression does not shift; he knows exactly what she means.

"Eat your dinner," he says. "We've a long way to go yet."

"Are you sad?" she asks again. "The way you were at Stav Kesh . . . like a child, jealous of those around him with better toys."

Dal raises an eyebrow and then laughs out loud. "Is that what you think?" he asks.

"Well . . ."

"You really think I'm jealous of you? Of Mother and Father, and those others we trained with back there? Jealous that none of you are your own masters?"

"Of course we are."

"No!" He places his plate down and stands, not angry but frustrated. "No, not at all. You're *slaves* to the Force. You might think it serves you, but you serve *it*. You never have your own thoughts, because the Force is always on your mind. You never fight your own fights, because the Force fights for you."

"It's not like that, Dal, it's—"

"Well, that's what I see," Dal says. "I watch you use it, and when you do, you're not yourself. You're not my sister."

"I thought I knew what was best for you," she says.

"But you don't! Only *I* can say that! Our parents, you, the Masters who trained us, everyone wants to tell me what to be, to force something upon me. But I'm my own man. My own *master*!" His eyes go wide, as does his smile. And it's not madness or fury that Lanoree sees there. It's joy.

"What are you going to do?" she asks.

Dal looks to the dusky sky, where stars are already emerging and Ashla and Bogan peer from behind a haze of clouds. A hundred lights move high up, satellites and spacecraft drifting high above Tython's atmosphere.

"I'm going to learn," he says, "everything I can, from every temple we both visit. And then after that I'm going to the stars."

"The stars?"

"I'm going to find my way home." He says no more, does not elaborate, and Lanoree's overriding feeling is one of sadness that the home they have together with their parents is not enough for Dal.

Five days later, after journeying across the eastern extreme of Kato Zakar—where fungi forests gave way to swamps, and those in turn soon became sand dunes rolling kilometers toward the sea—they approach the coast from where the first of the Moon Islands is visible on the horizon. A hundred kilometers and seven islands beyond, the continent of Talss.

Though they talk and travel together, the distance between them is widening with every day. Lanoree can feel that, and she senses that Dal does, too. The difference is that he welcomes it.

* * *

Dal breathes in deeply. He is invigorated by the energy of the ocean and the violence of the waves.

"Beautiful!" he says. "Have you ever seen anything so beautiful, Lanoree?"

Rain is falling. The sea smashes against the sandy shore, the heavy dunes they stand upon fleeting in the lifetime of Tython. The waves are topped with a rolling luminescence in the dawn light, countless minute creatures casting their glow across the waters. She can feel the power through her feet. It is humbling and, yes, beautiful.

"It's amazing," she says.

"Puts your Force to shame, eh?" He grins, and the sea breeze blows sheets of rain that soak his hair.

Lanoree does not respond, though she could. She could tell him that the power he feels *is* the Force, because it flows through the sea as well as the air and rock, the plants and ground, the living things that fly and run and crawl, and the dead things that rot beneath the soil and under the waves. She could tell him, but he would not listen. Worse, he would not understand.

So she closes her eyes, and the rain and sea spray soak her as well.

Later, in the coastal port of Ban Landing, they are offered an escorted crossing to Talss.

"The gelfish swarms are farther south than ever this year," the woman says. She has not told them her name, but she wears a Ranger star at her belt. "I've been across the Moon Islands and back seven times, and each time the craft I was in was attacked. I'd advise a scheduled crossing, Journeyers. Those larger ships have special defenses to deal with anything the Moon Channel can throw at them, and if you go alone you'll only have a small sailing boat."

"We go alone," Dal says. "Eh, Lanoree? We're journeying to learn and explore, after all."

The Ranger objects, and yet Lanoree sees a flash of respect in her eyes. Perhaps on her own Great Journey she did the same, though she does not tell them.

They spend the night in Ban Landing, staying in a simple bunkhouse close to the water's edge. In the wooden beams that hold up the roof are carved thousands of names, Journeyers from years past who stayed here before their own dangerous crossings of the Moon Islands to Talss. Lanoree spends some time looking for their parents' names, but she does not find them.

Later, Dal sits out on the deck surrounding the bunkhouse. Great waves break on the beaches half a kilometer away, and lit by starlight only their swirling, luminous tops are visible, like giant coiling snakes in the dark. But she is looking at her brother. He lies on his back with his hands resting behind his head, staring up.

"Food?" Lanoree says. Dal takes the plate she has brought him and nods his thanks. "It'll be dangerous."

"Don't worry, little sister," Dal says, even though she is older than he. "I'll look after you."

Their journey across the Moon Channel takes only three days, but Lanoree will remember it forever.

The sea is calmer when they set out at dawn the following day. The Ranger meets them at the harbor and tells them how she has used the Force to confuse and combat the threat of sea creatures—the deadly gelfish most of all—on her previous crossings. Then she wishes them well.

They sail from island to island, stopping only to replenish water canteens before moving on. They sleep briefly on land, but spend all their waking time afloat.

A storm blows up halfway through their journey. A gelfish swarm hits their boat and starts climbing the hull, oozing, toxic tentacles whipping at the air and seeking flesh. Lanoree uses the Force to punch them back into the sea. Dal uses his blaster to blow groups of them apart before they even reach the boat. The swarm passes.

But they are not out of danger. A sea serpent appears as if from nowhere and almost capsizes the boat, its head as big as a person's torso, teeth dripping venom. Lanoree disorients the beast by touching its mind, and Dal stabs it several times with a boat hook. It slips away and flees, and Lanoree senses it going deep, seeking a dark hole to hide in and repair its wounds.

They battle together. Taking on Tython's dangers, weathering its storms.

But when they reach Talss at last, landing in a small seaport, Dal sets off from the moored boat without another word. For him there is no time to waste, no point in stopping to rest. It's as if Anil Kesh has something for him, and he is impatient to get there.

Storms thrash above Talss. Heavy rain strikes them like a hail of small stones, lightning thrashes, and Lanoree feels eddies in the Force. The Force Storm makes her feel sick and unsteady, and Dal grabs her arm and helps her along. There's a new purpose in him now, and Lanoree only wishes she knew what drove it.

The Temple of Science is still two days' travel inland.

"He calls it the Network," Tre said. "It's a loose collection of contacts, informers, and spies, not only in Greenwood Station but in almost every domed city on Nox. Sometimes beyond. So loose that any break in the Network protects everyone else. Any disruption to the links in its web cuts off everyone else. It's genius, really." He sounded almost respectful. "It's taken Maxhagan years to set it up, and he won't risk it unless we make it worth his while."

"And you've met Maxhagan? Used his Network?"

"No to both. But he and I have conducted business."

"Just what have you—?"

"It's him you need to know about right now," Tre said sternly. "I mean it, Lanoree. I like you. I have shadows in my past, and I'm sure Dam-Powl suggested that to you. But Maxhagan isn't someone to fool with. He's the real deal. A maniac. A monster."

They had crossed a stinking, polluted canal on a rickety bridge and were now in District Six. At its far end stood the rock and metal tower that acted as Greenwood Station's central buttress, every gigantic spine of the immense dome curving back and down from the tower's pinnacle. At ground level it was so wide that it would take half a morning to walk around, and its top was hidden within a haze of smoke and steam. Craft buzzed to and from the tower, both airships and powered vessels. There was even some green up there, Lanoree noticed. Garden balconies overflowed, and all across District Six, petals and leaves were crushed into the pavement by countless feet. It was as if those in the tower teased the rest of the dome with what they had.

District Six itself was a mix of large factory buildings, storage warehouses, and contained outdoor parks for larger produce—Lanoree had seen a large area half-filled with ranks of ground assault vehicles of various shapes and sizes—and a network of squares around which hunkered accommodation and administration towers. The squares bustled with people going to and from work, and the largest housed a huge market where workers spent their pay.

They were closing on that square now, a huge factory belching and thundering to their left, a soot-smothered five-story office building to their right. Lanoree wondered how people managed to live and work in such a place. But she knew that many did not have a choice. People were born and died on Nox, their lives mapped out from beginning to end. Most earned just enough to survive in one of the domes, sometimes affording a few luxuries from time to time. But to leave the planet would cost more than most could ever save in a lifetime.

No doubt the Corporations liked it that way.

Lanoree looked up at the high dome, barely visible above them, and the noisy, stinking factory to their left. Dal could be anywhere here. She felt a rush of urgency, not only to catch him but to see him again.

"I've dealt with monsters before," Lanoree said.

"Yeah, and fought them, I'll bet. But Maxhagan is a monster with brains. Four years ago he was crossed by a family from Volke House on Shikaakwa. They'd bought some information from him that helped them establish a production base in Crystal City, a dome eight hundred kilometers south of here. Then they refused to pay. Killed three of his messengers and withdrew to Shikaakwa with all their business gains intact." They paused as a train approached, moving to one side, and letting the massive transport trundle by along its tracks in the middle of the road.

"So this is a tale of revenge, and what terrible retribution he brought down on them," Lanoree said. She knew what to expect. Her previous visit to Nox had been brief, but she knew people like Maxhagan. She'd met them all over the system.

"In a way," Tre said. "It took him a while. But he conspired to initiate a feud in Crystal City, and that resulted in a skirmish that left three thousand dead. Wiped out the Volke family's entire network on Nox, and there was no link whatsoever to Maxhagan. He wasn't interested in ego, or in anyone knowing it was he who caused it. He didn't want infamy. He just wanted revenge."

"Yet infamy is his."

Tre shrugged. "These things become known."

"A sharp mind, then."

"Sharp and brutal. The three thousand included many children. I doubt he had trouble sleeping that night."

"So he makes all his money from information?"

"The best way there is to make money." Tre gestured around them at the buildings, the air hazy despite the air-treatment units drifting and thundering around the dome's massive airspace. "This is all fleeting, constantly assaulted by the atmosphere. Or it can be destroyed, as we saw on the way in. Information is eternal, and that's where Maxhagan places his faith."

"So is the Force," Lanoree said. "I'll put my faith in that."

"My faith is here," Tre said, touching the bulge of the blaster on his belt.

"Imported water," Lanoree said. "Seems ironic that he deals in something that represents purity."

"Good cover," Tre said. "And I don't know about you, but I could do with a drink."

They moved on, and soon District Six's huge central square came into view in a shallow valley. It was a sea of movement, and for a moment looking down into it Lanoree felt queasy. Countless people swarmed and swirled, market stalls and more impressive structures strove to take their money from them, the smells of cooking mixed with the dome's manufacturing stenches and made her stomach turn. Somewhere down there, the head of the Network, and perhaps her way to Dal.

Lanoree led the way down a gentle slope and into the melee.

In the end, Maxhagan was easy to find. Perhaps he believed that concealment would make him seem more suspicious. Or maybe he was simply too confident to hide.

He was certainly one of the most unobtrusive men Lanoree had ever seen.

"Well, I'm *pretty* sure that's him," Tre said, frowning. They were standing in a food stall, mounds of root vegetables and racks of curing meat all around. Across the wide walkway from them was a water stall. That's all it sold—water, in various container sizes. The sign above the stall exhorted THE FINEST WATER, IMPORTED FROM KALIMAHR, CERTIFICATE OF AUTHENTICITY AVAILABLE TO THOSE WHO DOUBT. The man standing behind the stall talking with a family of human workers was short and fat, his dark skin wrinkled with laughter lines, and the few remaining tufts of white hair on his scalp gave him a comic appearance. His eyes were filled with good humor, and with just a few words he had the family laughing along with him.

"It is," Lanoree said. "He has four people around him. The Noghri at the lizard-fighting pit along the way, three stalls away, that tattooed woman selling fate readings we passed a hundred paces back, and up in the buildings around the square one sniper with a blast rifle and another with a rocket. All watching."

"You Je'daii," Tre said, but he could not hide his admiration.

"Best not use that word here. So, let's buy some water."

They waited behind the family, and after they left, Lanoree smiled at Maxhagan and approached the stall. She kept herself sharp, reaching out with her Force senses to those hidden guards she had already recognized. The last thing she would do was let Maxhagan's appearance deceive her.

"Ahh," Maxhagan said when he saw Tre. "What brings you here, Tre Sana?"

Tre could not hide his surprise at being recognized. Perhaps they hadn't dealt face-to-face, but it seemed Maxhagan always knew who he did business with.

"He's my guide," Lanoree said. "And we'd like to buy some of what you're selling."

Maxhagan glanced back and forth between them, and never once did his smile slip, not even from his eyes. He scratched at the corner of his mouth, and Lanoree tensed, hand drifting a little closer to the sword hidden beneath her robe. She probed at him gently, but before she'd even touched his mind, she flinched back. His thoughts were such a pit of filth that she could almost taste their rot.

"Je'daii," Maxhagan whispered.

"And so?" Lanoree asked. Tre stood frozen at her side.

Maxhagan stared at her, still smiling. He poured three cups of water from a plastoid container without even looking, lifted one to his lips, sipped.

"Don't see many Je'daii here."

He'd sensed her instantly. Ready this time, Lanoree reached out to read him, but he was closed to her now. The wall he'd thrown up was solid and vast, and it had the feel of something enhanced. He had tech implanted somewhere in his skull—under one of those tufts of hair, no doubt—and it was top-grade stuff, high-end military. His protection went far deeper than simple bodyguards.

"I'm doing my best not to be seen," she said.

"I've nothing against Je'daii," he said. He put his cup down and handed one to each of them. Lanoree took hers and nodded for Tre to do the same. "Just don't—" he waved his hands above his head "—you know, mess with my mind or any of that crap."

"That might be hard," Lanoree said.

Maxhagan laughed out loud, and it was so infectious that she actually found herself smiling. "Well, protection is always advisable, especially in a pit like this. Eh, Tre?" He grunted and sighed. "So. Time for my lunch break. Come with me and we'll talk."

He took them beneath the square, descending one of the many staircases. There was machinery down there that powered lights and air filtration, and also places where less-acceptable business was conducted. Brothels, drug bars, fighting rinks, Lanoree sensed and saw them all, built in ruins that were testament to Greenwood Station's past. Sometimes, it was easier to build new upon old

But Maxhagan had no interest in such underground endeavors. Through three doors, along several corridors, and then down a secret staircase concealed behind a locked wall panel, they emerged eventually in a room that might have impressed those Corporation officials in their high tower.

"Nice," Lanoree said as he led them inside. They were on their own, yet she had no doubt Maxhagan was well protected here. She felt the weight of battle droids buried in the walls, and suspected that his implanted tech probably controlled everything about this room. One wrong move and chaos would erupt.

"I do enjoy some comforts," he said. "Oh, and don't think for a moment that I'm imparting any sense of trust by bringing you here. I have dozens of these rooms all over the dome. I haven't been to this particular one in a long time, as can be witnessed by—" he picked up several bottles from a table and threw them into a corner "—the bad drinks selection. Apologies."

"Not here to drink," Tre said.

"Here to buy more mercenaries, Tre?" Maxhagan's eyes twinkled as Tre squirmed uncomfortably. But Lanoree did not take the bait.

"I'm looking for someone, and Tre says you can help," she said. "He might have arrived already, or his ship might be incoming. He'll have people with him. They call themselves Stargazers."

"Looking in your Je'daii capacity?"

"He's my brother," Lanoree said. It was no answer, but it seemed to satisfy Maxhagan.

"It'll cost you. But I'm a fair man in business, so I'll let you make me an offer."

"Half a million credits," Tre said. Lanoree held in her surprise, and was pleased to see Maxhagan's eyes go wide.

"A generous offer," he said.

Tre smiled. "I'm a fair man in business."

Maxhagan strolled around his opulent room, running his fingers along surfaces and tutting at the buildup of dust.

"His name's Dalien Brock," Lanoree said. "I need to know where he is. And he mustn't know I'm here."

"Are you going to kill him?" Maxhagan asked.

"That's none of your business."

"True. But every time I use my Network, I put it at risk. And as I'm in business for pleasure, there's always a price over and above money. Generous though your offer is, Tre."

Lanoree did not respond.

"Added to that," Maxhagan continued, "do you have any idea how much business would suffer if anyone knew I was helping a Je'daii?"

"We won't tell anyone," Lanoree said.

"Oh, I know that." He spoke with such assurance, such confident control, that Lanoree felt a shiver down her spine. Only one other person had ever made her feel like this—Daegen Lok, the one time she'd seen him during her short retreat on Bogan. None of the others with her party had seen him, and the Master supervising them had told her that it was impossible, that prisoners were kept separated by force fields. But though he had been little more than a shadow on a distant hillside, she had felt his eyes upon her and the weight of his regard. Heavy. Dark.

"So," Maxhagan continued, "an answer to my question is also part of the price. Will you kill your brother?"

Lanoree considered the question. It was one she had confronted and struggled with already, and it had caused more distress in her than finding Dal's bloodied, torn clothing nine years before. But the answer was already firm in her mind. "Only if I absolutely have to."

Maxhagan nodded. His eyes were on fire.

"My stall, dusk," he said. "If he's in Greenwood Station I'll know by then." He plucked an electronic device from his belt and held it out to Tre. "I'd appreciate untraceable bonds, if you will. And the transfer should be the full amount."

"Half now, half—" Tre began.

"The full amount is fine," Lanoree said. "I can see you're a man of honor."

Maxhagan frowned for a moment, trying to make out whether Lanoree was playing him. Then he laughed out loud again, head back, hand pressing his side.

This time she felt no urge to laugh with him.

"I need a shower," she said. "I want to change my skin. Buy new clothes. The man's a disease."

"I did warn you."

"And where do you get so much money?"

"You don't want to know."

I do, Lanoree thought as they walked as quickly as they could out of District Six. *I do want to know*. She made sure they weren't followed. Maxhagan would have his eyes on them somehow, she knew, and his attention was something they had bought along with his help. But someone following them would be too much of a threat to ignore.

And she *did* want to know about Tre, and where his money came from, and dusk was a while away.

"I know a place we can go to—" Tre began.

"No. We'll walk. I don't like his knowing I'm here. He'll have a trace on us somehow, but I'll feel more comfortable on the move. Beside . . . I need to know this place more."

"Why?" Tre asked.

"Useful if it comes to a fight." She nudged Tre's shoulder. "Come on. Let's buy a couple of tankards, drink while we're walking. We'll fit right in. And you can tell me something about yourself."

They bought drinks and walked, and all the time Tre was talking, Lanoree was taking in their surroundings. Getting the lay of the land. Locating herself in relation to the rest of the dome and the damaged sector and possible exit routes to the outside, if the need arose.

She tried hard to make herself believe she wasn't being helplessly fooled by Maxhagan.

"I made my name in violence and my money in secrets." Lanoree's own silence had encouraged Tre to speak, and she was not about to interrupt his flow with questions.

"My third lekku set me aside, even among the Twi'lek community on Kalimahr. It invited ridicule. You wouldn't think that, would you? That in a society filled with so many shapes, species, and creeds, a simple *extra* something would set me apart?" He snorted. "I suffered as a child, and that set me on the course I took all through my young adult years."

He fell silent, and they passed a square where small, sick-looking creatures were kept in metal-fenced stalls. The animals were completely silent, and it was the humans and other species who made the most noise as individual subjects were hoisted up on an apparatus, hung from their back legs, and butchered. Meat and money changed hands. The cattle watched, eyes heavy with knowledge.

"What course?" she asked.

"The path of violence. I killed my first man when I was seventeen. A street fight outside a tavern on one of Kalimahr's less-salubrious islands. No one cared that he was dead, and after a day neither did I. It had helped me. His mocking, his violence against me, were washed away." He looked down at his palms as he walked. "By his blood on my hands."

"Killing should never be easy."

"But it was. And I became really good at it. Defending my honor, I'd discovered that I was a fighter. Others soon noticed. I slipped into crime. There was always a part of me that resisted, but the rewards easily helped me fight back. I drove down the doubt and embraced the new worlds opening up for me. Wealth, power, status. I became feared and revered in equal measure. A name. I gathered others around me and formed my own criminal organization from the bottom up. It was unintentional, really, that creation of a gang. But it just happened, and I relished every moment."

They left the square with the doomed cattle and entered a warren of narrow alleys between low buildings. The sounds of life flowed from open windows—screaming infants, arguing parents, entertainment channels, music. Lanoree felt apart from all that, and the weight of her mission bore down on her even more. Her heart beat with its urgency. She should have found Dal by now.

"You don't look like a crime lord," Lanoree said. "You don't seem like one now."

"Now, I'm not. Like I said, I made my name in violence. Once that name was made, and I'd moved my operations to Shikaakwa, I became . . . one of many. I was lost. On Kalimahr I'd had an empire, on Shikaakwa I was just another upstart. The real crime lords there looked down on us, picked those who they thought could help them, sometimes slaughtered those who looked beyond their station. And that was something I could not help doing. I expanded too quickly, reached too far and too fast. I was noticed."

"And?" Lanoree asked. Tre's lekku betrayed his nervousness and how uncomfortable he was with his memories.

"And they gave me a chance. Killed many of my lieutenants but saw something in me that they thought might be of use. They were . . ." He shook his head as if finding it difficult to explain.

"Like Maxhagan," Lanoree said.

"Only the very least of them were like him," Tre said. "The worst . . . monsters. Beyond anything I could ever want to be. They repulsed me. But they gave me a chance to live, and I took it."

"What chance?"

"To make money by keeping secrets. I was on my own once again, and lonely. Two of the Nine Houses employed me to be their messenger. They gave me secrets that could not be entrusted to the written word or technology, could not be transmitted or relayed by unreliable droids. I carried such secrets for them, and if any ever escaped, I would die. I still would. I could tell you such things, Lanoree. . . ."

"But you won't."

"No. And even the greatest Je'daii could not pick them from my mind after what Dam-Powl has done to me."

"She's protected you," Lanoree said, understanding at last. By making Tre Sana impenetrable even to Je'daii probings, she had given him the perfect mind in which to maintain those secrets from the past that could be the death of him.

"It's a small part of what she promised," Tre said, his voice dropping. "Because I want my life back. The gangsters haven't called on me for almost a whole Tythan year, but they will soon. I don't want it anymore. I want everything that Dam-Powl promised—a new identity, new face, new home. And to forget everything I've done." He laughed softly, touching his third lekku. "Surgery. I want to fade into the crowd instead of stand out. I want to be . . . normal."

You'll never be normal, she thought. *Not after what you've seen and done.* And Lanoree should know. But she said nothing to shatter his dreams. While he still dreamed, he could help her. She felt sorry for him, but she also recognized that a wish to leave such a life did not absolve him of the guilt he had earned. He'd told her only a small part of what he had done. His red skin was stained with blood, though of how many victims she would never know.

"After this, Dam-Powl will set me free," he said. He seemed so confident. So sure.

"She's a Master of her word," Lanoree said. "And she gave me a large part of what I am, too."

Tre raised an eyebrow and his lekku formed the questioning touch. But Lanoree said no more. He might have opened his heart, but her story was not one to share with someone like Tre Sana.

Lanoree nodded to the dome's western expanse where filtered yellow light bled weakly across the city. "Dusk is close. Time to hear Maxhagan."

CHAPTER TWELVE
CHASM

Ashla. Bogan. They're just moons. My own destiny lies elsewhere . . . and it has such gravity.

—Dalien Brock, diaries, 10,661 TYA

Lanoree wakes from a dream of home in which she is dreaming of the stars, and Dal is sitting beside her. He is bathed in firelight, but most of his face is in shadow. Still she can read him from his stance and his stillness—he is staring at her with a terrifying coldness.

"What? Is there something . . . ?" But she knows there is no threat from outside. They are a day away from Anil Kesh, camped beneath a copse of heart berry trees. They have eaten several berries each, and Lanoree's stomach is warm and comfortably full, the berries' goodness thrumming through her. There is wildlife in these foothills that might mean them harm—acid spiders, and rumors of a family of flame tygahs that crossed the Moon Islands—but she would sense if any of them came close. She would know.

"I am the Chasm," Dal says. His voice is lower than before, deeper, as if echoing from somewhere deep.

"What do you mean?" She sounds like a scared little girl. She *is* scared.

Dal shifts, turning toward the fire so that its light reveals his face. He is still her brother but he looks older than before. Wiser. As if she is seeing a Dal who has already completed his Great Journey.

"I have depths waiting to be filled. Places you can never see, and go, because you're Je'daii, and my depths are my own. Not steered by something else."

"The Force doesn't steer me, Dal."

He snorts. She is even more scared. She went to sleep still knowing who her brother was, but now . . . ?

"What happened?" she asks.

"I am the Chasm. I have depths to explore and fill."

"Depth implies mystery and fullness. But in you I sense only void."

"Your Force tells you that," he says, almost spitting the words, "and you believe it."

"No. I know that because of my love for you as a brother."

For the briefest instant a look of regret seems to cross his face. But perhaps it is merely a flame from the fire casting a sympathetic shadow.

"My own Great Journey ends soon," he says. "After I've taken everything I can from Tython, bled it of everything that can be of use, I'll be leaving. Don't get in my way."

At dusk the next day they approach Anil Kesh.

Lanoree has heard many stories about this place, but nothing can prepare her for the reality. The temple itself is an incredible structure, graceful and brooding, huge and yet insectile in its shape and proportions, an engineering marvel that surpasses any other on Tython. Its Tho Yor floats about it, sometimes close, sometimes farther away. It's believed that it drifts with the Force.

Beneath the temple, the Chasm. One of the most amazing places on Tython, and also one of the most enigmatic and dangerous, the Chasm is a seemingly bottomless pit within which Force Storms rage and mystery resides. No Je'daii has ever gone deep enough to find the Chasm's bottom . . . or if they have, they have never returned. The stronger one is with the Force, the greater the Chasm's detrimental influence—disorientation, pain, and eventually death. Many have tried. Some have died, and some have gone so deep that they returned insane, deluded. Suicide is common among those who ignore all warnings and their own better judgment to try.

One of Anil Kesh's main aims is to plumb the depths of the Chasm, because it is Tython—and the Force—at its most mysterious. Lanoree has seen holos of Temple Master Quan-Jang discussing the Chasm, and even through these she can sense his awe and fascination. The Je'daii, he says, will find the bottom one day. It's what might exist there that possesses them to keep trying.

I am the Chasm, Dal said. Standing close to Anil Kesh now, Lanoree expects him to be staring at this strange wound in the land, but he seems untouched and unconcerned. Unlike him, she can feel the draw of the Chasm and its incredible, primeval power. The Force is in turmoil within her. She feels sick.

To manage that sickness, she knows, will be one of her first lessons at Anil Kesh.

This is not the final destination of their Great Journey. But Lanoree cannot help feeling the sense of an ending hanging over them both.

Greenwood Station was a city that never slept. The sun had set and the dome was now illuminated by hundreds of huge lights suspended beneath the massive support ribs. They were a poor substitute for the sun, but Lanoree supposed this was their night. Shifts were changing, the air was filled with the smells of industry and cooking and sewage, and she and Tre were once again approaching Maxhagan's imported-water stall.

She saw him from a distance, closing broken shutters across his tables and instructing several helpers on where to store those bottles not yet sold. He waved away a couple of late customers with an apologetic smile, then saw Lanoree. His smile remained, but it was no longer soft.

Lanoree did not break her stride, but she did feel comfort from the Force flowing through her. Muscles tensed, her sword sang with power, and her senses—always alert—became attuned to danger. Maxhagan was her focus, but if he meant her harm, then he would desire that focus. Any attack would come from those around him.

"Tre Sana!" Maxhagan called. "Lanoree! So good to see you both again!" Tre glanced around nervously to see if anyone else had heard his name, and Lanoree could not help smiling. She wondered how many enemies the Twi'lek had made over the years.

"I'm surprised you'd close up shop," Lanoree said.

"Only for a while. People travel to work now, intent on their journey. Or others go home, or to the taverns, where water isn't their prime concern. Also . . . I find that information is at its driest at this time of day."

"I expect you're filling and resealing the bottles, too, eh?" Tre asked.

Maxhagan looked genuinely hurt. "You doubt my product?"

Tre didn't answer.

"Other water merchants come and go. They fill bottles from poisoned springs in the caves below Greenwood Station, drop in a few purifying tablets, seal them up, sell them as pure. None of them last long. That's why I'm still here, selling purity after four years. That's why they always come back to me."

"Everyone buys their water from you?" Lanoree asked.

"Everyone that matters," Maxhagan said. His face dropped abruptly. "But that's enough about water. Follow me." He turned and pushed his way through curtains at the back of his stall, and Lanoree and Tre had to climb over the tables to follow.

He led them across the busy square toward a doorway in one corner. At first she thought he was taking them down into one of his opulent rooms again, but then she heard the sounds of revelry and smelled spilled drink and spiced food. When Maxhagan entered the tavern, only a few inquisitive eyes turned their way. Most lingered more on Lanoree than the water seller, and she kept the hood of her robe raised. She never could shake the feeling that her Je'daii heritage was easy to see.

"In the corner, round table," Maxhagan said. "I'll bring drinks."

"We're not thirsty," Lanoree said.

"But I am." He shoved his way toward the bar, and Lanoree scanned the tavern. It was filled with workers, their jobs sometimes apparent, sometimes not. All manner of people, species, creeds. None appeared to be armed. She glanced at Tre, pleased that he'd concealed his blaster well.

By the time she'd examined the corner booth to make sure it appeared safe, Maxhagan was with them again. He *must* have had his bodyguards. But Lanoree was slightly disturbed that she could not make them out in the crowd.

"Did you find him?" she asked.

"Your brother? Yes." He took a huge drink from an opaque glass.

"Where is he? Still on Nox?"

"No," Maxhagan said.

Lanoree's spirits slumped, but she kept her eyes on Maxhagan. Inside he was laughing. Playing with her.

"He's not *on* Nox. He's aside from it. In a place that in diplomatic terms is not here at all."

"Explain," she said.

"You're young for a Ranger, aren't you?" He sat back on the bench and relaxed, resting his hands on his ample stomach. It was the fact that he made his smile touch his eyes that troubled Lanoree the most.

"Not particularly. And what has my age got to do with anything?"

"Young Je'daii often don't know as much as older Je'daii. They're not told as much. Secrets have a way of being . . . passed down. I should know. I deal in secrets."

Lanoree drank, taking the opportunity to look around the noisy, smoky tavern. She didn't like Maxhagan using the word *Je'daii* so much, but no one seemed to be listening. Her Force senses alert, the irony that both men she sat with were shielded from her was obvious.

"Your brother is visiting a place that still sometimes carries out commissions for your people. It's called Pan Deep. It's in the base of the central tower, in its roots, its oldest foundations. Close enough to the surface to benefit from Greenwood Station's life-support systems and infrastructure but deep enough to survive when the Je'daii bombed us during the war. Closed off enough to be . . . somewhere else."

"I've never heard of—" Lanoree began.

"Of course not. It's a secret. But don't you wonder why Greenwood Station only suffered a flesh wound? The domes around were reduced to nothing. The people fried or crushed or blasted. But here . . ." He raised a hand as if indicating the ruptured dome, repaired now, where a Je'daii attack had scooped out a small portion of the city.

"So how do I get there? What does this place do?" she asked, but she already knew. Dal was having his device built there. A sense of urgency took her, and she calmed her excitement.

"High-end tech stuff," Maxhagan said. "Very high. Military. Sometimes beyond. Really advanced science that I can't even be bothered to try to understand." He smoothed a hand back over his bald head and past his ear, smiling softly. "I've used the place myself, on occasion. I have an interest in it, and even more of an interest in those who would use it."

"He's there now?" Lanoree asked. "With his Stargazers?"

"He landed two days ago, and his ship is still in the spaceport outside the city. But I don't know how many people landed with him."

"Tell us how to get into Pan Deep," Lanoree said.

"You're that desperate to speak with your brother, Lanoree? And, Tre . . . you're that eager to help?"

"Yes, and yes," Tre said, answering for both of them.

Maxhagan glanced aside, and for the first time Lanoree saw movement across the tavern that sparked her senses. Two human men, short but strong, and neither seemed to be paying their drinks any attention. They stared down at the table where they sat, concentrating. Listening. The glint of metal in their ears.

Lanoree leaned across the table, pleased to see Maxhagan pull back. "You know who and what I am," she said. "You might mock my youth, but you're an older man who's survived all these years doing what you do. That's because you're wise. You court safety. So you'll know not to mess with a Je'daii, Maxhagan. We've paid you for information, which is gratefully received. So now we'll be on our way."

Maxhagan's smile remained on his lips but faded from his eyes. "Are you threatening me?"

"Yes."

With the three of them frozen that way, Lanoree ranged her senses out across the tavern. The two men, staring at the table. A Wookiee at the bar. A Zabrak just outside the door, a triple-barreled blaster concealed in her backpack but within easy reach. Three Noghri laughing uproariously in another corner, blades tied to their legs, claws equipped with artificial poison sacs. All Maxhagan's people, all watching her.

If things went wrong, it would be a bloodbath. And Lanoree did not have time to be killing.

"Nice doing business with you," Maxhagan said, grinning. He pushed a small memory pod across the table, holding out his hand palm up. Lanoree swept up the pod. And against all her instincts, she shook his hand. "Good luck."

"I don't rely on luck," Lanoree said. She left the tavern without looking back, sensing Tre behind her all the way. Eyes followed them out. They passed the Zabrak waiting outside, and Lanoree nodded at her.

"He could have told us more," Tre said as they walked back across the square. "You're not expecting there to be much on that pod, are you?"

"There was plenty he wasn't telling us," Lanoree said. "But the place will be easy to find. Trust me." As she walked, making sure they weren't followed, she slipped the pod into her wrist computer and accessed the Peacemaker's main computer. She instructed it to read the pod—carefully, and with full protective protocol in case Maxhagan had tried to pass on a parasite—and search for construction plans of Greenwood Station. "Come on. No time to waste."

She imagined her parents' faces were she to tell them that Dal was still alive. And she remembered their expressions the one time she had gone home since becoming a Ranger—as if they had lost her as well.

Lanoree could not breathe a word of this to her mother and father until it was over. And even then, she would only tell them if everything ended well.

If she had to kill Dal, that secret would follow her to the grave.

The ship located the newest construction plans it could find for Greenwood Station's central core and transmitted them to Lanoree's wrist unit. As the midnight siren sounded across the dome, Lanoree and Tre entered an abandoned warehouse in District Four. They were very close to the central column here, and, looking up, Lanoree could see the countless lights belonging to those who lived there. So many up there profited from what lay below, but that was always the case. The ruling classes always set themselves higher.

From the plans, Lanoree could see that the subterranean Greenwood Station was not a quiet place. The foundations of the newer city were made from old, tumbled buildings of the past. There were artificial structures deep underground, their uses not always obvious. There were also transport routes, massive tunnels carved into the city's substructure along which the largest of its products were transported to its spaceport ready for export. Along with life-support systems, water reservoirs, waste-management plants, power centers, and storage facilities, the city was almost as expansive belowground as it was above.

But the place she sought, Pan Deep, was not actually that far below the rest of Greenwood Station. What set it apart was that it was built within the central tower's deep foundations.

It took some time to negotiate their way through the first subterranean level toward the tower. Lanoree sought to keep their movements covert; she was already uncomfortable that Maxhagan knew their destination and certain that he had withheld information from them. But she'd grown weary of his games. She was sure he was a consummate liar, but she had to assume he was telling the truth about Dal and Pan Deep.

It certainly fit what she knew her brother was attempting. And that was something that, she hoped, Maxhagan could *not* know.

The descent from the warehouse was down an old, rarely used spiral staircase, their feet clanging on metal treads, glow rods making shadows dance. Lanoree recalled all her training at Qigong Kesh, craving the peace of that Silent Desert as she cast her senses out and around them. She smelled for danger, listened for held breaths, searched the deep shadows with Force-enhanced sight, and if her mind touched one other mind intent on violence, she would know.

After a while they reached a long, winding tunnel that led toward the tower. She flicked on her glow rod. Just as she judged that they were beneath the central core of the tower, the tunnel opened out into an excavated cavern, a massive place with a floor sloping in from all sides toward a sinkhole in the middle.

"Oh," Tre said. "Oh!" He pressed a hand over his nose in disgust, and Lanoree could only agree. They'd been smelling the rank tang of sewage for a while, but actually seeing this place seemed to make everything so much worse.

The effluent of the whole tower flowed here. Perhaps ten thousand people of a dozen species, all venting their waste into toilets and disposal units in dwellings and offices, taverns and restaurants. Rainwater already stinking with pollutants was used to flush, and now they could see the resultant rain of shak showering down from the high ceiling. Countless pipes and gullies led here, their stinking contents falling in blessed darkness to splash onto the floor. And the floor was moving, a thick stew of repulsiveness flowing slowly down the slope toward the large hole in the cavern's center. From there Lanoree guessed it fell into an underground lake or a deep fault in the planet's crust; thousands of years of a city's refuse rotting in the darkness.

"You bring me to the nicest places," Tre said.

Lanoree didn't reply, because that would have meant opening her mouth. She consulted her wrist computer one more time, then switched it off. The plans were of no use to them now. Pan Deep was somewhere not shown on the schematics, and she thought she knew how to find it.

Tapping Tre's shoulder, she pointed around the perimeter of the massive cavern with the glow rod.

"You want to walk around *there?*" he asked.

Lanoree nodded and moved on. She had already seen the overhang at the left, the space beneath protected from anything falling from above. It led to the entrance of a corridor hidden behind a projection in the wall, and once inside the floor immediately sloped upward.

She paused. Tre almost walked into her.

"What?" he asked.

"This is a hidden place, not on the plans. Might not be the right place. But I'll soon know. Give me a moment." She tried to relax, closing her eyes and breathing deeply, letting the Force flow. In moments the stink was gone, her senses cleansed and purified by the Force, ready for what she sought.

"What are you looking for?" Tre asked.

"Energy source." She cast her senses outward.

It was a dark place, heavy with the weight of Greenwood Station's central tower above and the many people who lived there. The air itself seemed to carry a taint of wrongness. Perhaps it was because of the city's military manufacturing, but she thought it more like a trace from the minds of those who worked and lived there. She had seen many people, and all of them seemed to be constantly moving, or talking or eating and drinking. Few stood still for a moment simply to muse upon their lives. Perhaps to do so would be to admit the awful truth of their existence.

Lanoree shivered. Nox was long known to be a planet out of balance, and here more than anywhere.

She delved beyond that shadowy trace and searched for power. In the tower above there were countless sources, but down here there were only a few weak, old generators winding down.

And then she encountered a dark void of heavy shielding. She probed deeper, pushing hard, and her Force senses forged through.

Bright light. Heavy potential. Staggering *power.*

"This way," she said. "We're going up again. But not too far."

More corridors, and every step took them farther away from the stink. They'd been moving for some time, and Lanoree was hungry and thirsty. But she was also excited. The last time she'd been this close to Dal had been on that dreadful, painful morning at Anil Kesh.

"Here," she said. The tunnel they were moving along had rough walls and an uneven floor, but up ahead she could see a steady glow. And nearby, the gutter thoughts of a violent man.

She flicked off her glow rod. Darkness fell, but it was not complete. She grabbed Tre's arm and pulled him close, breathing against his ear. "Guards."

Drawing her sword she moved forward. Tre came behind her, blaster in hand. Her heart beat fast. She touched the guard's mind again, wincing back from his thoughts of violence and—

Only at the last instant did she realize her mistake. His thoughts had been a screen, a ploy. And as the blaster fire erupted she touched his real mind and the visions of starlit triumph that burned within.

Lanoree flowed, and the Force flowed through her. Movement and reality slowed, yet she moved with it, her perceptions and reactions enhanced. She swept her sword around and deflected two laser blasts, and advanced quickly.

The man crouched behind a column attached to the tunnel's side. He wore a loose robe, similar to those of the Dai Bendu monks, but any semblance of holiness was wrecked by the weapon in his hand and the fury she sensed in him.

A shot came from behind her and impacted the wall far along the tunnel, smashing rock into dust and blasting a flash of fire along its length. In that light Lanoree saw more figures rushing their way. Time was short.

I won't lose him again! she thought, and in three leaps—sword sweeping aside laser blasts meant for her chest—she was on the man. She saw a moment of fear in his eyes and then she parted his head from his shoulders, crouching and facing the approaching Stargazers even as she felt blood splash across her neck.

Tre scurried along the tunnel and pressed himself to the wall opposite her, aiming and firing his blaster along its length. A grunt, the sound of an impact, and then a woman started screaming.

"Wait here!" Lanoree said.

"But—"

She did not pause to answer his rebuttal, instead running forward with her bloodied sword raised before her. She Force-shoved ahead and heard three voices cry out as their owners were flung back. A blast sizzled past her ear and she smelled burned hair, scorched clothing. That was good. *The Force gives you power, and power breeds confidence,* Master Kin'ade had told her at Stav Kesh, *but confidence can be your enemy.* Lanoree was never one to forget her mortality.

Tre fired past her, keeping their attackers' heads down as she closed the distance between them. *Don't discount the injured one on the ground,* she thought, and then she was among them, slashing left and opening a Noghri woman from throat to sternum, ducking and rolling, standing, thrusting to her right and catching a man beneath the arm. He cried out and stumbled sideways, her sword jammed between his ribs. He fell. As she was pulled forward he turned—tearing blade through more flesh, bones cracking—to point his blaster at her face.

Lanoree clenched her left hand and aimed a Force punch, sending the blaster spinning away. Two of the man's fingers were still clasped around the grip.

He slumped away from her, dying, and she stood on his hip to withdraw her sword.

A blast from behind her and a brief, gurgled cry. She spun around. The injured woman was slumped against the stone wall, her throat and lower jaw an open wound, raw edges still sizzling from the laser blast that had killed her.

Ten paces along the corridor, Tre lowered his weapon. "She was almost on you."

Lanoree nodded her thanks. That was too close. *Clumsy!* she thought. But now was not the time to analyze her mistake.

"So now they know we're here," Tre said.

"I think they've known for a while. Come on."

They trotted along the tunnel, Lanoree casting her senses forward and around them. The flurry of terrible violence had set her heart pounding and blood rushing, and her pulse filled her ears. She knew control, and carried the talents to calm herself, but she also knew that the heightened awareness of the fight could be her friend. The Force complemented her; she was her own greatest weapon.

They ducked through a doorway, climbed a flight of stairs, and suddenly the stone wall disappeared and a metal corridor began. She probed ahead, but her vision was clouded now, her Force senses blurred. Pan Deep might sometimes serve the Je'daii, if Maxhagan was to be believed, but it also strove to protect itself from them.

She ran on. To slow down now, to take stock, would be to lose whatever advantage they still possessed. The fighting would have been heard, and perhaps Dal and his remaining Stargazers would not have expected her to win through so quickly. The confusion of combat would work to her advantage.

Through another doorway, and then there was a room.

Behind her, Tre gasped.

The room was large. Its walls were smooth, their lines clean. The ceiling and floor were white, like nothing they had previously seen on Nox. It resembled more the interior of a luxury spacecraft than a subterranean manufacturing base. At its center stood a wide table, upon which rested an object swathed in a loose white sheet. Scattered across the table were instruments and components, and around the room were several wheeled cabinets, home to more tools, parts, and obscure technology. It was more like an operating theater than a laboratory.

Huddled in one corner were six Selkaths dressed in plain white lab coats, all of them terrified.

And standing beside the table, Dal.

"Lanoree!" he said. His surprise was evident in his eyes and the way he threw up his hands, and as he grinned she was a teenager again, seeing her brother and reveling in his presence. A flush of emotion swept through her—pleasure and sadness, loss and love. He came forward as if delighted at her being there, and for a moment Lanoree was consumed by memory. And that was the only moment her lost brother required.

Tre screamed, and something struck Lanoree's head. As she saw the floor rising to meet her, darkness swallowed her.

CHAPTER THIRTEEN
OTHER WAYS

Alchemy should have no part in a Je'daii's experience. It is a dark force, arcane and dangerous. It has the power to upset balance. There are other ways.

—Temple Master Vor'Dana, 10,456 TYA

At Anil Kesh Lanoree finds herself, without even realizing that she was lost.

Their first few days there are strange. There is an orientation process to go through because of the disruptive influence of the Chasm below the temple, and Lanoree becomes immersed in the talks, meditations, and instruction. She and several other Journeyers spend their time in darkened, windowless rooms away from any sight of the Chasm, and a Sith Master guides them through varying stages of sickness and uncertainty. The Sith is a wise old man, and he has done this many times before. He sees their discomfort fade—not lessening, because the Chasm will always affect anyone strong in the Force, but simply tempered.

And in his wisdom, he perceives that Dal is enjoying all this.

Lanoree's brother says very little over those first few days at the temple, but he exudes a sense of peace that she has not seen in him before. He enjoys witnessing his sister and the other Journeyers suffering.

They are given several tours of the Anil Kesh Temple, which is even larger and more incredible than Lanoree thought. Each of its three giant support legs houses a complex honeycomb of living quarters, the structures designed to afford as much strength as possible to the supports. Within the legs are dampeners the size of Cloud Chasers, designed to absorb the incredible pressures placed on the temple by frequent and violent storms originating in the Chasm. Huge tanks of pneumatic fluid are stored at regular intervals, and there are also several access ports in each leg for escape craft. None has ever been used, and their tour guide assures them that none are needed. Everything here is large and amazing, the architectural and engineering talent on display awe-inspiring. Their guide seems to take some satisfaction in this.

The massive central body of the temple is supported by these legs, hanging directly above the Chasm. And floating around the temple itself, the Tho Yor. Hanging by means unknown, it drifts around Anil Kesh, so it is believed, in tune with the Force.

This central area is the heart of Anil Kesh. There are several large laboratories here, along with teaching rooms, private studies for Temple Masters, libraries, holo suites, and meditation chambers. There are also launch bays from which drones and other equipment are sometimes dropped into the Chasm. Lanoree is surprised to learn how infrequently this now happens. Every experiment that could safely be carried out on the Chasm has already been performed countless times, and still so little is known about the bottomless gorge.

Future discoveries, they are told, must arise from more esoteric means.

Yet a blazing, pulsing beam of energy is still fired down into the Chasm from the very heart of Anil Kesh, seeking information and readings.

On the fourth day, the Sith Master frees them from his instruction and tells them that their new Masters will be introducing themselves that evening. The rest of the day is their own.

"I'm going to look at it," Lanoree tells Dal. "I'm going outside to see." She means the Chasm. Even uttering those words causes a flutter of trepidation and excitement in her stomach. She is about to confront something that is still a mystery to even the greatest Je'daii, and she wants to do so with her brother.

But it's too late.

"It's nothing, really," he says matter-of-factly. "Deep. Stormy. I've been out there four times a day since we've been here. I'm more interested in the temple than the Chasm, though. Have you *seen* how long the temple legs are? Have you *felt* how much it flexes in the wind?"

He is toying with her, and he knows that she knows. But he doesn't care. His vision is elsewhere now, always, and soon something is going to happen. Maybe one day she'll wake up, Dal will be gone, and she'll never see him again. Or perhaps it will be worse than that.

"I'm going to look at it," she says again, and as she pushes past Dal she feels rather than sees his silent chuckle.

There are steps that lead up onto a gangway and outside. The heavy metal doors are always kept locked on the inside, as though something from beyond might wish to gain entry. But the dangers are far less physical. She spins the locking handle on a door, and it swings inward.

The blast of air is shocking. Loaded with warm raindrops, gushing against her like the breath of an unimaginable monster, it carries the smell of something mysterious and deep. Rain patters across the floor and spreads inside, and Lanoree feels a moment of panic—what has she let in?

She makes a quick decision and steps outside, pulling the door closed behind her.

Above her arcs one of the three great curving arms of the temple. They act both as counterbalances to the legs and also as transmitters and receivers, gathering atmospheric charge to fuel Anil Kesh's experiments and sending out messages from the Temple Masters to other Je'daii across Tython and beyond. Its mass shelters her somewhat from the storms.

But she can still look down.

She walks to the edge of the wide viewing platform and grips the railing. She feels the weight of Anil Kesh behind her, and the protective arms seem to hold her within their shadowy grasp. The temple feels on the breath of the Chasm, and its sturdy legs absorb every subtle impact of the wind. "'You always move, seeking to draw my eyes,'" she says. It is a line from a love poem she once read in an old paper book of her mother's, and she wonders whether the poet had ever visited this place.

Looking down, she wonders whether all Je'daii are in love with the Chasm.

It is mystery. It is depth and infinity on the surface of this world they deign to call their home. Its breath is warm and loaded, and deeper down through the mist of torrential rain, she can see the frequent flash of Force lightning, erupting in the darkness and illuminating nothing. It is dizzying and thrilling, terrifying and wonderful. She grips the railing so hard that her fingers hurt and her knuckles turn white, not sure she can ever let go.

There is a brief, ecstatic moment when she is tempted to lift herself over the railing and fall. It will end in death, but she will also get to see the Chasm's depth, to know its secrets.

It cannot be bottomless. They only say that because no Je'daii has reached its bottom and lived.

"Or none have gone down there and returned," she whispers, the words immediately stolen by the wind. She is drenched through by the rain. The storm whips curtains of water back and forth across the Chasm below her.

She feels a hand on her shoulder, and instantly fears it is Dal come to do her harm. *I am the Chasm,* he said, perhaps meaning that he is a mystery to her now, with a mind that no Je'daii will ever be able to fully understand.

Lanoree freezes. She cannot fight back because she is too shocked and too overcome with a sense of infinity.

But then a warm voice says, "Come inside, Lanoree, where we can begin our talk."

That first meeting with Master Dam-Powl extends long into the night.

* * *

"I told you to never get in my way."

Darkness. Pain. She heard her own ragged breathing, felt the troubled beating of her heart. Her head throbbed and pulsed, the core of a raging sun in the center of her brain. And she knew that voice.

"I never thought they'd send you after me."

She opened her eyes, but the brightness hurt. She closed them. The pain was a weight crushing every part of her. Her scalp was wet and warm, and everything was red.

Normally a calm sea, the Force within her was now a raging river of confused currents.

"I thought they'd have more sense."

Dal, she thought, and tried to sit up. Someone helped. That surprised her, but she was already gathering her senses. *Stay like this. Be weak. Be wounded.*

"I knew you were onto me on Kalimahr—"

"How?" Her voice echoed and thumped in her head, pounding her skull, but she could not help asking the question.

Dal did not answer. "Didn't think you'd be able to follow. Thought I'd shaken you. But you're *persistent*."

Was that something conflicted in his voice when he talked about her? Lanoree could not tell. He had changed so much, and she knew that without even seeing him.

In the distance, a deep rumble. *What was that? Where is Tre?* She remembered his scream, guessed he was dead, and felt a surprising sadness. Tre was not a good Twi'lek, but he was trying to make himself better. Trying to make up for his past.

Lanoree opened her eyes again and looked at her brother. He was blurry to begin with, swaying in her vision like a scar serpent waiting to strike. She closed one eye and her sight settled. Dal manifested, down on one knee before her as if questioning one of the elder gods.

"You've grown up," Lanoree whispered. Dal laughed. She recognized the sound, but there was something grating in it, something mad.

And he *had* grown up. Gone were his boyish good looks, replaced by a weathered countenance that carried every day of every year that had passed. He'd lost some of his hair, and what remained was speckled gray. There was a scar on his left cheek. He could have done something about the hair and scar, but she saw no vanity in him at all, no evidence of self-awareness about his appearance. His robe was plain and rough. Everything that Dal was now resided in his mad, glittering eyes.

Another thud! She felt it through her behind rather than heard it. Dal glanced up at the ceiling.

"I've grown in every way," he said. "See. Feel."

"I don't want to—"

"But I'm telling you to!" he screamed. Lanoree winced as his voice seared into her head, driving spikes of pain into her eyeballs. Perhaps she'd fractured her skull. She tried to feel, to sense, as they'd taught her in Mahara Kesh when she finished her Great Journey without her brother. But she was confused. The Force flowed through her, but it seemed to stutter. She could not examine herself, so instead she delved toward Dal's mind.

And withdrew just as quickly.

He grinned, nodding slowly. "You see?" he asked. "You feel?"

Lanoree nodded, tides of pain washing through her. She sensed nothing at all of the Force within him. No light, no dark; no Ashla, no Bogan. But he bore an incredible strength that she had only just started to recognize nine years before. It had grown into something solid. She could only call it madness, and yet . . .

And yet Dal's aims and ambitions were defined, and his route to achieving them firmly set. His madness had method.

"Not many people are completely without your Force, eh, Lanoree? Not many. Not him." He nodded toward a corner and Lanoree looked, relieved to see Tre propped there. He bled from a wound across his forehead and left eye, and twitched in unconsciousness. "Not even most of my Stargazers." There were three other people around the room, now, other than the Selkath technicians. They were of differing species but all dressed similar to Dal. Their look resembled that of a religious order, but they were much more than that. And few religions went that heavily armed.

"Not many people want to be," Lanoree said.

"See, that's why you didn't find me," Dal said. "Down there in that old dark place. Because you were looking the wrong way. You were searching as if I'd lost something and fled, not found something and set off on my own path. You were looking for a wounded, dying animal. Not the man I've become."

"I was looking for my brother."

"And I've already told you, you left the brother you always wanted back in Bodhi with our parents. He's dead, now. Long dead."

There was another distant impact, and Lanoree absorbed it, examined it. She was more conscious and aware now. She thought it was an explosion.

"What's happening?" she asked.

Dal stood and approached the covered object on the table. It was the size of a Noghri's head, and beneath the sheet it appeared completely spherical. "It's almost finished," he said. "Almost ready. You know what this is?"

"Yes," Lanoree said, bluffing. She knew his aims, and what he planned to use to make them real. But really she had no idea what the device was.

Dal rested his hand on the object almost reverentially. "Everything I always wanted." He whispered it almost to himself.

"Dal—"

"Shut up." He didn't even look at her as he spoke, and a sudden change came over him. "You're sure?" he asked the group huddled in the corner. "You're *certain*?"

"Yes," one of the technicians said. He took one step forward. "Your request was . . . forgive me, vague. We've worked hard. It was a task we relished. And the device is ready to do everything you want of it. It's . . . perfect. One of the finest of our creations, and it pushes at the edge of all our accumulated science. Once it's charged—"

"Enough!" Dal said, holding up a hand. He glanced at Lanoree.

"You have no idea what you're doing," she said.

"And you have no idea what I've seen." He nodded at his Stargazers.

The violence was sudden and shocking. The Stargazers—a human, a Twi'lek, and a Cathar—drew blasters and power bows and opened fire on the scientists. Lanoree winced but watched, unable to close her eyes. The Selkaths danced and juddered as blasts and bolts ripped into them. Blood splashed, fire sizzled across skin, clothes erupted into flames. In the space of five heartbeats the scientists were dead, the last one sliding down the wall to slump across her murdered companions.

Calm, Lanoree told herself, *calm*, and she sought the Force, readying to use it to save herself. The time must come soon. She had to stop him here and now, and nothing here would end well.

Dal looked at Lanoree. She could not read his eyes. She felt for her sword, but the scabbard was empty. *And now me?* she thought. Panic came and she washed it away, seeking the familiar Force to prime herself for action. But her pain was still raw, and shock stoked the storms and uncertainties inside her.

"You'd lose," Dal said. "Maybe you'd take a couple of us with you. But my Stargazers are ready for you. The first touch on their mind and a blaster would open your skull, or a power bolt would cook your heart."

Lanoree breathed long and slow, and the moment stretched on.

"I wish . . ." Dal said. She looked for weakness but saw none. He was expressing frustration, not regret.

"Wish what?"

"I wish you'd understood. I wish you could have opened your mind to our past. Your Force is so *constricting*! You think it gives you power, you're taught that it's great, but it binds you. You're *blinkered* by it, but my eyes are wide open. We see the stars! We have a place in the universe that was taken from us by the Tho Yor. They stole us away, brought us here, denied us the future we deserved. And I'm going to take it back."

"You'll kill everyone."

"No," Dal said, smiling. "I know what I'm doing."

"Dark matter? Gree technology, Dal? You're playing with something beyond anything we can even hope to understand." Lanoree nodded at the bodies still steaming and twitching in the corner. "You heard them. Even they said that thing is at the edge of known science, and edges break away."

"Gather it up," Dal said to his Stargazers. He turned his back on Lanoree.

There was another explosion somewhere far away.

"Dal, what have you done?" she asked. She stood slowly, holding onto a wheeled tool cart for support. The Cathar watched her, his gun at the ready.

"Started a little fight." Dal turned to face her again. For an instant she felt a flush of memories, but they were all good ones of her time with her brother. They did not belong here.

"With whom?"

"I arranged that the Knool Tandor dome would find out about Pan Deep's continuing business with the Je'daii, and they *hate* them. Many survivors from the bombed domes live there now. Landed one of my Stargazers there, and by now she'll have killed several of their corporations' presidents with a Je'daii sword."

"Where did you get—?" Lanoree asked, but then it fell into place. "Kara."

"Greenwood Station will be blamed for the murders and its alliance with the Je'daii," Dal said, his expression unchanging. "Skirmishes are common on Nox. And it won't be the first conflict between Knool Tandor and another dome."

"Covering your tracks," Lanoree said.

Dal shrugged. Behind him, his Stargazers had wrapped the device in the sheet. It did not seem at all heavy, and the Twi'lek held it to her chest. They were waiting for Dal to leave.

"Just like you did on Tython," Lanoree continued. One hand delved into her utility belt beneath the robe, rolling the item she sought between thumb and forefinger. A tracker, small and sharp. "Leaving your bloodied clothes for me to find. Letting our family believe you dead."

"I liked being dead," Dal said. "It gave me freedom from your constant efforts to push the Force on me when I never, *ever* wanted it." Another low rumble and a vibration from above. "Soon I'll be believed dead again, and gone from here. Free to pursue my own fate."

"Dal, you don't know what—"

"I should kill you." Dal pulled a blaster from beneath his robe and stood with it pointing down at the floor. He was incredibly still, like a statue. Even his eyes seemed to have died.

He's inside, Lanoree thought, and she wondered what he was finding in there, what he was thinking and the decisions he was making, and she knew that now was the time to push. She would push hard and violently, smashing aside those mental defenses he might believe he had built against her.

"But I can't," Dal said. He turned aside and holstered his blaster.

Lanoree brought out her hand and flicked the tracker, closing her eyes, concentrating, and guiding it quickly across the room until it attached to Dal's right boot. Then she opened her eyes and looked around, but no one had seen anything. Perhaps she had been lucky. Perhaps.

Dal did not even spare her a final glance. With a single nod at the Cathar he left the room the same way Lanoree and Tre had entered. The Twi'lek carrying the device followed, along with the human Stargazer.

The Cathar remained, gun aimed at Lanoree. It was a heavy blaster, and its muzzle still glowed warm. Lanoree clenched her fingers, readying a Force punch.

"Try," the Cathar said.

"You know I can't just stand here and let him leave."

"You won't be standing there for long."

Lanoree twitched her finger and a tool flipped from the wide table, clanging against the wall. The Stargazer didn't even blink.

"He doesn't want to hear you die," the Cathar said.

"That's kind of my brother."

"He *is* kind. The only kind man I've ever met."

Lanoree glanced at the huddled, bloody bodies in the corner.

"They were unkind," the Cathar said. "They hid down here instead of looking to the stars."

She sensed movement from the other side of the room. She did not look, but she knew that Tre was stirring.

"He's going to kill everyone," she said. "Once he initiates that device, the dark matter will form a black hole and everyone in the system—"

"He knows that won't happen. The stars call. They tell him."

"Oh, so the stars speak to him," Lanoree said, laughing softly. "And he's not mad?"

The Cathar blinked slowly, but she was not even putting a chink in his convictions. *Come on, Tre*, she thought.

Tre groaned. The Cathar glanced his way. Lanoree Force-shoved with everything she had. Tools and loose components rattled across the table and flew at the Stargazer, a cabinet tipped and bounced across the floor, a hail of bolts and snipped wires became a stinging rain that raked across his chest and face, ripping skin and blinding him.

She ducked down and Force-punched, shoving the Cathar back against the wall beside the door. His blaster fired, the shot smashing a hole in the ceiling. Molten material and rock fragments showered down. Then the Stargazer clasped at his belt, weeping blood from ruptured eyes, and a look of ecstasy broke across his face.

"Oh, no," Lanoree muttered. She looked at Tre and saw that he was barely conscious, and with every shred of strength and effort she had of the Force, she reached for him and dragged him halfway across the room toward her. His eyes opened comically wide as he slid without being touched, and as he reached her and she clasped his clothing Lanoree shouted, "Bomb!"

The explosion was deafening, shattering, assaulting her body and mind and senses, and she felt herself thrown around like a snowflake in a storm.

With her parents it was the arts. Her mother wrote the most beautiful poetry, and her father was a sculptor, his work venerated all across Masara. But Lanoree's calling lay in science and alchemy, and how the Force could be used for both. She discovers that at Anil Kesh. And she revels in it.

Master Dam-Powl shows her the way. The Cathar Temple Master has taught at Anil Kesh for sixteen years, and at the end of their first long night of discussion, she tells Lanoree that she has the potential to be her greatest pupil.

"Do you say that to everyone?" Lanoree asks, proud but suspicious.

"I've said it to no one before," Dam-Powl replies.

Over the next few days the studies begin, and Lanoree is amazed. She immerses herself in Dam-Powl's instruction, and in doing so her troubles with Dal fade away. They don't disappear completely—there is always a shadow and a sense of impending change in her life—but she sleeps better than she has since leaving home, feels happier, and realizes that her mind has always been too focused on her brother. Dam-Powl makes her understand that this is *her* Great Journey as well. And though Lanoree cannot give up on Dal, for the first time she places herself before him.

With the Chasm beneath them, Anil Kesh has a different feel from all the other temples. Every moment there is rich, filled with potential, and edged with a sense of danger. Lanoree has never felt so alive. It is as if the cells of her body are charged, her mind on fire. When she mentions this, Dam-Powl smiles and nods.

"We balance on the precipice of knowledge," she says. "The unknown lies below us, always threatening to draw us down or rise up and swallow us. The Force is charged and powerful here. Anyone familiar can feel and sense it, but if you're *powerful* with the Force . . ." She grimaces and presses a fist to her forehead. "Sometimes it hurts. But it's a hurt worth weathering."

Dam-Powl introduces her to sciences that Lanoree has only ever heard or read about. She knows of Je'daii who are disturbed by some of what occurs at Anil Kesh, but she listens to the Master wide-eyed and with an open mind. She finds plenty to concern her but so much more that fascinates. She's aware of Dam-Powl's watching her carefully, taking stock. She is eager to please.

In the storage pens in one of the temple's supporting arms are the altered animals. Taken from the Abyss of Ruh, a dangerous place deep in the Rift six hundred kilometers to the east, these strange and fearsome creatures have been genetically manipulated using the Force to serve the Je'daii. Lanoree is amazed at the changes in them—none are hurt or damaged, and it's as if their alterations are the true wish of evolution.

Dam-Powl takes her through a network of laboratories. In one, weapons are altered and adapted using Force-driven metallurgy. In another, weapons specific to the Force are being tested. Chemicals are changed and transmuted; solids have their structures re-formed; and the wild power of the Chasm beneath them is harnessed in thick-walled compounds, dancing and flashing, striking and snapping like a living thing.

It is in the last room that Dam-Powl shows her that Lanoree knows her future lies.

"The talents needed for this are deep," the Je'daii Master says, "the risks great. But the rewards are huge. I'm going to teach you."

Lanoree stares at the two Je'daii in the center of the room. Before each of them is a shape. Something that should not live, yet it flexes and breathes. A thing that should not be, yet here it is.

"Wrought from their own flesh and blood," Dam-Powl says, "and nurtured using the Force."

Lanoree is terrified and thrilled. She has heard of this, but never thought it was true. Never suspected she would see it for herself.

"The alchemy of flesh," she whispers. Despite her fear, she is eager to begin.

"Tell me you can get us out of here." Tre's voice. His urgency pulled her quickly back to her senses. That, and the stench of sewage and death.

Everything ached, and in a few places she hurt terribly. Her head still throbbed as if someone were jumping up and down on it. She smelled blood, and knew it was her own. But Tre was far from gentle as he grabbed her beneath the armpits and tried to haul her upright. Lanoree shoved him back and sent him stumbling into the shattered table.

She looked around and tried to take stock. It looked bad.

The Cathar Stargazer had exploded his suicide vest, demolishing the wall and bringing down most of the ceiling. The doorway was blocked by torn metal and smashed stone, and fractured rock had fallen behind it. The rest of the ceiling was spattered with his blood, a great swath of it burned black by the bomb's fire flash. The remainder of the large room was a mess—scientists' bodies scattered from the corner where they'd been massacred; tools and components everywhere; the large central table ruptured and splintered. If she hadn't pulled Tre behind there with her, they'd have both died.

There was a wide crack in one wall, and through this seeped a steady stream of effluent. A pipe or chute had been ruptured somewhere, and the leak was speeding up rather than slowing down.

"Look," Tre said, pointing. "Another door there." He was almost shouting, and blood ran from his ears. Lanoree also heard the fading whine from her tortured eardrums, but that was the least of her worries.

"That Cathar's bomb can't have done that," she said, pointing at the rent in the wall. It was on the opposite side of the room from the doorway the explosion had blocked.

"There was another explosion when I was trying to wake you," Tre said. "Far away, up there. To feel it down here it must have been big. What's happening? What have we started?"

"A war. And Dal started it. Come on. We've got to stop him leaving Greenwood Station."

"I feel sick," Tre said. "It stinks. My head hurts. I think my skull might be—"

"I'll break it myself," Lanoree said. "Come on! Help me with this door." She searched the room for her sword, knowing she would not find it, mourning its loss. Tem Madog himself had forged that sword for her. She'd rather have lost an arm.

Perhaps it had been dropped somewhere beyond that blocked doorway. Or maybe Dal had taken it with him.

They tried the door, but it was electronically locked.

"Cover your ears," Lanoree said. She concentrated on the lock and Force-shoved, crushing the mechanism and shorting the circuits. The door slid open, and a flood of sewage washed in around their feet. She and Tre clasped hands to keep their balance. The thought of falling into that mess . . .

When the levels of filth had equalized, they left the room and emerged into one of Pan Deep's corridors. It was long and empty, and several other doors led off it. They were all closed, marked only with laboratory numbers, and Lanoree had no wish to open them. Soft, reactive lighting glowed behind ceiling panels, and on the walls were touch panels, 3-D holo screens, and several indentations that might have housed implement printers. This was advanced tech for a place so hidden away. The money pumped into Pan Deep must have been vast.

They saw no one else. Perhaps the six murdered scientists were the only ones who worked here. Or maybe Dal had paid others to stay away.

Not much of a head start, she thought, *but he'll know his way up, would have an escape route planned from here and from the city*. She could barely believe the enormity of the events that Dal had set in motion. Initiating a battle between two domes—cities whose specialty was the design and manufacture of weapons of war—was as good as murdering the battle's victims himself. All to cover his tracks.

It was brutal. It was inhuman. He claimed freedom from the Force, but willingly removing himself from its influence had made him a monster.

Pan Deep was not as large as she'd imagined. At the end of the corridor they emerged into a rough cavern, at the other end of which a string of lights led into a tunnel that sloped slowly upward. The cavern floor was swilling with sewage and the stink was almost unbearable, but Lanoree knew that a person could get used to a lot in extreme circumstances. Even Tre was surprising her. He'd quickly stopped complaining and wiped the blood from his face and ears, and now he nudged her shoulder and pointed.

"Think he'll have set traps?"

"He thinks we're dead," she said.

Another blast rumbled down from above, spilling grit and dust from the cavern ceiling. From somewhere close by came a shattering, grinding crack, shaking the floor and setting the air itself vibrating.

"And we don't have time for caution," Lanoree said. "I think they're using plasma bombs up there. We've got to get clear of Greenwood Station and back to the Peacemaker, or this will be our grave."

"Laid to rest in a bath of shak," Tre said. "Well, I guess I had it coming."

Lanoree laughed out loud. Tre's eyes went wide with surprise. And then they ran.

It was a journey through a nightmare—flowing sewage, crumbling walls, three security grilles that Lanoree had to Force-shove open before they could continue—and what made it worse was the uncertainty of what they were moving toward. The farther they went, the louder the noises of battle. But they had little choice.

Frustration and fear drove her on. Not fear for herself so much as for the countless people who Dal's scheme would put at risk, and not only those now dying in the conflict initiated here. Seeing the shape of the device beneath the dust sheet had been strange—that something so small might contain such energies. The pursuit had clouded her thoughts about the hypergate, and the truth or not of its existence. But seeing Dal again, and his madness, and being so close to the device that might be born of Gree technology had all combined to focus her thoughts.

It was just possible that the device would work, which would be amazing, and the consequences of that she could not allow herself to consider. But it was much more likely that it would doom them all.

The farther they fled from beneath the massive tower's foundation, the greater the impact of the explosions. When she reached her Peacemaker she would contact the Je'daii Council and tell them of events here, and maybe they could intervene in time to prevent a greater tragedy. But doing so might be admitting their continued interest in Greenwood Station and the laboratories and expertise of Pan Deep. Perhaps they would be happier to let the domed city meet its fate and fade away from memory.

Their route took them upward, and Tre commented several times that they should have already reached street level. But they had no time to pause, and when Lanoree consulted her wrist unit, the schematics were confused. She could not pin down their location on the plans.

People passed by them in both directions, none sparing them a glance. They were all wide-eyed and scared.

At last they reached a set of heavy blast doors. Lanoree used the Force to fry their controls, and Tre found a heavy iron bar to pry them open. Heat and noise flooded in, the stenches and sounds of chaos, and Lanoree stumbled through onto a wide balcony several stories above the ground. They had emerged just above the base of the central tower, overlooking Greenwood Station's western side. The sounds, sights, and chaos of war were almost overwhelming.

They were confronted with a scene that took their breaths away.

CHAPTER FOURTEEN
SAD HISTORY

*Perhaps there is a madness in remaining on Tython while not strong in
the Force. One would not submerge long beneath the surface of the sea if
one did not possess gills. One would surface. One would escape. So to stay
here, now . . . that way, insanity lies.*

—Unknown Tythan, circa 9,000 TYA

When Master Dam-Powl knocks on her door and disturbs her from
sleep, Lanoree knows that something is wrong. She has been expecting it. Like the sense of imminent danger always apparent at Anil Kesh
because of the Chasm below, her own perception of Dal has been of a
coiled spring. Now, the time has come. Dal has sprung.

"He's a fool!" Dam-Powl says as they march along the corridor. "I
saw trouble in him the moment you arrived. As did Master Kin'ade."

"At Stav Kesh?" Lanoree asks.

"Of course. You think the Je'daii Masters don't talk among our-
selves about those on their Great Journeys?"

"What has he done?" Lanoree asks.

"He fled into the Abyss of Ruh. Put lives in danger."

"He's gone?" breathes Lanoree.

"Oh, no. Not gone. They pulled him out and are bringing him back. They're just coming in to land." Dam-Powl climbs a staircase and a heavy door slides open before her. Wind roars, rain splashes in across the floor, and Force lightning thrashes about the square of night sky revealed.

Oh, Dal, what have you done? Lanoree thinks. He has been gone for four days, taken with others by Master Quan-Jang on a visit to the Riftlands to collect specimens for the alchemical labs here at Anil Kesh. At first she welcomed his absence; it gave her the opportunity to study in peace with no concerns about what Dal might be doing. But her dreams these past three nights had been troubled. It was almost as if she knew that something terrible was going to happen. She follows the Je'daii Master outside. There is someone else out there already, standing at the edge of the platform and looking east. A Cloud Chaser is visible, drifting down toward one of Anil Kesh's landing zones.

"Master," the young man says, turning to greet them. He barely glances at Lanoree. "Master Quan-Jang reports that the Journeyer said nothing. But he appears fit and well."

"Good," Dam-Powl says. "The others?"

"Sickened from their time in the Abyss." He looks pointedly at Lanoree then. "It is a place of dark, dangerous energies."

Lanoree glances over the handrail and looks down into the Chasm. She feels woozy, and it's Dam-Powl's hand that steadies her.

"Breathe long and deep," the Master whispers. "The Force is very strong in you, and so the Chasm plays with you."

"That's what you think it is?" Lanoree asks. "Playing?"

Dam-Powl smiles enigmatically. "A turn of phrase."

"So what will happen?"

"Happen?"

"To Dal?"

It's the other Je'daii who replies. "We ensure that he's fit and well, unharmed from his escapades. And then we will arrest him and escort him from Anil Kesh first thing in the morning."

"Escort him where?"

The Je'daii's face is grim. "Once beyond the temple, he can go where he wishes."

"Banishment," Lanoree says.

"I think we'll actually be saving his life."

So is this how my brother's sad story ends? Lanoree wonders. But she thinks not. Dal has a weight to him, increasing the farther he removes himself from the Force. In her dreams, at their worst, his end comes with terrible greatness.

"I'd like to wait here for him," she says. The Cloud Chaser has touched down now, visible between skeins of low cloud. "Speak to him when he arrives."

"I'll wait with you." The Je'daii bows. "Journeyer Skott Yun."

Lanoree starts to object, but she realizes it was not a request. "Lanoree Brock," she says.

"I know." Skott Yun smiles.

"Afterward, bring him down to me," Dam-Powl says. "I'll go to make sure the medical bay is ready to receive those others still sickening."

Yun bows his head as the Master turns and leaves.

Lanoree watches her go, surprised at Dam-Powl's confidence in Dal's well-being.

"I'll fetch your jacket for you," Yun says. "It can grow cold out here."

It takes Quan-Jang and the others a surprisingly long time to reach the temple from the landing zone. Yun tries talking, but Lanoree is too distracted and troubled to enter into any meaningful conversation. Most of the time she stands with her eyes closed, her thoughts her own.

It is Yun who finally announces their arrival. They arrive at the temple on foot, Master Quan-Jang in the lead. There are ten people behind him, three being carried on stretchers. Even though she sees Dal with them, he seems to walk alone.

"I'll go to meet them," Yun says. "Wait here and I'll bring your brother."

Lanoree waits, and watches. They climb the leg onto the temple, and Yun meets them at the far end of the viewing platform.

Dal seems even more apart from them all than she first thought. There is no expression on his face, and he doesn't seem to acknowledge where he is at all. *He's more hurt than Master Dam-Powl let on*, Lanoree thinks. But she still wants him close so that she can assess his condition for herself. And she realizes that though it has only been four days, she has missed her brother.

Quan-Jang and the others move off into the temple, and Yun touches Dal's shoulder. Then the two of them walk toward Lanoree, across the viewing platform that is buffeted by winds from below and heavy, warm raindrops from above.

"Dal," she says as they reach her, but his expression gives her pause. So serious. So adult. There's something expanded about him, as if since she saw him last he has grown to fit the world he will live in. He seems assured, too, and confident, even though his skin appears burned, his eyes puffy and red.

"I came to say good-bye, Lanoree," he says. The words are strange and unexpected. He turns to leave, and Skott Yun stands before him.

"You're to be arrested and—" the Journeyer begins.

"There are such depths," Dal says. He is speaking directly to Lanoree. She wonders whether these are the last words they will ever share.

"What did you see?" she asks.

"Things you never can." His eyes are so bright they seem to glow. "Such promises and opportunities down in the Abyss! Such depths, of history and potential. And now I must go elsewhere, to find something more. And so—"

"Dalien Brock," Yun says, "you're to accompany me to—"

Dal strikes out. Lanoree sees it coming and is surprised that Yun did not. But though the Journeyer may be comfortable at Anil Kesh, he has yet to visit Stav Kesh to learn the martial arts. Dal's fist connects with his chin, and as Yun leans back, Dal spins and kicks him in the face. Another punch as he falls, and Lanoree hears bones break even before Yun strikes the metal platform.

"Dal!" Lanoree shouts, but she sees her brother's determination. *I cannot lose him now!* She goes for him, reaching out, wishing to hold him and try to undo everything that has passed between them since leaving home. It is a naive wish, and one that suits a child more than the Je'daii woman Lanoree is becoming. But familial love is a powerful force in itself.

From the corner of her eye she sees Skott Yun lift himself on one elbow and then raise his other hand, pointing toward Dal.

"No!" she shouts. "Don't try to—" She will always wonder whether her voice gave Dal warning, and whether in fact she wanted that.

The moment she speaks, Dal crouches and spins on one heel, his robe billowing as he brings one hand out from beneath its folds. His blaster coughs. Skott Yun cries out and is shoved across the platform by the impact. Blood bursts from his back, and his clothing smokes.

"Dal," Lanoree breathes, feeling weak and suddenly hopeless. This is the point when everything goes too far.

"Good-bye, Lanoree," he says again. And then he is gone, dashing across the platform and climbing a sloping ladder fixed into the temple's curved wall.

She should stay to help Yun. She kneels briefly by his side and examines the wound, and though still breathing, she knows that he will not survive. Lanoree should stay to tell Master Dam-Powl what has happened.

But instead she chases her brother. Up onto the temple's high wall, across its curved roof where deep ditches channel water and moss makes the surface treacherous, following his distant shadow through the increasing downpour until he scurries down one of the massive legs toward solid ground.

Her first Great Journey ends, and her pursuit of her brother begins.

"Your brother did this?" Tre gasped.

"So he said."

"But *how*?"

"A word in the right ear. A rumor, a threat, a challenge. A murder."

"It's . . . monstrous. It's *terrifying*."

Lanoree could not argue.

The air was filled with violence. Smoke, screams, the pounding and roaring of weapons, and the groaning and grinding of the giant dome under stress. They had emerged onto a balcony just above the base of the central tower. To the west was the previously damaged area of the dome, with its massive buttresses and chaotic-looking repairs sealing it from the toxic air outside. And to the south, an attack was under way.

Several large parts of Greenwood Station's dome had been destroyed, the ragged holes still smoking and dropping burning, molten detritus to the buildings and streets far below. The dome's atmosphere screamed as it was vented to the outside, as if in distress at mixing with the toxic clouds beyond. At the nearest of these wounds in the protective skin, Lanoree could see several large, bulky shapes—battle droids—hunkered low by the hole and firing laser cannons into the city. The barrage seemed to be indiscriminate, and many fires were already taking hold. The battle droids edged forward and the first of them dropped, retros beneath its many arms firing to ease its descent.

A missile streaked from the tower above them and struck the droid. It bloomed fire, fell out of sight into a manufacturing district, and exploded. More missiles curved away from the tower, sweeping in graceful arcs and impacting the dome around the shattered area above. Some droids erupted in fiery death, others tumbled across the outside of the dome. More dark shapes replaced them and the barrage began again.

At another smashed section an attack ship hovered. A plasma cannon started pulsing into the ground close to the column's base. Each impact was huge and shook the city, the ground, the air itself. Explosions of fire and smoke mushroomed up, and Lanoree could not help wondering how many people were dying with each impact. *Beneath the central column,* she thought, *just where Dal would have told them Pan Deep lay.* More rockets were fired from the tower, but as they approached the dome's underside they evaporated into clouds of blazing white vapor. The attack ship had defenses. Lanoree could hardly imagine the destruction involved if it succeeded in getting inside.

"We've got to go!" Tre shouted above the noise, grabbing her arm. The balcony vibrated with each impact, and if the attack ship shifted its targeting by just a few degrees . . .

"Come on," Lanoree said. She grasped Tre's hand as he pulled away, squeezed to calm him. "Trust me!" Then she hauled him to the edge of the balcony and tipped over.

Any normal person would have been killed instantly by the fall. But

Lanoree eased them down with the Force, slowing their descent and landing them with barely a jolt on the street below. People ran around them in confusion and terror. No one even seemed to notice them.

"Don't *ever* do that again!" Tre shouted, almost hysterical.

"Next time I won't hold your hand." Lanoree ran, and Tre went with her.

Far to the south, hidden by smoke and the haze of many weapons, a ground battle seemed to be taking place. She could not make out the details, but she could just see the sparking impacts of artillery fire speckling the outside of the dome's shell several kilometers in the distance, and the constant thump, thump of returning fire sang through the air. Hundreds of bright lights dropped from punctures in the dome. Battle droids, or perhaps even ground assault troops.

A much heavier impact sounded, like Nox itself shrugging. Lanoree felt a deep vibration that set buildings swaying. Glass smashed, wreckage showered down all around as weaker buildings started to break down. The air inside the dome seemed to momentarily blur, and outside the city's huge skin the skies lit up.

"Incoming plasma bombs," Lanoree said. "They're being diverted for now. But they'll get through soon enough."

"So how can you help?"

"Help?"

"You're a Je'daii, aren't you?"

"We're not magicians, Tre. You know that as well as anyone."

"But this is—"

"We get out," Lanoree said, "as fast as we can. Dal thinks we died down there, and all this is just to make sure. Whatever escape route he had is hidden to us, and he'll be away and gone by now. But this, what he's caused or initiated, is all for nothing. Because we're going to survive, and we know he's still alive."

"Look!" Tre pointed. In the distance to the north a section of dome had slid open, and several ships rose from across the city and headed for the outside. Lanoree could tell from the way they moved that they were battleships, not civilian transports. This was not yet an evacuation.

As the first ship passed through the dome opening it exploded, blossoming into a ball of fire and erupting ammunition that rained down in a beautiful, awful shower across that part of the city. The other warships powered through the destruction, another of them exploding outside and then impacting the dome half a kilometer away. The others rose clear, and though they were little more than blurred shapes beyond the dome, Lanoree saw them swing around and streak to the south.

"Come on," she said. "I don't think we have long."

"Until what?"

"Until we're a part of Greenwood Station's tragedy."

Lanoree led the way. She headed for the portion of dome already bombed years ago by the Je'daii. What she had learned of Pan Deep—that the Je'daii had spared it because they commissioned high-end military tech themselves—did not sit well with her. But it was not relevant to her mission to consider that right now. And she more than anyone knew that the Je'daii often harbored secrets.

She spoke into her comlink. "Ironholgs, prep the ship for takeoff. There's trouble—we'll be coming in fast. Initiate ship's defenses. Shoot anything that comes close that isn't us. Got that?"

Her ship's droid crackled and spat in reply.

"And start the tracker scanner, frequency two-four-zero. You should find the signal soon enough, probably just off planet. Lock on and track it."

"What signal?" Tre asked.

"I put a tracker on Dal's clothing," she said. "I just hope he hasn't found it."

"Or changed his outfit." Tre was trying to joke, but Lanoree could not smile. Such a small thing as a change of clothing might doom everything she had ever known. She was already living in history in the making, the tragedy of Greenwood Station that would become known across the system. If she failed to catch Dal, and his attempt to initiate the Gree tech went wrong, then *everything* would be history. And there would be no one left to know it.

There's still time! she thought. Because she knew the device was not yet ready. The scientist had mentioned that it needing charging. She'd sensed no energy source there, nothing that might indicate that its dark matter drive had been primed or loaded. She would have known. Her teachings with Dam-Powl had given her an insight into such shadowy matters.

An arcane device that only needed charging before it was ready . . . a tracking chip that might or might not remain on Dal—everything was suddenly so nebulous and unreliable.

A war played out around them as they fled. People ran back and forth in panic—parents herding children, adults running in shouting groups—but Lanoree could see some organization starting to become apparent. Though they wore no sign or uniform, one group of men and women seemed to be part of some sort of Greenwood Station security force. They were breaking down the fencing around a compound housing several militarized Cloud Chasers, airships supporting heavy gun platforms and with grav units fitted to landing gear to aid flight. As Lanoree and Tre passed, the first of the airships started to hum with power.

Other people bearing weapons rushed across the street ahead of them, heading south toward where the bulk of the fighting seemed to be taking place.

"They'd do better to flee," Lanoree said.

"They're defending what they have!" Tre said.

"This is a full-on assault, ultimate destruction. Not an invasion."

They paused beneath the cover of an old factory's slumping wall. Perhaps one day this place would have been repaired, but it looked like it hadn't been used for some time, and the building's metal framework was corroding beneath the toxic atmosphere.

"Look. Invasion." Tre pointed south at another cloud of lights drifting down from the many damaged areas of dome. Gunfire was being exchanged, and it took several seconds for the crackling sound to become audible.

"Droids," Lanoree said. "They're not sending troops in because—"

A massive explosion rocked them from their feet. The ground pounded at her as she fell, and the air itself seemed to vibrate in her lungs, through her chest. Lanoree rolled against the building and looked back and up, astounded and sickened by what she saw.

A plasma bomb had found its way through the city's defenses and impacted close to the dome's highest point, more than a kilometer above the ground. The explosion had ripped the dome open, the shattering destruction running down through the central column and bursting from it in blooming flowers of flame and blazing metal. The wide tower was crumbling from the top down, and around it the dome's mammoth support structures were cracking and dipping, great spreads of dome rupturing and falling away. The explosion continued to expand, probing inward and touching the ground at last. A firestorm swept across the air, incinerating everything in its path. The destruction was so huge, and so far away, that it seemed to happen in slow motion.

"Lanoree," Tre said. He grabbed her arm. "Lanoree!"

"Yes," she said. Tre helped her up and they moved on.

They reached the building through which they'd entered the dome not so long ago. As they went inside, they left behind a very different Greenwood Station.

They worked their way back through the ruined and hastily repaired area of the city, retrieving their masks from where Lanoree had hidden them. But the masks had leaked away the last of their oxygen, so Lanoree cast them both aside.

"We've got a kilometer to go across that landscape," she said. "Follow me. Step where I step. Run as fast as you can. And try not to take deep breaths."

"We'll die out there," Tre said.

"No. And once we're on the Peacemaker, I have medicine that will clean your skin and lungs."

"I don't have skin and lungs exactly like yours, human," Tre said, smiling nervously.

Lanoree grabbed his shoulder, squeezed. "Close enough. Come on."

She Force-shoved the exterior air lock door open and ran out onto the toxic, poisonous surface of Nox.

Behind them, the battle raged and the destruction continued. Out of the dome they could see more, though the air was constantly hazed with stinking clouds of gas. Attack ships stood some distance off, firing at the dome. Way beyond the dome a huge glow filled the sky, and Lanoree guessed that the spaceport adjacent to the dome in the east had been bombed. Those few defensive ships that took off from inside and made it out without being destroyed streaked south toward the attackers, and most were blasted from the air before even entering combat. One or two made it through, spiraling up and around as their laser cannons opened up. Explosions bloomed. Burning wrecks arced down to the planet's surface. It was only the skill of their pilots that kept them aloft, but the attacking force appeared to be far superior.

Lanoree already felt the acidic burn on her skin and tasted it at the back of her throat, and the destruction and deaths behind her weighed heavy. Her spine tingled. The back of her neck smarted as if the accusing dead stared.

"Ironholgs!"

The droid responded immediately. The ship was ready for take-off, the tracker was acquired and locked on. But Dal's ship was already breaking away from orbit, and soon he would be beyond the range of their instruments.

They reached the Peacemaker and boarded, and Lanoree did not feel as pleased, as safe, as she should have.

"Okay?" Lanoree asked.

"Perfect." Tre nodded, though he looked ready to vomit. His lekku hung pale and sickly, and his eyes and nose were running.

"Strap in," Lanoree said. "They'll probably see us lifting off and—"

Greenwood Station took three more direct impacts from plasma bombs. The blasts shook the Peacemaker, and Lanoree quickly fired the engines and took her ship aloft, afraid that the explosions might cause tremors or eruptions around the city. She flicked on all sensors, checked systems, initiated weapon systems, and only then took time to look toward the dome.

The ruptured dome was falling in great burning, melting sheets. The city inside had become a pit of molten chaos, and billowing pillars of smoke and flame rose high above it. The sparkling, expanding clouds from the plasma impacts bloomed outward; and when they met the rank atmosphere, they formed sickly rainbows that in other circumstances might even have looked beautiful.

Lanoree punched it. And even flying up and away from the dying city, the stark flashes of its demise lit up the interior of the Peacemaker's cockpit.

"All those people," Tre said, and Lanoree had never heard him sound so wretched. "We went there, and this is the result."

"It wasn't us," Lanoree said. "It was Dal."

"But if we hadn't chased him here—"

"If he's not stopped, this could happen everywhere!" she said. "It shows how determined he is. And how mad." She lowered her voice, almost talking to herself now. "There'll be no reasoning with him."

A chime on the control panel, and Lanoree groaned.

"What?" Tre asked.

"Company." On the scanner three sparks were following them, closing rapidly. Lanoree banked the ship steeply and accelerated, the hull shaking around them, groaning with the huge stresses she was placing it under. But she knew her ship as well as she knew herself—its breaking points, its capabilities.

Still the shapes closed on them.

"Fighters from Knool Tandor," Lanoree said.

"And now they have a Je'daii ship to add to their score sheet," Tre said.

"I'll draw them out of the atmosphere—the Peacemaker's better in space."

"I can shoot."

"You told me you'd never *been* in space!"

"Well, maybe once or twice. But I've fired land-based laser cannons a hundred times. I have a good eye."

"Top turret. Go."

Tre unclipped and scampered back into the living area, and Lanoree charged up the laser cannons.

"And put on the comlink so we can talk!" she shouted back at him. Strange. Right then, she was almost glad she had Tre here.

She saw the terrible irony in the situation. Dal had made Knool Tandor believe that Greenwood Station was in league with the Je'daii. Not only that, but some of that city's highest-standing residents might already have been assassinated by a Je'daii sword. And now here they were, in the midst of their attack on Greenwood Station . . . and a Je'daii was attempting to flee the planet, the Peacemaker ship giving her away. She had come here incognito but might be leaving the seeds of a wider war behind.

Right now, escape was her priority, and stopping Dal. Everything else could be smoothed over afterward.

A few moments later she heard the static and scratch of Tre turning on the comm headset in the top laser turret.

"Okay," he said. "Okay. We're fired up, I think I have this. Foot pedals to turn the turret, tracking screen, combat display, touch trigger."

"You damage my gun and I'll gut you!" Lanoree said.

"Yeah, yeah, Je'daii, you and which army?"

Lanoree laughed softly, always keeping her eyes on the closing targets. They had fanned out behind the Peacemaker and were approaching in a wide pincer. Soon the shooting would begin.

"Front cannons will be in my control," Lanoree said. "But I'll be busy flying this thing as well. You've got the best field of fire behind us, and you'll have visual."

"I've *got* visual."

"You see—?" Lanoree was cut off by the dull thuds of the upper turret's laser cannons firing. Eyes on the screen, she twitched the ship to the left and hit the boosters. Then she switched on the Peacemaker's deflector shields and kept one hand hovering over their control lever. She'd have to angle the shields in accordance with which direction the next attack was coming.

"Missed!" Tre shouted into her ears. She heard the gentle hum of the turret's motors working as Tre turned, and then the first ship streaked ahead of them.

They were still in the upper reaches of the atmosphere. Lanoree swung left, but heat flare glared across the windows, and she had to rely on scanners to keep tabs on the attacking Knool Tandor ships. They were fast and very maneuverable.

"Tre?"

"Can't see much—think I winged it."

Lanoree flicked a switch so that the targeting computer display sprang up before her. Even before locking on she let off a burst of fire, strafing across where the lead ship might fly. It twitched left and climbed.

She thrust forward with all the power the ship had, and the attackers fell back a little. But she knew hers would be a momentary lead; their ships would be at least as fast as the Peacemaker.

"Right," Tre muttered, and his cannon let off several sustained bursts. "Yes! One down, one down!"

"Good shooting," Lanoree said, but she was distracted. "Shift deflector shield to the rear, angle the ship out of the atmosphere, keep an eye on trajectories and the bright sparks of the two remaining ships." Still talking to herself even though Tre was there. For a moment she wondered what she'd have done if he *weren't* with her . . . but then everything would have been very different. It was through his contacts on Nox that she'd been able to find Dal.

The ship reached the highest extremes of Nox's polluted air, the stars speckling into view, and it was almost as if she felt it come alive in her hands. The Peacemaker was fine in atmospheres, but it was in the vacuum of space where it truly came into its own.

"We're away from Nox."

"Good, I can see again," Tre said.

"Grav units phasing in," Lanoree warned.

"Oh, great, there goes my stomach."

She grinned. "They're following."

"Didn't think they'd give up. You'd be a good prize."

"And you?"

"Oh, I don't think they'd worry about—"

The Peacemaker shook as a volley of shots smacked across its left flank.

"Where'd that come from?" Tre shouted.

"Two more from out of the sun."

"Yeah, but . . ." His laser fired again, and he was muttering all the time, words Lanoree could not quite make out. On the scanner she saw another ship flare briefly into a hail of smaller parts, then expand into a cloud, then fade away.

"Still three out there," she said. Another ship powered toward them . . . then disappeared. "I've lost it."

"Me, too."

"You can't see it?" she asked.

"No. Gone. Can't you Force-see it, or something?"

Lanoree ignored the quip and swung the ship sharply left and up, aiming for where she thought the ship might have gone. Climbing directly away from the Peacemaker and above them, it might for a moment have disappeared from her scanners, shielded by its exhaust and angle of climb. It was a good trick, but one Lanoree knew. She'd used it once or twice herself.

She saw the glimmer of starlight on metal before her scanner even picked it up. She closed her eyes and breathed deeply, comfortable in the Force. Then she looked again, past the grid lines of the targeting computer, past the pulsing lights and scrolling figures of laser preparedness, target distance, altitude and attitude. And when the time came, she touched the fire pad once.

A single shot streaked ahead of them, and eight kilometers away the ship flowered into a blazing bloom.

"Whoa," Tre said. "Good shot."

"Those last two are coming in fast," Lanoree said. "One port, one starboard."

"I'll take starboard."

The laser cannons thudded. Lanoree took the ship through a roll and then powered directly up and away from Nox. Gravity grasped the vessel as if sad to let go. The whole ship shook. She took manual control of the underside turret and swept it to port, watching the targeting grid on the left of her screen as the central four quadrants turned red. She fired several bursts, but already knew that she'd missed.

Tre shouted, "Look out, they're—" and then the whole ship shook as a plasma torpedo exploded half a kilometer away, ignited by the ship's shielding system. Lanoree let the blast tip the ship to starboard, knowing that fighting the effect would waste time and effort. Then she took control once again.

"Everything at that port ship," she said, opening fire. Tre's cannon thumped, and she saw the streaking trails of laser blasts converging in the distance.

On the scanner, the blooming star of destruction.

"Yes! One more down!" Tre said.

"The other's making a run for it," Lanoree said.

"Let's go! I'll put a shot into its afterburner."

Lanoree considered for a moment, then turned away from the fleeing ship. It was already thirteen kilometers away, the distance between them growing fast. "No time," she said. "And no point."

Tre was silent for a while, then she heard his sigh. Relief, perhaps. And gratitude that they were still alive.

"Stay up there awhile," Lanoree said. "They might have gotten a message off, could be we have more company."

"Yeah," Tre said.

Lanoree muted the comm. In truth, there would be no more company, because she'd blocked the fighters' communications as soon as she'd seen them. But she wanted to take a moment on her own, compose herself, submit herself to the Force and every soothing, empowering aspect it meant to her.

She breathed deeply and took a final look back down at Nox.

Even from this far out, the dying city of Greenwood Station was the largest, most obvious feature on the planet they were leaving behind.

CHAPTER FIFTEEN
RAN DAN'S FOLLY

Je'daii must know their limits. There are places we should not go, things we should not do, powers we should not seek. The Force has an incredible strength, but a Je'daii's true strength is in knowing when to use it, and when not.

—Master Shall Mar, "A Life in Balance," 7,541 TYA

She chases him across Talss, alone, without weapons or supplies or equipment, following his trail where she can find it, doing her best to sense his presence and direction when she cannot, and it is three days before she has an inkling of where he is heading.

Lanoree knows she should not have simply run. She should have waited for Dam-Powl, and now fears what the Je'daii Master will think of her. But she is confident that she will not be a suspect in Skott Yun's murder. And if she is, the time will come to put things right.

Lanoree is doing what she can to avoid losing her brother forever. Everything feels unreal, nightmarish. *Dalien is a murderer!* She has been made to grow up, and her world has changed forever.

Talss is a wild, sparsely populated land, and the farther south she goes, the more alien the landscape becomes. It is sometimes called the Dark Continent, and she is beginning to understand why. She descends from the hills onto a wide, endless plain, almost devoid of any plant growth over waist height. She wonders why for a while, and then half a day across the plain the first of the winds strikes. An initial gust steals Lanoree's breath and knocks her sideways, and she curls into a ball against a low rock as the most powerful wind she had ever known rips across the landscape. The tall, thin grasses that she has come to hate—her lower legs and hands are crisscrossed with cuts from the grasses' sharp tips and sheer edges—whip around her, lying almost flat across her body and yet weathering the storm. She feels the dribble of blood from fresh grass-cut wounds, and now lying down her face is lacerated as well. She struggles to breathe.

All the time she is trying to make herself as small as possible, and find as much shelter as she can behind the rock, she fears that Dal will continue walking through the storm.

She pushes for him, taking comfort in flowing with the Force. He is somewhere ahead, his mind a riot of confusion. It has been the same since leaving Anil Kesh, and Lanoree is not certain whether it is intentional. He knows her so well, knows how she will try to reach him. Perhaps this is his best defense.

Just before dusk the winds start to ease, and she stands and hurries on. She is thirsty, hungry, and cold. Frost sheens countless blades of grass, hardening them, forming a landscape of glimmering jewels for as far as she can see in every direction. It is beautiful and is like wading through a sea of blades.

Dal, stop, for me, she thinks, pushing the thought as hard as she can ahead of her. There is no telling whether he hears.

She has come to believe that the Old City might be his destination. *That's where the true Tythans lived*, he used to say. So little was known of the city and its former inhabitants that she could not argue, and he had built a romanticized view of those tumbled ruins, pyramids, and the unplumbed depths of its caverns and canals. Some say the Gree built the Old City and lived there for tens of millennia. Others postulate that the Gree merely borrowed the place for a while and that its true builders were lost forever to the mists of deep history. It is a mystery. And mysteries of the past are what Dal seeks.

The Old City lies in the southern regions of Talss, a wild, remote place called the Red Desert, frequented only by explorers and those desiring to leave civilization behind. It's said that blood spites stalk the nights and haunt the underground. It is rumored that they are half plant, half animal, untouchable by Je'daii talents, and that they feed on warm blood. She feels a frisson of fear when she thinks of it.

Once there, what will Dal do? She cannot know. Perhaps he doesn't know either, and in that doubt might be her one chance to win him back.

But he's a murderer.

She tries to ignore the thought. She will confront that fully when she finds him, and decide what to do then.

Confused, conflicted, Lanoree finally leaves the plains of slashing grass and chases her brother into the first rolling dunes of the Red Desert.

At dawn the next day, Lanoree shivers awake from a dream.

She is down in the darkness beneath the Red Desert. The weight of the Old City hangs around her, crushing her from all directions with its enigmatic history and a million untold tales. She is in a network of elaborate caverns, all of them illuminated by flickering firelight burning somewhere out of sight. The walls and ceilings are beautifully inlaid with pictograms of the timeless Gree, and though she is certain they tell of long-forgotten histories, she cannot perceive the true stories. It's as if even with the truth laid out before her, she can never understand what happened here.

And then the blood spites appear: soundless, deadly, batlike things the size of her head with clasping tendrils and dripping teeth. She has no hope of fighting them off. They circle her in the confined spaces, darting in and biting chunks from her face, her neck, her waving arms. She feels no pain, but her blood flows. She cries out for help.

Her brother watches from the shadows.

Lanoree sits up and stares at the wide, star-speckled sky. The dream is already fading, as most dreams do, and she recognizes the blood spites from the few times she has read about them and how she imagines them to be. She has never seen any holos or pictures. In her dream they are monsters, but the real beast merely watched.

It's a chilling sensation. As she rekindles her fire and looks for food and water, using survival skills taught to her by her parents from a young age, the idea of Dal as a monster does *not* fade. Her dream spills into waking hours. Or perhaps in dreams, she could merely see the truth.

She has only slept for a short time, and she hurries to pick up Dal's trail again. Trying to recall maps and legends of the Red Desert, she calculates that the Old City might be eighty kilometers farther to the south. And though she has lost Dal's physical trail, she is now certain that the ruin is his destination.

Lanoree has always been fit, and she starts to run out across the larger dunes and into the Red Desert. She runs for ten hours, pausing now and then in areas of ragged plant growth to dig for water. She overturns rocks and eats bugs and ants, and at one stage she scares some desert wraths from a recent kill. The meat is rich and tough, and she eats it raw.

The Red Desert is beautiful and daunting, barren and silent. It is a place that would inspire poets and madmen, and she does her best to remain inwardly focused as well as outwardly alert. It would be easy to lose oneself out here. Her sense of who she is remains firm, and there is a familiarity that gives her great comfort—the Force, strong in every sun-bleached rock and grain of sand.

Just before dusk, she sees the first ruin. It is a tumbled wall at the base of a gentle slope, little more than a pile of blocks half-buried by shifting desert sands. But it is obviously not a natural formation. And the cold chill the sighting provokes convinces her that she is almost there.

Lanoree climbs the slope, and toward its summit she sees footprints. Pausing, she looks around, but Dal is nowhere in sight. She places her hand, fingers splayed, across one boot print in the sand and closes her eyes. But the sands here are hot and ever moving and imbued with a timeless history the breadth of which startles her upright.

"Dal, we shouldn't be here." It is the first time she has spoken aloud since leaving Anil Kesh three days before. Nothing answers.

Reaching the top of the hill she emerges into the last of the day's sunlight once again. A kilometer to the west, the sun sinking into its ruin as if that place has always been its home, lie the sprawling remains of the Old City.

Wishing desperately that everything could be different, Lanoree walks toward it.

As she enters the shadow of the Old City's largest pyramid, the first blood spite attacks.

In the Peacemaker, pursuing Dal and his Stargazers past Malterra's orbit and toward Sunspot, Tre Sana was quieter than Lanoree had ever known him. But she did not question his silence. They had seen terrible things, witnessed a tragedy of shattering proportions. And though she knew of his past as a bad man, Tre's shock could not be feigned.

The tracker seemed to be working well, and Lanoree had plotted the projected course of Dal's ship three times. Each time the destination came out the same—Sunspot. And she thought she knew why. The incredible device had been built for the Stargazers by the scientists of Pan Deep, but to charge it with its driving force Dal had to visit Sunspot. The mines there were deep and incredibly dangerous, but the rewards for working there were great. Exotic elements that could be used for fuel or weapons. Crystals that sang with Force power. And perhaps, exposed to the correct technology, a touch of dark matter.

Dal's ship had an eight-million-kilometer head start. Lanoree had tried plotting a more direct course to Sunspot, but following Dal would be the fastest route. She had pushed her Peacemaker to its greatest speeds, aware that the modifications she had commissioned made it one of the fastest ships in the system. Yet Dal remained out of reach, matching her speed, forging the fastest route to meet Sunspot on its quick orbit of their star, Tythos.

Settled into their route, Lanoree initiated a contact with Master Dam-Powl. It took a while for the signal to be acknowledged, and a while longer for the chime of an incoming connection.

"Lanoree," Dam-Powl said, and even before the flatscreen snowed in to show her face, Lanoree knew that the Master knew.

"I can't believe he did it," Lanoree said, "just to cover his tracks. To make others think he was dead."

"Perhaps there's more to it than that," the Je'daii Master said. She looked tired and drawn, and Lanoree could only imagine the conversations she had been having with the Je'daii Council. The diplomatic fallout with Nox, the efforts to calm a volatile situation . . . but that was beyond Lanoree. She had to stay focused.

"What more?" she asked.

"He must have shared rare knowledge with Pan Deep for them to make his device. To ensure his uniqueness, he'd have to kill them all."

"But the whole of Greenwood Station?" Lanoree said. "It's monstrous."

"Not everyone died," Dam-Powl said. "Some transports got away before the final strike."

"How many were lost?" Lanoree asked quietly.

"So many that the numbers mean little." The Master sighed heavily, then she seemed to gather herself. "So. What progress have you made?"

"Dal and the Stargazers are traveling to Sunspot, I believe to arm the device. I have a trace on him and I'm following, but I'm hours behind."

"You can't get in range to destroy his ship?"

And kill my brother? Lanoree thought, but she could not share that thought. "No, Master. Whoever is funding his madness bought him quite a special ship. I can't read its signature, but it wouldn't surprise me to discover it's Je'daii."

"Stolen?"

"I can tell you more soon."

"Sunspot and Malterra approach each other in their orbits," Dam-Powl said, frowning. "You know what happens once those planets draw close. Magnetic interference, space storms. Any space travel in their region will be impossible."

"Then he's timed this to the heartbeat," Lanoree said. "He's planned *everything* in great detail. I'll have to catch him on Sunspot."

"Do anything you have to, Lanoree."

"Of course."

"Anything." The Master's gaze softened.

Lanoree did not reply for a moment, and the silence between them was loaded. Then she thought of that madness of Dal's that she had barely touched down in Pan Deep, and how all-consuming it had felt.

"Be strong, Lanoree. I know you are. But the responsibility is heavy, the price of failure might be unimaginable. So be *strong*. Experiences like this, such tragedies, can be what makes a good Je'daii great. May the Force go with you."

Lanoree nodded and broke the communication. She remained sitting in the cockpit for some time, thinking things through, saddened and afraid. And she surprised herself by finding comfort in Tre's presence.

Her Twi'lek companion came to sit in the seat beside her. The last time they'd traveled like this there had been a lightness to him, a protective bluster. No more. The silence was heavy, yet neither of them broke it. Lanoree checked the ship's systems and kept an eye on the scanner, always aware of him sitting silently alongside.

It was a long while after her communication with Dam-Powl that Tre spoke at last.

"I feel sick."

"As do I," she said. "Whatever Dal has become I can't believe he would—"

"No, I mean . . ." Tre trailed off and then vomited copiously between his feet. Ironholgs crackled in alarm, and Lanoree climbed from her seat and surveyed the mess. The ship's support systems sprang into overdrive, but the air filters could not work fast enough to swallow the stink.

"Oh," Lanoree said.

Tre was panting and wiping his mouth, sweating, shivering. "S-sorry."

"Nox," she said. "We breathed too much of its atmosphere."

"You?"

"I feel fine." *Do I?* she thought. She assessed herself and found nothing of concern, save her mixed emotions about Dal. But there were still two days' traveling until they reached Sunspot. If Tre sickened, there was nothing she could do but practice the medical skills she had learned at Mahara Kesh. And if he died, there was the air lock.

But *she* could not fall ill. She only hoped that Tre's sickness was a result of Nox's poisonous atmosphere, not something more insidious he might have caught. If at any point he appeared contagious, she might have to take action.

She looked away from Tre for a moment at the cockpit screens. The signal from Dal's ship was still on the tracker, still eight million kilometers ahead of them. She could not take any risks.

But she knew she could never throw Tre from the air lock alive.

"Use my cot to rest," she said. "I'll clean it up. Drink plenty of water."

Tre did not argue. He pushed past her, lay on her cot, and slept almost instantly.

Lanoree looked down at the vomit spread across the cockpit floor. "I wish you had arms," she said to Ironholgs. The droid grated something that sounded like a chuckle.

Over the next two days Tre did not grow any worse, but neither did he improve. He ate small amounts of food, but more often than not brought it back up. He drank plenty of water. Shivering and sweating in Lanoree's cot, his sleep was troubled, and his dream mumblings were incoherent and disturbing.

Lanoree spent most of the time in her cockpit seat, keeping track of Dal's ship and catching brief, uncomfortable naps. Her dreams were vague and unpleasant. She woke more than once with the idea that something was flapping silently about her head, slashing with barbed tendrils and seeking her blood.

And she had one dream where she watched from outside the system as Tython itself, and Tythos, and then every planet and moon that orbited it, was swallowed to nothing. Billions of lives and loves and dreams wiped out almost in the blink of an eye.

As they approached Sunspot at last, she accessed the ship's computers to remind herself about the damned place. She knew that environmentally it was even more unwelcoming and harsh than Nox. Her research reminded her how much so.

Sunspot was the first planet of the system. Its orbit sometimes took it as close as forty-eight million kilometers from Tythos. It was considered a solid planet, yet much of its surface was in constant turmoil, volcanoes and quakes changing its landscape almost from day to day. Its more settled areas were mainly at the poles, and it was here that the scattered mining communities were located. It was perhaps the harshest inhabited environment in the Tythan system, yet the rewards for the miners were huge. Most only lasted one or two seasons before leaving the planet and vowing never to return. Around 10 percent of those who went to Sunspot seeking their fortunes died there. It was a hungry planet, and though it gave, it also took as much as it could.

It was also a curiosity in the system, because it orbited counter to every other planet. There were those who speculated that it was a rogue planetoid, tumbled into Tythos's gravity well in the distant past. This raised some startling ramifications, and three thousand years ago there had been a series of exploratory missions visiting the planet, searching for any signs of previous habitation. But none had ever been found: no trace of civilizations, no ruins, no evidence that any sort of life had ever flourished there. Sunspot was a dead planet that breathed the white-hot breath of molten rock, and the rest of the system regarded it merely as a resource.

Even approaching Sunspot's dark side, the violence of its surface was obvious. It radiated a steady glow from a fine network of volcano ranges and magma lakes and rivers, and the shadows of noxious gas clouds the size of a continent filtered the light, turning it an almost attractive pinkish hue.

"Southern pole," Lanoree said. Dal's ship had slowed considerably and was entering the atmosphere, swinging around to approach Sunspot's south pole from the planet's dark side. She had already calculated a similar path, and the Peacemaker's computer was taking them in.

There was a possibility that Lanoree could even close the gap between them and shoot Dal down before he landed. Her customized laser cannons were powerful and accurate, and the Peacemaker carried four drone missiles that were effective at eight hundred thousand kilometers. But if she missed, he would be alerted to her presence.

Yes, that was why she didn't open fire. The advantage of surprise. She convinced herself of this as she made ready to take to the surface, and Tre watched her every move.

"I wish I could come with you," he said for the tenth time.

"No, you don't," Lanoree said.

"True. I don't. You take me to the nicest places."

"Says the Twi'lek who took me to the Pits."

Tre watched as Lanoree prepared herself. She changed her clothing, and lacking her lost sword, she plucked a spare sword from a cabinet beneath her cot. It was the weapon she had trained with before Master Tem Madog had forged her own. She hefted it in her hands, swung it several times, and remembered its weight. It was a surprising comfort.

"It becomes you," Tre said.

"It'll have to do." She sheathed the sword—the screech lizard sheath remained at her hip—and knelt by the cot again. She removed two blasters from the cabinet and slipped them into her belt. Tre watched, eyebrows raised. Lanoree only shrugged.

A chime from the cockpit signaled that their descent had begun. She felt the familiar shifting in her stomach as they entered the atmosphere and the Peacemaker's grav units faded out, and she watched Tre, wondering if he'd vomit again. But he held himself together.

She indicated that he should strap himself in, then sat next to him on the cot.

"You don't want to land the ship yourself?" he asked.

"I will. Once we're close to the surface. But Tre"—she squeezed his shoulder—"I'm leaving you in my Peacemaker. My ship. This is my home, and I'm trusting you to treat it well."

"I'll guard it," he said.

"Ironholgs can do that, and the ship has its own defenses. Just . . . don't touch anything. Anything!"

"Trust me," he said, smiling. His eyes were watery and weak, his skin pale, lekku limp.

"I have to," she said.

The Peacemaker rocked and kicked as it sliced down into Sunspot's violent atmosphere. Lights glowed, warnings chimed from the control panels, and the screens darkened as heat burned across the hull.

Lanoree climbed into her flight seat, taking control of the ship. She checked the scanner, uploaded a terrain map onto another screen, and accessed the ship's computer to download as much information as she could find about the area.

Dal and his Stargazers had landed at a small mining outpost called Ran Dan's Folly. According to her records the mine worked a deep source of petonium and marionium, both elements used to power ships' drives and that could also be weaponized. The mine had been in existence for almost a hundred years, and there seemed to be nothing spectacular about it that set it aside from any other Sunspot business concern. A tragedy thirty years ago in which a hundred miners lost their lives. A strike eighteen years ago that led to violent riots and an eventual buyout by the workforce and their families off planet. Shipping and trade deals with parties on at least three planets, including Tython. If Ran Dan's Folly was a source of dark matter, nothing had ever been noticed, and no one knew.

No one but Dal.

Lanoree experienced a brief, chilling fear that her brother had found the tracking device she'd planted on him and placed it on another ship. She'd followed for three days, and all the while he had been heading for Tython. Perhaps he had a supply of dark matter already sourced and waiting to be implanted in the device. Maybe even now he was on Tython, down in the Old City, going deeper than anyone had ever been and readying to activate the hypergate. Any moment now . . .

"If it's even there," she muttered. She was still unsure. In all this, the hypergate's existence was the one nebulous factor. But whether it existed or not, the danger was just as pressing.

"This is Dal," she said, watching the scanner as it tracked his ship until it landed. The red spot became blue as it fell motionless, and Lanoree dipped the Peacemaker to the south so that she could approach Ran Dan's Folly over a blazing rift in the planet's surface. She needed as much cover as possible.

She also needed a plan.

But time was short. Malterra and Sunspot grew closer. Dal was still one step ahead.

She would have to make this up as she went along.

Lanoree crouched behind a rock, looking at the mine and the haphazard collection of buildings around it, and wondered how anyone could live there. The minehead itself was at the base of a slope of shale and tumbled rocks, encased in a rickety steel structure with two giant lifting cranes protruding through the roof. The surrounding buildings were low, built almost entirely from rock, and connected by chains, presumably for navigation between buildings during the terrible storms that swept the area. There were no windows. Three heavily armored land cruisers were parked close against the buildings' walls, and the wrecks of several more were scattered around the area, slowly corroding into the sterile ground.

Further along the low valley were three landing pads for whatever freighters and other craft could be used in such an atmosphere. Dal's ship rested on one of these pads, and Lanoree knew now why she had not been able to run him down. His ship was a Deathblaster, and one that had seen action, perhaps even during the Despot War. A great swath of its left flank was scorched black, and areas of the hull had obviously been replaced and repaired judging by their color and styling differences. It was a mean-looking craft, sister ship to the renowned Deathstalkers, except large enough to carry a payload of bombs, equipment, or passengers. They were even rarer than Deathstalkers now—many had been destroyed during the Despot War; many more dismantled afterward by the Je'daii; and those that survived were usually in the hands of mercenaries, Shikaakwa warlords, or at remote criminal settlements out on some of Mawr's moons. From the speeds Dal's ship had attained, there was a good chance that it had been customized.

She checked the area one more time from behind the rock pile, then ran at a crouch toward the Deathblaster. She kept to the shadows, knowing that Dal would have left some of his Stargazers preparing the ship for a rapid escape. Probing out gently, she sensed two minds, their thoughts untroubled. The Stargazers were excited; their plans were coming to fruition. She wondered what Dal would say if he knew how much they had lowered their guard.

The moment begged for action, not diplomacy. And though disabling them would have been her preference, Lanoree could not risk even the slightest chance of these two coming around while she was down in the mine. Before she moved, she sought comfort in the Force for what she was about to do. *Desperate measures for desperate times,* she thought. And she remembered how so many had died in agony on Nox.

Close to the ship's still-hot engines, the Iktotchi woman didn't know what had hit her as Lanoree's sword parted her head from her shoulders and severed the long, distinctive horns. She darted up the ramp into the ship, where the second Stargazer stood comically motionless, head cocked at the strange sound of steel cleaving flesh he'd heard from outside.

"Don't—" he said, and Lanoree stabbed him through the heart. He was dead before he slumped to the deck.

She glanced around the ship's hold. Empty, and now deserted but for the dead. She ran back down the ramp and headed for the mine. The blazing air burned her lungs, and she knew she should have donned a protective suit and breathing apparatus. But she did not want her movement and senses impeded in any way, and soon she would be belowground.

At the main mine building she paused and crouched down, peering inside through cracks in the old, dilapidated structure. There was no movement, and she sensed no one inside.

She heard an explosion in the distance. Startled, she turned and raised her sword. Kilometers away, beyond a low rise to the north, the sky glowed with the huge, pulsing fires of an active volcano. Clouds of smoke and ash billowed kilometers high, lit from within by wild electrical storms. Deadly lava bombs arced through the air. The ground rumbled as if from fear.

Inside the enclosure she approached the two elevators that provided access into the mine. Both were still, shaft doors open, but only one of the cages had descended. If she activated the other, she would alert anyone below.

She looked into the dark, empty elevator shaft. It was a long way to fall.

Sheathing her sword, Lanoree delved into her utility belt and brought out three short lengths of thin, strong rope. She tied two together and formed a harness beneath her arms and around her wrists. Then she clasped the end of the third length tightly in her left hand and, without giving herself time to consider the madness of what she was doing, she leaped, swinging the rope around one of the taut elevator cables, catching the other end, bracing her feet against the steel cable and pulling tight. She shook for a moment as she found her balance, and the air was filled with a gentle hum as the cable vibrated from the impact.

Starting to slide down, she tested the strength of her boots dragging against the cable, only hoping the strong leather would not be burned through by friction in the descent. That would hurt.

She sped up. Darkness whisked by. She probed outward with her Force sense and felt the open space around her, the shaft square and braced at regular intervals with heavy steel props.

Faster than she'd expected the bottom rose toward her, and she pulled at the ropes and pressed her feet hard against the cable to slow down. She misjudged slightly and struck the elevator cage's roof hard, driving the wind from her lungs and causing a clanging thud that would have been heard by anyone nearby. But there was no reaction, no shout of alarm. After she'd gathered her breath, Lanoree lowered herself down between the elevator car and the shaft's wall.

At first glance the mine reminded her of the tunnels beneath Greenwood Station's central tower. There were occasional, flickering lights along the narrow corridor leading in two directions, and the walls and ceiling were roughly formed. But it was *hot*. Heat simmered from somewhere down below, the floor sizzled her worn boots, and a faint glow seemed to flood into the corridor far away to the left.

She sensed something moving rapidly toward her along the corridor. Holding her old practice sword before her, Lanoree was struck by the gust of hot air and thrown to the ground. She rolled to one side and tried to catch her breath, but the fearsome wind stole it away. The scorching blast—the result of drastic temperature differentials, perhaps—simmered her clothing and stretched her skin. She squeezed her eyes tightly shut.

Sunspot was trying to bake her alive.

The hot wind growled against the walls and then faded away, and Lanoree took a deep breath.

She smelled sweat.

Opening her eyes, trying to stand, she sensed the heavy rock swinging for her head, gathered all her Force talents to deflect the injury, but she was far too late.

A brief pain, and then darkness fell.

CHAPTER SIXTEEN
THE ALCHEMY OF FLESH

A Je'daii needs darkness and light, shadow and illumination, because without the two there can be no balance. Veer to Bogan, and Ashla feels too constraining, too pure; edge toward Ashla, and Bogan becomes a monstrous myth. A Je'daii without balance between both is no Je'daii at all. He, or she, is simply lost.

—Master Shall Mar, "A Life in Balance," 7,537 TYA

The blood spite is a shadow with teeth. It trails long tendrils around her that, though thin and easy to break, constrain her. She plucks and kicks at them, and the smell and taste when they snap reminds her of the grassy plains at Bodhi Temple, long summer afternoons, evenings of music and talk with her family. The thing's body darts in again and again, carried on feathery wings that make no noise at all as they beat at the dusky air. Lanoree sends a clumsy Force punch and the spite reels. Its tendrils flail and teeth clack at nothing.

Its teeth are its hardest point. Wings, tendrils, body, all are light and airy, giving it the feel of a fancy or memory more than a living thing. Its teeth give it form.

The spite attacks again. Lanoree feels warm fluid spatter across her neck, and she's not sure whether it's the spite's sap or her own blood. Her moment of panic abates. She is without weapons, but never without the Force. And while this being's strange nature might make it immune to any mental assault, Lanoree has studied at Stav Kesh.

She clenches her fist, gathers a Force punch, and heaves it toward the spite.

It is flung back with such speed and power that many of its fine limbs are torn off, drifting to the ground and catching the setting sun. The body drops and squirms for a moment before growing still. Lanoree examines her wounds. The bleeding is not too bad.

Having no wish to wait for more blood spites, she hurries toward the pyramid.

And there is a power here. She is awed by the city, and aware of its deep history, but what she starts to feel is something beyond or apart from that. It is nothing physical—no throbbing in the ground, no charge to the air—but still she is flooded with a feeling of such coiled potential that her teeth grind, her heart thuds. It is the most delicious fear.

Nothing will deter her. She follows Dal's trail, the only human prints visible on the wind-driven sand and dust. And when his trail disappears for a time she continues anyway, instinct guiding her onward. She has entered something of a dream zone. This is Tython, but she no longer knows when. This is home, but she has never felt so far away. The power she feels below and around her is divorced from the Force; and though she asks that strong, protective energy that is always within her, she finds no answers.

I'm being repulsed by this place, she thinks. Sadly, she is not surprised that Dal is drawn here.

The ruins are so ancient that most of them are long buried by the effects of time or worn down by wind and sand, rain and sun. But here and there among these small hills and shallow valleys are the tips of pyramids, the slouch of fallen walls, or the deep hollows of openings into the ground.

These dark pits yawn and seem to exhale the strange energy she feels. And it is into one of these pits that Dal's footprints lead.

Before she can consider the folly of her actions, Lanoree goes down.

* * *

The small glow rod she always carries gives a gentle but consistent light, but in a way she wishes she could not see.

The alienness of this place strikes at her. Everywhere else she has been on Tython has been created by and for those sentients who inhabit the planet now—humans and Wookiee, Twi'lek and Cathar, many others. Their appearances might be different, but their basic physiologies are the same. The Cathars are relatively short and the Wookiees usually taller than most, but there is a similarity to their features that makes the places they live and work comfortable for all.

These ruins are different. Lanoree drops several levels that she eventually realizes are huge steps, as though built for giants. A passageway she moves along is tall and wide. The very air she breathes—still and stale, old and loaded with the dust of ages—seems suited more to something *else*. She shivers as if watched, but knows that it is only the depth of history that observes.

But she is not the first to come down here.

Dal's footprints draw her onward, pressed into the dust. They are far apart and deep, as if he is running, and she wonders how he can find his way down here and what light illuminates his path.

That crushing energy seems to throb through the passageways like a pulse through the veins of a giant, sleeping creature. It is a discomforting image that Lanoree cannot shake, yet she knows it is foolish. The Old City is just that . . . an old city. Archaeologists have been here. Historians. Some have been, seen, and left again, intrigued but not possessed. Others have spent their lives researching this place. A few have never been seen again, and there are stories of such depths . . .

But she wonders whether any of them have ever felt this terrible, pulsing potential, and what they thought of it.

"Dal!" she calls, surprising herself. Her voice echoes from walls and ceiling, fading into the distance yet seeming to persist far longer than she could have believed. Later, descending another giant staircase, she thinks she can still hear her brother's name traveling through the darkness. Or perhaps it is simply a memory.

* * *

Deeper. She starts to wonder what walked these passageways millennia before, and tries not to. So little is known of the Gree, if indeed this was originally a Gree structure. Legend has it that they possessed amazing, arcane technologies that allowed travel among the stars. That they were a nomadic species, exploring the galaxy for unknown ends. There were rumors of Gree sculptures somewhere in the Old City. But some believe the expedition that supposedly found them fabricated them.

Sometimes Dal's footprints fade in areas where the floor has seemingly been blown free of dust, perhaps by underground storms. Power surges as that incredible energy breaks free, maybe once each year, or once in a lifetime. So much is unknown, but Lanoree's attention is fixed. Her intention *is* known. Dal needs saving from himself, and she will strive for this as long as she can.

Lanoree loses track of time. She thinks perhaps a day has passed since she left the surface and ventured down here. She is worried about finding her way back out, but there are footprints—both hers and Dal's now—and there is the Force. It is a comfort to her, and the only reason she can stay her course.

She's hungry and thirsty. Water runs down the walls in places, but she cannot bring herself to touch or drink it. She has no idea where it has come from or what, over many centuries, it has been filtered through. There must be countless places that time has forever hidden from view, and countless things that will never be known.

She starts calling after Dal more and more. The echoes of her shouts seem to argue, and sometimes she thinks she can hear choirs of Lanorees imploring her brother to return, to turn around, to come to her and home. Lanoree thinks she is hallucinating but can't be sure.

The ruins are so old that nowhere is untouched by time's finger—sometimes they are ravaged, sometimes merely stroked by a reminder that entropy cannot be denied. She passes along large passageways with smaller tunnels leading off, and sometimes by alcoves in the walls that might once have been doorways but that have long since been closed off. These smaller tunnels offer tantalizing and terrifying possibilities, but Lanoree will not be shaken from her course. This is not an exploration, it is a rescue. There are much larger caverns—almost hallways—with strangely shaped pits in the floor that might once have held water, and upright structures with the remains of metal shapes. Perhaps this is technology, rotted away over time.

She feels she is closing on Dal.

A metal bridge spans a deep, dark ravine, from the depths of which flows a warm breath. The bridge groans as she crosses it. The darkness beckons. It smells of dusty bone and wet fur, and Lanoree crosses the last third of the bridge at a run.

Beyond is another large cavern where ranked levels all around look much like seating areas, and a central dais bears the remains of several upright mechanical objects. Lanoree pauses to catch her breath.

In the distance she hears a scream.

Lanoree was being dragged. Voices sounded, urgent and angry, making no effort to hide. She felt heat on her body as they threw her down. She rolled onto her side, feeling for wounds. But there were only the bumps and bruises she was already familiar with, and a few more besides. She still wore her weapons and wrist unit. They hadn't even bothered disarming her. Either they were clumsy, or they no longer viewed her as a threat.

Hit on the head again, she thought. Master Kin'ade would be disgusted. She tried to see away some of the pain, losing it to the Force, and a calm numbness descended.

"I'm almost done. I'll let you watch."

Dal! But he was dead, wasn't he? She'd come down here looking for him and found—

But, no, that was another place, another time. That was in the past.

Lanoree opened her eyes and gathered herself, sitting up, hugging her knees to her chest.

The air in the mine shivered with heat. Several humans, growth stunted and dressed in reflective clothing and visored helmets, fussed around some mining equipment. Dal stood close to her, blaster in his hand aimed in her direction, and five Stargazers accompanied him. They were faceless to her, followers of his madness. It was Dal who held her attention.

"You left me for dead," she croaked. Her throat felt dry and swollen, her tongue like a rock in her mouth.

"Yes, left you. I can't make that mistake again."

Woozy, weak, Lanoree tried to touch his mind.

Dal pointed the blaster at her face, his lips pressed tight, whole body tensed. She could Force-shove him aside, and perhaps she'd be able to get to her feet before the other Stargazers shot her. Maybe, somehow, she could distract them all. Perhaps, like Master Tave, she could lose herself in the Force, become unseen by them for long enough to disarm and defeat them.

But she thought not.

"So shoot me," she said to her brother. As she spoke her mind was deluged with a flood of memories of their childhood, their dear mother and father, and the good times that were all now past. She was sad but incredibly angry as well.

"You and your Force—"

"Enough with the talk, Dal! Just shoot me and get it over with!"

"You've come this far," he said, smiling. "Don't you want to see my second-greatest moment?"

"Second?"

"The greatest is yet to come." He nodded past the mining equipment at where the device rested on the ground, exposed now, the Stargazers standing at a respectful distance. It was surprisingly plain: a round metal shell, several connecting ports around its circumference. It did not look amazing.

The miners were checking display screens and working the machinery, and though it ran with barely a whisper, Lanoree wondered whether the deep rumbling she felt was caused by what they did here.

"No," she said. "I'm bored. You're going to kill me, so why not now instead of later? Brother." She spat the last word, hoping for a reaction. But his gentle smile remained. She was trying to goad him into action, hoping that before he pulled the trigger there would be a moment of hesitation, an instant of regret and doubt of which she could take advantage.

But Dal was in charge here. Lanoree felt the flow of the Force and knew that she was just as powerful and rich in it as ever, but her sick, mad bother was still in control.

"There," a miner said. The machinery before him vibrated slightly and then grew still, and a square metal box rose from a hole in the floor of the mine. Lanoree had seen this before in holos and knew what it was—a marionium cube, bearing one of the most unstable yet desirable elements found in Sunspot's mine.

But what of the dark matter? Was everything she had seen, heard, learned wrong?

"In the device," Dal said. "You know what to do."

Three Stargazers stepped forward and lifted the cube, moving it toward the device.

Lanoree thought of Force-shoving them against it, but she didn't know what effect that might have. They were dealing with arcane, ancient technology, and she remembered her journey down into the Old City nine years before, the power she had sensed there, the fear it had instilled.

I have to stop them! she thought. *But I can't risk triggering the device.* Stuck between the two, she felt the gravity of both possibilities tearing at her.

"No," she said as the Stargazers slid aside a panel. The insertion was simple. The marionium glowed softly as they tipped it into Dal's device, and then they closed the panel and stood back.

"So what will it—?" one of the miners asked. He did not finish his question.

The device finished it for him. It started to turn.

Dal gasped, and Lanoree realized with dreadful certainty that he really had very little idea what he was doing. He was following old plans, chasing a childhood dream. He was running blind.

She tensed, readying to act whether it meant her death or not. Because this could not happen.

There was a soft grinding noise as the device turned on the gravelly ground. Then it rose and hung in midair, spinning faster and faster until it seemed to fade from view, return, fade again. Lanoree felt suddenly sick. It was a physiological reaction to something very wrong.

"Oh, Dal, you don't know what you're—"

The Force itself recoiled. Lanoree fell onto all fours and vomited, and she felt a *flexing* of the Force, like the natural reaction of a person wincing away from fire. For a flicker, the Force was absent from that mine, and in its place was only the device, still spinning and fading in and out of existence.

And then the thing slowed to a halt in midair, exuding such a sense of malignant power and unfathomable energy that Lanoree vomited again.

Weak, head spinning, she looked up at the others around her. The miners were on the ground, holding their heads. But the Stargazers were jubilant, and Dal was the happiest of all.

"It worked," he breathed, awed and delighted. "It worked! We've done it! It's ready, now. It's made its own dark matter and it's ready—and, oh, Lanoree, I so wish you could travel with me."

She wasn't certain whether that was a veiled plea, and she did not try to see. She didn't care. "You've become a madman and a monster, Dal. My only aim is to bring you down."

"Then this is the end for you," he said softly. Elation quickly fading, he aimed the blaster at Lanoree's chest and pulled the trigger.

Lanoree runs, drawn by the cries, knowing she should be running *from* them because they are so terrible. But she has come down into the Old City to save her brother, and now she fears she is too late.

She finds his clothes close to an underground lake. They are shredded and wet. She sniffs the blood. It smells like family.

The surface of the lake shimmers as ripples calm to nothing.

Without caring what might hear, Lanoree screams her grief at the darkness. She sinks to her knees and gathers the clothes to her chest, and even while Dal's spilled blood is still warm, his sister starts to mourn.

CHAPTER SEVENTEEN
REPULSION

Immersion in the dark side of the Force can seem stronger, more freeing, more triumphant than existing within balance. But only from the outside. Do not be tempted. Those who are swallowed by the darkness lose not only balance and control. They lose their souls.
—Master Shall Mar, "A Life in Balance," 7,541 TYA

At the last moment she grasped the Force with everything she had and brought it before her.

Then there was darkness.

In her dreams she chases Dal through the Old City forever. He is always only just ahead of her—a whisper around a corner, a laugh in the next ancient cavern, and on the surface his shadow is just out of reach behind walls or around the sides of dunes. One step ahead, however fast she runs, however slow she walks. But she has no sense that he is teasing her. There's a repulsion between them, and as she moves toward Dal, he moves away from her. Perhaps that repulsion has always been there, even from when they were children. She remembers many times playing together, but now it also seems to her that those times were shadowed by the knowledge of Dal's growing wanderlust and his resentment of his family; and her childhood self was able to ignore these aspects of him. She sees his child's expression with adult eyes, and knows what will come.

"I feel terrible," the voice said, "but you look worse. Can you open your eyes? Open your eyes. Please, Lanoree." Lanoree tried, but her eyelids were too heavy, her head throbbing and expanding to squeeze them closed.

"Squeeze my hand if you can hear me." She tried to squeeze and a white-hot sun of pain exploded in her chest and across her torso, stabbing into her neck, jaw, and skull. She tried to scream, but taking in a deep breath only ignited the pain even more.

"Okay, lie still and . . ." The voice faded, and Lanoree felt herself falling. The depths below her were dark and filled with malignancy. They might have been in the Gree caverns and halls beneath the surface remnants of the Old City, the stinking sewers of Greenwood Station, or the blazing mines on Sunspot. Where she was did not matter. The darkness promised death.

She swam in the dark, but had no strength to stop her fall.

She was moving. Heat buffeted her from all sides. The stink of burning overrode everything else—an old, deep-set burning, molten rock and singed eons. *I'm still in the mines*, she thought, and she tried to open her eyes.

Whatever she was lying on struck something and jarred her, and she screamed at the pain that surged through her veins like acid. She tried using the Force to smother some of the agony, but it was only partially successful. Movement ceased and a shadow appeared above her.

"Lanoree?"

She saw Tre Sana's outline as he bent over her, his lekku silhouetted against the soft red glow of their surroundings. *What's happening?* she wanted to ask. *Is the mine on fire, is Dal destroying everything behind*

him again, have they taken the Peacemaker . . . what are you doing here?
But all that emerged from her mouth was a deep groan.

"I'm getting you out," he said. "Ironholgs is pulling. What did you
do to him? He's not like any droid I've ever . . ."

Senses fading again, Lanoree tried her best to hang on. But she
knew that she was gravely wounded. She felt hollowed out, and wondered how much of a hole Dal had blown in her with his blaster.

Dal, her brother, with his blaster . . .

This time when she fell the Force was there to catch her, and
through agony she had a moment of ecstasy as she felt it surround and
flow through her.

The roof of the mine was on fire. Tre must have dragged her into a
huge open chamber belowground, though she could not remember
moving through any on her way down. The high ceiling was a splash
of red and orange, yellow and white, swirling so slowly in boiling flame
that she could make out shapes and features. Some civilizations worshipped fire, and now she knew why.

But if they didn't move soon, they would be consumed.

"Almost at the ship," Tre's voice said. "Lanoree . . . you awake?
We're almost at the ship. And for shak's sake I'm going to need you,
then."

Almost at the ship? she thought. Then she realized what she was
seeing, and for a moment the all-encompassing pain was swallowed by
a creeping, prickling fear crawling from her mind and across her whole
body.

They were on Sunspot's surface heading for the Peacemaker, and
the planet's sky was ablaze.

Given context, the sheer size and scope of the scene above her
made more sense. The air itself appeared to have been ignited, and
great swaths of flame rolled in random directions, exploding against
one another in cataclysmic impacts. Lightning arced across her vision,
purple streaks parting into thousands of white-hot forks. Sheets of
lightning waved. Even greater explosions boomed deep within the
fiery atmosphere, billowing outward in gouts that must have been ten
kilometers in diameter.

"Malterra . . ." Lanoree whispered, and Tre's shadow closed on her, lekku twitching frantically.

"What?"

"The other planet . . . Malterra . . . draws close."

"You're telling me." He stood again and continued pushing. From somewhere she could not see, Ironholgs clattered and clicked, and she heard the rapid padding steps of the droid's feet as it helped transport Lanoree back to her ship.

Whose choice was it to come? she thought. But she knew right away. However much personality she projected onto Ironholgs, it was still just a droid. It would have taken a person to make the decision to venture out in this heat and chaos. Tre had come for her . . . and she had no idea how long it had been.

"Tre."

"Not now. Almost there."

"Tre!" She groaned as waves of pain radiated from her chest. But the stretcher stopped again, and he bent down so he could hear her above the lightning and fiery roars. "How long . . . ?"

"Almost half a day," he said. "On the scanners I saw the other ship take off, and when you didn't come back . . ." His lekku shrugged.

"Oh, no . . ."

"Lanoree . . . you've got a hole in you the size of my fist. I've no idea how you're still alive. So shut up while I get you back to the Peacemaker, and then . . ." He started pushing again, and she felt suddenly bad for him. He had no idea what to do.

But she did.

She remained silent, floating in a sea of pain as Tre finally reached the Peacemaker and pushed her inside.

As the door hissed shut, Tre struggled to shift her from the makeshift stretcher to her cot. She was hardly any help. She rested her head to one side and examined the stretcher, and she was filled with admiration. It was a door from one of the mine's elevator cages, one side ragged from where it had been removed from its mount, and at one end was fixed one of Ironholgs's suspension units. It seemed to be smoking a little, ready to expire.

Lanoree lifted her hand. "Tre. Here."

He sat next to her on the cot, sweating, exhausted. She remembered how sick he had been when she'd last seen him. Such a short time ago, but already he looked thinner than she remembered, and older.

"Take my hand," she said. Speaking sent pain lancing through her chest, but some things needed to be said.

He did so, breathing heavily.

"Thank you." She squeezed his hand and nodded, grimacing at another wave of agony but never breaking eye contact with him. "And now . . . you have to . . . trust me."

Tre's expression barely changed as she instructed him which cabinet to open and what to bring out. Even when he saw *what* he brought out, he seemed almost unmoved. Perhaps he had seen more of what Master Dam-Powl could do than Lanoree had first suspected.

"Now help me sit up," she said. "I don't have very long."

In that room long ago with Master Dam-Powl, before the tragedy with Dal and while Lanoree was still wide-eyed with wonder and potential, the lessons she learned had felt amazing.

Your future lies in the alchemy of flesh, Dam-Powl had said. I saw it in you the moment we met, and nothing has dissuaded me from that. It is a talent, for some, that lies on the edges of acceptability. It is a strong, challenging power, and you must be firmly balanced to attempt it. You must not let heavier desires tempt you. The dark side lurks close to what I do here, Lanoree, and I am always vigilant. Don't be tempted. Don't be drawn. Maintain your balance.

The words had always remained with her. Remembering them now Lanoree did as instructed, but there was too much pain, too much pressure. Her mind wanted to find balance in the Force, but her heart forged onward. Dal would not wait for her to be ready. Every moment she wasted here brought them all closer to tragedy.

"You might want to turn away," she told Tre. But Tre only shook his head and sat in the corner of the cabin, eyes half-closed. After she had saved herself, she'd do what she could for him.

The experiment was as she had left it. Traveling alone, she had long spells when she could concentrate on perfecting such alchemies, and though she was still young, she knew that her talent was great. Proof of that lay before her now. She lifted the cover and the flesh throbbed. Blood dribbled from imperfect yet adequate veins. Vestigial limbs waved weakly and without purpose. At one edge a blind eye opened, pupil milky white. Even if it did see, there was no mind to understand.

The iris had her coloring because it was a part of her.

The life that animated this flesh was formed by Lanoree and drawn from the Force. Over time she had molded the single collection of cells—taken from her own arm, a splash of blood, and marrow—into this, an object with a form of life that was all her own. Its movement still troubled her, as did its partial familiarity. But where there was no brain, there was no mind, and without a mind it was meat. That was all. Living, pulsing, replicating meat. She continued to tell herself that even as she wondered whether it felt pain.

The power she sometimes experienced as she molded flesh to her own desires was shocking, but right now she found meaning in her experiments at last. *It's not just alchemy,* Dam-Powl had told her. *It's not just learning the art for the sake of it. It's practicing to be the artist.*

Lanoree gathered herself, resting her hands on either side of the experiment's small pedestal. Her wound was deep and wide, its edges weeping and its depth burning. But at the moment Dal had tried to kill her, she had gathered herself behind the Force, and it had swallowed much of the impact. If she hadn't done that—an instant, an instinctive action—her heart and lungs would have been blasted across the mine's floor. Her brother believed her dead. At least she had given herself a chance.

She breathed deeply and welcomed the Force flowing through her. Closed her eyes. Shut away the pain that threatened to make her sick, the tiredness that lured her down to sleep, and death. The Force grew stronger in her, tingling in her fingertips and toes, her neck, her wounded chest, and she directed it into her experiment.

The alchemy came alive within her. It was a burning star with a dark heart. *That, I have to watch,* she thought, but agonies swept through her, distracting her. The power was wonderful. She smiled.

The flesh before her started to bubble and boil, and without opening her eyes she stripped off her tattered robe and undergarments and leaned forward.

The smell of burning flesh filled the Peacemaker.

She heard a pitiful whine from Tre but did not look. If he was afraid, he could cover his eyes.

Bogan loomed and she opened her mind's eye to embrace its darkened surface, and at the same time she felt a warm, wet touch between her breasts. It caressed the angry wound and numbed. Lanoree welcomed the contact and sought more, leaning farther forward until she was directly over the pedestal of flesh. *My flesh, my experiment, my very own alchemy of self.*

She sought and found Ashla, a bright spark within the Force. And experiencing herself in balance, the talents she had been made aware of at Anil Kesh, and which she had been practicing for so long, began to flow.

Flesh flowed with them.

Bogan is in her dreams. She was there before becoming a Ranger, but only briefly in the company of others. A visit, an education. And in her memory Ashla was always a constant light that drew her away from darkness.

But in these dreams there *is* no Ashla. She stands on a hillside on Bogan, beside the ruins of stone buildings thousands of years old, looking up at another Bogan staring down. Two moons, both of them dark. No hope of light.

Lanoree sprang awake and sat up, clutching her hands to her chest. She was on her cot, still naked but with a thin sheet gathered around her waist. Ironholgs clacked. Tre sat slumped in the corner, head to one side and eyes barely open.

"The sleeper wakes," he said weakly, and he looked very sick.

Beside her cot, on the floor between her and Tre, was the experiment. It was withered and dry now, the petrified remnants of something long dead. Even the blood that had dripped onto its base was dark, dry, and flaked, as if it had fallen long ago.

She looked down at the wound in her chest and took in a deep, startled breath. Her skin was rough and scarred, and there was a definite depression in her chest. But the blaster hole had vanished. She closed her eyes and breathed deeply, twisting to the left and right, and felt no pain inside. Nothing out of place. Nothing missing.

"You look better," Tre said.

"You look worse." Lanoree stood from the cot and quickly snatched up her clothes, pulling them on, then knelt beside Tre, resting one hand against his cheek.

"I think whatever poisoned me on Nox has reached somewhere vital," he said. "My heart staggers. My breathing . . . light." His lekku were limp and pale, and she had never seen his red skin so wan.

"I can help you," she said, but then she frowned. *That withered thing, dry and old . . . there's nothing left.* "Not how I helped myself, but I can use the Force to cleanse your blood, perhaps. To purge you."

"No time," Tre said. "I'll be fine . . . had worse . . . no time."

And Lanoree knew that he was right. There *was* no time, and perhaps even now they were too late. Dal might not have killed her with the blaster—

But he meant to, he wanted me to die, he shot me to kill me!

—but if he reached the Old City and initiated the device, then he might succeed in killing her anyway.

Lanoree slapped a compartment open and dropped a medpac into Tre's lap. "Here. Drugs. I'm sorry, Tre. Do what you can for now, and I'll . . ." He waved her away.

She rushed into the cockpit and ran her hands across the Peacemaker's controls. It felt like coming home. She fired the engines and then paused as the ship shuddered around them. "Thank you, Tre," she said. "For coming to rescue me."

"Only 'cuz I can't fly your ship," he said from behind her. She smiled, pleased that he was nowhere near the bad man he had once been. She only hoped he had more time to make things even better.

The scanners flashed, warning lights chimed. She switched on comm to send a message to Tython, but the flatscreen was a haze of snow and crackles. Nothing manifested, and its level indicator fluctuated rapidly. She could have examined the readings closer, but there was no need. Sometimes instruments gave voice to what was visibly obvious.

Outside, the skies and surface of Sunspot were in turmoil. The fiery clouds and lightning she had witnessed as Tre and Ironholgs pulled her from the mine had increased. Now they looked cataclysmic. Fingers of lightning thrashed down all around, making the ground shudder and the air bend. The skies were deep red and violent orange, streaked here and there with white-hot flame that ignited massive, thundering explosions high up.

Malterra was close. Gravities fought as each planet exerted influence over the other, and it seemed that both sought dominance.

They could retreat underground into the deepest mines, as most of Sunspot's miners did on every such occasion. For four days they would live down there, feeling the world around them shaking and sensing the great energies being expended above. And then they would climb to the surface to repair any damage, and the mining would begin again.

Dal planned this, Lanoree thought. *He must have. Once in a Malterran year, a quarter of a Tythan year; such coincidence can't be an accident.*

But Lanoree knew that she had no choice. If she desired, she could consult the ship's computer and calculate the odds of her being able to pilot the ship out through such a storm. But she never liked hearing the odds.

"Can you make it up here, strap in?" she asked Tre. She heard a groan, and then his shuffling footsteps as he came to join her. He stank. His breathing was ragged.

"I'll probably puke again."

"Don't worry. Ironholgs, prepare for takeoff."

The droid clacked and clicked.

Lanoree increased power to the engines. The ship felt strong and confident around her, and as she took in a deep breath, she felt the same. *I am renewed*, she thought. She knew that the sense of power and superiority she felt was wrong; her alchemies were talents that should be borne lightly.

Ashla and Bogan be damned. She had a more immediate fight on her hands.

"Here goes nothing," she said, and the Peacemaker blasted from Sunspot's surface and into cosmic chaos.

* * *

The most direct route from Sunspot to Tython would have taken them straight through Malterra. Lanoree programmed the route four times, and each time the ship's computer threw out a different alternative. So in the end she took manual control, switched on four screens with different scaled space charts, and trusted her instincts.

There is no fear; there is power, she thought, and she worked with the Force to see them through. She felt queasy. She convinced herself that it was the result of her healing, as opposed to an unsettling of her balance. *But the flesh was strong. The strength, the* potential! She could not hold down the excitement she felt at such arcane alchemies.

"We should wait," Tre said beside her, weak and scared. She did not answer. He knew as well as she how much was at stake, and how much of a start Dal had on them. They had to travel as fast as they could. There was no other way.

The Peacemaker took a pounding as she curved them up out of Sunspot's atmosphere, but the craft had been built to last. The noise was tremendous, and she could hardly hear her own shout. The straps cut into her shoulders and chest. The windows shimmered with heat on the outside. Her seat creaked in its mounting, loose panels rattled and shook, and the flight stick vibrated so hard in her hand that soon her fingers and forearm grew numb. She could not let go. She fought the storm through the ship, and calmed herself with the Force, and Dal was large in her mind's eye.

She remembered his face as he'd pointed the blaster and his eyes as he'd pulled the trigger, and there was nothing there.

Scanners showed that they were almost fifteen kilometers above the planet's surface, and she increased the power to break them into space. Once there, she hoped the abuse the ship was undergoing might lessen.

But she was wrong. Space itself was being rippled and torn by the forces exerted between the two planets as they rapidly closed on each other. They would pass within half a million kilometers of each other, and that sounded like a comfortable distance. But flying between them felt like dropping a feather into the winds of Talss's grassy plains. Her instruments went haywire from the magnetic and gravitational chaos dancing between worlds. Ironholgs skittered across the cabin behind her and tipped onto his side, sparks arcing from several slits on his head.

"Your droid's exploded," Tre said. Even his voice sounded dismantled, broken into constituent parts by the incredible assault on the ship and everything within it. "How long till the Peacemaker goes, too?"

"The Peacemaker *won't* go!" Lanoree shouted. "Your brain will fall from your butt before that happens."

"I think it already has," he shouted. She was pleased to hear humor, because perhaps that meant Tre was feeling better. Maybe the medicines he'd taken had helped. But she could not fool herself. She had cured her own terrible wounds using arcane and dangerous Force alchemy, but Tre was different. The poisons eating at him might be slowed, but to stop them would require expert attention.

She tried to communicate with Tython, to warn them, but all comm systems remained down. An hour after the attempt, her own message came back to her, surprising her with its air of desperation. She felt sick, and Tre vomited beside her. At least this time he turned away from her before letting go.

"That's the second time you've done that to my ship!" she shouted. No reply from Tre. She glanced across, and he was sitting with his chin touching his chest. His lekku hung limp and unmoving. She switched on the grav unit, but it was malfunctioning in the storms. Her stomach rose and fell. She pressed back into her seat. Something seemed to have come loose in her chest, and she probed delicately, using the Force to feel out the geography of her wound. It felt fine; her fix had been good. Perhaps it was simply her held breath.

Time moved on, every moment an eternity. The Peacemaker shook and vibrated, and more rattles developed. The ship was being shaken to pieces. Arc lightning struck them three times, the third time such a heavy charge that every seam and hole in the hull, control panel, and structure lit up as if they were being burned apart. Lanoree screamed out loud but could not hear, and she quietly prepared herself for death. *I'll feel nothing*, she thought, but she knew what she would see at the moment of death: the madness on her brother's face.

But the ship held together and they did not die.

* * *

When they were a million kilometers out from Sunspot, Malterra passed its closest point to that planet. Lanoree watched the passage on one of her scanner screens, and wondered at the immense forces and pressures being exerted there right now. In those deep mines, miners huddled. She had every respect for them and wished them well.

At last, as the storms seemed to be getting better instead of worse, she ran a full systems check on the ship. Ironholgs was still out of action so she had to do it herself. They had taken a battering. Life support was damaged, but would last them to Tython. One of the laser cannons had been fractured; she shut off the pod supplying it in case of leakage. A fuel rod had ruptured, and she jettisoned it into space. But the hull integrity was good, and all vital systems were functioning. The Peacemaker was well enough to get them to Tython, and that was her only aim.

She plotted the fastest course that would take them to the Old City and handed control to the ship's computer.

As she unbuckled herself and stood to squeeze back into the main cabin, something struck her.

Lanoree gasped and sank back into the seat. A vision. A blow. A ripple in the Force, far greater than she had ever felt before. *A ship*, she thought. *A battle. Death and chaos, and one among them* . . .

Then the vision was gone, leaving barely an echo in its wake. Dal's ship? She thought not. There was no sense of recognition at all; indeed, a coldness had taken her, and an alienness seemed to haunt the shadows of her mind. Soon, that too was fading.

Lanoree shook her head. Then she lifted Tre from the copilot's seat and carried him to the cot. His eyes opened as she lay him down.

"Half a day and we'll be entering Tython's atmosphere," she said.

"Just blast me into space. I'll feel better that way." He sat up slowly and squinted at Lanoree.

"How do you feel?"

"How do I look?"

"Covered in vomit."

"That's how I feel."

Lanoree sat next to him, frowning. "Everything feels so strange."

"Well, you did just heal a hole in your chest. You should be dead."

She thought of her experiment and the life she had coaxed into it.

"Maybe," she said. "I need rest." She leaned back and closed her eyes. "Wake me when we're approaching Tython." Without even hearing Tre's response she fell into a deep, troubled sleep.

Her dreams are strange. She is aware that they are dreams, yet they are more chilling than ever before. She constantly tries waking herself, but she does not feel in control.

There is a figure. Tall, cloaked, armored, an unmarked helmet hiding its features. In its hand is a weapon the like of which she has never seen before. A sword, but strange, with pure Force as its blade.

The same dream, again and again.

Only hands on her shoulder and a familiar voice bring her up from that vision.

"Lanoree. Tython. But something's very wrong."

Approaching Tython, the chaos on the planet's surface was evident.

"What's that?" Tre asked.

"Force Storm." Lanoree had never witnessed one from space, but it looked far more violent and widespread than any she had experienced before. She tried contacting Master Dam-Powl again, but though her comm unit was now functioning, no signals could pierce the storm.

"He's started already," Tre said. "Whatever it is your mad brother's trying to do, it's begun."

"Maybe," Lanoree said. And that was her great fear. If Dal initiated the device, perhaps Tython's first response would be a shudder of the Force and storms to rip across the planet's surface. "Maybe I'm too late."

She jumped into the cockpit and steered them into a dive into the atmosphere that was all but suicidal.

Every moment might be their last. She would make them all count.

CHAPTER EIGHTEEN
THE DESCENT

Never forget that we were brought here. Tython is a planet rich in the Force, but it is also a place of mystery, unknown to us, existing here for eons before the Tho Yor arrived. Its age is deep, its stories deeper. We are but residents here; our true home is in the Force.

—Master Deela jan Morolla, 3,528 TYA

For Tre, the descent must have been terrifying. The Peacemaker blazed, hull creaking in protest at the incredible forces and terrible heat, flames smearing the windows, acceleration pressing him back against the seat with enough pressure to make his ears and nose bleed and his lekku drain of blood. Lanoree barely noticed these physical effects. The Force was in turmoil, and the closer she came to home, the more lost she felt.

But though she sought Dal and his mad plans, she was not convinced that this storm was connected to him. She sensed it all across Tython, erupting from the deep places of the world and springing from the widest skies. The disturbance was powerful, but the planet still stood solid.

She thought again of that vision in her dream and the strange feeling she'd had flying through the violent space between the inner planets.

Dal is my focus, she thought. Gripping the flight stick she urged the Peacemaker into an even deeper, more dangerous descent. She was forcing the ship past its design constraints and thrusting it into the danger zone. But there was no other way. Every breath she took between now and finding Dal might be one breath too long, and her last.

The Peacemaker burst from the clouds above Talss. She headed west, skimming hilltops, watching scanners confused and disturbed by the ongoing Force Storm, and an urgent chiming marked a partial return of her comm signal.

She immediately sent a signal for Master Dam-Powl. It was answered in moments, and the flustered Master appeared on the Peacemaker's flatscreen.

"Lanoree," she said. "I . . . the worst."

"Master! Dal gave me the slip, but I know where he's going, and I know what he has." Dam-Powl's image seemed not to be hearing the message. She looked older than before, distracted, and she was not as well presented as usual. Lanoree could not even tell where the Master was transmitting from; the room around her was clean, modern, empty.

" . . . ship from out of system . . ." Dam-Powl continued speaking, but Lanoree could not hear. She adjusted some controls, checked transmit levels. But the storm's effects were insurmountable.

"Master, I'm almost at the Old City. Are there Je'daii there waiting for him?"

" . . . withdrew, but there are safeguards," Master Dam-Powl said. She seemed to gather herself and stare at Lanoree from the flatscreen. "He must be stopped. Whatever is happening now . . . end it all."

"Master?"

"I sense that everything is about to change," Dam-Powl said. She went to say something else, but the screen snowed and her voice disappeared into a crackling haze of interference. Lanoree tried one more time, then turned the comm unit off.

What had she meant? A ship from out of system? One of the Sleeper ships returned? Lanoree was more than intrigued, but she was also set on her course, and Master Dam-Powl's words did nothing to dissuade her.

"Please, just land this thing," Tre said. "I've got nothing else to throw up."

"Almost there," Lanoree said. She looked across at Tre, pleased that he seemed a little better. Perhaps whatever had poisoned him on Nox could be treated, given time.

"What's the plan?" he asked. His lekku were stroking either side of his face as if giving comfort.

"Plan?" she asked.

"Is she always like this?" Tre asked Ironholgs over his shoulder, and Lanoree smiled. The droid issued no reply; some of its circuits were fried, and it was in need of repair. Again, given time.

The ship jolted as a streak of Force lightning arced down and split the sky. Lanoree cringed and jerked the ship to one side. To crash now would be—

A chime from the sensors. She leaned to the left and shielded a scanner from reflected light from outside, and then she saw it. Several kilometers in the distance, and at least thirty kilometers from the first ruins of the Old City.

"What now?" Tre asked.

"Crashed ship." She tweaked the sensor controls, then sat back and sighed in satisfaction. "Something going for us, at last."

"His?"

"Yes. Deathblaster. Let's take a look."

She brought the Peacemaker in low, the remaining laser cannons at the ready for any aggression. The Deathblaster might have been a wreck, but that didn't mean it didn't have fight left in it. She circled at a distance, scanning for life-forms. There was nothing. If the Stargazers and her brother were still on board, they were dead.

She felt a pang at that, unsure whether it was grief or regret.

"Why not just blast it?" Tre asked. The ship had landed hard, gouging furrows from the soil across a low hillside, and then broken up when it struck a rocky outcropping. There was no sign of fire or explosion.

"Can't in case the device is still inside," she said. But that was not the whole reason. "Setting down."

They landed with barely a jolt, and the Peacemaker seemed to croak and sigh with relief. As she was about to speak, Tre held up one hand.

"Who's going to look after you if I stay here?"

"I was just going to say you don't need to come," Lanoree said. "This was never really your fight."

Tre's face darkened and his lekku dipped to communicate anger. "It's *everyone's* fight," he said. "We just happen to be the only two here."

"You sound like a bad holo." Lanoree smiled and opened the hatch. Hand on sword hilt, Force senses fogged by the storms that raged across Tython's surface, she stepped down onto her home planet one more time.

They split up as they approached the crashed Stargazer ship, and Lanoree's nervousness grew. She did not want to find her brother dead among the wreckage. Whether that said she was a good person, whether it spoke of an unreasonable sense of forgiveness, she did not know. It simply was. She had always held out hope for him. Even as he turned that blaster on her and she had a split second to partially shield herself with the Force, she had felt so sorry for him.

A fool, perhaps. But a sister for sure. She hoped her parents would be proud.

Lanoree closed on the ship and probed outward with her Force senses. She could not detect anyone inside at all. Tre approached slowly from the other side, and when he hefted a rock and threw it at the hull, she ran forward to tackle anyone who emerged. But all was silent.

She climbed the tilted hull and shone a glow rod through a smashed door. The insides were a mess—crushed paneling, hanging wires and cables, a tumbled seat, and hardened impact-foam formed around the empty shapes of at least four people. She could see two bodies still encased in foam, and the parts exposed were badly mutilated by the crash.

Lanoree signaled for Tre to wait where he was, then climbed inside. Neither body was Dal's. She breathed a sigh of relief, then jumped at a particularly strong crash of lightning from outside.

There was no sign of the device. And no evidence of a battle or being shot down. The Force Storm had downed this ship, and she wondered at the stroke of luck.

She touched the hull on the way out, then slid down the ship's back to the engine cowls. They were still almost too hot to touch.

"Thirty kilometers to the Old City, and they're on foot," she shouted.

"How long ago?" Tre asked.

"Not long. Still hot. But we need to hurry." They ran back to the Peacemaker, and Lanoree took off and drifted them quickly across the landscape. Tre sat beside her and kept his eye on the scanners as she steered them through valleys and around rocky summits. She was more than aware of the element of surprise they had on their side once again. Dal thought she was dead.

Approaching the Old City, she experienced flashbacks of the last time she had been here. After finding Dal's bloodied clothing and believing him dead, she had returned to Anil Kesh to face the repercussions of his final acts. Following the inquest into Skott Yun's murder—for which blame was laid squarely on Dal—she had been granted a period of leave, during which she had traveled home and told her parents everything that had happened.

They had blamed themselves. And Lanoree had blamed *her*self. A distance had grown between them, and when the time came to embark upon the rest of her Great Journey—alone this time, a situation she would grow to prefer—she had grabbed at it.

She had never returned to the Old City. Dal was dead and gone, some *thing* had taken him down, and there was nothing to be gained from visiting that place again.

Besides, there was the sense of fear that had flooded her, which she had attributed to the immense age of the place, the unknown history, the mystery that even the Force could not enlighten. She had never spoken of it. She believed that place should always be left alone.

And now, here she was again.

"Sensors don't show any life-forms," she said.

"No Je'daii here? Surely they'd be guarding against him getting past you?"

"I think Master Dam-Powl said they withdrew." She pointed up at the sky. "There's something else going on. Connected or not, I think we're on our own."

"You Je'daii and your mysteries," Tre said, lekku shrugging. "So where are they?"

"They must have gone down already."

"Down?"

"There are tunnels beneath the ruins. Caverns. Lakes. Deep places."

"I've had enough of the underground."

Lanoree looked at him, one eyebrow raised, although this time she did not say, *You don't have to come.*

"Let's make it quick," Tre said.

"You're feeling better?"

"Your drugs are keeping it at bay."

Lanoree landed the ship, and together they approached the Old City.

The landscape seemed overfamiliar, though she had been here only once. Almost as if she had always wished to return. She led them through a shallow valley and past a hill that might once have been a pyramid. They followed the footprints of four people in the long, damp grass. Her heart was beating fast, and a sense of impending dread crushed in around her. *They really believe they're here to start a hypergate!* she thought, and the idea was staggering. If everything went wrong, they might doom the system. But if the hypergate was real and the device actually worked, Dal might be building a step to the stars.

What explorer could not feel a thrill of excitement at that?

At last they stood close to an entrance to the Old City's underground, and Lanoree recognized it as the way she had come before. A sense of déjà vu struck home, hard, and much that had happened since that first fated descent felt like a dream.

"I don't like this place," Tre said, snapping her back to reality. "Feels . . ."

"Strange," she said.

I sense that everything is about to change, Master Dam-Powl had said.

Once again Lanoree pursued her brother beneath Tython's surface, not knowing what might lie beneath.

* * *

Not long after descending from the light they came across the first of Dam-Powl's safeguards.

The Cathar Stargazer woman had been sliced into several parts. Her head had rolled down a slight slope and now rested, staring up at them. The rest of her lay scattered across the tunnel floor. The blood was still wet and warm, its smell sickening. Her eyes reflected Lanoree's glow rod light accusingly, and Lanoree sensed the Force about the trap that had been sprung here. Set into the wall was a series of laser pods, all of them expended now. But they had fulfilled their purpose.

"Only Dal and two others left," Lanoree said.

"And now they know there are traps."

"I doubt they'll fall for the next one."

"Let's hope we don't," Tre said.

"These are set by my people," Lanoree said.

"Then there must be something down here worth protecting."

Lanoree did not reply, because she had thought the same. The Je'daii Council had charged her with stopping her brother, and they had surely assumed that she would have succeeded long before now. This was the final step in his plan, and still he was ahead of her. But they would not have guessed that. These traps were here to prevent *anyone* from entering the deeps of the Old City. And they had been placed recently.

They continued their descent. Lanoree probed ahead, her senses less befuddled down here. Perhaps the Force Storm on the surface was calming, or maybe the solid bulk of Tython between her and the storm acted as a shield. The Force felt disturbed, but settled. She used it with confidence, and the next trap was obvious.

Dal and the others had also been aware of it. They had filled a robe with rocks and thrown it ahead, and the shredded material and cracked rocks bore the scorch marks of spent laser pods.

"They're moving quickly," Lanoree said.

"How can you tell?"

"That's my brother." Lanoree drew her sword as they moved on. She recognized some of the caverns and tunnels, the large stepped descents and the strange engravings on some of the walls, but she kept focused. The pursuit, the Je'daii safeguards, they were all that mattered.

If it existed, she had no idea how far down the hypergate might be.

As they crossed a hallway with carved stone pillars and plinths bearing strange, time-worn sculptures, she saw a flash in the distance. It illuminated a high, arched doorway for a moment before fading, then came again. The white-hot scorch of a laser blast.

"Another trap triggered," Tre said, and Lanoree nodded. They were close. She ran.

Perhaps expectation smothered caution. The chase was almost at an end, and her determination to face Dal again before he triggered the device was a hot, driving thing. She probed with her Force senses, detected nothing amiss, and trusted that. She did not take into account that her senses were obscured and that the Force was once again shivering at the storms above.

Whatever the reason, she led the way into danger.

The laser trap had been set across a wide tunnel, and smoke was still rising from the heavy object that had been used to spring it. The rock had been neatly sliced in two, severed parts glowing. *They can't be more than a hundred steps ahead*, she thought, and as she concentrated on running quietly, shielding her mind, and readying herself for what was to come, she saw a flurry of movement on her left.

"Lanoree!" Tre shouted behind her, and he pushed her forward. Maybe he tripped, shoving her as he fell. Or perhaps he did so on purpose.

The hail of blaster fire echoed across the tunnel, smashing rock to molten pellets, and the Stargazer had fired five times before Lanoree raised her sword. She deflected two more shots and leaped across the tunnel with barely any effort. She landed beside the man and swung the sword, severing both of his arms just below the elbows. Forearms and blaster fell to the ground. The man gasped quietly, and took two steps back until he was standing against the tunnel wall. He looked down at his gouting stumps, then up at Lanoree, eyes wide.

She swung her sword through his chest, cutting him almost in two. As he dropped dead, she turned around, ready to encourage Tre onward and tell him to be careful, because now Dal and the last Stargazer knew they were close on their tail.

But Tre did not need telling, because he was dead. One blast had struck him high on the side of his neck, scorching across the back of his skull. He had fallen onto his front, arms still outstretched.

"Oh, Tre," Lanoree whispered, because she didn't know what else to say. She dashed to his side, ready to snatch up his blaster and run on.

A bubble of blood formed at his nose.

She touched his hand, his wrist, and felt a weak pulse fluttering like a bird in a trap. The wound looked bad, yet he still breathed.

But Lanoree knew there was no time.

"I'm sorry," she said, and she left Tre in the dark and ran on. Her only comfort was in knowing that, were he conscious, he would understand.

As she had been that first time in the depths of the Old City, she was now alone.

Soon, Dal was alone as well.

Careful now, more attuned than ever to the ebb and flow of the Force through these ancient subterranean rooms, Lanoree sensed the last Stargazer long before he knew she was there. He was hiding on a high step that led up one massive wall, blaster aimed back the way he and Dal had come.

Lanoree climbed higher. She moved quickly and quietly, barely even disturbing the air around her, and every moment she watched for the movement that would show that he had heard or seen her. But she was a shadow. When she was high enough, she moved forward and dropped on the Stargazer from above.

She thought of questioning him about where Dal had gone and how he was armed, but she could not take the chance. She'd seen one of these Stargazers explode suicide belts without a second thought. And, she supposed, there was also anger behind the swing of her sword. The Stargazer's head bounced down three large steps, and she landed softly on the ground just as it settled beside her. She was already running again. Dal might not know that the last Stargazer was dead, but he would assume that he was on his own now.

Him, and the sister he had shot and left for dead.

"Dal!" Lanoree shouted, surprising even herself. She paused, then smiled. It felt good to call his name. And not because he was her brother and she still held out any hope for him because, at last, she did not. No more hope. She enjoyed calling his name because in her voice she could hear the anger and disgust she was feeling. So many people he had killed to fuel his fantasy. Even his sister.

If their parents were to suddenly appear, he would kill them as well.

"Dal! I'm coming to stop you, now. No pleading! No more chances! Just you and me, and last time down here you spilled your *own* blood." Her voice echoed away, filling huge rooms and grand tunnels that might never have heard such language before. She wondered at the Gree tongue and what these places had seen and heard so long ago. She felt the heavy, dense power that filled the place, and did not care. She was tired and enraged. Her balance was unsettled, but she let the anger drive her on. It sharpened her senses.

Deeper, and her glow rod fought harder against the darkness than ever before. Perhaps the farther down she went, the heavier the dark.

And then Dal was there, standing in a room that might once have been a bathing place. He'd thrown several glow rods in a rough circle around him, and resting by his feet was the device. He must have been carrying it on his own, and Lanoree was amazed that something so powerful did not bear more weight.

"I think this is far enough," Dal said.

"I'm not stopping now," Lanoree said. She slowed, but kept walking toward Dal.

"I don't mean you. I mean this. Here. It's far enough."

"Here?" She looked around. "But where is the—?"

Dal bent down to touch the device.

"Don't!" She drew a blaster and aimed it at Dal's head, sheathing her sword. And she knew without any doubt that it would take nothing for her, now, to pull the trigger.

"Not a very graceful weapon for a Je'daii."

"You stole my sword."

"Looks like you have another, and you're not afraid to get it bloody."

"This one isn't special."

"Oh. Right. Yeah, I dumped that other one in deep space." He was still half crouched, fingers splayed, and she watched his other hand.

I should shoot him right now.

"Come with me," Dal said.

"You shot me."

"And yet you're here. My tough sister."

"The Force saved me. Ironic, don't you think? You mock it so much, and yet it'll be your undoing."

"It looks like a blaster will be my undoing."

They stood that way for a while. Lanoree did not relax for a moment—her finger on the trigger, her eyes on Dal, her Force senses ranging and yet never quite fully aware. The storm was abating, but the Force on Tython was still stirred.

"You're a bad man, Dal."

"I'm fighting for what I believe in!"

"That doesn't mean you're not evil."

"I won't stop," he said. "I won't give this up, Lanoree. Not after so long. Can't you feel it? Can't you *sense* it? You have *no idea*—"

"I don't care," she said.

Dal stared at her, the older, madder Dal she still did not know. "Can't you just wonder?" he asked softly. "Aren't you at least curious about what might be out there?"

She did not reply.

"Where we came from," he said. "Our origins. Our birth planets. Places where we belong but which we were torn away from. Our heritage in the stars, Lanoree. Doesn't even a small part of you wonder?"

"Yes," Lanoree said after a brief pause. "But not at the risk of everything I know and love."

"Then shoot me." He reached lower.

Lanoree's finger tightened on the trigger. And eased again. Instead, she closed her eyes and took the greatest risk of her life.

She pushed a memory of them together. Pushed it with all her might. The Force left her with a *clap!* and for a while she was actually alive in the memory as it formed in Dal's mind, as real there as she was in this ancient subterranean bathing place for the Gree.

They walk together beside the river back at Bodhi Temple, young, almost carefree, watching the weave birds nesting in the trees and the river water carrying clumps of roundweed as large as small islands. The young Lanoree laughs in delight and sees Dal do the same. His eyes are wide with surprise. For that moment he is back there with her—and Lanoree saw her brother's eyes grow wide and wet where he hunched over the device, and she thought, *Now!*

She shoved again, but this was no mere memory. She gathered every flaming, blazing, wretched image she had witnessed over the past days—the explosions and death across Greenwood Station, the mines deep on Sunspot, those who had died beneath her sword, the violent conflagration in the skies of Tython—and heaved them at Dal. His mind recoiled and for an instant his face was a child's, displaying shock and anger at her deception.

Then her brother began to scream

He staggered back, crying at the wretchedness, the pain, the suffering she had pushed his way. Lanoree Force-shoved him back. He stumbled, then tripped over his feet and went down.

She moved beside the device, blaster clasped in one hand. *I stopped him!* she thought, and a great weight vanished from the depths of her chest. She pressed her hand there and felt the heat of her healed wound.

Dal's scream lessened. He stood, shaking his head, rubbing at his face, and running fingers through his hair. His breathing remained labored, each inhalation shuddering.

Defeated, she expected him to run. And she would have let him. He'd have lost himself down there and died, or maybe he'd have gone farther than Osamael Or and disappeared into the Old City forever.

But he did not run. And when he looked up she saw a completely different expression on his face.

Rage.

"Stay out of my head!" he roared, and he came at her.

Lanoree raised the blaster, but Dal, somehow, was quicker. His hand flashed out, she saw something flitting through the air between them, and then a cool pain erupted in her hand. She dropped the blaster and staggered back, looking at the slim metal blade stuck through her palm and slicing the heel of her hand in two.

Then Dal was on her, and every second of attention he had paid at Stav Kesh came to the fore.

Startled, Lanoree failed to deflect the first punches and kicks. Dal's skills had always been in combat, and she reeled from the blows he rained down on her. She held her wounded hand to her side but he aimed for it, one kick catching the blade and slicing deeper, a punch pressing her hand back against her hip and snagging the blade's end on her clothing. Lanoree cried out in pain. Dal grinned.

He came at her again, but this time she had recovered enough to be ready.

As Dal fought with every martial talent and all the strength he had, so Lanoree drew on her training. Her years as a Ranger. Her closeness with the Force. Everything Dal hated, and she used it all against him.

A punch caught Lanoree across the shoulder and she shoved with her uninjured hand, Force-punching him across the cavern. He struck a column and slid down, struggling to stand again. Lanoree snatched up the blaster and did not hesitate to pull the trigger.

Nothing happened. The dropped blaster must have been damaged.

Dal crouched, picked up a rock, and threw it.

Lanoree deflected it with the Force and it shattered into dust.

Dal drew two short knives from his belt and attacked once again. Lanoree dropped the useless blaster and drew her sword, parrying his knife thrusts. She held the blade one-handed, but even then she knew she had the better of him. She almost felt sorry.

Then he threw a knife at her face, and as she Force-shoved it to one side, he leaped at the device.

Lanoree had no time to think, and if she had she would have done the same. She swung the sword in a high arc, up over her head, down toward where Dal would meet the device.

She closed her eyes at the last moment and felt the sickeningly familiar sensation of sword parting flesh.

Something moved and hit the ground, and Lanoree had to look.

Dal's right arm lay severed beside the device, fingers still splayed. The blade was buried deep in the side of his head. He slumped down, moving slightly, eyelids flickering. He looked at Lanoree, his body seeming to relax, and for the first time since childhood she truly saw the Dal that had once been. But he no longer knew himself.

Dal's eyes flooded red, blood ran from his ears and nose, and then he was still.

The sudden inaction and stillness came as a shock, and Lanoree let out one heavy, startled sob of relief and sorrow. She probed out gently, expecting to feel rage and hate, his familiar anger at her touching him with the Force, and his determination to complete what he had begun.

But there was no more Dal. Her brother was gone, and all that was left was this sad, broken body.

She turned her back on Dal while she made sure the device was stable. She thought so. She also thought that the strange power she'd sensed down here nine years before existed now as something like a held breath, matching the shattering potential of the device. The darkness at its heart was horrible. But she was not the one to deal with it.

She had left the sword with Dal. It was not her real sword. And she had no wish to wipe her brother's blood from its blade.

Soon, she would carry the device back to the surface and into the Peacemaker, and if Tre still lived she would do what she could for him. Poor, brave Tre. She would transport them both to Anil Kesh, the Temple of Science. More talented Je'daii than she would examine and make safe the device, and better healers would give Tre their full attention. She would demand that of them. She would insist.

After that, she would meet the Je'daii Masters who had set her on this mission. She would tell them everything that had happened, and request permission to recover Dal's body so that she could take him home. She had decided that she would tell her parents everything.

After all that, there was one more journey to take, and some final questions to ask.

Temple Master Lha-Mi would grant everything she asked, because she might have prevented a cataclysm.

What she would *not* tell the Je'daii Masters, *ever*, was just how long she sat there next to her brother's cooling body, staring at his device's activation panel.

Wondering.

Only wondering.

CHAPTER NINETEEN
MIGHT

I can never tell anyone what I saw in the depths of the Old City. There are no words. But I hope one day I can show them.
                                              —Dalien Brock, diaries, 10,661 TYA

In the end, she decided her parents could wait. That was a reunion she dreaded, and not only because she had killed her own brother. She dreaded it most because she had failed to save him a second time.

Storms still raged across Tython as she coaxed her damaged Peacemaker down onto one of Anil Kesh's landing pads. The ship needed repairs, and her droid required some special attention from those expert in such technologies. Most of all, Tre was balancing between life and death. She had done her best for him, but her brief ministrations might have been worthless. He needed the attention of someone experienced in Force healing. She had spoken to him every moment of their brief flight to Anil Kesh, and though he was in a deep coma, she hoped it had done some good. It certainly made her feel better, no longer talking to herself.

But Lanoree's dark matters were not yet over. And even though her mission was all but completed, she sensed something greater occurring on Tython.

Master Dam-Powl met her on the landing pad, hood raised against the rain.

"Lanoree," Dam-Powl said with genuine affection. Lanoree went to kneel, but Dam-Powl pulled her into an embrace. She submitted to it and rested her head on the shorter Master's shoulder. "Your balance is unsettled," Dam-Powl whispered.

"Yes, Master. I killed my brother."

Dam-Powl sighed heavily. "These are dark times. Please, come with me so that we can talk. We'll eat, and drink. I'll welcome the company. I'm acting Temple Master here in Master Quan-Jang's absence."

"Where is he?"

"Away. Now come." Dam-Powl held out her hand. "Tell me everything. And then I have plenty to tell you."

"I thought it was over," Lanoree said, looking up at the skies to the east. Lightning danced there, and powerful winds swept stinging rain across Anil Kesh's exposed surfaces. Beneath the temple, the Chasm roared. Darkness seemed to rise from there, though it was almost midday. Even after everything Lanoree had seen and done, it made her shiver.

"Your mission *is* over," Dam-Powl said. Together they watched three Je'daii Rangers who were carefully carrying the device from the Peacemaker, place it on a stable trolley and wheel it toward an open door. It was destined for one of Anil Kesh's laboratories. Lanoree only hoped that the Je'daii could learn from it. "But a greater story is beginning."

Master Dam-Powl told Lanoree of the alien ship that had entered the system, exploded above Tython, and then crashed somewhere near the Rift. Perhaps in the Abyss of Ruh itself. Its arrival had caused the dreadful Force Storms that still rippled across the planet, and the Je'daii were unsettled.

"Master Quan-Jang is one of many seeking news of the crashed ship," Dam-Powl said. "I fear it means changing times for Tython."

"Fear?" Lanoree asked.

"There was a disturbance in the Force before the ship crashed. A wave of darkness. A terrible voice of pain, and then silence as death fell."

"I sensed that also," Lanoree said. "On my way from Sunspot."

"Many Je'daii did," Dam-Powl said. "Those on the ship were Force sensitives."

"From out of system?"

"We believe so." Dam-Powl nodded gently but said no more. She could sense Lanoree's need to talk. "So now, your story," she said.

They sat in Master Dam-Powl's laboratory, and Lanoree told her everything.

"Bad things," Dam-Powl said when the story was almost over. "Such bad things. I hope Tre Sana can be saved."

"He's a strange man," Lanoree said. She was surprised to find herself smiling. "So hard when I met him. Harsh. Selfish. He had troublesome views, and he even told me some of the things he'd done. Not the worst things, I'm sure. But he was very open about his past. Some would have called him wicked, or even evil. But he helped me several times, and I saw the better man inside."

"I sensed that also," Dam-Powl said. "That's why I chose him to be my ears and eyes."

"You really promised him what he said?"

"I did," she said softly. "If he survives, I'll keep my word."

"He came for me on Sunspot, saved me. And I think he was willing to sacrifice himself to save my life again down in the Old City. He knew what was at stake. If he hadn't put himself in the way of that laser blast, I might have died."

"Your alchemical skills are . . . quite remarkable."

"Only what you taught me, Master."

"No. What you did cannot be taught, Lanoree. You're a natural. Just be careful when you continue your experiments."

"I'm not sure I *will* continue," Lanoree said.

"Oh, you will." Dam-Powl smiled, but it quickly faded. "But what you did . . . the dark tempts you. It teases with the power it could give. And killing your brother has pushed you that way, also. You feel conflicted. You feel . . . confused."

"Yes, Master."

"Brush aside the confusion," Dam-Powl said. "That is the first step to confronting any imbalance. Know that you are troubled, or be comfortable that you are not. Be honest with yourself. And . . . I am here, Lanoree. We are all here to help. Every single Master, because . . ." She shrugged. "It could be you saved us all."

"I feel that my balance has swayed, Master. But I have not fallen. And I will not."

Dam-Powl raised an eyebrow, took a drink, delicately wiped her mouth. "So, the threat is quashed, and another rises in its place. You'll be wanting to rest before your journey back to Bodhi and your parents."

"No," Lanoree said. "I'm not going home just yet. And rest will wait. I still have questions."

"Oh," Master Dam-Powl said, but she knew very well that Lanoree had more to ask.

"The hypergate. I felt it."

"You felt something in the Old City, as anyone particularly talented in the Force will. Just as the Chasm causes disturbance, and the Abyss of Ruh, and other places on Tython. Your brother was right in one regard, at least. This is not our planet."

"But I felt such power. Like something waiting."

"The wine's finished. I need to fetch another bottle." Dam-Powl stood and went to turn away. Lanoree grasped her robe and pulled her back around so that they were face-to-face. It was an audacious move, handling a Master like this. But Lanoree felt justified.

"Master. *Is* there a hypergate down there?"

Dam-Powl looked down at Lanoree's hand on her sleeve, waiting until it was released.

"Whether there is or isn't—whether anyone knows for sure, or not—doesn't change what you did, Lanoree. If that Gree device had been turned on . . . well, we might not be here now. Friends. With wine. The whole system might not be here anymore."

"Might," Lanoree said.

"Civilization is built on the word." Dam-Powl smiled. "You serve the Je'daii well, Lanoree. You remember when you and your brother first came to Anil Kesh? I saw the potential in you then. And when you returned to complete your training after you thought he had died, and we spent long days together here, in this laboratory . . ." She gestured around at dark corners and flickering candles. "That's when I knew for sure you would one day be a great Je'daii. I was not afraid to tell you so. And today, I'm not afraid to claim an element of pride, because I was right. You *are* a great Je'daii. And on your journey, you *might* need to learn when to confront things, and when to turn away. When to obey your Masters, and when not." She shrugged. "Hmm. That word *might* again. It means 'perhaps,' and it also means 'strength.' Maybe it's doubt that gives true strength, eh, Lanoree? Balance is easy. Shifting from balance and finding it again means you have to be stronger than most. And I have every confidence in you."

The Je'daii Master turned away again and walked across the laboratory, past benches where she and Lanoree had practiced alchemies and manipulation. As she returned with a new bottle of wine, Lanoree had one more question to ask.

"Master, where did the information about Dal, the Stargazers, and their device come from?"

Dam-Powl nodded, as if affirming something to herself. "It's Kalimahr you need to visit."

"Yes," Lanoree said. "Kalimahr." She held up her glass for one more drink.

On her way to Kalimahr, Lanoree had time to reflect on what she had done.

Your balance is unsettled, Master Dam-Powl had said, and Lanoree could not disagree with the Master. Darkness haunted her dreams, and sometimes she found herself dreaming of Bogan. All that troubled her, yet this journey was not yet done. When it was over, soon, she was confident that she was strong enough to correct the unbalance herself.

She was surprised to find herself lonely. Ironholgs remained at Anil Kesh, being repaired by a young Journeyer whose talent was mechanics; and without Tre here, her cabin felt too large, her ship too silent. She spoke to herself again but was sad that there was no reply.

Tre's prognosis was good, she had been told. She held on to the delight she felt at this fact. She thought perhaps she had made a friend.

A group of Journeyers led by Master Kin'ade had searched for Dal's body for some time, but it was never found. *Creatures*, Lanoree thought. *There could be anything down there. There are depths.*

She sat staring at her experiment for some time. It was shriveled and denuded, and it should have been blasted into space. Yet she could not rid herself of it. Darkness danced around the petrified flesh, and Lanoree tried several times to find life still within it. At first it was simply dead. But then, half a day out from Kalimahr, her Force senses perceived a speck of flesh that pulsed with life once more.

Given time, she would relearn the alchemy of flesh. Its draw was too great to ignore. And she was strong.

On Kalimahr, there was nothing to find.

Kara's high apartment was abandoned. The damage caused by the battle she and Tre had fought with the fat woman's sentry droids had been repaired. The secret room Lanoree had discovered was clean and empty, now opened up as part of the apartment. Everything personal was gone. Kara had left her apartments for the first time in thirteen years, and they should have been desirable real estate. And yet no one had chosen to rent it. There was something dark about that space.

Any enquiries she made as to Kara's location were met with a blank wall. Most claimed not to have heard of her. The several times Lanoree used a subtle Force trick to read her associates' minds, she found confused images of Kara as friend and threat, but no indication of where she was now. They had all known her, and they were lying about that. But when it came to her whereabouts, they told the truth.

Kara had vanished.

With her, so the militia captain Lorus told Lanoree, had gone several other high-profile members of the Rhol Yan community. One day they were there, the next . . . not. Their homes were abandoned, sometimes still filled with personal possessions. Their business interests were left without directors. There was never any trace.

"Maybe you're better off without them," Lanoree suggested.

"And why would you say that?" Lorus asked her.

"Because they weren't what they seemed. They were darker. They had their sights elsewhere, and when it suited them they fed information to the Je'daii. Brought me here. Made my brother and his cronies speed up their plans. I think perhaps Kara and her like are the *real* Stargazers."

She left Kalimahr the same day that she arrived, sensing that Lorus was glad to see her go. And she was glad to leave.

She thought of Ironholgs being repaired. There were the machines and there were the masters; the tools that function and react, and the programmers who use them for their own ends. She suspected that Dal had been a machine, a tool, and that Kara and her missing comrades were the real masters.

Perhaps Dal had been moving too slowly with his schemes, and his masters had wanted to encourage him to speed up. And what better way than to set the Je'daii on his trail? Lanoree did not like the feeling of being used, and yet it was something that haunted her.

But now Tython was her destination once more. Her parents awaited, and it was time for their daughter to come home.

After the second remembrance service for Dal, she would stay for a while. She would wander the grassy plains around Bodhi Temple alone, perhaps swim in the river, and watch the weave birds making nests. And when darkness fell she would lie back and contemplate Ashla and Bogan, and her place of balance between them.

ABOUT THE AUTHOR

TIM LEBBON is a *New York Times* bestselling writer from South Wales. He's had almost thirty novels published to date, as well as dozens of novellas and hundreds of short stories. His most recent releases include *Coldbrook* from Arrow/Hammer, *London Eye* (book one of the *Toxic City* trilogy) from Pyr in the United States, *Nothing as It Seems* from PS Publishing, and *The Heretic Land* from Orbit, as well as The Secret Journeys of Jack London series (co-authored with Christopher Golden), *Echo City,* and *The Cabin in the Woods* novelization. Future novels include *The Silence* (Titan). He has won four British Fantasy Awards, a Bram Stoker Award, and a Scribe Award, and has been a finalist for World Fantasy, International Horror Guild, and Shirley Jackson awards.

Film rights to The Secret Journeys of Jack London series have been acquired by 20th Century Fox, and he and Christopher Golden wrote the first draft of the screenplay. A TV series of his *Toxic City* trilogy is in development with ABC Studios in the United States, and he's also working on new novels and screenplays, both solo and in collaboration.

Find out more about Tim Lebbon at his website www.timlebbon.net.

Read on for the short story
Star Wars: Dawn of the Jedi: Eruption
by John Ostrander

Hawk Ryo drifted in and out the shadows, a shadow himself. The moon world, Zerist, was located far from the sun, and most of the available light was reflected off the gas giant, Obri, around which the moon orbited. Kainnan was typically bustling with activity, but the workers' town was now deserted. Like all the surface towns on Zerist, Kainnan was located near an active volcano for its much needed warmth, despite the risk of occasional eruptions. The authorities usually predicted the eruptions in time and evacuated the threatened areas, just as they had recently done with Kainnan. No one was left in the town except Hawk.

In theory.

In reality, the Je'daii Ranger spotted two figures atop the flat-roofed building less than a kilometer away. Only five stories high, it was still the tallest building in the area. They were Twi'leks, like himself. And armed. Hawk opened his comm and called his partner.

Her surroundings, Lanoree Brock decided, were beautiful. Underground seas flowed through large caverns smoothed with high vaulted ceilings, and natural minerals gave off enough light to create a twilight effect. It was no wonder the rich of Zerist chose to live in the warm caverns rather than the cold surface of the moon. It was calm on this island, lending itself to meditation.

Peaceful.

The negotiations were not. The management of Dessain Mining and the manual laborers were now simply shouting at one another; ill will was building. Lanoree was finding it difficult to maintain balance between the light and the dark sides of the Force as she was taught.

Management consisted entirely of the extended Dessain family, which was headed by Emin Dessain, the tall, pale, patrician head of the clan. The workers, both human and alien, were led by short, weather-beaten Arko Santis, and demanded a voice in how the company was run. They left Zerist to labor at the gas-mining operations floating above Obri. The pay was steady, if not generous, but it was a hard life.

For their part, the Dessains were loath to cede control to anyone who was not family. The solution, it was decided, would be a marriage between Brom Santis, Arko's oldest son, and Oma Dessain, Emin's youngest daughter. Brom would become part of the Dessain family and a voice for the workers. Lanoree had gotten stuck with the role of negotiator, and though it wasn't the solution *she* would have suggested, if it satisfied all parties concerned, then it satisfied her.

That was before Oma Dessain vanished.

Each side blamed the other for her disappearance. Work at Dessain Mining had ground to a halt. Tempers flared and open class warfare looked not only possible, but likely. Lanoree and Hawk had been sent by the Je'daii Council on Tython to prevent violence and find the girl.

Lanoree's comm buzzed. The Ranger swung her long legs out of the chair, turning away from all the shouting. "Please tell me you found the girl."

"I *may* have found her," Hawk replied. "I went to the spaceport to check who arrived or left around the time of the kidnapping. I discovered a Shikaakwan ship registered to Baron Volnos Ryo."

"Your brother."

"My brother the crime lord." Lanoree could picture Hawk's lips twisting in distaste. "He owns interests in the mining operations on Obri's two other moons, but he's never been able to get a foothold with the Dessains. One of the ways to increase the value of his own holdings is to decrease the value of his rival's holdings. Are you growling?"

"Maybe. Will Oma still be alive?"

"Her body hasn't been found, so it's likely. If they intend to kill her, it'll be when the two sides are at each others' throats."

"Which will be soon."

"You have to keep them from reaching the boiling point. I think I've spotted where Oma is being held, but you can't say anything until I know for sure. I'll let you know what I find. Keep the workers and management from killing each other."

"Right. You get the easy job."

"The Force be with you."

Lanoree turned back to the round wooden table and narrowed her gray eyes. Both sides were already at the breaking point. Violence was ready to erupt. But Lanoree had a theory: Sometimes the best way to cut off violence was to use it first. Her right hand dropped to the slug thrower at her hip. She didn't often carry one—didn't need it most times—but something told her to wear one today. If there's one thing Lanoree learned through her experience, it was to listen to her instincts.

With one fluid move, she aimed the slug thrower straight up over her head, and fired three bursts into the ceiling. The arguing stopped dead and all eyes went to the auburn-haired Ranger. Je'daii were mysterious beings to most of the sentients of the Settled Worlds. They went where they willed and intervened where they chose or, they claimed, as the Force directed. They had strange powers and were both respected and feared. Right now, Lanoree was feared.

Good. That meant she had their attention.

The slug thrower still in her hand, the Je'daii Ranger sat back in her chair, placing the weapon on the table before her, the barrel pointed at the now silent delegation. She spoke quietly. "The last time I was a negotiator was on Ska Gora. Before I was done, forests were ablaze and one of the parties was dead."

She leaned forward. "I was hoping these negotiations would go smoother."

In truth, the deaths and the burning forests on Ska Gora haunted

Lanoree. The negotiators here on Zerist, however, didn't need to know that.

"Perhaps we should begin again," she suggested in a low murmur. They did, quietly, and with nervous glances in her direction.

Certain he hadn't been seen by anyone, Hawk reached the side of the five-story building and glanced upward. One guard was directly above him and the other would be across the roof. It was vital that he silence both before they could give alarm—assuming the girl was alive.

The Ranger brought his sword out of its sheath without a whisper, holding it in his right hand as he let the balance within him slip into the dark side. Hawk knew the dark side well; he dwelled too deeply in it once and it got him sent to Bogan, a moon of Tython where those who drifted too far to the dark side were sent by the Je'daii Council for solitary reflection and meditation until they returned to the balance. Right now he needed to use aggression, however, which meant channeling the dark side. He eased into it with a comfortable familiarity while he crouched and then leaped straight upward, letting the Force carry him. Hawk cleared the edge of the roof, right in front of the very surprised Twi'lek guard, and without hesitation slashed his sword across the guard's neck. He died silently.

The other guard sensed something amiss and started to turn. Hawk gestured with the Force and pulled him across the roof. The guard gasped for a moment before being impaled on the Ranger's sword. Their eyes met and Hawk recognized him. Deon Aarlaa —one of his brother's personal guards. Aarlaa's eyes registered recognition as well, and then life faded from them. Hawk felt his death in the Force, and part of him, the part that fed on the dark side, felt a deep satisfaction.

The Ranger let the body slide off his sword and took a deep breath, centering himself again in the balance. It was tempting for Hawk to just stay in the dark side as he had once before. It was seductive but dangerous.

Hawk found a stairway in the middle of the roof leading down into the building and descended cautiously. Two floors down were two large rooms on either side of the stairwell, the doors left wide open in the haste of the evacuation. At first blush, they appeared to have been used as dormitories for workers that were unmarried; cots were overthrown and debris littered the floor.

Hugging the stairway wall, Hawk glanced through the doorway and found Oma. The girl was bound and gagged on a cot next to the wall opposite the door. A large and surly-looking Twi'lek stood guard, a slug thrower at the ready, but he was looking at the far end of the room.

Focusing his senses through the Force, the Je'daii heard two more Twi'leks at the other end of the dormitory. Neither sounded happy.

". . . thought this would be over by now!"

"You got other things to do?"

"Other than sit next to a sokar volcano? Yes!"

"The problem is that Je'daii sitting at the table. Not for long, though. Our contact will take care of her. Then we off the girl, leave the corpse where it can be found, and get gone."

Hawk couldn't risk comming a warning to Lanoree. His best bet was to settle things here and hope his fellow Ranger was still alive. However, the moment he made a move the two guards at the end of the room would see him and the guard closest to Oma would certainly kill her. He needed a diversion.

The volcano provided a spectacular one. Ahead of schedule, the eruption started with a clap of thunder as plumes of pumice, flaming ash, and molten lava were belched into the air. Everyone was stunned for a moment, but then Hawk Ryo moved. His sword in his right hand and a long knife in his left, he swept into the room. Hurling the knife toward the guard standing next to Oma, he guided it with the Force into the Twi'lek's neck. The guard's finger tightened on the trigger of his slug thrower as he dropped; the shot went wild but was audible even over the roaring volcano.

Hawk pivoted toward the two other guards and sped toward them as they turned to the source of the slug fire and spotted him. A moment for their reaction. A few steps for Hawk. A moment as they brought their slug throwers around. Another few steps. They aimed their weapons. Hawk threw himself into a forward roll beneath their shots and pushed off of one leg as he came forward and up. Flipping in midair over the guards, the Je'daii shoved his boot down hard into the upturned face of the one to his right. Nose bone and cartilage cracked as the Twi'lek fell backward. The Je'daii landed, spun, and thrust his sword into the fallen Twi'lek's chest—a quick and clean kill. His partner kept firing, but always where the Je'daii *had* been. Hawk landed in a crouch and, with a gesture of his hand, delivered a Force blow that sent his target backward through the window. The Twi'lek's scream was covered by the volcano's roar.

Hawk preferred not to kill when he had the option, but there was no time and no other choice. Still, the dark part in him exulted and he struggled to bring himself back to the balance.

Hawk squatted next to Oma. "I'm Je'daii Ranger Hawk Ryo and I've been sent here to rescue you. Try to be calm." Picking the teen up, Hawk threw her over one shoulder and raced back up to the roof. Superheated volcanic debris rained down on the town, the wooden buildings starting to catch fire. Hawk again tried to warn Lanoree, but the ash jammed the comm's signal.

It was hard to see through the ash and the Ranger tightened his grip on Oma. Calling on the Force once more, he leaped to the next nearest roof, ran across, and then jumped to the next roof after that. He could barely breathe and was jumping blind, but he hoped he could trust in the Force that he was taking them out of danger.

And that Lanoree was not dead.

Ranger Brock eased back into her chair. The discussions were still going nowhere, but at least everyone was civil. A servant brought her a goblet of wine, a Vaisamond red, something she had developed a taste for on Ska Gora. Lanoree raised the goblet to her lips—and paused. She knew the bouquet of the wine and something bitter underlay the aroma.

Lanoree turned her head to glance at the servant who had given it to her: a nervous little man, as old as Emin Dessain. Fear came off him like a wave, a bitter aroma of its own. The servant turned to run. Lanoree caught him with the Force, lifted him up, and dropped him onto the round table. Thrusting the goblet in his face, Lanoree whispered, "I think this vintage is off. Please. Taste it."

The man's eyes went wide as he babbled incoherently. Lanoree growled, "Drink it, little man, or I will *make* you drink it." She didn't have that ability, but it was commonly believed that the mysterious Je'daii could seize your mind. That fear, that superstition, sometimes served the Je'daii almost as well as the Force did.

The servant certainly believed the stories. "No! It's poisoned!" he blurted.

Lanoree folded her arms, keeping her eyes on her would-be assassin. "Master Dessain, you have a traitor in your midst. The kidnappers would have needed someone on the inside to reach your daughter. That traitor is this man."

Emin Dessain looked at his servant, appalled. "Betolo? All these years, you have been a trusted servant, almost a member of the family . . . why?"

"Because all these years I have *only* been a servant." Betolo said quietly. "*Never* a member of the family. I wanted to have something of my own before I died. A chance to leave this wretched rock."

Dessain's voice seethed with fury. "Where is my daughter, Betolo?"

"With any luck . . . *dead*. My lord."

Lanoree's comm buzzed. "With any luck, my lord, she is not," she said as she activated the comm. "Hawk?"

"Lanoree, someone is going—!"

"Yes, I know. He tried and failed. Is Oma Dessain with you?"

"She is," Ryo said, "but we have another problem."

"What do you mean you refuse to marry Brom Santis?!" Emin, while relieved to have his daughter back, was furious.

Oma Dessain stood alongside Hawk Ryo with the delegations on the island in the cavern. She, like him, was covered with ash, making her pale skin even whiter and powdering her dark hair the same hue. Free from her bonds, she stood glaring defiantly at her father.

Oma's chin jutted out. "I mean I won't marry him! No one asked *me* if I wanted to get married! I don't and I won't!"

"You have your duty to the family!"

"I have a duty to *myself*! I don't know this Brom, I don't love him, and I won't marry him to settle some dispute!"

This set off another round of arguing between father and daughter, with Santis pitching in.

"This is breaking down quickly," Hawk murmured.

"Actually, my sympathies are with the girl. She shouldn't be a clause in a treaty," Lanoree murmured back.

"If she doesn't relent, the negotiations will likely collapse and everything we've done will be for nothing."

"I think I may have another solution," Lanoree said. "First, I'll need their attention." She shot her slug thrower three times into the air. And again, with the same effect.

Very pleasantly, Lanoree spoke. "In other parts of the solar system, rival interests have a practice called *fostering*. I suggest you try it. Oma would become a foster child in the Santis household and Brom would be the same with the Dessains. Each would be treated as a full member of the family they are with. They would spend six months with one family and six months with the other. The workers would have a voice through Brom, and Oma would learn firsthand about the workers' lives."

"I think this is a very reasonable suggestion," Hawk added, equally pleasant.

But the expressions on the two Je'daii firmly suggested that all sides accept the deal. Oma looked pleased; at least she wasn't getting married.

Details were worked out, Hawk cleaned up, and the two Je'daii met at the spaceport to take leave of Zerist and of each other.

"The Council has summoned me back to Tython for a special mission," Lanoree said. "It's been four years since I've been back; it's time."

"I'm heading out to Furies Gate," replied Hawk. It was the outermost planet in the system. Great Generation ships left from the small world, seeking a path through the maze that was the Core and looking for ways back to the rest of the galaxy. The Settled Worlds jointly maintained a station there. "I like to look out into the stars and meditate," he said.

A small shadow passed over Lanoree's face. "My brother used to look out at the stars and wonder if there was a way back to the rest of the galaxy. He was never very happy on Tython," she said softly. She was quiet for a moment, then shook it off and said, "It was good working with you, Ranger Ryo. I look forward to the chance to do it again."

Hawk nodded. "I do, too, Ranger Brock. The Force be with you."

Lanoree smiled. "And you," she replied. The Je'daii then crossed to their waiting ships and took off into the star-flecked skies.